Three Short Novels
Clarence Cooper, Jr.

Black!

Old School Books

If this is your first foray into the shadowy world of rediscovered black fiction we call the Old School, welcome. If you've got the taste for adventure, we think you're going to like it here. If you're joining us for another go-around, nice to have you back.

Our latest offerings feature four more slippery and subversive works. They haven't been excavated to make you feel good about your life, validate your existence, or put a smile on your face. This is a hard-boiled, blood-drenched fiction—untamed and unbearably suspenseful.

It is a slice of real life that will keep you up late nights, and chill you to the bone.

This time we offer you an inside look at the numbers racket, the dramatic rise of an unlikely drug kingpin, an anguished novelist's final revenge, and a middle-class family whose love for each other has turned to hate—until their home is invaded by a couple of bungling black nationalists.

Don't bother looking for role models; you won't find them. Old School heroes are a tortured and tormented breed—alienated, existential, and disaffected men for whom success is measured in terms of survival and escape is just a pipe dream. On the fringe of so-called respectable society, they may win, they may lose, but at least they go down swinging.

But for all their creeping menace and crashing violence, we think you'll agree that these are landmark works told with terrible honesty and explosive brilliance. Adventurous, ambitious, and aggressively undogmatic, these premature postmodernists weren't afraid to gamble for high stakes.

What was their reward? Obscurity. Poverty. Rejection. But for what it's worth, they also gained the self-knowledge that they hadn't minced words or sold out their genius. And that's why we're celebrating them.

Lost since their original publication, they've been dead and buried—impenetrable as a tomb and inaccessible as a dream. Here in the Old School, they are born again.

So if you think you're ready, pull up a stool, have a round on the house, and read your way into oblivion.

See you next time.

Black!

OLD SCHOOL BOOKS

edited by Marc Gerald and Samuel Blumenfeld

Black!

Three Short Novels

CLARENCE COOPER, JR.

Old School Books

W · W · Norton & Company

New York · London

Copyright © 1997 by Marc Gerald and Samuel Blumenfeld

The text of this book is composed in Sabon, with the display set in Stacatto 555 and Futura.

Composition by Crane Typesetting Service, Inc.

Manufacturing by Courier Companies, Inc.

Book design by Jack Meserole.

Library of Congress Cataloging-in-Publication Data
Cooper, Clarence L.
    Black! : three short novels / by Clarence Cooper, Jr.
      p. cm.—(Old school books)
    Contents: The dark messenger—Yet princes follow—Not we many.
    ISBN 0-393-31541-X (pbk.)
    I. Detective and mystery stories, American. 2. Afro-Americans—Fiction.
Title. II. Series.
PS3553.O5799A6 1997
813'.54—dc20
                            96-30313
                            CIP

W. W. Norton & Company, Inc., 500 Fifth Avenue, New York, N.Y. 10110
http://web.wwnorton.com

W. W. Norton & Company Ltd., 10 Coptic Street, London WC1A 1PU

1 2 3 4 5 6 7 8 9 0

TABLE OF CONTENTS

CLARENCE COOPER, JR.

CLARENCE COOPER, JR. should've been sitting pretty in 1961. Only one year earlier, the 27-year-old's first novel, *The Scene*, had been published by Crown to near-universal praise. However, far from basking in the literary spotlight, Cooper was languishing in a federal prison, wondering how things could have gone so wrong, so fast.

In truth, Cooper had to look no farther than the jailhouse mirror. A charter member of the live fast–die young school, the native of Detroit, Michigan, was a lifelong dopefiend, and had been in and out of jail since his teens. But psychiatrists delve, fighters fight, and rather than whiling away his three-year sentence examining the reasons for his addiction, Cooper wrote.

Shunned by the more respectable hardback publishers, these three short works—along with the rest of Cooper's early-60s output—was originally published in slash-and-crash paperback editions by the Regency House, a Chicago-based outfit, edited by a young Harlan Ellison. Though marketed as standard-issue pulp, in its short, three-year history, Regency also published the iconoclastic writings of Jim Thompson, Robert Bloch, Philip Jose Farmer, and Ellison himself. "The Dark Messenger" originally appeared in 1962 as a stand-alone paperback; "Yet Princes Follow" and "Not We

Many" first appeared in 1963 in a volume titled *Black!*—which we have borrowed for this Old School Books compilation.

"Clarence Cooper, Jr. is black and can not get along with this world," Harlan Ellison wrote in a brief 1963 foreword. "No special star shone at his birth to tell anyone that another dark face or a special talent had come to stare at us and wonder what place it could find for itself. He had to find his own voice for his own message and that message is here."

Sadly, that message has been thoroughly unappreciated over the years. At the time of Cooper's death in 1978, none of his six books were in print. Boldly experimental, fiercely original, and utterly modern, Cooper's time has finally come.

Black!

The Dark Messenger

CHAPTER ONE

*L*EE'S BLACK FACE was almost pink when he arrived at the *Messenger*'s offices Friday morning. Somehow it had taken more than a little effort to get up, and the angry, squalling bastard of Winter had frozen his eight-year-old Plymouth into an almost unstartable condition. Yet it did not allow him an excuse for being late, starting up whiningly at the last minute, like an apoplectic old hag, and he damned its revival. Of all the days of the week, he hated Friday the most.

The only thing to help ease the burr would be Diana and, perhaps a little later in the day, his friend Tobey. But right now was the thing—this drab office of the city's largest Negro weekly, and its Negroless Negroes.

"Good morrr-ningg, Mr. Merriweather," purred the bright-eyed receptionist, Joan.

Lee nodded self-consciously, shaking himself free of the new falling snow, and strode toward the back and the one dirty door labeled *City Room.*

Opening it was a monumental task, more so this morning than any other. And it had been getting harder to open day by day. It wasn't so much of what lay inside, this hesitancy, this minimum of fear that had freakishly grown out of proportion; it was, instead, the knowledge of what he was not and what he could not make himself seem to be. Say: his face was the blackest of all. Say: he could not always G his Ings the way they could, the ofay way they spoke. Say: his one year of journalism at State U qualified him as a member of the *nouveaux Negro elegante*, and he would be telling the goddamndest lie he ever thought of.

Every time he opened that dirty door to the *City Room*, he had to masticate and swallow a little bit of himself. The CR seemed to dissolve about him like instant coffee, a shelter of shotgun confusion. It plunged narrowly to the rear of the building, where French windows peeked with frosted cataracts on the desolation of the back alley.

The CR was *grime*, that was the word that rang the bell in his head each day—grime, a paste-like, indelible residue bequeathed by countless generations that had made home in the tiny space. The cluster of desks and rented typewriters was like the squashed corpse of a night bug that had been lured into the crushing mouth of a highway vehicle. Data of all sorts littered the desks and spilled onto the floor, even crawled, it seemed, upon the walls and skewered itself with tacks and straight pins.

Smiling lusciously down on all this, the sexually enthusiastic faces of overgrown female cherubs, the gatefolds of slick men's magazines, beckoned with a leg, a thigh, a plump, pink-tipped breast or two, a slitted bouncing butt made immobile by the leering orb of the camera, the stars in their eyes still innocent of the fact that Hollywood Heaven was still a long way off despite the obvious visual assertion that they showed up well in Technicolor.

"Morning, Lee." Phillip Meyer, the managing editor. "Kinda hard pulling your ass out of the sack this morning, huh?"

"I had car trouble," Lee told him.

"I had bar trouble,"—with a hair-of-the-dog grin, Cy Venson, city editor.

From a dusty, piled-high desk of UPI dispatch envelopes, the day reporter, Joe Richards, threw a reticently pleasant grin Lee's way. Of the three, Lee liked Joe the best. Perhaps it was because Joe, a year younger than Lee's twenty-five, was barely a shade lighter than himself, or that their writing objectives were somehow paralleled by tenacity and the need to have every printed word bear an unforgettable impact. He didn't know why he felt so strong a kinship with Joe this morning, but he was strangely aware of a need for alliance this day.

"Hi, Joe," he said.

"We're gonna have a visitor today," Meyer proclaimed from his desk, "The Great Him." He sat high in his swivel chair, a short, chunky man. His hair was straight and shortcropped. He was a Negro, but everything about him resembled a Jew; the long nose to top lip, the hazy orange color of skin—even the surname Meyer—it was all an unfunny conjunction Lee could never quite adjust himself to.

Now Meyer sat back on the hinges of his chair, in a special way he had, and contemplated, overhead, the pink behinds and ripe red breasts of various white girls, as though he were making the last and final decision to their fate.

"Gentlemen," he said in mock proclamation, "today we will all participate in a most momentous occasion. For those of you, like Lee here, who have never felt the persuasive hand clasp of a living moneybags, this will mark a high point in your literary career. Hail to our grand leader, esteemed publisher—and meal ticket—D. S. Sandersford."

"Heil, D. S. Sandersford," Cy piped up.

"Listen to these guys, Lee," Joe Richards said a little sardonically. "When the Great Him pulled in last year, you'd think they were all wearing a three-in-one coat—that's how close Phil and Cy were hanging onto him."

"Hold to, Horatio," Cy said, with an upward pointing forefinger. "Lee's only been here a year, so we don't want to give him anything but the straight wire, since he's never met him."

This was it, mostly—this way they included him—that Lee disliked more than anything else. He excluded Joe, but he felt Meyer and Cy cooperated in some sort of private, pervertedly jocose conspiracy against him. He went over and sat down behind his desk, the smallest in the room. A draft from the French windows swept in under his feet, and he didn't take his coat off until his hands and body were sufficiently warmed.

"You see, Lee," Cy went on, "it's something like a once-a-year seminar we have here at the *Messenger*. The Great Him comes through. We sit and listen. He drops us our bonuses. We wave good-bye to him when he leaves, a tear in every croc's eye."

"Don't pay any attention to that bastard Cy," Meyer grinned over at Lee. "Him's really a great guy. Don't think, because he lives in New York, he's not in constant touch with what goes on with his newspaper—or employees, for that matter. I've always found, in my case, that D. S. is capable of responding like an uncle. Even a father. I don't wanna form any snaps of the man before you meet him, but you'll never find an easier brain to get along with, Lee. Take you, for example . . ."

"What about me?" Lee said, on guard.

"Well, hell—me, you and everybody else on the *Messenger* knows about your background . . ."

Lee tensed in a manner that was unusual, feeling every tendon draw bowstring taut. "What about my background?" And, as he watched Meyer's mouth open casually, like two crooked pink lines of badly ruled type, he thrilled with an insensate urge to slam his fist into the pasty face.

"Aw, shit, Lee," Meyer said like a brother, "it's nothing to be ashamed of. You couldn't help it because you were an orphan—"

"Or that I graduated from a foster home to a vocational school," Lee said, his stare becoming a thing that ached on Meyer's smiling, dispassionate face. ". . . That they kept me there until I was twenty—from the time I was sixteen until the time I was twenty . . ."

Meyer obviously felt the tone of his voice, and became silent. But he never stopped smiling. Vaguely Lee was aware that his fists were clenched. Slowly he came out of his overcoat and hung it behind the desk on the wall rack.

"I hope you got the gist of what I was trying to say, kid," Meyer said, still smiling. "I only attempted to show what kind of personality the big man has. He knows all about you—you know—all the things I guess are damn unpleasant for you to think about, but he's got nothing but praise for your work, believe me."

"Thanks," Lee said, straightening the crook of his fingers, listening to the diminishing thud of his heart, glad the thunder of it had ceased in his eardrums. He noticed that Cy had been quietly observing him, his smile very much like the one Meyer wore—but it was a background smile, unimposing, cunningly inoffensive.

18

"I don't know why you're looking at me that way, Lee," he said innocuously. "I'll *switch* reputations with ya, if you want to, and I'll guarantee you'll get the short end of the stick."

"Or no end at all," Joe contributed laughingly.

Finger on cheek, Meyer watched him musingly. "I've noticed, Lee—you don't wear a hat. Doesn't your head get cold?"

"Not very."

"Uh huhn," Meyer said. "Ever thought about that, Lee? How the Brother came from Africa with that thick head of hair? Why'd he have all that hair in the first place?"

Lee touched the keys of his typewriter gingerly. "Might make a good feature. Want me to take a crack at it?"

"No, really," Meyer appealed, "I'm serious. Why the hell would the Brother have such a thick head of hair in the hottest goddamn spot in the world?" He briskly stroked his own shortcropped hair. "Here he's been in the U. S. going on four hundred years, and he's still got it."

"It's something to think about," Lee agreed, "I just never wear a hat, that's all."

"I'm not talking about *you*," Meyer said emphatically. "I didn't mean you personally—don't take everything to heart."

Lee felt his face begin to burn. "I didn't *think* you were talking about me."

"I think you've got a nice head of nigger hair, Lee. I was just wondering why the Brother hadn't lost that stuff all these years."

"I still say it'd make a nice feature."

"It's got something to do with genes," Cy grinned in a half-hearted contribution to keep the peace. "I read about the whole thing somewhere."

"But that's silly," Meyer insisted. "It doesn't explain anything."

"The whole damn thing is silly," Lee said, feeling a release to anger. "The white man hasn't lost *his* hair; there's no reason why the black man can't keep his."

"But you don't get my point, Lee—I'm just saying that the goddamn Brother had no business with all that hair in the *first* place. As hard as his head is, it'd make just as much sense to put hair on a cueball."

Lee felt an intense warmth about the collar of his shirt. "It's just as right for the black man to have a full head of hair as it is for the white man."

"Sure, if you take the Constitution seriously. What I'm trying to get across is the fact the Brother didn't have a physical practicality for all that hair in Africa. Actually, he should've been baldheaded."

Cy snickered. "Phil, you're just like a bulldog, the way you hold on to a guy's ass!"

"I just like to be realistic—it's Lee who loves to hold onto these things."

Abruptly, Lee raised the lip of his standard typewriter and let it slam down hard on the desktop. "*You* brought it up—you started talking about my hair—"

"I wasn't laughing about *your* hair, Lee," Meyer laughed harmlessly. "I was talking about the Brother's hair."

"Who gives a damn?" Joe shouted above their voices. "Let's get some work done around here!"

"You know nobody does any work around here on paydays," Cy giggled.

"You'll start hoppin' when Him gets here," Joe reminded him. "I'll betcha the whole office picks up then, hair or no hair."

Meyer was smiling at Lee. "I just can't understand why you'd get mad because I said the Brother didn't have any business with all that hair."

"I didn't get mad . . ."

"Why, you sure as hell did, Lee."

"I just said it didn't make any difference, that's all I said."

"Haven't you ever thought about it?"

"Why have hillbillies got red necks?" Lee said, with no hint of amusement.

"Now you're playing in semantics," Meyer said disapprovingly.

Lee made use of the sudden advantage. "I've seen billies who've been away from the hills for a whole generation, but they've still got pepper-red ears and necks."

"It's not the same thing. The hillbilly's red neck is functional—it's got something to do with pigmentation and climate. It's nothing like that hair business."

Lee found some copy paper in a bottom drawer and twisted it into the machine angrily. "I don't understand why you keep raking this crap over. If you've got something to say about my hair, go on and say it. You don't have to go by way of Africa."

Meyer lapsed into an apparently amused and thoughtful silence.

Lee took a deep breath. For a moment he closed his eyes, staring into a red-black, abstract darkness. He was briefly confused by an inward pain which was accentuated by Meyer's mention of the word orphan. It had been a long time since he had reminded himself that his social birth was stigmatized in a manner that exceeded the self-consciousness of his black color.

He opened his eyes to see Meyer sitting apparently oblivious of the dark stone he had unearthed from the uneven plain of Lee's awareness. And Lee became quietly furious.

It seemed that, today, the initial course of events had conspired, with Meyer's aid, to precipitate what Tobey called the "awakening black giant" in his soul.

Were it not for Meyer and his unsubtle sarcasm, Lee would have relished Fridays. On this day, his tiny salary of $70.00 was most heartily welcomed. Among other things, it enabled him to buy a fifth of Scotch and visit his friend Tobey, an unorthodox young man who never drank, preferring the intoxication of marijuana. And later, Diana would come to his small apartment and they would spend the remainder of the evening together . . . and they would make painful, searchingly exquisite love . . .

And Lee couldn't get over the feeling that Meyer was afraid of him for some reason, despite his barbs and outward calm. This morning, more than at any other time he sensed an unusual maliciousness in Meyer's racial jibes.

It had been Meyer who arranged for his position on the *Messenger*, but Lee felt the last puff was about to be blown into some invisible competitive balloon. Was that it?

Perhaps, at thirty-nine, Meyer was threatened by a man fourteen

2 1

years his junior—that would, in part, explain the shift in his affections. But once, Lee remembered, he had said, "I like the way you work, kid—you honestly seem to have a knack. You've rough at the edges yet, but I'll educate you and see you adjust to this lousy goddamn routine. When I die, maybe you'll inherit the job."

Lee felt a little guilty at the recollection. Of several rewrites he found one about desegregation that he was interested in, and began to do the job over. But he continued to watch Meyer from the corner of his eye. He couldn't help envying the man his education at NYU, his popularity in society, his weekly check and asides that more than doubled the one he received. And, also, there was Meyer's glibness, his ready wit, his near whiteness, his comely, half-white wife . . . his passion for all things white . . .

Lee thought of Tobey's contemptuous regard of the Negro press. It was, at first, rather difficult for him to understand—the Negro press was a tradition in the black community, a pompous black overlord that sat beyond the bounds of censure. But, during the last year, having a chance to watch the workings of the specialized organ first hand—gradually awakening through a new surge within himself, and the acid probings of Tobey Balin—Lee had frightenedly begun to suspect it was all a damn lie.

He continued, with little enthusiasm, the piece he was working on.

That thing about the hair had hurt quite a bit. Not that he was ashamed of the thick, wiry mass at the top of his skull (which he was): but it stood out as an added something against him here among people he barely recognized as his own. His people, yes. For the first time in months he again experienced those overpowering feelings of insignificance, of unimportance—those things which caused him, against Tobey's protests, to ditch State U and take a try at the selective journalism of the *Messenger*.

Outside his vision, he seemed to have heard a twitter of laughter, but he saw that each man had his attention elsewhere. It was as though life, the big bastard, were laughing at him.

The desegregation story was going badly. He finished it in a page and tore a piece of copy in half, inserting a half sheet of carbon for the dupes. In the left hand corner, he typed out the size of type for the printer, then typed out the head in caps:

DIXIE SOLON AIDS
FIGHT IN SCHOOL
INTEGRATION

And there it was, that easily: a story full of the dailies' quotes, void of any creation whatsoever, the hallmark of Negro newspaper reporting. A shameful thing, he admitted to himself. He passed it over to Meyer for an okay.

After reading briefly, Meyer said, "Don't you think you missed the point, Lee?"

"It's big as a barn. I don't see how I could."

Meyer began to edit with his copy pencil. "The point is, this hillbilly is committing political suicide. Why? Who's gonna give a damn one way or the other if he thinks white kids and black should go to the same school? I mean, how many of our readers are gonna give a damn? Here's your story: He *thinks* they should—and in thinking that, he's made a sacrifice of himself. Get what I'm driving at?"

It was a little surprising, but Lee *did* see now.

"Here's this Southern bastard who's worked ass-high in ignorance all his life to get where he is today," Meyer pointed out. "He's had nothing but a Dixie-eye view of the whole racial mess. Now—isn't he a phenomenon? He thinks nothing is *wrong* with mixing the schools! The man is a freak."

"Now that you mention it—"

"Here's your goddamn lead, Lee: This courageous old redneck is going against every Southern covenant in order to demonstrate that the Brother is just as good as anybody else. Maybe to him the Brother isn't important. What's important to him is the fact that every man is entitled to that inalienable fair shake, and for this he's doomed—his political career is finished. Now, that's quite a thing to give up for a handful of pickaninnies, *s'il vous plait!* Do you see the light?"

He couldn't help feeling a tiny glow of admiration for Meyer's insight. "I'll start it over, Phil."

"Give it that pathos, kid. This is a story with plenty room for creativity. Pour it on. Give me about three pages, okay? Remember the piece you did for the *State Review,* when the home team lost the ball for the tying score on the one yard line? It's tragic, buddy, tragic."

Lee began the story again, revitalized. He felt the burden of the Senator, the wrath of his Southern contemporaries. In thirty minutes he finished the story and handed it to Meyer for comment.

"That's the business!" the managing editor said, beginning to mark the dupe with page instructions. "I think we'll run this on the first page. If nothing better comes up, maybe we'll make it the lead."

The door to the outer office opened and a tall, melon-colored young woman came in.

Cy gave a happy shout. "Well, men, we're about to be remunerated for the past week of blood."

"Everybody but you," the girl laughed. "The boss doesn't think blood was what you gave most of last week."

Cy popped his eyes comically. "Aw, Diana honey—you gotta give me a check! What makes better blood than gin?"

"Ever try blood?" Joe Richards snickered across the room. "The kind distilled from grapes, I mean."

"That's for the Italians like you," Cy sneered back.

"This is some pressroom," Diana Hill said, looking at them with mock distaste. "Don't you guys ever get any work done around here?"

"How can we?" Meyer said. "With pretty young things like you busting in all day, it's no wonder we're distracted."

Lee felt the hair at the back of his neck rise up. No one in the office was aware of the affair between him and Diana, and they preferred to keep it that way, since Boss George Hooker, editor-in-chief, frowned on interoffice relationships. Yet there were people like Ken Bussey, one of the ad men, and Cathy Jones, one of two sisters who laid out the society pages, who were carrying on openly, and not a word had been said about it. It was common knowledge about the office that Bussey was married to a devoted young woman and had several children.

As Boss Hooker's private secretary, Diana was particularly envied and watched by the other women in the office, and she couldn't afford to lose the job. Lately, Lee had become more than ordinarily concerned about her job. It would be Diana's salary, and his meager savings, that determined the imminence of the marriage they had been planning for the last five months. The nightmare that it might all fall through, caused by the bombastic interference of some unseen intervention, haunted Lee no end. It had become an obsession of unlimited scope that he marry Diana as soon as possible, but he could not motivate the origin of his intensely fearful, irrepressible desire. . . . In Boss Hooker's estimation, no one was indispensable, not even Diana who had worked for that peculiar monarch nearly three years.

For one moment, he was unreasonably tempted to throw it all to hell—actually cause some crazy kind of violent, physical demonstration right here and now—watching the way Meyer, the lust evident in the twitching of his thin lips, was evaluating the slim, neat hips, the tiny but erect breasts, the tasty, moist blossom of mouth pursed undramatically in Lee's direction . . .

"And your check, Mr. Merriweather," she said, handing him a white envelope that would have been anonymous, except for his neatly penned-in last name.

Only a flicker of her big brown eyes, impersonally—and deceivingly—focused on the disturbed rush of inner wrath which had begun to tint itself on his smooth, dark features, said there was anything special in their surveillance of Lee.

"And, finally, Mr. Venson," she said, stopping before Cy's desk. "I'll make a personal exception of the Boss's orders . . . here's your check!"

"Hallelujah!" Cy shouted.

Casually, Diana gave Lee's silent face a last look that was almost imperceptible and exited, lauded by a broad wolf whistle from Meyer.

"That's quite a piece, boys," Meyer said, rubbing a hand across his mouth. "A man'd be a damn fool if he didn't try to give that backside a working over. She's got class."

Lee got up, experiencing a falling sensation he knew would result in Meyer's collision with an irresistible force, if he didn't get the hell out of there. "I think I'll walk over to the bank and cash."

"Wait a minute, Lee," Cy said, getting up. "It's almost lunchtime. I'll walk over with you."

Outside a petulant blizzard rose and abated irascibly. The blanket of snow had risen boot high.

The two men trudged slowly down Farrell Street. "How about a drink?" Cy suggested. "We could stop off at Al's."

"I don't give a goddamn," Lee said darkly.

Towering a few inches over Lee, Cy investigated him with concealed appraisal. "What's the matter? Phil get under your skin?"

"It might not be a good thing if he did," Lee said, with an inscrutable, but wire-taut, promise in his voice.

Cy grinned and clapped him on the back heartily.

"Welcome, buddy," he said. "This club's one of the oldest in town!"

CHAPTER TWO

IN SOME WAYS IT WAS GOOD to be a weakling, Cy told him.

Hahah . . . drink, drink the gin.

You see, a weakling could forget a whole lot easier than a strong man. He didn't have to be bothered with scruples and pride and all the other things that made men out to be worth more than they actually were.

Drink, drink the gin . . . Hey, Al!

Cy watched Lee brood over his glass of beer. It was safe to say that he didn't like the young man, but it was one of the lesser dislikes he reserved for individuals he might eventually make use of.

His hands trembled as he lighted a cigarette and offered one to Lee, who declined. "Oh, that's right, Lee buddy; you don't smoke, do you? Hey, hey, what's the matter there, boy? You look like you got road troubles. Who's the broad?"

Lee looked at him cautiously. "There's no broad."

"Don't gimme that."

"Why should I lie to you?"

Cy twirled his fingers expertly around the shot glass of gin. "I'm a mathematical sonofabitch, Lee. I've been married twice, both times what you'd call society girls. I had more road trouble with those girls than you'll ever come across. Funny things about society girls in this new Negro uprising—they're the biggest whores in United States history."

"It's all psychological."

"Sure, it is. If you wanna call the hairy monster psychological, maybe it is. But it hurts a hell of a lot when your woman gives that psychological monster away to all comers."

Though he was well on the way to extreme intoxication, Cy could tell that his revealing patter was provocative to Lee.

"You don't make sense, Cy."

Cy puffed out his sallow cheeks in a comic gesture and called for the dark, squat little bartender to refill his glass. After he had sprinkled the coals of his insatiable thirst, he resumed. "Naw, course I don't make any sense. That's what makes everything so funny."

"Now it's funny."

"Sure it is! I'm thirty-five years old, right? Right?"

"If you say so."

"I've been working with the *Messenger* going on fifteen years. I was here when we had to load the press run on our backs and distribute them, me and Phil."

"You and Phil . . ."

Cy grinned owlishly. "That's right, you hate Phil, don't you? You hate him because of that girl."

"You're crazy as hell!" Lee said too quickly. "Why should I hate him because of Diana?"

"Ahhh!" Cy breathed with easy discernment. "So it *is* her!"

"You're in your goddamn gin," Lee told him.

"How long's it been going on, Lee old buddy?"

"There's not a thing going on! Say, what is this? You act as though I've committed some heinous crime—"

"I *like* the way you say 'haynous . . .'"

"I can't tell you about something that doesn't even exist."

"You can't hide it," Cy scoffed. "I've noticed you, old buddy, I've seen the way you and that little peach look at each other. Don't you think a guy who's been married to two society broads can tell?"

"Right now," Lee said contemptuously, "you couldn't tell your ass from a hole in the ground."

"*Is* there a difference?"

"Listen, Cy," Lee said earnestly. "You're all wrong. I don't even know the girl. All I've got for her is a hello and a good-bye. Now don't you go back to the office spreading any false rumors."

"Me?" Cy said, aghast. "Why, I wouldn't tell anybody a damn thing, Lee, you believe it. I'd like to see you with that kid a helluva lot better than I would Phil."

"What Meyer does is his own business!"

Cy called once more for a refill. "That's all right, Lee. Go ahead and get mad at me. Vent your suppressed kill images. I'm just trying to save you from a fate worse than death, and such is your reward if you fool around with those Diana Hill kinda society girls, even though she does seem like a nice kid. I wouldn't want you to get *married*, get what I mean?"

"There's not much danger in that," Lee said, looking at the darkness of his face in the wall mirror behind the bar.

Cy sipped at his gin. "Oh, you'd be surprised, my boy. You got talent. When I was your age, I had talent too. That's what the girls in this new Negro uprising are looking for—talent. They can take and sink their dirty little claws in and rip it out; then they'll eat it,

28

they'll feed on it. Yeah, that's what the girls of Sigma Chi are, a bunch of cannibals. You know something, Lee?" he said, becoming unusually talkative with the intake of gin and, Lee noticed, a good deal more forthright. "I've watched these girls. I've seen them try to emulate their white sisters at every turn of the stile. And do you know one thing? They've become accomplished at it; even in the matter of destroying their men."

"You're getting my shoulder wet," Lee said disgustedly.

"Sure, sure, I cry," he said, and it seemed for a moment as though he actually were. "I'm crying; I cry, cry. The road trouble you've got don't even compare with mine. As much as I disparage those fine, upstanding, downlaying Missusvensons, I loved them both. That's the trouble; you get to love those girls."

"That's what you're trying to save me from?"

Cy's eyes became misty. "If it hadn't been for the *Messenger* I'd still be married to one or the other of those girls. The *Messenger* took them away from me."

"Now it's the *Messenger's* fault!" Lee said. "Do you think *you* had anything to do with it?"

"Of course I did! I drank! And why did I drink?"

"You tell me."

"I took too much kicking!" he diagnosed with hot self-pity. "I give my whole goddamn life to that stinking Nigger paper and what do I get? What do *I* get? I stand still at eighty bucks a week for ten years!"

"Why haven't you asked for a raise?"

Cy snorted. "Don't be ridiculous. The *Messenger* can never stand the expense, that's what Boss Hooker says. But what about the expense I go through every week, setting up two pages of editorials and six pages of theatricals and society? What about *that* expense?"

"If that's the club you want me to join," Lee said, "you can count me out. The *Messenger* is my bread and butter . . ."

"Oh, sure! You wouldn't bite the hand that stuffs your black mouth, would you?"

Lee pushed his beer away carefully. "Listen, Cy, I don't have anything personal against you. We've never had any buddy-buddy

29

relationship. You're imposing on me, and you're going to push me just a little too goddamn far!"

"Do you wanta bust my face now?" Cy said in a high, injured voice. "Would that make your mouth any less black? That's your trouble, Lee: you're black and you want people to act like you've got one of those unmentionable diseases."

"I only want respect," Lee said with forced coolness. "That's all I've ever shown you or anybody else at the *Messenger*."

Cy was not too drunk to stop himself before he completely alienated Lee. His wrath was not against the younger man but only for the newspaper to which he had been restricted and imprisoned for fifteen years, and the man who held the job he felt he was fully entitled to. Hadn't he come to work for the *Messenger* several months before the Great Him had sent Meyer in from New York?

Somehow it was difficult for his mind to differentiate between his hate for Phil Meyer and his hate for the *Messenger*. Over the years, they had merged, schizoid, in the dark pits of his mind's loathing.

It bothered him little that Lee should see him thusly, stripped of his phony, devil-may-care facade, garrulous and bitter of his circumstance, contradicting with his sodden presence the theory that a weakling could forget a lot easier than a strong man.

He tried to pick up the thread of happy carelessness. "I didn't mean to hurt your feelings, Lee old buddy! Here, have a drink on me. Al!"

"That's okay . . ."

"Don't get sullen on me, boy! You're gonna have a drink! Al," he bellowed, "give my good buddy here a drink!"

The little bartender came over. "What'll you have?"

"A Scotch," Lee said reluctantly. "Martin's V.V.O."

"Don't let me get under your skin, Lee," Cy said, clapping him on the shoulder in a brotherly manner. "We have enough trouble with Meyer getting under our skins, don't we?"

"We sure as hell do," Lee confessed, then revised it with a stony look at Cy and: "*I* sure as hell do!"

"Well, he bothers *me* too!" Cy complained.

30

"You seem to get along all right with him."

Cy winked a red-veined eye. "Don't let him fool ya! He's smart, real smart; you gotta fight fire with fire. Like that Diana: he's *subtle*. He's been trying to screw her for the past three years. He doesn't give up; he tries all sorts of ways. He keeps me informed on his progress." He saw Lee's mouth tighten. "But you can relax, Lee. He's not making any progress, not any at all."

"It doesn't make me one goddamn bit of difference."

"Aw, why don't you come off it, Lee? Aren't we good buddies? Aren't we both suffering under the iron heel of the new Negro uprising? You can tell me . . ."

"I've told you."

"Aw, c'mon, good buddy!"

"I'm telling you, Cy, I hardly know the girl."

"Aw, c'mon, good buddy! Have you screwed her yet?"

Lee stood up from the bar. "I've had all the digging I'm gonna take from you!"

"Hey, Lee! Siddown, siddown! I promise I won't say another word about it." He pressed Lee's shoulder gently, and the younger man sat once more.

"I'll tell you something," Cy said confidentially. "You know why I hate Meyer? I'll tell you: Meyer laid my first wife. AhHah! Didn't know that, did you? I could see the surprise in your eyes! And you know what? He damn near screwed my second wife!"

"You're blaming Meyer for that?"

"Oh, sure, I know it was my wives' fault for putting themselves in the position—but Meyer was supposed to be my best friend. It happened around nine years ago. We were pretty tight together, me and Meyer, going out together, drinking together, whoring together. Is a guy like that supposed to stick a knife in your back?"

Lee didn't answer.

"We went on a fishing trip," Cy remembered. "His wife Alene and my first wife Barbara. We got split up, me and Alene and Phil with Barbara, in the woods. They didn't get back to the cabin until the next day. They said they'd been lost, but me and Alene knew better. Later Barbara confessed that Phil had her heels up that night, after I received the final decree. Now is that a friend, I ask you?" He called for another gin and swallowed it quickly. "But that wasn't enough for that bastard, was it? I got married to Georgia a year after the divorce. Phil was even my best man! About a month later, on the press day, I worked late. Phil left early. When I got home, Georgia told me how he'd tried to get in the apartment." A gobbled sound bounced back as he laughed in the thick glass mouth of his shot glass. "She might as well have left him in—she'd been letting in an old boyfriend for the entire month we'd been married!"

"You didn't say anything? To Phil?"

"Why should I?"

"Why are you complaining?"

"Complaining? Well, I'll be damned if I am complaining! But even if I was, don't you think I got reasons?"

Lee didn't hide his contempt. "Why bitch at this late date? If you'd been any sort of man, you would've kicked Meyer's ass in. I would have. If he could get away with it once, why shouldn't he try again?"

"You don't understand," Cy whined. "I had my job to think of. If I had said anything—"

"You're a dumb bastard," Lee told him. "You're trying to initiate me into a dumb club! The only thing the matter with those society broads was you. It makes you feel good to be walked on! The *Messenger* and Phil Meyer haven't done any more to you than you've done to yourself."

"I wouldn't expect you to understand!"

"Of course you wouldn't . . ."

"An ex-con like you!"

Lee got up.

"AhHah!" Cy said with satisfaction. "There—he makes his escape! You think you can run and hide?"

"No more than you," Lee said tightly.

"You think Meyer won't be able to screw Boss Hooker's secretary?" Cy hissed maliciously. "I'll just tell you something: Phil's been able to screw every woman that ever came into the *Messenger*'s office. He's even screwed Miss Joy For The Boys, Cathy Jones—and he'll screw your Diana, black boy!"

Lee turned and walked out of the bar.

Cy was dazed in his anger. He hadn't meant to lose himself so completely. Sensing Lee's dislike of Meyer, he had wanted to use the man in Meyer's destruction. Of course, he was assured of Cathy Jones' cooperation, but wouldn't it have been fun to make Lee the emissary of death to the career of the managing editor?

It wouldn't really matter that much. When the Great Him arrived today, he and Cathy would be able to accomplish their goal.

It seemed as though the seething angers of a thousand years were within him. He would only be appeased by the extinction of Phil Meyer's influence on the *Weekly Messenger*. Today was the day he had waited on for fifteen years.

"Hey, Al!" he yelled, raising high the empty shot glass, "Hey, Al! Come fill the cup of glad revenge!"

CHAPTER THREE

*A*LTHOUGH PHILLIP MEYER was a man of intense devotion, he worshipped not God; not his wife Alene or their twelve-year-old son Thomas; not the memory of a father, who had prospered and become prominent in the sale of last-ditch real estate to unsuspecting Negroes; nor even of an anemic, gentle mother who had died before her time.

Some fifteen years before, Phil Meyer had joined in holy union with the *Weekly Messenger*, and he worshipped it as a man worships the breath of life within his body.

In reward for his faithfulness the *Messenger* had repaid him with things he might otherwise have never had. He was respected in society circles and often asked to speak at their gatherings. He was well known and deferred to by top members of the police department, and it was by this token that the *Messenger's* crime reporters could get into news areas forbidden the city's two other Negro newspapers, the *Eagle* and *Tribune*.

But most rewarding of all was the fact that his editorship on the *Messenger* gave him access to many bedrooms in the homes of society matrons, or those of dusky debutantes; and the only payment they required was that his editorial power should deign to display their names and pictures in the weekly pages of the *Messenger*.

Of his dumpy little body and odd pigmentation, Phil Meyer was secretly more self-conscious than Lee Merriweather. The self-imposed caste system which the Negro had created for himself had, for Phil Meyer, no special category. He was a man with and without, riding on the coattails of the *Messenger's* circulation supremacy, burrowing under the security of edition after edition of what he clearly recognized to be yellow journalism.

It had been many years, however, since he had allowed himself to care about that.

When Lee came back in, Meyer was considering an appointment he had just received by special messenger, placing him on the mayor's commission for better community relations. The appointment carried a yearly stipend of $4,500.

He considered the message with happy triumph. Added to the $6,000 yearly *Messenger* salary, plus an additional $5,000 he received in gratuities from political trusts, for services rendered, the appointment would do nicely to supplement his ever mounting personal expenses. His only regret was that he wouldn't be able to keep the appointment from Alene. Boss Hooker would most certainly expect him to exploit the news in the next edition of the *Messenger*.

Getting up on his short legs, he threw the letter over on Lee's desk with an expansive gesture. "You're the first to see this, Lee."

Lee took off his coat and hung it on one of the wall racks, then sat down to read the appointment.

"Phil, this is great!" he said presently, with unfeigned sincerity.

"Of course it is," Meyer said. "It's unprecedented! I'm the first Negro to be appointed to the commission."

Lee nodded, similing. "But wasn't it inevitable? The Negro population is growing bigger, it's expanding. We've got growing pains in this city, and we damn sure can use the representation."

"Sure, sure," Meyer said, waving his hand impatiently. "But the important thing is the appointment itself! There's any number of big shots the mayor could have appointed, but I got it. And do you know *why* I got it, Lee? It's because I worked my ass off to get it. Who was it put the mayor in office? Who turned the Brother's vote in last year's election? *I* did, Lee. It was my editorials that gave him the plurality he needed." He saw that Lee was not convinced. "Well, hell, boy, you can see for yourself!" He came over to Lee's desk and began to expound, slamming a fist in the palm of his hand for emphasis. "When has the Nigger vote ever been turned to a non-partisan candidate in this city? Ever since Roosevelt, the Brother has been Democrat clear up to his burr head. The only time he'll vote different is when he's made to believe that the opposing party can give him just a few more ham hocks than the Democrats. The Nigger is a lamb, Lee—you remember that, for as long as you work on this paper. The Brother is a dumb little bastard who'll go for anything that glitters. Always write down to him so he'll understand. Give him third grade sentences and a lot of tinsel, and he'll think you're God Himself."

"That's a hell of a theory," Lee said quietly.

"Well, certainly, it is!" Meyer applauded, mistaking Lee's meaning. He snatched the letter from the young man's hand and went back to seat himself. "Do you know one thing, Lee? There are 550,000 Niggers in this city, all in a population of two million. The *Messenger* reaches 150,000 of these Brothers every week, which gives us a reading potential of 400,000 or better. Only 220,000 Brothers are registered to vote. In the last election 190,000 of these Brothers voted, and 95 percent of them voted *non-partisan.*"

"And you're saying the *Messenger* made them," Lee said calmly.

"What else?" Meyer said with smug grin. "What else could have suddenly switched staunch Democrats to a non-partisan ticket? The

Messenger and *my* editorials," he answered. He waved the letter at Lee's somber black face. "And this is my reward; this is what a systematic psychological campaign can do!"

In his elation Meyer failed to see the impact his views had on Lee. Vaguely he sensed there was a difference, but he attributed it to his constant use of the word Nigger. However, his use of the word was only a twisted brand of therapy he used on himself. It was as though, with reiteration and acknowledgment of the thing called Nigger, he could in some degree, sever himself from the too real proof that it was all he could or ever be. And wasn't it true that the Nigger he spoke of was altogether different from the Nigger of himself?

He needed no textbook, no cracker's abuse, to tell him that he was indistinguishable from the black herd. However, he was outstanding in his own element, but the distinction begged of him no responsibility of comradeship.

When he said Nigger, he meant the *other* Niggers: those black little bugs who clung with disreputable adhesion to the singular abilities of individuals such as himself; who paid with unfailing regularity 15 cents each week for the childish, innocuous puffings of the *Weekly Messenger*. When he said Nigger, he meant power, stupid, directionless power; power to be guided by the inflexible steel of his desire for personal and social gain.

Consequently, he really didn't give a damn what Lee thought, not Lee or anybody like him. And at the same time he silently and graciously admitted that Lee was one of the few *real* Niggers that he liked. A little moody, perhaps, but that was the significance of the man. Temperament was what the *Messenger* needed; pure, guileless temperament. Being a *real* Nigger, Lee could touch the other *real* Niggers with his written word. When the time came, Meyer would be able to use him to best advantage.

The door to the City Room opened and Boss George Hooker came in. The Editor-in-Chief was a big man, well over six feet. He was almost bald and light-complected. His wide nose, which had been flattened in a football game while he was a student at Tuskegee Institute, spread out over his round, bulbous face and gave the impression that he was much older than his fifty-eight years. A weak, unfertile mustache, practically gray, perched unhealthily beneath the multilated proboscis and accented the wide, thick lips. He wore no coat, and his shirtsleeves were rolled neatly at the cuffs.

Between him and Phil Meyer, there was no love lost, but since Phil was a favorite of the Great Him, Hooker could do little but bury his dislike. On two occasions Hooker had informed the Great Him of shady deals wherein Meyer had been an accomplice, but the august gentleman had only wired back from New York: "Doesn't everybody?"

"Good afternoon!" the Boss said in a high, deceptively feminine voice, and blessed them with a rare smile. "I just want to alert the staff that D.S. may be expected today."

"I think we're all aware of it, Boss," Meyer informed the big man.

Boss Hooker swung his shining globe about on thick shoulders. "Where are Cy and Richards?"

"Joe's gone to the bank," Meyer said. "I can't say where Cy is." The implication was broad enough.

Boss Hooker put both hands behind his back and shook his round head with what appeared to be woe. "Drinking again, I'm sure. I don't see how long we can put up with this, Phil. It seems to be getting worse."

"He never loses any time," Meyer said in Cy's defense. "But it doesn't look so good around the office, Boss. We've got people coming in here all day long. They get the impression from Cy that we're all a bunch of winos."

Lee was concentrating on a rewrite and didn't look up.

Meyer didn't purposely seek to injure Cy's standing with Boss Hooker, but his feeling of guilt about the man was matched only by his desire to rid himself of that guilt. It was a Boss Hooker fallacy, in Cy's case, that no one was indispensable, for Cy was like a machine on press day, instructing the typesetters, riding herd on the late news round-up at City Hall, dispatching the trucks and drivers. It would be practically impossible to find someone to take over a job which had been done by one man for fifteen years, moulded for expediency by his idiosyncrasies.

Still, if Cy weren't around, Meyer would not have to look in his face and know that Cy knew—knew that he had enjoyed the sweet crush of Barbara's thighs more than once.

"Oh, I'd like you to see this, Boss," he said, seeking to change the subject with the letter of his appointment.

Boss Hooker read with some interest. "Well, *well!* Isn't that what I told you, Phil? We've got the mayor right in our back pocket! Now all we need is a project. Something to play up your role on the commission, you understand."

"I've been thinking about that new public housing outfit down by the river," Meyer said. "They've got segregated units."

"That's a damn good start, in my opinion."

"It ought to sell some papers, too."

"Naturally it will! Next week we'll put your appointment on the front page. Get one of the photographers to go with you down to the mayor's office and get a picture of him shaking hands with you."

"We ought to have the commission chairman in on that," Meyer suggested.

"Who's that?"

"Kalinowski, the alderman for Polack town."

"That shouldn't be a problem. Why don't you give him a call and arrange things?"

"I'll do that right away."

"This is wonderful!" Boss Hooker said in his high voice. "Mr. Sandersford'll be wild about it! This is the first appointment the *Messenger* has had since I was given a seat on the board of health five years ago."

"I must say it all came as a surprise, Boss," Meyer said with humble mien.

Boss Hooker waved a big hand. "Nonsense, Phil boy! With the work you did during the election, the mayor couldn't help but show his appreciation. He's done the *Messenger* a great honor."

Meyer knew there was no envy in Boss Hooker's congratulations. In fact, he knew that Boss Hooker was even more happy than himself, for the appointment opened up new areas of profit for the *Messenger*. Through connivance and immoral sycophancy in each weekly edition, the paper had been able to ring down many political favors. It was simply a matter of knowing when to open its big mouth in behalf of its black readers.

The phone rang on Meyer's desk and he picked it up quickly.

"Mr. Meyer," the switchboard operator said, "there's a Mr. Harvey on the line. He wants to speak to you. He says it's about our running contest, The Best Story of the Week."

"Well, why don't you handle it, Joan? I don't have time to answer every damn silly question these people call in about."

"He says he has some news for you, Mr. Meyer. He sounds very urgent."

"All right, all right. Put him on."

There was a clicking sound and a deep, guttural voice came through. "Hello?"

"Hello?" Meyer said.

"Hello?" again. "Hello?"

"Hello!" Meyer said. "Who is this?"

"Hello, Mr. Phil Meyer, editor of the 'Senger?"

"Yes, this is Meyer. Who is this?"

"My name's Robert Harvey. Ah live at—"

"Yes, yes, Mr. Harvey, what can I do for you?"

"Is you Mr. Phil Meyer?"

"Yes, I'm Phil Meyer! What is it you want?"

"Ah'm callin' 'bout you' contest—"

"Well, why didn't you talk to the girl about it? I'm very busy, Mr. Harvey—"

"Is yo' contest still runnin', the twenty-five dollar contest?"

"Yes, it's a regular spot," Meyer said with exasperation. "I don't have anything to do with that. If you'd like to talk to the young lady who handles it—"

"No, Ah wonts to talk with you, Mr. Meyer; Ah just wonted to find out if you still gives out twenty-five dollars for news stories."

"Yes we do, Mr. Harvey! Now if you'd—"

"Well, Ah got a story Ah think you'd give twenty-five for: my next door neighbor just killed hisself . . ."

Meyer perked up. "When did this happen?"

" 'Bout ten minutes ago. Me and my wife heard the shots and we run over. Ah already done called the police."

Meyer took his pencil and a half sheet of copy paper. "Where do you live, Mr. Harvey?"

"Ten-two-three-six West End. My neighbor lives at ten-two-three-four."

"What was his name?"

"Stanley Hardwicks."

"You say this happened ten minutes ago?"

"Yes, sir, Mr. Meyer, just ten minutes. Me and my wife run over to see what happened, and there was blood all over the place."

"Did you know Mr. Hardwicks personally?"

"Yes, sir. Me and him was first cousins . . ."

"*Cousins?*"

"We worked at the same place together until we was laid off four months ago."

"I thought you said he was your neighbor?"

"Well, he was! And he was my cousin, too."

"Was he married?"

"Oh, yeah. Had four kids."

"Where's his family?"

"Oh, they's layin' over there with him."

"Laying?" Meyer said incredulously. "You mean he's *killed* them?"

"Ever' lass one of 'em," Harvey avowed. "Wife, kids, ever'-thang . . . he even shot the dog. Blood all over the place."

"Why the hell didn't you say so?" Meyer yelled.

"Ah was gonna tell you 'bout 'em. Ah wonted to get my twenty-five dollars straightened out first. Ah wonted—"

Meyer slammed the receiver down and looked up at Boss Hooker. "That's the stupidest goddamn Nigger I've talked to in my whole life! A man just butchered his entire family, and he's talking about twenty-five bucks!" He swiveled around to face Lee, tossing over the half sheet of paper on which he'd written the dead man's address. "Lee, get the hell over there and get this story. On your way out, tell Joan to get one of the photographers to meet you there—Scotty'll be okay. Tell him to get some good, close horror shots. We'll run 'em right on page one. Get the guy's background, everything; you can probably pick that up from the idiotic bastard next door. Get a move on now before the cops padlock the joint! And don't come back here without a good set of pics!"

Meyer didn't have to repeat himself; Lee was almost out of the office before he finished speaking.

Meyer smiled after him, generously. "That boy's gonna go places."

Boss Hooker pursed his thick lips. "I hope his fervid application doesn't shy off in the wrong direction. I understand he's been doing some feature articles on a boys' club downtown."

"Yeah, he's created a sort of series out of it. I think it's kind of cute."

"You know the club I'm speaking of, then?"

"Certainly."

"You know it's sponsored by Ray Irving, the numbers man?"

"That's news to me."

Boss Hooker bobbed his bald head. "Irving usually pays for what he wants, Phil boy. Understand what I mean?"

"You think Lee's logging those articles? Irving's paying him to?"

"I've got it from a very good source," Boss Hooker enlightened him. "The boy may very well regard the payments innocently. I understand it's a sort of 'expense account' arrangement, since Lee does the pieces on his own time."

Meyer wanted to say "So what?", since there was nothing unusual about such a liaison. It was no secret that practically everyone on the *Messenger* staff, from Boss Hooker on down, took a taste every now and then from the sundry mounds of ready sugar in the city. Some of the biggest pay-offs on the paper were made through the advertising and editorial departments. Cathy and Teresa Jones, who laid out the women's section, were known to have one of the more prosperous weekly shakedowns.

Involuntarily, he flinched at the thought of Cathy Jones and for the thousandth time cursed himself for a fool—not only for getting involved that way but for letting Boss Hooker find out about it.

On high, the Editor-in-Chief smiled down in a manner that briefly gave Meyer a chill, as if reading his thoughts. "You understand we must have some semblance of integrity here, Phil. It's even in our masthead: *Integrity*."

"Certainly, Boss, but—"

"I don't want you shielding him," the big man warned. "I know he's a sort of protégé of yours. I won't allow him to consort with this gambler, for the sake of the *Messenger*'s good name. I want you to do something about it, Phil—I won't have it bandied about that *Messenger* reporters are for sale."

"Well, I'll certainly get at it, Boss—"

The door burst open and Cy Venson weaved in tipsily.

"Hi, Boss!" he said half-drunkenly, trying to right his wobbling gait under the big man's disapproving stare. "What's up, fellas? What's the latest?"

Boss Hooker crooked an ominous finger at him. "You may follow me upstairs after you get our of your things, Cy." Then he left quickly and silently.

"What the hell's wrong with him?" Cy scowled, pulling awkwardly at the buttons of his overcoat.

"You're drunk!" Meyer said. "Don't you think that's enough? You make it hard as hell for yourself. You know what a sonofabitch he is."

"Well, thanks for your concern, Phil buddy," Cy sniffed. "But it seems to me that, if I wanna drink, I can *drink*."

"You smell like a goddamn distillery."

Cy finally got out of his overcoat and straightened the lapels of his drab little suit. "I'll just go up and give him a piece of my goddamn distillery," he piped, and staggered out of the door.

Meyer's phone rang.

"Hello?" he said.

"Hello?"

A thin series of clickings told him that Joan had unintentionally given him a direct line.

"Hello?" he said again.

"Hello? Hello?"

"Just who the hell is this?" Meyer flared.

"Is this Mr. Meyer?"

"Yes, who is this?"

"Mr. Meyer, this is Harvey again . . ."

Meyer forgot himself. "Goddamn it, Harvey, what the hell do you want?"

"Ah's callin' 'bout my twenty-five dollars, Mr. Meyer. Y'all wouldn't be thinkin' 'bout not payin' me, would ya?"

"Listen, Harvey—"

"Ah give y'all a good story—"

"Yes, it's a good story—"

"And now you don't even wanna talk with me."

"I *want* to talk with you, Mr. Harvey, but it's just—"

"*Am Ah gonna get my money?* Yeah or naw, one t'other!"

"You're going to get your money, Harvey, I'll write the check myself!"

"You just better be damn sure Ah do!"

The phone clicked in Meyer's ear, and he began to curse.

When he spoke of Niggers, those were the people he was thinking of: the majority.

CHAPTER FOUR

WEST END STREET was two normal city blocks long. Its homes were legion, a twisted disorder of dwarfish wooden buildings, the snow piled high on their sway-backed skulls. The accumulated snow was left unshoveled on the walks, and from no home did there appear evidence of entrance or exit. Even the whiteness of the snow could not hide the scars of dirt and filth. The many windows of the houses, unprotected by storm windows, were steamed over by the heat of the interiors, or by the body breaths of the inhabitants, and only the idle finger marks of children on the damp surfaces implied that there was life of any sort behind the walls no thicker than cardboard.

It was as though through some post-natal recollection that Lee felt instantly afraid when he turned onto the street. He felt suddenly intimidated and apprehensive of the things and people he was about to encounter.

Mama and Daddy . . .

A strange and instantaneous turmoil bubbled up in his throat. For a long, long moment, he could not find himself, could not place himself or his destination, and he tasted the sharp new fear avidly, enjoying the bitter manifestation in his mouth.

Manodad . . .

Of course, again.

And with that thought, he was not Lee Merriweather, nor had he ever been. His was the round black thing in soft black arms, and in his mouth was the coarse black teat of a breast . . . *titty, Boo-Boo?* . . . and the smell of collard greens and fat back rind was unmistakable, intensified somehow.

Ho Ho!

And could he see the man's face! Could he *really* see it?

It was like the tom-toms of Africa, a thing he could not remember having ever heard or even seen in reality, but a thing as instinctive and natural to him as sleep. It was almost a greenness of the tropical leaves and the footpads of silent, huge and horrible things, and the music of the drumbeats accompanied his racing heart. He soared within and without—there was the *Chi-Chi* of monkeys, the *Jukkkaw* of the dancing green and yellow birds . . . and all this time was the goodness of the black, mouth-sucked teat and the strange liquid hubbub his stomach made as the thick milk nourished him . . .

Big Man see 'Merica, Big Man, Mama, Little Boo-Boo, ride Merry Weather boat . . .

44

"What the hell is wrong with me?" he shouted in the car, shuddering with a fear he could not understand.

Involuntarily, he took his hands from the wheel and clasped his head, where strange, garbled words and flashingly distorted color scenes had suddenly and painfully exploded. The car swerved in the thick snow, its rear end twisting, and slammed over the curbstone, almost up on the sidewalk. He put it in reverse and tried to back up, but the rear wheels had mired themselves in the soft stuff and merely spun until they laid down a thin layer of ice.

"Goddamn it!" he cursed, getting out of the car and taking a closer look at his predicament. He put the gears in neutral and tried to push the automobile back into the street, but he could gain no firm footing. At last he gave up and decided to walk the rest of the distance.

At the far end of the block he could see a number of the street's citizens and several police cars gathered in front of one of the wooden homes. He quickened his steps in the thick snow, wondering at the thing which had made him lose control of himself.

Partially he attributed his unrest to Phil Meyer and his brutal conception of the Negro race. It seemed doubly fantastic that a man in Meyer's position could so completely detest the people from whom he earned his living. Why hadn't he seen the man's attitude before? It was as though he were really *seeing* Meyer for the first time.

He couldn't understand it. Meyer was a Negro himself, wasn't he? Then, in a moment of desperate unreasoning, he considered the possibility that perhaps Meyer wasn't a Negro. He didn't necessarily look like one, and if a person who didn't know any better happened to be in the office when Phil's wife Alene made one of her infrequent visits, he'd swear that she was white.

Wouldn't that explain Meyer's maneating credo, if he were white? In his tenure with the *Messenger,* Lee never ceased to be amazed at the various fortifications of racial distinction the Negro had erected about himself. There were the Kappas, the Urban League, the Brotherhood of Masons. Within all of them were the higher and lower echelons of importance, and they ceased not in organizational intercourse but were carried over into the individual's daily social life.

It was as though the Negro felt in this petty autocracy a means by which he could cushion the blow of rejection he received at the hands of his white brother. In this, the Negro was superior to the white man in that he could discriminate any number of times, while his pale-faced, powerful master could exhaust his prejudices with but a handful of inferiors.

Lee was puzzled, and he was gradually becoming angry as the little light of awareness flashed on in his brain. He couldn't yet bring himself to believe his friend Tobey Balin's theory that the Negro press was doing an injustice to the Negro race, but he could not help admitting that Tobey had been searchingly correct in his estimation of the people who ran the press.

Closeted with his thoughts, he had come to his destination before he completely realized it. Several policemen in thick blue overcoats stood about the ramshackle, one-story frame house, chasing away the curious, staring neighbors. In the snow there were footprints which had blood in them.

Lee went up to the big, chalk-faced officer at the front door. "Merriweather," he said, "from the *Weekly Messenger.*"

"The what?" the cop said.

"The *Weekly Messenger* newspaper," Lee told him.

"Never heard of it," the cop said. "You better get on down there with the rest of your people."

Lee took out his press card and let the cop take a look.

"Oh!" the officer said with recognition. "You're from that Colored newspaper. Well, what do you want?"

"I want to take a look around, if it's all right. We got a call about the killings . . ."

"Well, you'd better hurry it up. The cor'ner's men'll be here in a minute and we're gonna shut this place up."

He was admitted without further delay into the drab, dark little front room of the house. In the far corner was an ancient coal stove; ashes poked out like fat, gray excrement from the grate doors. The walls of the room were scarred and the wallpaper hung off in patches. A dirty blue couch, possibly ten to fifteen years old, sat under the stringy curtains of the front window, the only piece of furniture in the room.

Two Negro detectives, with whom Lee was acquainted from police headquarters downtown, were hunched over the body of what appeared to be a child. Pools of blood lay over the floor, and in some of them was the lifeless gray muck of brain matter.

One of the detectives, a short black man with a mustache glared up at Lee. "What the hell do you want?" he asked irritably.

"I'm Merriweather—" Lee started.

"I know who the hell you are," the detective cut him off. "You guys are right on the ball, huh? This'll make a big spread next week, won't it?" The man's face was sick. He stood up, and Lee could see that his snowshoes were black with blood. "C'mere, Merriweather, and take a close look. I'm gonna help you make your spread."

Lee came over and looked down. The child's face was indistinguishable. The head looked as though it had exploded, and one side of the face was blown completely off, exposing raw, red tendons and a portion of the jawbone. The child was dressed in a summer polo shirt and summer shorts; whether it was a boy or girl, Lee couldn't make out. The right arm was twisted under the upper part of the body and looked as though it were broken. The feet were shoeless.

The other detective, a tall, light-skinned man, got up and went to the front door. He leaned with both hands on the door jamb, his head down.

"Kinda pretty, huh, Merriweather?" the black cop said. "This boy was six years old . . . six years old! You think this is something? You come with me, boy, you just come with me! I'm gonna give you your goddamn spread, believe me!"

They went into the next room, a bedroom, where a mattress, blood-soaked and formlessly submitted to the tithes of time and tons of unknown bodies, was the only bit of furniture. On the mattress lay three small children, one scarcely a toddler. Their bodies and arms locked in a sleep without waking, each one of them possessed a round, nut-sized hole in its forehead.

Drawn closer by the horror, Lee saw that each small chest had been crushed, as though the heavy iron foot of God had mercifully aided in speeding their lives away. The dirty, plaster-broken walls were streaked scarlet with blood, published with the frenzied red fingermarks of the killer.

Lee began to puke. He couldn't stop himself; the contents of his belly sprayed forth and some of it stained his overcoat.

"Oh, no, *no!*" the detective hollered at his senseless ears. "Not *you* guys! Not you guys on the *Messenger!* This kinda stuff sells papers, don't it, Merriweather? Just think what the press run'll be next week!" He grabbed Lee by the scuff of his overcoat and fairly dragged his retching body into the next room.

"Murder and mayhem! That's the life blood of our black papers! That's how they stay alive from week to week! Well, Merriweather, the *Messenger'll* get a hell of a shot in the arm next issue! Take a look! Take a look, goddamn you!"

The man lay on the floor. There was little left of his head.

"He ran outa bullets on the kids, but he still had a shotgun!"

Now look at the woman. Eyes gouged with steel spikes, the shock struck him so deeply.

"She was pregnant, Merriweather! When he aimed that shotgun he made sure neither one of 'em came out of it!"

Manomom.

There was only an iron bedstead and rumpled mattress, and the woman lay on it. Her face was undamaged, and it was a beautiful face, with fine lips, and the eyes were closed as though sleeping. The mound of her belly in the housedress was a mushy, red formlessness.

The murderer had murdered himself completely. The shotgun was still clutched in his dead fingers, and his legs were crossed, one over the other, as though he were leisurely napping on the bloody floor. The remains of what had been the top of his head were sieved upon the ceiling and walls.

"Do you wanna see the dog, too, Merriweather? It's out on the back porch . . ."

48

It was too much for Lee. He sank to his knees. The convulsions of his stomach became so violent he could barely breathe. He was horribly aware that his hands and fingers were spread in the blood of these people, on the floor, but there was nothing he could do about it.

He died for them again; he could feel the pain of the bullets entering his skull, the crush of the father's foot lay against his throbbing heart . . . The birdshot against the belly of his mother was most painful, and he knew in his pain that he would never, ever see her again, only now realizing he had wanted to so desperately . . . or know more of her than the huge, maternal breasts: The memory, the knowledge of death, was too much; it was a red, digging spear which unearthed an unknown heritage buried deep in his belly and accused him of crimes of which he had no cognizance.

". . . and do you know why, Merriweather?" the detective asked repeatedly from a far-off fog. "He was *tired* of starving to death! He wanted to eat, and he wanted his kids to eat! Is that so hard to understand? When you write your goddamn spread, you be sure to say he was crazy—crazy with hunger!"

Lee got up screaming. "He killed my mother! He killed my mother!"

"Hey . . . Merriweather!"

"He killed her!" he screamed, and screamed again: "He killed her! He killed her! He killed her!"

The detective's palm came across his mouth, meat-slamming, stinging the flesh, releasing the salty, reviving taste of blood to his tongue. He crumpled without strength into the arms of the man, beginning to sob. The tears came, hot and blinding, and ran over the brims of his black cheeks. He buried his head against the hard fiber of the man and cried until his throat felt dry and his brain was throbbing with pressure.

"I'm sorry, kid . . ." The voice of one who newly understood seemed to whisper in a frosty tunnel. "I'm sorry as hell about that . . ."

But for Lee it was just beginning. In the midst of this death he had glimpsed a bit of the searing reality of life. In no way could he

49

assure himself that what he felt was not real, that each significant part of himself was not in some way linked to these bodies of drying gore. Never had he been so shocked; not so even on the day when mental development informed him that he had no mother or father, that he was like an inane piece of heavenly firmament, caused not by the force of inception and conception . . . but simply *there,* as though it had always been.

He clung to the detective so that his sanity would not be completely unhinged. In this he could feel the warmth and breath of life, and he was not entirely beseeched by the unanswerable question, Why? In this he could know that *he* was real and the man, too, was real and in this moment not even death could separate them.

He wished for Tobey and Diana, for now he was unquestionably frightened; and they were so liberally endowed with that virtuous element of honesty—of strength at least, since total honesty seemed to be beyond the grasp of man . . . and even God.

Mano—

"Look, kid," the detective continued to whisper gently. "I didn't know it was your first time. First time or last, it's not something you get used to. Nobody ever gets used to dying."

He put a fatherly arm about the sobbing Lee and led him again to the front room. The coroner's men were just entering with wicker baskets in varying sizes. Behind them a tall, cigar-puffing Negro came in with a press camera and flash attachment.

"Quite a mess, huh, Merriweather?" he said, coming over to them. Then he noticed Lee's reddened eyes. "Got to ya, huh? Always does, the first time. What kinda shots you want?"

Lee didn't answer.

"Look, Scotty," the detective told him, "you better hurry up and get the hell out of here, or I'm gonna run you out!"

"Okay, okayyyy!" the photographer brayed appeasingly, "This looks like a fine start," he said, looking down at the child's body. He moved around with cold efficiency on the blood-stained floor, snapping his pictures, reversing the film plate with slapping expert's hands. "Where're the others? I wanna lock this up tight before the basket boys goof everything. Boy, I wish I could run this in technicolor!"

"You got a good stomach!" the detective told him disgustedly.

"Why should I care? The *Messenger* is only gonna pay me four and a half for each pic they use, anyway. They'll probably wind up using just one—that don't even pay for my gas money."

The detective grudgingly told him where the other bodies were, and he was back in a moment, grinning and patting his camera. "Boy, this baby is gonna be fine on that detail! I got a close-up of the old gal's face. It's gonna be a beauty, a be-uu-*tee!*" He pointed the camera at the detective and Lee and snapped the shutter. "Dusssh!" he said.

"I'd like to give you a douche," the detective told him, "right up your—"

"The *Messenger* wouldn't let ya," Scotty warned. "They've got a *special* douche they give the employees!"

"All right, you guys can get the hell on out of here." To Lee, who was still in a fairly dazed state, he said again, "I'm sorry, Merriweather. I shoulda remembered you only work for that rag."

"Death and destruction, copper!" Scotty called back cheerily.

Slowly, Lee moved out into the bloody snow of the front yard. For the first time he noticed the blood on his hands, and numbly he took a handkerchief from his pocket and began to wipe the mess away.

Behind him, the photographer had paused to take a shot of the dark, one-sided little shack. " 'This is the house where death struck violently Friday afternoon,' " he stated. "That'll make a fine cutline. Whaddayou think, Merriweather? This is the juiciest bit the *Messenger* has had in some time, huh?"

"I don't know." Lee's eyes had brought themselves to focus on the faces of the people crowded about the front yard. The lust and smell of death was about them, and it seemed to him that in the jumbled pattern of black faces he could see the faces of the dead children, of the dead mother and father. He moved with difficulty into their midst.

Scotty caught up with him and chattered happily. "This is the

5 1

best thing we've had since the nut cut off his mother's head last year and buried it in the backyard . . . Hey! Merriweather! Where ya going?"

"My car . . ."

"Yeah, I saw it down the street. What'd you do, have a wreck or something?"

"No . . ."

"Well, you need a hand." He pointed to his late model sedan parked in front of the house. "C'mon, get in. We'll go down and dig ya out."

A small, thin Negro, about forty and wearing a torn dirty parka came over to them. "Say, you fellas from the 'Senger?"

"That's right," Scotty told him.

The man's face lighted up in a smile. "Well, don't y'all wonna talk with me?"

"Who are you?" Scotty asked him distastefully.

"Ah'm Harvey!" the man said expectantly. "Them folks in there was my kinfolks!"

"Here's the man you wanna talk to. This is Mr. Merriweather, a reporter on the *Messenger*."

"What about my twenty-five dollars?" Harvey asked Lee anxiously, his dark, elf-like face bobbing up. "Mr. Meyer said he was gone send me a check. Is you got it?"

Lee shook his head. "You'll probably get that in the mail, Mr. Harvey."

"Well, whenim Ah gone get it?" Harvey insisted, sticking out a threatening chin.

"That's something I couldn't tell you, Mr. Harvey. I imagine you'll be getting it pretty soon, though."

"Ah give y'all a good story!" Harvey said. "Ah coulda told the *Eagle* or *Tribune*, but they don't give no 'ward like the 'Senger."

"I can assure you that we appreciate your calling us first, and I'm positive the *Messenger'll* pay promptly for the information."

"Ah coulda even called one of the white papers," Harvey's voice said, beginning to rise with his anger, "but Ah didn't, and Ah coulda if Ah'da just wonted! Ah betcha *they* woulda paid me right off for the news! But naw! Ah wonted to give the news to my own color, and they ain't even thinkin' 'bout payin' me! That's the way Niggahs is!"

"In the case of Niggers like you," Scotty said scornfully, "maybe that's the way they should be."

"If y'all don't pay me," Harvey shouted, shaking a long finger under Lee's nose, "Ah'm gonna have my law'er sue the hell outcha!"

A group of interested spectators began to circle them.

"There's no sense in me arguing with you, Mr. Harvey," Lee said. "Nobody at the *Messenger* refused to give you the twenty-five dollars."

"Ah got witnesses!" Harvey claimed. "Ah got witnesses kin say the '*Senger* promised me my twenty-five dollars!" He turned to the faces in the crowd. "Ain't that right? Ain't that what Ah told y'all?"

"Dass right," the witnesses witnessed. "Dass what you say, Harv man . . ."

"They ain't gone pay you, Harv man, they don't ever pays . . ."

"C'mon, Merriweather," Scotty said. "Let's get the hell out of here!"

"See dere!" Harvey yanked accusingly, turning on them. "See how they runnin'!"

"We're not running!" Lee barked at him suddenly, the blood vessels standing out on his smooth, black forehead. "Why the hell should we run?"

" 'Cause you owes me twenty-five dollars and don't 'tend to pay!" Harvey yelped his indictment. "Y'all big soshalities don't do nothin' but soak up all the news you kin with a lie! You sits 'round at yo' big parties off what the poor black folks pays for the news you sucked off 'em! You never 'tends to pay for nothin' but yo' big parties and yo' big soshalite dances!"

"Why is it y'all don't take pitchers of nothin' but half white gals in that paper?" a black woman inquired from the crowd.

"Dass right! Dass right!" someone else said. "The on'y time they takes pitchers of black folks is when they get blood in they eyes, like Harv man's cousin!"

"Dass s'posed to be the black man's paper, but ever' week they got mo' white faces in it than black," mumbled the black face of the crowd.

Harvey was stirred to a frenzy. "Ah wonts my money! Ah ain't gone let y'all cheat me the way you been cheatin' the black folks!"

The coroner's men came out of the house with six baskets, and the crowd was hypnotically possessed, it seemed, by a collective moan of lamentation. The policemen came to clear the people back as the bearers of death deposited the corpses in the dark hole of a waiting police paddy wagon with rough indifference.

"Po' Harv man!" the people cried for the living.

"Oh, my po' cousin!" Harvey wailed for the dead. "My po' cousin an' his fam'ly!" He followed after the men with the baskets. "Oh, po' cousin Stanley and yo' fam'ly, please God rest you in peace!"

Death's handymen closed the door of the van, oblivious to Harvey's cries of mourning. Then they got in and drove off.

"All right, folks," the cops said. "Break it up! Break it up! Go on home; there's nothing else to see here."

But the people were not convinced, hovering like vultures about the front walk.

Harvey took this opportunity to resume his harangue against the *Messenger* and its employees. "See my po' cousin and his fam'ly gone to God? The *'Senger*'ll sell a million papers on account of that! All them half-white folks'll profit 'cause of my cousin an' his fam'ly, but they won't give me my due! They's gonna use my twenty-five dollars to buy likker for they bigshot parties and pretty dresses for they half-white women!"

"Here!" Lee cried at him, sickened by the exhibition. "Here's your goddamn lousy twenty-five dollars!" He took twenty-five dollars from the seventy-dollar pay he had received that afternoon and pushed it into Harvey's hungry fist.

Harvey was mollified. "You's only givin' me my just due. You's only givin' me what Ah had a right to." He shoved the money into his pocket. "Now, if you ever needs any mo' news—"

Lee opened the door of Scotty's car and got in. Scotty went around to the driver's side and slipped under the wheel.

"You can't help feeling ashamed when you meet a Nigger like that," he said. "Ashamed that you belong to them. You know what I mean?"

"The man doesn't know any better," Lee said.

Scotty started the car's engine and warmed away its chill before putting it in gear. "He knows enough to squeeze twenty-five pieces out of you. He was a crafty little sonofabitch!"

Lee watched the crowd slowly and reluctantly disperse. "You can't blame these people. It's their environment; they've never known anything else."

"Don't make excuses for 'em," Scotty snorted.

"So we're just a little bit more fortunate; so maybe we're just a little bit more educated," Lee said. "That doesn't give us the right to condemn them."

"It doesn't give us the right to kiss their dirty asses, either! That bastard never would have gotten twenty-five bills out of *me*."

Lee turned to watch Scotty chew belligerently at his cigar. "Doesn't it make you feel sort of funny?" he asked.

"What?"

"That these people should feel the way they do about the *Messenger*?"

"Hell, no. Why should I?"

"Some of the things that man said were true . . ."

Scotty shrugged. "Maybe." He put the car in gear and made it slide off smoothly from the curb. "Street's too small to turn around on, and I don't wanna get stuck like you. We'll have to go around the block."

Lee broached the subject again. "Scotty, the *Messenger* is supposed to represent these people. How can it represent a people who don't even trust it?"

Scotty shook his head. "That's no concern of mine, kid. I catch enough hell in my darkroom without trying to figure out world problems. As long as I get my four-fifty, I don't give a damn what happens on the *Messenger*. If it wasn't that I was just getting my own shop started, the *Messenger* could throw its sloppy jobs somewhere else. Four-fifty for each lousy shot! Yahk, yahk, yahk!" He squinted thoughtfully at Lee. "You'd be surprised how many pics I make for the *Messenger* each week—and just how many show up in the pages, without even a credit line! For four-fifty! And will Boss Hooker pay more? Not to save your neck, he won't." He laughed the queer yahking sound again. "You think I give a damn what people think about the *Messenger,* especially *those* people? I wish I could give you some small idea what I think about it myself. Four dollars and fifty stinking pennies! I'll tell you about us guys who work as photographers for the *Messenger,* Merriweather—we don't give a damn. How can you, when you get a poor engraving or a botched-up Fairchild?" He winked. "You'll learn soon, Merriweather, that the *Messenger* doesn't give a damn about you, and then you'll get so you won't give a damn about the *Messenger.*"

"There has to be more to it than that—"

"Now you're trying to defend the *Messenger,*" Scotty said.

"How could I—"

"Exactly—how could you? The *Messenger* can't even defend itself! Just name me one solid achievement it's made, just *one.* It's been a rag for more than two decades, and that's all it'll ever be.

"Who buys the *Messenger,* Merriweather?" he asked. "Who do you think keeps that paper going? It's people like where we just came from, that's who. A hundred thousand of them, every week. Why do they buy it, do you think? It's because they're bloody little bastards, and they know that the *Messenger* knows it. They can pick up any week's issue and read about Joe Jones beating his old lady, or some other drunken slouch who's being held for assault and battery. But first, they read column four on the first page and find out how many black sisters were arrested last week for accosting and soliciting. Or maybe the lead streamer'll be about Johnny Jones, Joe's brother, who stuck a knife in some guy in some bar about some bitch." He was bitter now. "Merriweather, I've been clicking the shutter for Boss Hooker for nine years and I know what I'm talking about. And don't you think the *Messenger* doesn't consciously slant its news. It slants its news just like it slants its salaries. Down, brother, down! Everything about it is low: low news, low salaries, low people. That's why a guy like Douglas Sandersford is rich."

Lee could muster but a mute defense for the *Messenger*. He could not tell Scotty that until recently the *Messenger* had been like an umbilical cord to him, nourishing him with the opportunity to write. Scotty made him feel like a conspirator against a group of dumb, lamb-like people.

What was happening to him? He felt as though the earth had moved and left him standing on the airless waste of nothing. Scotty honestly believed that what he said was true. And if it was true, then the earth had really shifted its position, leaving him to reenact, in fact, a vaguely-remembered dream role in a nightmare that had recurred frequently when he was a child.

Then, as now, he had felt on awakening the special terror of the import in his dream seclusion.

As a child he had suffered from a sense of difference from the other children in the Ward home—the seclusion had been real and self-imposed.

His head began to ache, and he could smell the blood of man and woman upon his hands. He rubbed his hands against his coat, but it did no good.

Now, Lee's two worlds of child and man were merged—still, his sense of difference presented an elementary interpretation.

Now, however, he would sooner face damnation than the bewilderment and horror of a nightmare come true.

But this time he would not face exile so easily. The escapist world was going to come up with some reasons—it would be damned sure about that.

Manodadmanomom

CHAPTER FIVE

IT WAS AS THOUGH GRACE and capriciousness had both arrived incarnate at the *Messenger* offices when Teresa and Cathy Jones entered that afternoon.

It was easy to see by their light-skinned, tear-drop faces that they were sisters, but it was there all resemblance ended. Teresa was short and stocky, heavy-limbed, and although Cathy was bequeathed the same thickness of bone she was tall and wide-hipped.

Their clothes contrasted their general personalities: Teresa's were sensible and quietly expensive, giving the subtle impression of the height she lacked, while Cathy's were nebulous and frothy, accenting the round, round hips, disdaining with their summery blossoms the severity of winter.

"Doll!" she said to Joan when they came in. "And how are *you* today? You're looking wonderful, dear! I like your style, I must say. I've been considering a fashion extravaganza at the Gaymount, and you'd make the *too* perfect model! Is Mr. Meyer in? Any calls for me today?"

"No calls, Miss Jones," the girl replied. "But you've got some mail."

"How nice!"

"I left it on your desk," Joan told her.

Teresa lighted a cigaret and leaned across the front counter. "Do you have our checks, or does Miss Hill?"

"Miss Hill told me to tell you she left your checks with Mr. Meyer, Miss Jones."

"Why not out here?" Teresa said in her deep, man-like voice. "We usually pick 'em up from you or Miss Hill on our day off."

"Didn't you know, Miss Jones? Mr. Sandersford is getting in some time today. I think Mr. Meyer wants to talk to you about his arrival."

"Not the old man?" Teresa said with pleased surprise. "Well, that's a wonderful change of pace! D.S. is one of the few *men* I know, even if he is as old as Methuselah."

"Darling Terry," Cathy said. "Didn't I tell you the Great Him was getting in today? It must have slipped my mind."

"That figures," Teresa told her with unsister-like coldness. "Has Mr. Sandersford come around yet?" she asked Joan.

"No, Miss Jones. I just received a wire for Mr. Hooker, from Mr. Sandersford. He said he might be delayed."

"But this is our day off, darling!" Cathy cried. "I thought he'd be here by now!"

"Why all the sweat?" Teresa asked her. "You don't have any appointments today. Or do you?"

"I just thought he'd be here by now, that's all."

Lee Merriweather and the photographer Scotty came in the front door just then.

"Hi, gals!" Scotty greeted them.

"Hail mighty Casey, Crime Photographer!" Teresa said. "You look like you just had a fine serving of catfish eyeball stew, Front Page. I bet you've got some beauties in that little box."

"Bee-uu-*tees!*" Scotty said with a broad wink. "Merriweather and me just covered a joint with five murders and one suicide. When I carry the film through the mix I'll give you girls a couple copies for your albums. On dark, snowy nights, when you're sitting around the fireside with your grandkids, you can show 'em what the good old days were like when you worked for the *Messenger.*"

"You'd better give them to the poor woman's Abby Van Buren, here," Teresa said, nodding at her sister. "They'll go over big with her collection of etchings."

"Etchings?" Scotty said. "Maybe I oughta come up to your place and borrow a few, Miss Jones."

"But you can't, Doll, because that's how I got them—on loan. Anyway, for a man who's just covered five murders, they'd seem mighty tame."

"And one suicide," Scotty amended.

Cathy shuddered. "I think it's just horrible! Don't people have better things to do with themselves?"

Scotty winked at her slowly. "*Some* people don't."

Without a word, Lee went down the hall to the City Room and closed the door behind him.

"What's the matter with junior?" Teresa said, staring after him.

"He was kinda shook up," Scotty informed her. "It was his first glimmer at so much blood at one time."

"Oh," Teresa said, and her tone was understanding.

Scotty followed after Lee. "I'll see you gals later. I'm gonna let Der Führer know I've accomplished his mission."

"I think that Lee is kind of cute, don't you?" Cathy asked her sister.

"Lee?" Teresa pursed her lips and stared hard at the willowy young woman. "You getting ideas again?"

Cathy fluffed the hair at the back of her skull. "I just said I thought he was cute. He's so black and—and *African.*"

"You better pull in your claws, big Sis. It takes two to tango, and I don't think Lee knows how."

Cathy burst out in a pearly little laugh. "That goes to show how much *you* know."

"What?"

She swished away smoothly on her high heels. "I think I'll go upstairs and freshen my face a little."

"I think I'll go with you," Teresa said, patting her hips suggestively, "but it won't be my face I'll freshen."

They went up the long steps to the second floor of the ancient building, where the women's rest room and lavatory were located. In a straight line on the second floor were situated the business offices of the *Messenger,* disemboweled rooms which had been originally intended as apartments by the architect. All six doors were closed and only a faint chatter of typewriters and voices could be heard. Boss Hooker's office, with a large placard on the door making it impossible to mistake the majestic occupancy, adjoined the women's room.

"Sometimes I think that guy's got his office here purposely,"

Teresa observed. "I bet he can tell exactly who's made the movement by the way they flush the john."

She went back to the toilet area, which was divided from the sitting room by a swinging plywood door. Cathy sat down at the small public vanity near the far wall and began to apply a light, pink lipstick.

"Hey," Teresa called from the toilet. "What did you mean, that shows how much *I* know?"

"What's that?" Cathy said absently, poking her lips at her reflection.

"You know damn well what I said," Teresa called. "You were talking about Lee."

"Oh."

"What did you mean?"

"Oh, I didn't mean anything."

"Don't give me that," Teresa said.

"Well, mercy, Terry, if you didn't see it why should I tell you? All you have to do is *look* at them."

The toilet flushed tiredly, and in a few moments she could hear Teresa washing up at the basin in the rear. In several seconds the shorter woman was standing behind her at the vanity.

"If I didn't see what?" she said. "And all I have to do is look at *who?*"

"Oh, nothing, Doll," her sister said petulantly. "Why do you keep bugging me about it?"

"Because I know the way you work," she was answered bluntly. "If you know any dirt about that kid, you just keep it quiet. Maybe he's a little green, but Lee is as gentle and innocent as a rabbit, and I don't want to see you or any of the other buzzards in this office start tearing at him."

"But of course he's nice, Terry! I didn't say he wasn't, and I don't know if the dirt we're talking about is dirt at all."

"Just what is this dirt you don't really know is dirt at all, if any?"

Cathy caressed her smooth lips against themselves. "You mean to tell me you haven't noticed the way they act around each other?"

61

"Who?"

"Lee and—well, let me tell you this way, darling. I've got friends, you know."

"That's about the nicest name I've ever heard them called."

"Nevertheless, one of them happens to live in the same apartment building that Lee lives in."

"Is this friend a man or woman? But that's a silly question, isn't it?"

"Well, naturally I find my most lasting friendships in the male sex, honey!"

"Naturally!"

"Well, as I was saying, this friend lives on the same floor that Lee does—"

"Ah, the plot thickens."

"As a matter of fact, his apartment faces Lee's. And who do you suppose has been coming up to keep our little black boy company?"

"I'll take just one quess. A little black girl."

"Certainly it's a girl, but the lady I'm talking about is a good deal fairer than either one of us."

"Honestly, big Sis, you're full of surprises!" Teresa said with mock astonishment. "It's a revelation to hear you admit something like that."

Cathy grinned at her sister in the mirror. "Well, *isn't* Diana Hill?"

"Diana? Not Boss Hooker's—?"

"My friend has very good eyesight, and he happens to be acquainted with Diana from one of the *Messenger*'s social whirls I invited him to."

"Diana?" Teresa said again, as though the word were impossible. "Kate, do you suppose—? But, no, he couldn't, could he? Boss Hooker, I mean?" She smiled happily at the information. "I think it's wonderful! They're the two nicest kids who've ever worked in this rat mill. And, come to think of it, they make a fine couple." Then she looked at her sister with suspicion. "I want to say more power to 'em, but I'd like to know what you've got cooked up."

Cathy looked up with big-eyed innocence. "Not a thing, Doll!

I just happened to be in the way of the news, you know, and it really doesn't make me one bit of difference."

"I just *hope* it doesn't."

"Why must you always think the worst of me?" Cathy despaired.

"Because you never let me think the best of you, *Dahll*. I'm still trying to get over that Phil Meyer episode."

Cathy's face took on a venomous expression. "Don't mention that bastard!"

"To know him is to love him," her sister chirped. "You and I have been working for the *Messenger* for ten years, Kate. We *know* Meyer, or at least *I* do. I admit he has a way about him, but I saw through that the first time he shot me a proposition. I tried to tell you about him right after you came out of high school—I told you he was no good."

"And didn't I believe you?"

"Sure, you did, right up to the time you started believing *him*. And the only reason he hadn't been up your dresstail before then was because I had a firm hand on you. But after you got hip—after you started laying out with your fine 'friends'—"

"There you go bugging me!" Cathy said bitterly. "How long did you suppose you could shelter me from the world, Doll? In three years I'll be thirty, and I've had you hanging over my shoulder like my conscience for the last fifteen! All right, so you're the eldest, but don't try to give me any of your Mother Duck philosophy. Remember my advice to the lovelorn column: I haven't been wrong yet."

Teresa put a gentle hand on her sister's shoulder. "Look, Kate honey, we've been alone for most of our lives. I *had* to be the Mother Duck. All it takes to get along in this world is mother*wit,* something you were born with. Diana Hill is a good example of that. The kid's only twenty-two, but she told me she's been taking care of herself since her mother died four years ago . . ."

"Are you implying that I *can't* take care of myself?" Cathy said angrily. "Diana lives at the YWCA. If she's so great, why doesn't she get out in the world, pray why? It's because the YWCA is *safe,*

Doll, that's why. Oh, she's a great example of motherwit, if Lee Merriweather is any credit."

"And what's wrong with Lee?"

Cathy turned to survey her smooth features and apply a bit of mascara. "Nothing, Doll, except that he's black."

"Just a while ago he couldn't have been too black for you—he was so *African,* to quote you."

Cathy tinkled a high little laugh. "I was thinking of him in bed. Doll! What woman could appreciate such an atrociously black creature socially?"

"The same woman who could appreciate a wet-mouthed slob like Ken Bussey," Teresa said pointedly.

"Oh, Terry!" Cathy sighed. "Ken is just a fancy, I fancy, whose usefulness has just about come to an end."

"I'll lay odds that the only reason Diana doesn't make her relationship with Lee public is because her job is at stake," Teresa asserted.

"Not only her job, darling, but her whole life. How could you compare Diana with me? She's so *utterly* gauche!"

"At least she's honest, Kate, and that's a word I think you've forgotten the definition of."

Cathy sneered with an air of delicacy. "At the sake of forgetting that definition, I've learned others: comfort, money, glamour. And I've also learned that I don't need you to continually pull my coat. I like what I am and I like what I'm doing. I'll confess, Doll, that I've never had the relaxation I'm having now until I moved from your place."

"Neither have I, I'll have to confess."

Cathy looked up at her secretly. "As for Mr. Phil Meyer, the road is usually rocky to Rome, you know."

"What do you mean, Kate?"

"Please, dear, let's forget it, shall we?"

Teresa watched her sister with apprehension, for her referance to Phil Meyer was not without meaning. Their short love affair having been anything but idyllic, Cathy still bore traces of the hot, burning flames of its violence.

Teresa was almost frightened of her sister, and it was at moments like this, when she lost the voice of her arguments, that this fear was shamelessly apparent. But it was more a terror than fear, a terrified awe that respected the self-creation of Cathy, the still unleashed lusts within that fomented and boiled under a weakening outer crust.

She felt that there was more to know of Phil's and Cathy's relations than her sister had revealed to her. In the many years she had worked for the *Messenger,* Teresa had seen the women come and go in Phil Meyer's life, and never had any one of them been so coldly rejected as had Cathy. No, no woman ever had.

It might have been all right if Cathy had reacted as a normal woman, if she had cried the abuse of a woman scorned. But her cultured affectations, however seemingly pretentious, were psychologically real, Teresa knew, and they would not let her react as a normal woman. Therefore it was practically impossible for Teresa to read her motive. Read her? She had never really been able to *know* Cathy, or even to *love* Cathy. She had simply permitted herself to tolerate Cathy, for her sister was an iconoclast when it came down to the fragile little niceties of love. Trusting her with such a sacred symbol was like putting a new born babe in the arms of a wild gorilla.

It was this inability on Cathy's part to receive love which additionally frightened Teresa. Never had her lovely sister been called on to *give* her love, and such a thing might very well have occurred in the affair with Meyer.

If she *had* fallen in love with Phil Meyer, there was bound to be trouble, and Teresa knew no manner by which she could go about stopping it.

Without a further exchange, they went back downstairs and into the City Room.

"Hi, girls!" Cy Venson, only half sobered, waggled a hand as they entered.

"Hi, baby," Teresa said. "If they ever stop making gin I'll be able to tell it. All I have to do is look in your face on Fridays."

"If you ever wanna see why they *should* stop making it," Cy twittered alcoholically, "take a look in my face on Saturdays."

"Darling," Cathy said, placing a hand on his shoulder, "*I* think you look marvelous!"

"Cathy," Cy said, giving her body a wide-eyed examination, "have I ever told you how much you remind me of Elsa Maxwell?"

"Not lately, Pets. For the last two weeks you've told me I remind you of Bette Davis."

"That was before I saw how much you resembled Elsa!"

"Cy, really!" she pouted. Nimbly, her glance strayed over to Meyer's desk, but she saw that he hadn't paid any attention to their entrance. He was involved in a heated conversation with Lee Merriweather.

To Cy, she said: "Everything's arranged, Doll. Maybe you'd want to stop around to the Gaymount Hotel in a few moments? I'd like to buy you a drink."

"Not unless it's a double gin," Cy warned her. "Singles are no good unless they come in couples."

Cathy gave him a brilliant and knowing smile. "A double, I promise."

"Sold!"

She followed behind Teresa over to where Phil Meyer was berating Lee Merriweather.

"You had no business doing it," Meyer was saying. "I'm not going to be responsible, Lee, and the *Messenger* isn't either."

"But what else could I do?" Lee said.

Meyer swung back on the swivel of his chair adamantly. "I told that bastard when he called that he'd probably get the twenty-five dollars and that I'd send him a check. We have no way of knowing whether his story will lead the issue or not at this point. You had no business *doing* it, Lee!"

"Listen, Phil, if you could have heard what that guy was saying about the *Messenger*—"

"I don't give a damn *what* he was saying about the *Messenger*. If we listened to half of what those crazy Niggers say we wouldn't make a dime." He sat forward in his chair and looked up at Lee stonily. "What I'm saying is that you had no authorization to give that man twenty-five dollars. Now you're out of twenty-five dollars, that's all there is to it."

For the first time since she had known him, Cathy saw an angry glow come over Lee's dark features. "Then you won't give me a voucher?" he said quietly.

"Well, of course I won't!" Meyer told him. "If the loss of twenty-five dollars is going to effectively pound it in your head that your first responsibility comes under the heading of reporter and reporter only, not some goddamn paymaster to every black bastard who puts the bite on you, then it's twenty-five dollars well spent. I won't back up your patch-in-the-ass-idealism and neither will the *Messenger*."

"I don't think it's fair," Lee said, eyes unnaturally wide and flashing on Meyer's face. "I didn't go out there with the intention of paying anybody off. When I heard this guy kicking the *Messenger*, what else could I do? Wasn't I anything else but a reporter? Isn't it one of my duties as an employee of the *Messenger* to uphold its integrity!" He shook his head, almost trembling with a massive inner fury. "Maybe I'm stupid, Phil, but I don't understand! To that simple little man and those people standing around watching, I *was* the *Messenger*. In a situation like that, could *you* have divorced yourself so easily?"

"As easily as you divorced yourself from twenty-five dollars," Meyer told him blandly. "The point is, you stepped out of your place, and your place is reporter for the *Messenger*. Nobody authorized you to take up the *Messenger's* banner. You took it on yourself. And for what good? Those people out there have probably forgotten you now. Even that little bloodsucker has probably forgotten you. I'll bet a dime to doughnuts, if you were to go back to that guy's house right now you'd find both him and his squaw sloppy drunk. Now is that any good?"

"The point is, the man was *promised* the money! The *Messenger* promised him the money! What good are we doing the public when we back out on our promises?"

The flesh around Meyer's eyes became livid with his exasperation. "Goddamn it, when are you going to get it through your big Nigger skull that we don't owe these people a damn thing! The *Messenger* can afford to back its ass out of any promise it feels *big* enough to back out of! And when it comes to a promise we gave one of those black little nobodies out there in the street, we're big enough!" He stood up on his short legs and pounded his desk. "First of all, who do we serve? Not the public but the Great Him, a guy who founded this paper twenty-five and more years ago. He's the one to whom we owe fealty, and our jobs. Secondly, who do we serve? Our advertisers, that's who! You think we can run this paper on fifteen grand a week, the subscription rate? Why, it takes more than ten grand a week to job this paper! It's our advertisers who bring in the gravy, boy! Our nationwide contracts. Lastly, who do we *push*? We push the Nigger in the streets, that goddamn little kid. The more we offend him and tell him the white man's tromping on him, the better he likes it—and the more business he gives our white advertisers. The same whites who, in one way or another, keep Rufus running-drunk with a sore ass and a belt around his gut tightened to the last hole. He's gonna buy our paper regardless, and twenty-five dollars more or less isn't going to encourage him any."

Lee turned quickly and went back to his desk. He sat down and rolled a sheet of paper into his typewriter. His face was quiet, but his lips were drawn tightly together. He began to type.

"Lee—" Meyer started, but Lee didn't answer. Then he turned and saw the women staring at him. "Oh . . . how are you doing, girls?"

"Quite a lecture," Teresa winked, leaning over to poke a stiff finger in his chest. "I'd like to have it mimeographed in a pamphlet, along with Lincoln's Emancipation Proclamation. I'd also see to it that your byline was more prominent than Linc's; a dead rail-splitter doesn't cop any stars under our point system, does he, kid?"

Meyer sat down. "It'd be ambiguous, don't you think?"

Teresa made her eyes roll to the back of her head and groped about as though blind. "It'd simply be to show how two individuals of separate races and divided by about a hundred years could have held such opposing views about the same subject. Good thing for Abe he was born ahead of your time."

He looked up at her with annoyance. His gaze avoided Cathy, however, and she purposely made herself more conspicuous by placing an ample buttock on the edge of his desk.

"I guess you girls want your checks," he said.

"I don't see why Boss Hooker spends money on checks," Teresa said. "Why not make 'em out in food orders? It's a lot more convenient, and that's about all they're good for."

"Ahn, ahn, Sister," Cathy chided. "It's all for the sake of appearances. And it's a lot easier for Boss Hooker to keep a check on the canceled checks, isn't it, Phil?"

Meyer didn't answer her, but his eyes darted over nervously at the firm, flowered hip.

"For the sake of appearances," Teresa said dryly, "I think it'd be better if we *all* just disappeared."

Cathy's red mouth pursed slightly as she watched Meyer. "Isn't it a funny thing about canceled checks, Phil? They always keep coming back."

He squinted up at her. "What are you talking about?"

"She's talking about our money," Teresa said. "Now, if you don't mind, I'd like to have my starvation wage."

"What with the money you girls make sticking up the postdebs each week, I don't see why you cry so about your salaries."

Teresa wrinkled her brow in feigned concentration. "There's something so—so—how should I put it?—so *criminal* about the way we have to make our money on the side. Any outsider would be shocked to know how niggardly the *Messenger* is with its salaries, and what we have to go through to make up for it."

Meyer shrugged. "Don't ride me, girls. You know I don't make out your checks."

"And you don't care, do you, Phil?" Cathy smiled. "Not so long as your checks are as tidy as they are. Have you ever seen one of Phil's checks?" she asked her sister. "You'd be surprised to know how much he makes! Phil's got an expense account, too. Don't you have one of those things, Phil? He can sign over *Messenger* money for just about anything he wants—can't you, Phil? I've seen him, Terry—I've seen Phil sign over as much as five hundred dollars of *Messenger* money, haven't I, Phil?''

Meyer was visibly disturbed. "If you girls want your money, here it is," he said, handing them two envelopes from his desk drawer. "Oh, before I forget, Mr. Sandersford won't be arriving until ten tonight; he got held up. Mr. Hooker has asked me to advise all editorial staff members of this and ask that you try to come back. Of course, you're not compelled to."

"I wouldn't miss it for anything!" Cathy said exuberantly.

"I wash my feet on Friday nights," Teresa said. "But if it's okay I'll just bring my foot bath along—the slish-slosh'll help break up the monotony—although I don't think there'll be much of that with the old man here."

"I don't give a damn," Meyer said. "Just so long as you *can* get back."

"With bells on," Cathy said, getting up from the desk.

"Well, cheerio, folks!" Teresa said as she started out. "Don't let Der Führer fall off a swivel chair. I'm off to a banquet."

Cy grabbed her hand as she came by his desk. "Teresa, have I ever told you that you remind me of Eve Arden?"

"Not since you told me that I reminded you of Lizzie Borden," she rejoined. "But have I ever told you that you remind me of Willie Best?"

She went out, slamming the door of the City Room behind her.

Cathy lingered by Cy's desk. "Ready for that drink, Doll?"

"Wait'll I finish this," Cy said, pecking away on his typewriter at a couple of dupes. "All right, I'm ready," he said presently. He got his hat and coat from the wall rack.

"So long, Phil darling," Cathy called. "Don't write any bum checks."

Meyer started to get up from his desk, but thought better of it and remained seated.

"Well, let's beat it, m'fair beauty," Cy said. "I can hardly wait for that double!"

Cathy got into her things and they went out of the office.

Since the Gaymount was eight blocks away, they got in Cathy's four-year-old sedan and drove over, saving their conversation expectantly, as though the car might have been wired with microphones.

There was no other Negro hotel in the city as luxuriously comparable to the Gaymount. Towering some eighteen stories, the building was the cast-off venture of a disgruntled Jew, who had in turn been swindled by a calculating gentile. Due to the chameleon-like changes of the neighborhood, the Gaymount had never stood on financially stable ground. Thus when it was discovered that an enterprising Negro, who owned a substantial portion of the local numbers set up—though not completely subsidized on his own—had two million dollars to "invest" in a promising business venture, the Jew lost no time divesting himself of the white elephant.

The transaction proved to be quite a surprise—to the Jew. Now there entered through the refurbished swinging portals of the Gaymount the successive trains of Negro night life in the city: the showpeople, the big names, the stars. And following in their tracks came the hordes of "big" pimps and the more notable maids of the night, insinuating themselves on the graciousness of the showpeople, the big names, the stars, hoping in this to escape their labels of pimp and whore. And surrounding them on the edges, gawking like starving children with big bellies, their tongues and throats dry with envy, were the little people, the nothings, the waiters for nothing, hating the being-ableness and the Cadillacic mania of movement with which the "bigger" people seemed gifted.

Through the molecular miracle of glass, sidewalk unfortunates could look in on the grand glory, the wisp-of-mist loveliness, of the Gaymount's dining room, where the smooth, well-dressed government girls supped with the perpetually mustached boss. Or perhaps the man was just a man in the office. In the corner there might be a man from the mayor's office, discussing the latest trend in interracial matters with one of the city's more well known Negro ministers, whose congregation last week celebrated his fifth year under Second Baptist of God with a spanking new Cadillac.

"Let's go down to the bar," Cy said. "I prefer it because it's so much more bar-ish."

"Oh, there's the councilman!"

"Now, Cathy—"

"But, Cy, his daughter's having a coming-out affair next week! Maybe me and Terry can make a fine nickel out of this one."

"Have you forgotten?" Cy told her in a dry voice. "You might not *be* with the *Messenger* next week."

"I wouldn't count on that, Cy Doll."

"I don't want to bite the heads off nails without a drink. Let's go down to the bar."

Down to the bar they went; not quite a basement, it poised mezzanine fashion just under the dining room, with ultrasoft velvet bar seats and a cute, high-toned barmaid.

"I didn't know a drink could taste so good!" Cy gasped after his first swallow. "After what I went through with Boss Hooker this afternoon—!"

"Has he been after you again, Doll?"

"Just like Ex-Lax."

"The trouble is, you take too much of him. He and I *never* have a misunderstanding."

"I'd call you an unfair comparison."

"There's certainly no dividend in being anything else, is there?"

"Well, I'd feel a hell of a lot better if we could include him in our brief resumé to the Great Him tonight."

"Maybe we can," she said thoughtfully.

"Did you have any trouble with the check?"

"That's just what I was thinking of, Cy precious. No—I didn't have any trouble. I just told Diana I needed the canceled check file to trace the last payment of an advertising account. Then I merely had the copy of Phil's check photostated."

"I hope there's no mistake," he said, a bit warily now.

"But how can there be? I've got the check, written in Phil's own handwriting and endorsed by Dr. Fred Lowell. Lowell's already been involved with the government about his taxes. It won't be so hard for the Great Him to believe that Phil was a partner to Lowell's easy way out: abortion—and that I was one of his more grateful customers."

"But the proof—"

"The check is the only proof we need."

"But what if Phil just denies he was the father of that kid? Suppose he says he gave you the money just to give you a hand?"

"But, Doll, do you really believe he could lie his way out of it? The circumstances are too peculiar! If it was a loan, why didn't he note it as such and make arrangements by which I could pay it back? He just wouldn't *give* away five hundred dollars of *Messenger* money, would he? And if it was a gift, why did he fail to draw it from his own bank account? Because Alene would find out, that's why."

"Do you think Lowell's gonna stand still for this? It could ruin his career."

She shrugged. "There's nothing we can really do about Dr. Lowell. He's incriminated because he's the check's endorser. He'll be further incriminated when someone investigates his files and finds that I don't have one. There'd be no basis of services rendered for the five-hundred-dollar payment. Wouldn't the federal people be interested in that little item?"

"Cathy—"

"Believe me, Cy! I don't bear the good doctor any ill will. He was very nice and kind and gentle, and he had very soft hands. And I can't tell you how helpful he actually was."

Cy shook his head. "It's a shame we have to kick him in with that sonofabitch Meyer . . ."

"What's this?" she said, looking at him keenly. "Do I detect some regrets? Is the mastermind himself getting ready to back out? What's the matter, Cy Doll, won't that gin give you enough courage? You certainly had enough when you came to me with the idea! For the first time in my life I was glad of man's vain propensity for indiscretion. Phil really did me a favor by telling you."

Cy hesitated over his drink. "I haven't lost my enthusiasm, dear girl. It's just that I wanna make sure there's no slip-ups."

"There'd only be a slip-up if you fail to get the Great Him out of the clutches of Boss Hooker and Meyer and that big-bellied old advertising manager, Earl Morrell. You've got to get him where I can talk to him alone."

He took a quick, worried swallow from his shot glass. "That's gonna be tricky. You know how they get together for their closed door meetings after Mr. Sandersford arrives. I'm not even invited."

"Well, you'll have to invite yourself *this* time. Stick in his pocket. You'll be able to get him alone. But if push comes to shove, I'll tell him in front of everybody. And don't worry about Boss Hooker. That check makes it imperative for the Great Him to get both a new editor and editor-in-chief."

"Hooker—?"

"But *certainment,* Doll! Hooker keeps a tight zipper on all the checks in the *Messenger's* office. He *had* to know that Meyer wrote the one for five hundred out to me. If he knows that, you can bet he knows everything else. Hooker is an accessory after the fact."

Cy began to grin. "You're making this sound like a dream! But what about later? Do you think Mr. Sandersford will let you stay on?"

She tossed her head enigmatically. "I don't really care, you know. I just want to see our mutual friend out of the way. As long as I can accomplish that, anything else doesn't matter." She had a sudden, private thought. "I'm reminded that I have a very important engagement this afternoon—a person I should have visited a long time ago."

"The only thing we've got to worry about Hooker," Cy said, "is that he might change his field and say he was only waiting on the arrival of Mr. Sandersford, so that he could spill his guts about Meyer.

"I don't think Boss Hooker is that nimble on the field. However, I can take care of that when I get the Great Him alone. I'll purposely involve Boss Hooker, if that'll make you feel any better."

Cy's mouth made a hard grin. "I've got nothing against Boss Hooker. He just rides my back too goddamn much. Rrrowr! A goddamn tiger. I want him and Meyer completely out! I know I couldn't hope for Hooker's job, but I don't have any doubts about who Mr. Sandersford would put in the managing editor vacancy."

Cathy laughed derisively. "The conspirators, that's us! For once we can bring our feelings out boldly, and all the other goo that goes along with the subterranean mess."

"Just damn, downright dirty!" he whispered with an evil smile. "That's us!"

"Think what the *Messenger* has done to us. Look at you . . ."

"It wasn't so much, I mean about what Meyer did. Babies aren't so much. My sister and I used to live in an old place a long time ago, and it had roaches. I think about babies in a woman's belly just like I think about those roaches: they just get fatter and fatter— and smarter—and one day you just can't keep them from crawling over everything. They're not so much," she finished softly.

"I was just thinking about what Meyer *did* . . ."

"Oh, you mean the 'Dear Jane' routine?" She coughed at a sip of her drink, then grinned bravely. "Now that did hurt I was unworried right up until the fifth month. He told me he was going to tell Alene. Then, when he said he couldn't—! Cy, he was a bastard! He could have told me . . ."

"He could have told you," Cy mimicked, but she missed the malice in his eyes.

"I could have done something," she pleaded, more to herself than to Cy, more to the inner bit of herself—that soft bit—than to the stratified core of Cy. "If he hadn't told me he was going to marry me, I could have *done* something before it went so far."

"Plenty warm water and vinegar," he said with a lewd smile. "But you being the kind of *society* girl you are, I would have thought you'd get yours in a tube."

"You're a bastard!" she said, looking at him.

"Ooooh, gin!" he cried to the barmaid, then to Cathy: "More a sonofabitch than a bastard, beautiful thing."

"Cy," she said, betraying for the first time some hint of the soft, pliant woman within, "Cy, I was really *weak* for that guy!" And now she felt the sting of tears at the edges of her eyes. "Why didn't he just tell me in time? Why! All those times at the cabin . . . Did you know he had a cabin upstate?"

"I know that cabin *well*."

"Even a month before the—Dr. Lowell—we used to go up there. Why didn't he tell me then, Cy? Why couldn't he?"

"Mine is not to reason why—" he laughed, as the barmaid refilled his glass. "You're knocking yourself out. It would have all been the same."

"It wouldn't," she protested. "If he had told me . . ."

"Ifhehadtold me, ifhehadtoldme!" he snapped. "Quit lying to yourself! Meyer didn't *want* you—he only *wanted* to use your stupid body!"

She didn't notice the poisonous look on his face. "I would have understood better. And then I might have been able—"

"You sicken me!" he said, glaring at her. "All of you *sicken* me! You think your pretty little reasons really amount to something? They don't amount to anything!"

"Ho-de-ho-*ho!*" she said, looking at him in this new light. "Excuse me, Doll, I didn't know your claws were *that* long!"

"You're being disgusting," he said sullenly into his gin glass.

"I should like to think I was—if I were sitting anywhere but here with you."

"Look at us! Calling each other names! The *conspirators!*"

Her eyes scorched at him intensely, as though she were trying to look through to the back of his skull. "Sometimes it's necessary to remind each other just what it is we are, Doll. You're most delectable when that divine little ego of yours decides it's time to come out of the diapers and get into the jockey shorts."

He tried to laugh at this. "So *you're* the peeping Tom around my bedroom window at night!"

"Perhaps I've made a mistake in letting you peek through mine," she said thoughtfully. "It's difficult to trust you, Cy."

"How do you mean that?" he said carefully.

"I mean about the whole thing. Maybe I shouldn't have let you look in on me so clearly."

"You're being silly—"

"What have I got to lose but a job? But why should I lose that?"

"Now, Cathy," he said soberly, "you're talking crazy!"

"I was under the impression that you considered my motives commendable, Doll."

"But they *are,* Cathy—! I mean, Jesus A. Christ, you're not the only one who's got a stake in this. I mean, we're in this together, aren't we, and I've got just as much to lose as you, as much to gain?"

"You make me think it's more."

His mouth strained awkwardly. "You're mixing up words! You know I need you—*we* need each other!"

"Sure, I know it," she said resignedly. "I know we *need* each other. Well, all I'm asking is that you do your job. I'll do mine."

"Don't you worry," he assured her with relief. "I'll do my part. I'll do everything just the way we planned it."

She pinched one of his cheeks. "We're going to make it so hot for Phil Meyer tonight his skin'll peel, Cy Doll!"

CHAPTER SIX

*L*EE MERRIWEATHER WAS WRITING the story of Stanley Hardwicks.

The office rang with the insistence of his message, and before him again he could almost see the death masks of the people, scent the odoriferous, heart-shattering smell of their blood. A burrowing worm seemed lodged in his head; its overpowering reek of pestilence conquered his brain and reinflated the vacuum with an insiduously burning hate and need to swing out at someone.

The quickening, violent hate he felt for Phil Meyer was enveloping him; the full, blossoming pain of it was overloaded and dripping from the sides of him.

Into his story he wrote the pain of Stanley Hardwicks and his family, and the pain of himself. The whys he asked of the reader were the whys which tumultuously rained his consciousness, and into his story was also infused the angry awakening fetus of his confusion.

The story and Lee were soon indistinguishable. The two of them were hot, liquid rubber, molded into the bouncing idiocy of some child's ball; some bad and cruel adolescent. And into the hands of the child they passed themselves, spherically, inalienably, to be tossed and bruised against the rock-hard pavement of public apathy.

Public? What was he thinking of?

It was Phil Meyer, that's what it was! That's what it *had* to be. How could he have welded himself so closely to the abrupt conclusion that the public had anything to do with it? The public was the victim, the public was the prey—the public was Stanley Hardwicks and the others like him. The stupids. The black people. They would not *ever* understand, because *he* did not understand. The intricate questions, the pat answers. The *nothing* of it all!

His long black fingers pounded the keys of the typewriter. His face grew long, it seemed, and the corners of it grew tighter and pained him.

Possessed by a reminiscently dank comfort, he felt vaguely like a child crying out to its mother, crying and knowing through the exhaustion of crying that it would not be sated, that there was no one to nourish it. And he felt, like that child, a need to become a man before its time, in order to live. And in order to survive this child-man had to forget that its mother would not come and that its father had only been father out of the necessity of the word come. He had to conclude that it was impossible for him to have either mother or father under these conditions. He had to *forget* them and forget that they made him a man among men but not a man belonging to men.

The typewriter pounded, chattering out his need to destroy something . . .

. . . Through the veldt . . . The sound of the typewriter's clicks composed a sound similar to the clackbills of the watching birds, and Meyer's face was like that of the lion, the lion lazy and fat, his tongue huge and black with many meals, licking, like the moon covering the sun, as Grandfather had seen. And even as there was hate for Meyer, there was hate for this lion, but it was not Boo-Boo who hated the lion, for Boo-Boo reposed in strong black loins, and it would not be until after the moon of the First Death that he would be released to swim through the dark warmth of the jetdark valleys and anchor himself to the root of life . . .

O Master of Creation, this day protect thy son M'Tele, who becomes a man with thy will.

O Master . . .

O Master . . .

O Master . . .

And he saw the blood on Meyer's throat. He was trembling unaccountably, the smooth ebony of his face was streaked with a feverish sweat. Involuntarily he stood behind his desk, and for the first time in his life he noticed the tremendous strength in his wide, black hands; it was as though his eyes had been purposely blinded to their latent deadliness, as though the exposure of their potent capability had been reserved for this moment. He flexed the long fingers with excruciating pleasure. Slowly, in unprovoked deliberation, he came from behind his desk and advanced upon the oblivious back of Phil Meyer.

He knew that in a moment he would fall intransigently on that back, but he was helpless to stop himself. He was divided, senselessly, into two people, and there was a loud, weird voice yelling in his ears, *For my people! For my people!*

. . . It was the primordial instinct, the primitive vendetta, of a betrayed race. It was the flood of the Zambesi into the krall. It was the witch doctor who had sold them for a flock of Kilimanjaro's fruit—the strong-backed rams, the fecund ewes . . .

In his mind, the revenger knew the exact spot of throat, the precise moment at which to drive deep the strong fingers, the appropriate twist with which to break the lying, cheating bone and cartilage of neck and back, and—*for my people!*

My people . . .

He was in a virtual trance. He stopped when his belly twisted strangely, as it had when he saw the face of the beautiful dead woman, and he knew in an instant that it was not his mother. . . . Why had he said it was?

It was not his mother! He had no mother! He had no people! Meyer looked up just then.

"Lee?" he said slowly, the sound of his voice a question. For a moment Lee saw the fear, the precipitate fear, in his eyes, and was prompted on, almost sexually, with the need to destroy Meyer and feel his blood as he had felt the blood of the dead man and woman.

"Lee . . . ?" again, shrinking away. "Lee . . . what's the matter?"

Lee became conscious that they were alone in the room, that around them were the utensils of the *Weekly Messenger,* the ganglia of the *Weekly Messenger*—the desks and typewriters. This consciousness touched his very nerve ends, and he sagged suddenly with the knowledge of what he had been about to do.

He now watched Meyer guiltily, crushed by the implication of himself. For what reason had he wanted to kill the weak little man? What was it that had made him so *proud* to be mobilized with that intent?

My people! the voice still cried faintly in his ears.

But *what* people? What people could he call his own? Now, looking in the pale, unvirile face of Phil Meyer, the bastard blood of his dumpy body, Lee could not tell himself honestly that he belonged to the same race. How could he or anyone else delude themselves into thinking that there *was* a race, when the presence of Meyer and the others like him belied violently the claim?

There *is* no Negro race, he discovered with a shock. Negro?

Negro? *He* was not a Negro; Meyer was definitely not a Negro. They did not belong together; they were apart, and they had no meaning together, as individuals. They were only a Merriweather and a Meyer, and wasn't it funny how their names began with the same letter?

Where was the race? he wanted to shout. Where had it gone? What was he doing here without it?

"Lee . . ." Meyer pleaded—pleaded?—still frozen to his chair, but Lee barely heard him.

What am I doing here?

What was he discovering?

What am I seeing?

What was the vision?

Caught in the strange, wild, strangling vortex of himself, he could not go on; he did not want to see the truth, a truth so infinite and omnipresent that it ground him under the hard hell of gross despair.

It was truth that he was not Lee Merriweather, that much he *knew.* It was truth that he was so different from the thing that Lee Merriweather should have been that he felt like the creation of some mad genius, some Frankenstein. It was truth that he hated his creator, even if it were God, and it was revelation of revelations that he was unreasonably imprisoned in one of the darkest, most vilely stinking pits of man's evolution.

"Lee . . ." the little voice continued to implore, the little voice lost also in the fetid pit, the spawn of man's incongruous destiny: the anachronistic Nigger with the face, the everything, of a Jew.

There was something symbolic, ironic, something *Haw Haw!* about the two of them. It was as though they two were grotesque clowns the world did not dare laugh at, because the laughter would be self-deprecating. They were stunted, deformed little children of Mother Earth, and through her blind disregard for all her children, they were *not* brothers; there was nothing of them that demanded that they be brothers.

"Lee," Meyer said, regaining some of the strength to his voice; unable to quench the fire of fear in his small eyes. "Lee, what's the matter with you? What the hell's got in you?"

Lee turned away before his heart took wings and plunged outward from his chest; before he disintegrated and began to commit murder because of the abject futility of life—just like Stanley Hardwicks—before the guilt of living became too much and he absolved himself through the incarnate lust, the love, of death.

"Hey, look, Lee," Meyer said soothingly behind him, somehow

dimly alerted that the younger man had reached a final and danger-ous crisis in which *he* had been involved, "don't take it so hard—what I said." He laughed with a strange, relieved twitter. "I know you're an idealist and all that. I spoke too hard. Lee? Lee? You know what I mean, kid?" He came over behind him, and Lee felt his flesh crawl, hoping that Meyer wouldn't touch him.

"You know what I mean, Lee?" A grating, apologetic voice. "I'm sorry about that twenty-five bucks. Is that it? Is that why you're mad, kid? Tell ya what I'm gonna do, like the man says: I'm gonna write that voucher! Now don't tell me different; that's exactly what I'm gonna do, Lee. I'm gonna sit right down now, and write you that voucher for twenty-five dollars. I'm gonna go out of my way. I still think you're wrong as hell, but after all, it was your *first* mistake, wasn't it? But don't we have to have *some* semblance or order around here? Don't we have to have it? I'm asking you. If we didn't have any order, what would we do? We have to keep ourselves ordered, and we have to keep those people out there in the street ordered, too."

Lee went back and sat down, not trying to understand the order Meyer spoke of. He kept his eyes away from the man.

"You're too sensitive," Meyer said softly. "That's your trouble. Do you *want* to live off three thousand dollars a year for the rest of your life? Like Cy? Do you want that, Lee? Of course you don't! You want to get up in the world, just like *anybody* with good sense. Isn't that right? Of course it's right. And the only way you get to the apex is by crawling over people. Understand what I mean? *Any* people, it doesn't make any difference. You can't condescend, Lee. When people see you bending over with your rear unprotected, they try to ram you. You ask for it, you'll get stuck every time, brother, just like you got stuck for that twenty-five bucks."

"Sure," Lee said.

Meyer's face lighted up. "You understand what I mean?"

"Sure."

"Don't *ever* bend, Lee."

"No, you can't ever."

"You see, we're a different kind of people."

"Sure, we're different from the man in the street."

"Certainly, we are!"

"That's good."

"We always have to remember that."

"We can't ever forget it."

"That's right . . ."

"We can't ever forget what we're doing."

"Doing . . . ?"

"You know—what we're doing to that man."

"Now, listen, boy, we're not doing anything to that man! We're rendering him a service."

"Sure, just like a pusher."

"A what?"

"A pusher, who pushes dope. That's what we're doing. We're giving that man poison; we're selling it to him for fifteen cents a week, ounces of it."

"Now, listen—"

"But as long as that makes us a dollar, we don't give a damn."

"What else are we in business for?" Meyer thundered suddenly. "My God, Lee—"

"I go along with you. I'm beginning to see the sense of it."

"Now that's the spirit!"

"We don't give a damn about that black bastard in the street."

"Of course we don't!"

"He's just the means to an end."

"Right, Lee, right! Now you're thinking!"

"And the quicker I get it out of my mind that we're the means and *he's* the end, the better off I'll be."

"Isn't it easy, when you think about it?"

"It's terribly easy."

Meyer grinned with a sort of pride at his black face.

"We're not like those Niggers in the street, are we, Phil?"

"No, certainly not."

"We're professional people. We owe fealty to no one but the Great Him and that grafting little bunch of petty politicos who make this paper *go* from week to week—those advertisers, whose national contracts, those dictators of what it is we should or shouldn't print for the Nigger in the street."

Meyer's enthusiasm was reined up short. "What are you talking about?" he asked suspiciously.

"I'm talking about what *whores* we have to be," Lee said passionately. "What sellouts!"

"We're not whores!" Meyer said indignantly.

"No, we're not whores—we're a bunch of pansies, a bunch of fruits, that's what we are! We're not men, we're inside-out facsimiles. We're perverts! I feel like *Judas!*"

Meyer's face was strained. "I don't like the way you're talking, Lee!"

"Neither do I!"

"If you're so fired up, why don't you try to kick Roy Wilkins out of his executive post with the NAACP? That's where you'd be better off. You want a constant battle. For what? Let me tell you: the *Messenger* isn't fighting any battles, and it's not going to fight you! That's a warning!"

"I wouldn't have recognized it!"

"Well, you'd better take heed!"

"I have been . . ."

"I like you, Lee. I hate to see you kick yourself in the ass like this."

"I'm masochistic."

"That could very well explain it. Your attitude."

"It doesn't explain anything, and I have no attitude. I've been trying to tell you—you've finally convinced me." His face was quiet. There was no clue on the plain of his dark features as to his emotions.

"You know you're making an ass out of yourself," Meyer said finally, dimly, unconvincingly.

"I said I believe you," Lee recalled. "I told you I was ready to take on the yoke of the *nouveau* intellectuals, of the *leaders* of the Negro race. Is that making an ass out of myself?"

"You're saying it wrong!" Meyer balled impatiently. "Didn't you get enough coddling from your mother?"

"Don't bring my mother into this!"

"You're acting like a goddamn stupid kid!" Meyer fumed. "I had *hopes* for you!"

"So had I!"

"How long are you going to suck on that flabby, senseless titty of brotherhood? Nobody else does!"

"That's because they've exhausted it!" Lee shouted. "People like you! All people! Black and white—they sucked it until there's nothing left to suck! They got fat and sloppy off it, and they didn't give a damn for the people who had to come after them!"

Meyer began to roam about the office like a maddened bull. "The fact is plain and simple—you're *stupid!* You make yourself stupid when you think the way you do. You're no better than that Nigger you gave the twenty-five dollars to!"

"Are you?"

"Well, hell, yes!" he blazed. "There's no escaping it. Some of us are better than others, and that's no Aryan joke! Some of us *have* to be better than the rest. We have to govern them—and when necessary we have to eliminate them!"

"*Mein Kampf!*" Lee said with thick loathing.

Meyer shook a fist at him. "Now you're showing your intelligence, Lee! And don't you think it's right? Don't you think the Caucasian is stronger than the black? Don't you think he *should* be?"

"Hell, no!" Lee cried. "But he'll always be as long as he trusts in people like you—and me—and Boss Hooker—and Cy Venson! The black man will never have unity, because we'll *see* to it that he doesn't! We'll write down to him and give the dumb bastard a lot of tinsel—"

"Are you trying to make me eat my words?"

"That's impossible, and you know it. Nobody but you can do that."

"And I'm not about to!"

"I didn't expect that you would be. I wouldn't want you to. I want to remember everything you've said today. I would die if I couldn't remember it."

"You might regret ever having heard it."

"As far as that twenty-five dollars is concerned," Lee said solemnly, "you can forget it."

"I already have! I was trying to do you a favor, but you—"

"Phil Meyer," Lee said, rising, "I don't want *you* to do a damn thing for me! I want you and everyone like you to leave me the hell alone! That goes not only for you but the Nigger in the street, too. I don't belong to you!"

"You sure as hell don't!" Meyer growled with unaccustomed fire. "You belong to that neat little category of 'weakling'! You'll never be anything but a black nappy-headed Nigger!"

"Thanks! *Thanks!*" Lee yelled. "And not because you've said anything that wasn't true! Thanks for trying to make me think I'm something I'm not! I wish I *was* a Nigger! If I could really believe that, I wouldn't have to look at something like you and *know* that I wasn't!"

The phone on Meyer's desk rang.

They didn't move, because the broken thread between them instantly raveled itself about thrust away the hint of violence, leaving them naked with their wrath and ashamed of the origin which had brought them to this.

The phone rang again.

Everything progressed in slow motion, and Lee watched the ridiculousness of Meyer's short legs moving toward the desk, the practiced, devastating insouciance of his hand upon the receiver, the dread, the unfamiliar look of terror in his small eyes.

He let the phone ring again, then picked it up.

"Hello?"

And Lee felt drained, as though some monstrous Amazon of a woman had squeezed from him every drop of joy between her brutal thighs.

"Yes, Boss?"

There was no going back from here, and he did not care. He wanted to die, to die, to end, to be nothing, to never know that there were such things as sex, as money, as freedom.

"Why, no, Boss. I haven't talked to him yet. He's right here, though."

Upon his desk, the story was blurred in his eyesight, and Stanley Hardwicks now seemed elemental; he was a *so-what*, he was a statistic without statistical meaning, except to show that blacks were more murderous than whites.

"Well, if you'd like to, Boss! But I told you I'd talk to him."

He took the story and destroyed it, just as Stanley Hardwicks had destroyed himself: he shredded the pages in small bits, neglecting to commit them to the bowels of the wastebasket purposely, so that the cleanup man might curse, might pick up the gossamer of six lives, and curse the hand which dropped them to the dirty floor.

"All right, all right! I'm *not* trying to protect him! I'll send him right up."

So Lee got up. He got up, his mouth full and moving, readying himself, to say *Take your job, Phil Meyer, and shove it—*

"Boss Hooker wants to see you," Meyer told him, hanging up.

Lee came from around his desk.

Meyer apparently could not find his words. "Lee . . . when you come back, I'd like to talk to you . . ."

"No."

"We've *got* to talk!" Meyer said. "Do you realize what you're throwing away? I used to read your stuff in the *State Review* and say to myself, 'This kid's got the kind of talent that made Jimmy Cannon famous.' Don't you realize what a gift you have?"

Like a small child at a circus, Lee saw the goodness of the cotton candy; he *knew* the unadulterated goodness of Meyer's words, the words of a man who could do naught but classify talent and fear the loss of its presence. Even though its presence with him meant its gradual extinction, he longed to be present at its passing, to be impassive of its destruction, as a senile old man is impassive of his impotence.

"Lee . . . I'm sorry . . ."

"You can never be sorry, and neither can I."

"Listen," Meyer flamed. "I'm not gonna slobber over your black butt!"

"How would you react if it wasn't black?" Lee said.

Fearlessly, he left the room and bore his cross up the steps to Calvary.

CHAPTER SEVEN

*B*OSS HOOKER PUT THE PHONE BACK.

"I'm sort of worried about Merriweather," he told Earl Morrell, the heavy-set, yellow-faced advertising manager.

Morrell sat facing Hooker's desk, his big belly straining almost obscenely against his white shirt front, oddly resembling a woman carrying a child.

"I think he's getting the wrong ideas," Boss Hooker went on. "You know Ray Irving?"

Morrell had the deep, slurring accent peculiar of Negroes born in the South. "You talking about the numbers man?"

"He's affiliated with the Viconetti house . . ."

"Oh, yah, Viconetti. We used to run the figures each week in our 'Sammy' cartoon." Morrell rubbed his thick lips together with delicious recollection. "There was a pretty penny used to roll in from that house, George, a *pretty* penny!"

Morrell grunted. "If the Urban League hadn't jumped us about the 'indecency' of the thing, a pretty penny would still be coming in. We're still doing some work for Viconetti, but the take isn't as big as it used to be."

Morrell took a pink, almost effeminate cigar holder from his shirt pocket and inserted one of the long cigars from the humidor on Boss Hooker's desk. "What's this about Merriweather?"

"I think Irving's paying him to plug some stories."

"Ah," Morrell said, lighting his cigar. "Yah, I see. That's no good. I thought we got all the Viconetti business from his publicity agent downtown."

"Well, we *have* been. That's why I can't understand Irving. Why he's doing it."

"That's easy. He can cut out the middlemen by coming right to Merriweather." He looked at Boss Hooker keenly through the smoke of the cigar. "What are you gonna do about it?"

"That's why I called you in, Earl. I want you to get on Viconetti and find out why we're only getting a trickle from his account. Tell him what Irving's doing—tell him we won't stand for it."

"Yah, that I can do. What about Merriweather?"

Boss Hooker clapped his big hands together on the desk top. "I'm going to put the fear of God in Merriweather right now. When I get through with him, he won't be writing any more stories."

"Yah, you got to show him right from wrong," Morrell said piously. "That money belongs to us, whatever it is."

"It's no more than a few dollars, I'm sure of that. But if Irving had come through regular channels it would have been considerably more; and Lord knows he can afford it!"

"Oh, yah, he can afford it! I had Irving set up with a church spread two weeks ago—still gonna do it. He's a member at Congregational Baptist; on one of those building committees or something." He snapped his fingers at Boss Hooker's serious face. "Eight hundred, George! Just for one spread, pics and all."

Boss Hooker nodded. "Just don't forget my twenty percent."

"Yah," Morrell said, puffing at the cigar.

"You tell Viconetti we don't want Irving cutting corners. After all we've done for them, it's their *duty* to pay off when they should."

"Got another church spread," Morrell said with incidental casualness.

"Something good?" Boss Hooker said hungrily.

"I think so," the fat man said in a slow drawl. "It's the Rt. Reverend Joey Lejoie: God's Earthly Balm Sent To Redeem And Cure The Soul Of Man—or so the ticket blurb says."

"That miracle-healer? The Evangelist?"

Morrell wiggled his lips. "Thousand dollar deal, George, payable before publication. That's just for the spread; he's paying six-fifty more for a full page ad."

Boss Hooker was hesitant. "You've got me between the devil and the deep blue sea, Earl. That sixteen-fifty is the sea."

Morrell stared at him. "You're not gonna pass this up, are you? What is the 'devil'? The Urban League again?"

"If it was I could ignore it. It's the NAACP, this time. They think ads by soothsayers, palmists, number touts and the like are unbecoming to a newspaper of our stature."

"George, you're not gonna pay any attention to those sonsabitches! Any time they need a free spread, where do they come? Do they go to the *Eagle* or *Tribune*? Why, hell no, they come right to us! They've been living off us for years. To hell with 'em!"

Boss Hooker shook his head. "Twenty years ago, Earl, when you and I first came to this paper, maybe we could have said that. We can't do it in this day and age. The NAACP as a power you can't ignore. I don't want any hard feelings."

"Well, let's do it 'accidentally'," Morrell contrived. "Before they know what's going on I could shoot Lejoie's spread and ad through. You could tell 'em you didn't have anything to do with it and that you hadn't told me about the new policy. I can take all the blame, and you and the *Messenger* would be in the clear."

Boss Hooker let the idea sink in for a few moments. "It just might go over. When does Lejoie want this business?"

"He gets into town tomorrow night," Morrell said. "We could set him up for next week's edition."

"So soon?"

The fat man puffed his cigar contentedly. "You know how these boys work. They hustle ass in and out. By the time the marks wake up to the fact that they've been bamboozled with some kind of mass hypnotism, Lejoie's found greener pastures."

"That really is too damn much money to pass up, Earl. And I'd just as soon for us to have it than the *Eagle* or *Tribune*."

"They couldn't do him justice, and Lejoie knows it. His reconnaissance boys check every publicity angle before he moves into a city."

"All right," Boss Hooker said with finality. "Set it up. Don't forget to have Lejoie make out two checks—one for us and one for the *Messenger*. Better still, get it in cash."

"You don't have to worry; he's solvent. *I* checked *him*. He's really been raking it in for the past six months."

"Nevertheless, I'd feel safer with cash. We naturally only declare the ad for the records, and I have an aversion for putting my signature on anything potentially incriminating." He smiled to himself, and his big hands clapped again on the desk top. "I'm reminded of Phil Meyer, when I say that."

Morrell twisted his mouth suggestively about the cigar holder. "Cathy Jones?"

"It breaks me up every time I think of it!" Boss Hooker laughed in his high voice.

"Has anything developed since you spoke to him about the check?"

"Not yet, but I've got the little bastard sitting on pins and needles, Earl."

"You've never liked Phil," Morrell said ruminatively. "This is your chance to blow him. When Mr. Sandersford—"

"I've been thinking about that," Boss Hooker interrupted with a heavy tone of deliberation. "I haven't decided yet, and I'm not so sure Meyer couldn't squeeze out of it. The old man's quite fond of him, you know. No," he continued with an inner anticipation that made the flesh quiver about his mouth. "I think it'd be pleasant just to watch Meyer squirm. I've been thinking of a little trick, and I'm going to have myself a hell of a lot of fun. When I get through with that little sonofabitch he'll wish he was about a quarter of an inch high!"

They laughed together, their voices indistinguishable in a high, bubbling chatter, like the *salud* of hyenas who have stolen the sleeping lion's supper from under his nose.

"You know," Morrell said at last, lips still twisted in a laughing grimace, "I'd feel uneasy as hell if I didn't know as much about you as you do about me!"

Boss Hooker's face was slandered with mock indignation. "You know nothing about me, Earl—except that Martha and I have been happily married for the past thirty years."

Morrell leered obscenely. "Oh, no? What about that little piece you hide out with over at the Gaymount every weekend? I've got a little bellboy friend who's seen you slipping up the back stairway. Yah, I know a little something, George. I know you're not so old you're going through the change."

"I'd have to be as old as you," Boss Hooker said caustically. "And if one must 'change' from girls to boys, I can't say I'd like to get that old."

Morrell's eyes darkened in his yellow face, but his tone of voice was jovial. "You're hitting low, Georgie."

Boss Hooker laughed into the man's simmering eyes. "It's no *fun* unless you do, Earl! But here, here! We don't have any secrets hidden from each other, do we?"

"Nary a one. It's nice to be alive when you know some other guy is just as big a bastard as you!"

The door to the outer office opened and Diana Hill, her big brown eyes glowing with efficiency, flowed in briskly.

"Pardon me, Mr. Hooker, but there's a client calling Mr. Morrell," she said.

Morrell strained to lift his bulk from the chair. "I'll stop in a little later, George. It's probably that Chrysler account. I've been expecting a call on it."

"Be sure to get in contact with Viconetti," Boss Hooker reminded him. "I want a definite understanding."

"Yah, I'll take care of it," Morrell assured him, waddling ponderously out of the office.

To Diana, Boss Hooker said, "Has Merriweather come up yet?"

"Not yet, Mr. Hooker."

"Send him right in when he arrives. Oh, yes, did you finish that letter to the mayor thanking him in behalf of the *Messenger* for Mr. Meyer's appointment?"

"Yes, Mr. Hooker. It's right on my desk. Would you like it now?"

"No, that won't be necessary. I'll look at it later. But you can bring in the weekly debit sheet and circulation report when you have time."

"Yes, sir, Mr. Hooker."

As she turned to leave, he surreptitiously surveyed the round, neat suppleness of her young hips under the modest dress, the deep curve of her long, strong back.

Had what Cy told him about her and Merriweather been the truth, or had he been simply trying to distract attention from himself with that little plum of interest?

No, it was probably true. Cy had a way of knowing those things. He reminded himself to speak to her about it when he had time. Couldn't have that sort of thing. Not with her having ready access to executive business. No telling what.

Some man was going to give her a tummy full someday, he remarked silently. A tummy full.

It would have been nice if he could have accommodated her, but business and pleasure didn't mix, as he had found out on several sorrowful occasions. It was only luck that Martha hadn't discovered . . .

Ah, well.

That's why he preferred the arrangement with Nora, at the Gaymount. Even though it was expensive, it was well worth it. He sat thinking of how she would look tonight, and the saliva accumulated swiftly in his mouth. So young and willing!

The office vanished before his eyes. He could see her sitting on the edge of the bed, her hard, young buttocks planted with firm magnificence on the whiteness of the sheet, the almost hairless grandeur of her armpits and smooth brown stomach, the tiny, tiny breasts, like Diana's with their dark nipples round as half dollars.

Sigh, he sighed.

When he was with Nora he wished Martha were dead. Thirty years with any woman—even Nora—was too long. Man's only true expression was sex, and he needed freedom of expression.

93

Well.

Perhaps Martha *would* die soon. She hadn't been feeling well lately. As a matter of fact, she hadn't been feeling well for years; not since she discovered he made more than enough money each week to provide her with a maid and clean-up woman. As though she *needed* any help in a one-story Colonial!

Well.

How he loved Nora! He could bite her! Tonight, after that old bastard Sandersford got through running off at the mouth he was going over to the Gaymount and bite her, that's what!

He turned on the swivel of his chair to look out of his office windows on the snow-covered waste of Farrell Street.

They had to get out of this neighborhood; move into a neighborhood which befitted the dignity of the *Messenger*. He'd talk to Sandersford about that tonight. They needed to move; get away from the colored people. Maybe in a nice interracial, upper-class neighborhood. Couples living around. No kids to walk on the grass. A factory type office, one story.

He thought of Ray Irving. Pulling a fast one. Well, they'd see about that! And Merriweather, that little black ball, sucking in money which rightfully belonged to the *Messenger*. They'd see about that too.

And could you imagine Earl liking boys? At his age? What was it now? Almost sixty? How about that!

Well.

He would bite Nora on the softest spot he could get his teeth at tonight! He'd bite the hell out of her!

CHAPTER EIGHT

HER LOVE FOR HIM was something nerve-sundering, a thing which made her tremble with the effort to regain herself in his presence.

And why? He was not the idea of the kind of man whom girls like herself desired and longed for: His hair was not the even-patched, semi-straightness—nor his smooth skin the light, preferable texture—of miscegenation. He was black and *foreign*—but that was not the thing which made her love him. It was something else, an intangible *majesty,* about him that swept her heart.

"Lee," she said, and her voice sang the name with sweet abandon, her mouth caressed the word: and vaguely she remembered the fairy tales read by a long-dead mother, in which she always pictured the prince as a tall, handsome white man, small of bone and thin of lip, with the high pompadour of youth.

How could the same man be him—this Lee—this prince? It was as though some evil witch had mesmerized her into thinking that he could have been nothing else but white. Each time she touched him, each time she kissed his soft, wide mouth, each time his strong black arms crushed her into his desperate warmth, welded her into his searching, child-like fury, she was destroyed in the knowledge that never again through life would she experience such tremendous joy.

"Lee," she said again, merely to say it and know that he was here; merely to die, if necessary, with the word of him on her lips. "Lee . . . ?" And now a question, for she could feel through his singular magnetism a threat of something dangerous, something cataclysmic and horrible.

"Baby—" She got up from her desk and went over to the door where he stood motionless. "Lee baby," she whispered, placing a hand on his wide chest, where underneath his heart beat wildly. "What's the matter? Is anything wrong?"

"I don't know," he said softly, and she recoiled a little at the wild blaze in his eyes.

"Did anything happen?" she said.

"Yes."

"Meyer again?" When he didn't answer, she went on, "Lee . . ."

"More than Meyer," he said.

"Who, Lee?"

His head shook like a black boll of consternation. "I don't *know*, Diana! I don't know who or what it is."

"Please, keep your voice down. Boss Hooker's waiting on you."

He grasped her by the arms, suddenly, his voice hissing. "Diana, I'm going to quit! Right now. I'm going to tell Boss Hooker I'm quitting."

"But why, Lee? What is it?"

"I don't belong here," he said hoarsely. "Neither one of us belongs here."

"But, baby, I thought you liked your work—even though Meyer—"

"It's not altogether Meyer now," he told her irritably. It's something I can't explain. It's the *Messenger*. It's Boss Hooker and Cy Venson. It's *me*. Diana, what have I been *doing*? These men don't care how they hurt people. They don't even *care* about people."

She had to turn away from him, for he was vitally injured, and the pain was transmitted as if by electrical coils. The thought of him ruptured internally brought a quick anger to her, and with only a little influence she could have gone downstairs, without preliminary, and torn the eyeballs from Phil Meyer's head. Not only Meyer, but anyone who had dared hurt Lee . . .

She went over to her desk and got a cigarette from the open pack on the leaf next to her typewriter. She lighted it, then peevishly crushed it out in a tray on the desk.

"Diana, I'm changed all over today," he said, coming over behind her. "The things I thought I knew—things I felt . . . I don't know what I'm thinking!"

She turned to him, her fingers digging into his arms. "Lee, I wish you could just make me understand! I know something is terribly wrong, but I don't *understand*."

The agony in his face reached out and twisted at her heart. "We're wrong, Diana. The *Messenger* is wrong. I just had Phil Meyer tell me that human beings are *nothing*, that they've never been anything."

"Phil Meyer," she said, trying to scoff, "he's—"

"He's right," he said. "That's what's so damn crazy about it. Diana," he said, and his flesh trembled beneath her hands. "Diana, I saw six dead people today. Six horribly dead people. I saw those people and I got sick. I tried to figure out *why* I saw them like that. There was nobody who cared that they were dead, nobody but a crazy little man who wanted the reward for the best weekly story in the *Messenger*. Then, oh yes, there was the *Messenger*! The *Messenger* cared because it could capitalize on the deaths of those people. But other than that, there was no one. And I said, why?" His eyes became misty. "I said, how come? I said, what are we? Nothing? Just dirty stinking blood? I saw those black people, some of them as black as me—"

"Lee . . ."

"I saw those black people standing around. Hungry. Not belly-hungry; just plain hungry: and they didn't know what they were hungry for. Maybe they were hungry like Scotty. Maybe they were hungry like Cy Venson. But they were hungry, and it was nasty, and I knew it was nasty! I came back here to this office thinking about the blood and nastiness of those people."

"Lee, there is no nastiness! You make up the nastiness in your mind—you *imagine* it."

"I *see* it!" he told her furiously. "There's a nasty man in that office, that I've got to go in. There's a nasty man downstairs. There's another nasty man downstairs who tells me it won't be long before you're impaled in bed with that other nasty man. Diana, it—it scares me! You *do* belong to me, don't you? You're the only thing I can see that isn't dirty and fouled up . . ."

"Yes, Lee . . ."

"But how? How can *I* have nobody?"

"You have me. I'll never leave you. I love you."

"That's not what I meant, Diana," he said, pulling her into his arms. "I don't *have* anything. I'm different. I feel it. I can see it in peoples' faces; I'm not real; I don't belong—"

"But you do, Lee, you belong to me! I love you, can't you understand that? I love you. I'll do whatever you want me to do. I'm your woman!" she said vibrantly against him. "There's nothing else in the world for me but you. You do belong. You belong to me and you always will."

"Isn't it funny?" he said dimly. "When I lived with my foster parents, when I was at the boys' school, I used to think everybody was the same, just a different color. Maybe that's why I'm twisted; because of that childish conception."

"But they *are* the same, Lee. All of us are," she pleaded with him. "I was taking a nursing course here in the city, and sometimes we were permitted to watch dissections in the amphitheater. They're all the same, baby, white bodies and black; there's no difference underneath."

"How can you prove that to a man who's never been in the amphitheater?" he said cynically.

"I've never met a whale in person," she said pointedly. "But that doesn't keep me from believing that such a thing is real. Is true."

She could tell her reply angered him, and she wanted to take back the words, suck them once again to the vortical recesses of her brain.

How to delve into him? He was so unlike any other man she had ever met. His incongruity was that he was *good*, a pure and innocent, personified naiveté.

She hugged him against her breasts almost protectively, uncertain whether to release him in this state to the lair of Boss Hooker.

"Honey," she said, "Lee . . . tonight—"

"Meyer says we should come back tonight at ten, for Mr. Sandersford."

"But afterward?" she asked, demanding a promise.

He looked down on her, and the fire simmered defeatedly in his eyes now. "Why not earlier? I think I'll stop by Tobey's after work. Would you like to come?"

"Not tonight. I've got some work to finish up *after* work. Would you want me to stop by your place?"

"You know I'd die if you wouldn't," he whispered in her ear, then his head jerked up. "I just remembered—I have to stop off at the boys' club this evening, but I should be done about seven."

She smiled. "Then you're not quitting?"

He had to smile back. "It depends on a lot of things. I've got to think this thing out, make things right in my mind. I don't completely know yet, Diana."

"Think about it, baby—please think about it. How will we ever get married if you don't have a job?"

"I've got a little saved up . . ."

"A married couple doesn't live on savings. But I could keep on working—"

"Listen," he told her firmly, "if I ever decide to leave this place you're coming with me."

"Yes, Lee."

"Money or no money. Anyway, I think it's about time we put an end to this YWCA jazz."

"Yes, darling . . ."

"I'm just about fed up with the *Messenger*. If I stay here any longer I won't be able to stand myself."

"Lee," she said cautiously. "I don't know what Boss Hooker wants to talk to you about, but—but will you please try—well, to think about us?"

"I will think about us," he promised. "Regardless of what happens in there, I'll be thinking about us."

"And . . ." she said, "and if you decide to stay on with the *Messenger*, Phil Meyer—"

"Phil Meyer," he said slowly, like a man in a daze. "Diana, do you know I almost killed Meyer? After the things he said? After what he implied to me? I actually almost killed him!"

"Lee!"

"It was something I couldn't help," he said, his voice strained. "It was something like being in another person's body and being unable to direct it with your mind. After a while I started feeling better, but I think Meyer knew. He was scared, I could tell. He started talking, saying those things—"

"What things?"

"About the Negro people. He was cursing them, and it seemed like he was talking about me. But then, again, it seemed like I was a party to what he was saying." He looked down at her. "Diana, what's wrong with me?"

"Nothing, baby, nothing!"

"But why is it I feel this difference? Why do I feel this *responsibility?*"

"What responsibility, Lee? To whom?"

His head came forward against her hair; she could feel the surrender of him. "I don't know; I don't guess I'll ever know. Maybe if I talked to Tobey—I want to talk to him as bad as hell."

"Yes," she said caressing the wire-like forest of his head. "Talk to Tobey. You can probably explain it to him better than me."

"But I can explain anything to you . . ."

"This is something you can't *show* me. This is something you must tell to a friend, not a woman who loves you." She throbbed against him, and again she could feel the inexplicable anger for the many shadowy antagonists who had disrupted Lee's existence. Was it maternal, this thing she felt for him? A maternal sense of protection?

But she knew by the thunder of her heart as he crushed her to him that such an idea was ridiculous. It was *him.* It was Lee, the *man* of Lee, which bent her like warm plastic. Even now she wished for the seclusion of his apartment, the warmth of his bare arms around her, the endless acres of his deep black chest against her breasts.

And it was more than sexual, this love: it was a perfection spoken of in storybooks, in novels: the meeting of a strange and tumultuous twain.

Had Lee said that he was different? How could she have denied him the idea? He *was* different, different from her as a mule from a burro! Only now did she have the first glimpse of the clue to her love, the formula which she had for so long sought vainly—and she as quickly closed it out of her mind. It didn't matter.

Absently, as he pulled away from her, she noted the light tone of her skin contrasted against the proud jet of his own; for the hundredth time she noted this, and for the first time she was totally conscious of it.

For the sake of Lee she had excluded all others, in the abstractness of her mind, from personal contact with him. Selfishly, she had never guessed his pain of difference, since she instinctively *loved* that difference. She wanted to scream at him, "I *know*, Lee— darling, I've found out!" But would this have made her love, her intense love, any clearer to him?

She watched him approach the door to Boss Hooker's office, the wide chin upheld, the wide flat nose splaying nervously with the intake of breath, the big, cupid's bow mouth set and beautiful. And suddenly she was maddeningly jealous of Tobey Balin and the singular insight, an insight she did not have, into the soul of the man she loved.

He stopped at the door and turned to her.

"I've got to pick up the debit sheet from the cashier," she told him. "I may not be here when you come out."

"You *will* be up to my place, though? Around seven or eight?"

"Unless I'm snowed under a blizzard, I'll be there, darling!"

"Well," he said, taking a deep breath, "wish me luck."

"Luck," she said. "Good luck, my sweet."

Boss Hooker was scowling when he entered, the light upon his cueball head giving an impression that it was convex, and Lee felt for a moment that Meyer had called up ahead of him to complain of his attitude.

But he could tell by the solemn slur of Hooker's womanish voice as he told him to have a seat that it was something other than Meyer which made the big man look at him as though he had committed a crime.

As if signaling the interview to begin, Boss Hooker gaveled his big hands atop the desk. "How are you today, Merriweather?" he said formally.

"Pretty well, sir."

"Any problems?"

"Some," Lee replied, looking Boss Hooker squarely in the face. "But every problem has a solution, Mr. Hooker."

"Those are exactly my feelings," Boss Hooker said gruffly. "How long have you been with us, Merriweather?"

"Going on a year, sir."

"From State, weren't you?" he said, knowing full well Lee's record.

"Just one year. Mr. Meyer hired me in after he read some of my articles in the college paper; my sports articles."

"How come you didn't continue on?" Boss Hooker asked, almost accusingly.

"There were a number of reasons," Lee said hesitantly. "I had a small part-time job on campus, but I was in hock for my tuition. I figured I'd try to get a job and work a while, on the outside, then return to State at some later date."

"A man needs a college education, in this day and age," Boss Hooker said sternly.

"I'm aware of that, sir."

"Especially a Negro. The white man requires of us an education double his own in order to qualify for the most menial position. He has us pinioned, you understand."

"I understand," Lee said without conviction.

"That's why I sacrificed—yes, sometimes even went hungry— in order to obtain my Master's at Tuskegee." He stared hard, even more accusingly at Lee, but the young man's gaze was steady. "When do you plan to return to State?"

"I don't know, sir."

"What's that?" Boss Hooker said with surprise.

"I have no plans," Lee told him.

"What do you plan to do with yourself for the rest of your life? Do you plan to work on here at the *Messenger*?"

"I *have* no plans," Lee emphasized. "This is a sort of twilight period for me. Right now, I'm only sure of one thing I really want," he finished, thinking of Diana.

"May I ask what that is?"

"No, sir," he said boldly.

Boss Hooker was brought up short. Lee could tell that his first impulse was to become belligerent, but he knew that such an outburst would cause them both embarrassment.

Silence, silence between them. Lee's skin began to crawl with anger, for he knew that Boss Hooker was prolonging the interval deliberately.

"Mr. Hooker," he said with an uninhibited urge, "I think that you ought to know how I feel about the *Messenger*."

The big man made his face go casual, and for an instant there was a twinge of aloofness about him. "Yes? And how *do* you feel, Merriweather?"

And now that he was trapped, he didn't know *how* to say it— what, actually, his feelings were. How to call a parasite a parasite by a sweeter name? How to interpret the malignancy of the thing? How to blaspheme the parasite to its keeper?

"Go on, Merriweather."

"I think . . ."

. . . he thought of thick grass, of high blue skies, of the needlessness of death . . .

"I think it's wrong for the people!" he exclaimed.

"*Wrong* for the people—"

. . . as right is to wrong, as right as the mud between the toes after the K'ala, the monstrous K'ala, and the code of M'tuma is right . . .

He shook his head against the visions, and in the catacomb of his brain a virgin headache began. "We are the black people, the people together . . ."

"I think you'd better explain yourself in a hurry, Merriweather!"

"The things we put in this paper, Mr. Hooker—they're wrong. We're betraying the trust of the people we serve; we give them the death of themselves, the filth of themselves. Good outweighs bad, doesn't it? Why must we run this paper on the contention that evil is the force of movement?"

"We're not running this paper on some Socratic precept!" Boss Hooker thundered at him through a haze. "And we've got no room on this staff for philosophers!"

"But there's a *right* for the people," he insisted.

"There's a *right* for people to buy the *Messenger*. Just what the hell are you talking about?"

"But I'm trying to explain—"

"You're explaining nothing! You're talking yourself out of a job!"

. . . But there is no home bigger than the krall, M'Tele knows, no knife of truth sharper than the knife of circumcision to the clitoris, no adhesion faster than the blood of the clan . . .

Didn't he understand?

"We're nothing without *truth,* Mr. Hooker . . ."

"Let me tell you something, Merriweather! The *Messenger* is an institution! It's been in this city—successful in this city—for over a quarter of a century! Our format is simple and plain, and it doesn't change!"

. . . Was that a cry of his people he heard? A cry of death? From over the deep hills where the snake waters roared, was that the shriek of slavery? The thing which Grandfather spoke of? Was that the shackle clamped, the manacles clicking? Let him run! Let him flee! . . .

"And since we've come this roundabout way to truth," Boss Hooker was saying, "I might as well come right to the point. You're a *fine* one to come in here talking about truth . . ."

Truth, M'Tele said, but his coward's legs were swift and sure . . .

"I happen to know Ray Irving's paying you off to besmirch the moral chastity of the *Messenger*. Do you deny he's given you money?"

Lee looked up, his head throbbing, exploding. "Who . . . Who?"

"Ray Irving!" Boss Hooker shrilled. "Do you deny he's paid you to come over and do stories about that boys' club of his?"

"Why, yes, I've done stories, but—"

"And you've taken money for them?"

"Taken?" Lee said, almost confused. "He's given me gas money, expense money. Just for my transportation."

"Then you *have* received money from him?"

"Why, of course. It was only natural—"

"It was *not* natural," Boss Hooker proclaimed. "We who work for the *Messenger* do not accept money under any circumstances. We are looked up to and respected in this city. We have an integrity to maintain—*integrity*— a most conspicuous word in our masthead. We have a professional dignity to maintain! We do not let ourselves become the pawns of individuals who might exploit us for personal gain. Am I understood, Merriweather, completely understood?"

Lee looked at him with shock and horror. "Did I hear you right, Mr. Hooker?"

"You most certainly did," Boss Hooker assured him vehemently. "Ray Irving is a disreputable character in this city, and as long as you're a reporter for the *Messenger* you will *not* associate with him. If you're involved in anything like this again, Merriweather, I'll have to ask for your resignation."

Lee got up, wanting to punch the flat yellow face, wanting to destroy the big body. How could Boss Hooker live with himself? How could he sit on his big ass of hypocrisy and twist his mouth up to say those things?

He shook his head against the pain. It was all a big joke, wasn't it? It was a dream! Men couldn't look the knife in the face and spit on it. . . .

Where had that come from? *The knife?* It was so foreign yet so familiar: so appropriate. What was his mind thinking, intermixed and pummeled by this day of ambiguities? Couldn't he answer himself? Couldn't he answer Boss Hooker, sitting there so smug in his power, so bloated with conceit, so apparently the filial bastard of John Russwurm, so *finally* the end result of one hundred and thirty-odd years of Negro newspaper publishing: such a big dirty yellow bag of mongrel complexities, interwoven with the sores of this social monstrosity, the *Weekly Messenger!*

How could the *Messenger* dare associate itself with integrity, with honesty, with leadership?—when its editorship was clearly the gigolo of the current political state! When it glorified death and crime? When its employees bartered editorial favors in order to live from week to week? When it was hated and despised by the very people who bought it from week to week? When it manipulated these same, dumb, uncaring people for its own personal gain?

The knife stabbed his heart.

Iscariot!

Judas, Judas, Justice!

He turned and stumbled out of the office.

"Merriweather!"

But he did not hear. He stumbled out of the office, and it was as if he couldn't see any longer. There was no Diana. Gone. Leave him. Away. And then again, maybe Boss Hooker was right. Right. Wrong. Gone. Away. Unbelonging. And coward. Running. Away, away. Too far. And the big boat Merry Weather. Merry, merry, merry weather. Run, M'Tele, run, run, *run!* Forget your people. Leave them. Slaves. Hate them. Love die them again away damn coward shit of Merry Weather.

"Hey, Merriweather!" A hand grasped him, a grinning face, a yellow grinning face. Ken Bussey, was it? Yes.

"Hey, what's your hurry, Merriweather? Just saw Scotty a while ago. He told me about that slaughterhouse. Hey!" Face grinned. "Hey, you know what? We could make a nice wad outa that. I got an account. Right around the corner. Al's Supermarket. Now here's my idea. I just set Al up for this quarter page ad, roger? Altakesad. But we overcharge him, get the business? We tell him, Al You're Right Around The Corner From The Slaughterhouse—get the business? We set 'im up for maybe five bills. He pays it! Know why he pays it? For service, kid! Get me, Merriweather? You write a story about him being around the corner from the Slaughterhouse, see? It drives all the bims into his store. You think he can pass that up? Huh, Merriweather? You see the logic?"

Lee strained to see the face in the hallway, the grinning face.

"Huk, huk! You still in that coma Scotty told me about? Hell, come out of it, kid! They're better off dead."

His vision went red. The muscles behind his neck bunched themselves and drew back the long arm; his fingers closed until the fingers were a fist. The face grinned. The arm swung the steel fist: flesh squished against flesh, hard flesh, soft flesh. The face stopped grinning, and blood suddenly splattered the wall of the hallway.

Dazedly, he looked down at the crumpled body of Ken Bussey. His fist stung and it would not unclench. He looked uncomprehendingly at the black fist.

A door down the hall opened, the sound of high heels. "*Lee!*"

Away. Away. He ran, terrified. Down steps, stumble-fall, scared face of Joan in the reception room, eyes wide, bugging. Run. Again. Merry Weather. Fall. Cold outside. Run. Away. Again. No stop. Kailalah! Kailalah! Kailalah! Hoping again sometime stop altogether snow running cold feet cold killing. Killing killing killing.

FOR MY PEOPLE!

He ran, madly, down Farrell Street.

CHAPTER NINE

T HE YOUNG MAN'S BODY was like music in the confines of the ultra-modern apartment, almost like the music that stormed from the hi-fi—Beethoven's Ninth—sweet yet powerful and heart-rending to the sight, as the catharsis of Beethoven to the ear.

Tobey Balin was a tall, slim youth, tall without seeming thin; slim without appearing fragile. In his light-skinned, intelligent face, there was a feeling of effeminacy, but this was only a quirk of his characteristics. He moved with athletic grace; he mastered each bit of furniture on which he sat. It seemed that even the floor and walls moved away in obeisance to him.

There was a weird tenderness about him as he watched Lee, as he got up to hand Lee a stiff drink of Scotch and water, as he spoke to Lee in his deep mellifluous voice.

"You must be out of your mind, Othello," he smiled grimly. "Running around in the cold without a coat. Look at your feet! You're drenched. Suppose I hadn't cut classes today? Where would you be now?"

"Out in the cold," Lee said thickly, sipping hungrily at the liquor.

Tobey went over to shut down the volume of the hi-fi, but the spiritual insistence of Beethoven was something that could not be muffled.

He relaxed in the womb of a contour chair, the good cut of his dark ivy-league suit draping about him langorously.

"What is it, Lee?" he asked quietly.

"Nothing," Lee said irascibly from the couch.

"You drip your dirty slush all over my rug and have the nerve to tell me nothing's wrong?" A dry smile—was it pity?—played with his thin slice of mouth. "We've known each other quite a while, Othello. Remember State? I was the only one you could talk to. I know you; maybe I know more about you than you think. I know, for instance, that it's those Niggers at the *Messenger* who've got you upset."

"Look, I've had enough 'Niggers' today!"

"A Nigger is a Nigger is a Nigger," his friend announced defiantly. "Any way you look at it, it doesn't make him smell any better."

"Stop it."

Tobey smiled. "Hasn't it ever occurred to you, Lee? The word Nigger is a good deal less phonetically embarrassing than that pretentious misnomer, Negro. That word makes my skin bubble."

"Why should it?"

"It's simply that you know when whoever's using it uses it, what he really means is Nigger. It's like the subtle double meaning of the word pussy, and it has the same restrictions. I'm all for making Nigger an acceptable social word."

"It already is. To hear Phil Meyer say it, you wouldn't think there was any other name."

"Ah, Phil Meyer," Tobey said, eyes closed dreamily, head moving to the strains of Beethoven. "So it was the Nigger Meyer?"

"No, you're wrong: *he's* not a Nigger."

"Of course he's not. Neither am I. Neither are you—"

"Oh, *I* am," Lee said with heavy irony. "It's me that the quasi-Niggers speak of when they talk about Niggers."

Tobey's bull laugh warbled deeply. "See how easy it is, Lee? See how easily *Nigger* trips tipplingly to the tongue?"

"Why don't you quit laughing!" Lee flung at him. "I hate to talk with you when you're been smoking that—that gauge!"

Tobey opened his eyes with mock surprise. "But I'm *not* laughing, Othello. And it's not 'gauge,' my poor, uninformed friend, it's *Boo!* And it's about time I started Booing myself."

"Tobey, I wish you would stop using that stuff," Lee said worriedly. "It's against the law, for one thing."

"It's against the law to play the numbers. Or solicit a prostitute. Or buy Scotch after hours. But I'll wager that you and I have done at least two of those three things more than once." He stretched luxuriously in the chair. "Boo satisfies my psychotic lust for adventure, Lee. Psychology 501 at State tells me that I'm insecure when I do this, and I can't argue with it. But you've never had a well-to-do mortician father, or abstentious mother, who demanded of you that you *never* have adventure."

"I've had neither one. You ought to be glad."

Tobey shrugged. "The only thing I can be glad about is that they're both dead and I've got a tidy little trust fund which should last me another year or so."

"You're a bastard to talk like that."

"I'd be a bastard to think like that and not say it." He raised himself up slightly to look at Lee. "You know what's wrong with you, Othello? You're mid-Victorian. Where did you ever pick up your strait-laced stack of morals? Certainly not in your background."

"I read a lot—the best books. I had time to read in the boys' school."

"But that doesn't explain it. According to the mathematics of the swell-heads who are supposed to support the theses we're fed in my criminology class, you're a *freak*, Lee! It's you and not I who should be inclined, socially and mentally, to the so-called narcotic, marijuana. But not you—you'd rather cut off a hand than smoke a joint. As a matter of fact, you don't even *smoke*."

"They're more people like me to back up statistics than people like you," Lee said.

Now, it seemed, he was at his ease, here with Tobey. Where had the fright gone? Where had the confusion swept off to? Here, with Tobey, he was safe and calm, and his mouth could not stop speaking.

"That's all the people like me will ever be," he said. "Statistics, variegated smudges of all the things people over the world should not be."

"I agree with you," his friend nodded sagely.

"You agree?" Lee said, hurt a bit in that he thought Tobey would disagree with him, *wanted* him to disagree.

"Certainly," Tobey said. "Statistics prove that the Nigger is a congenital defeatist. Sure, he's kicked in the ass by prejudicial conditions, but so are the Jews, Indians, Mexicans, Chinese and Japanese. The Jew, for instance, can take the bigot's crap and churn it into dollars. This is not the post–Civil War period, Othello. We've got the people with the money and technical know-how to elevate the Nigger, but they won't because they think somebody's going to *give* them something. They think the white man is going to say to himself, 'What a bastard I've been to the poor Coon,' then eviscerate his entire constitution simply to show the poor dumb Coon that he's not such a bad guy after all."

"I don't see how you can say that!" Lee said, draining his glass angrily. Spitefully he got up and went over to where the miniature bar stood near the swinging kitchen door. He poured himself a double shot and swallowed it down; then poured another to bring back to the couch.

"That's it," Tobey said. "Give the Scotch hell. I only buy a fifth, and it's only for you. There won't be another until the first of the month."

"As I was saying, the Nigger thinks Uncle Charlie owes him a living, which is false."

"*We* were enslaved," Lee said defensively. "We didn't ask to come over here. We *are* owed something."

"If anybody owes somebody something, *we* owe it to the white man."

"How can you see that? How the hell can you figure that?"

"Simple, Lee. We're paying the price of living in the white man's civilization. If we hadn't been enslaved, we wouldn't be enjoying the luxuries of a white democracy today. We'd only be savages, taking each other's heads in the name of some pagan god, in some jungle swamp."

"How do you know we wouldn't be *happier* doing that? Maybe we'd be a hell of a lot better off still living in mud huts and fighting the tsetse fly."

"Use your head, Othello—it's elementary. Nobody *likes* to be in danger of losing his head, not even a savage . . . And don't tell me that savage isn't frightened when one of his children lies down to sleep forever. When you and the other black nationalists start spewing off at the mouth about how happy that wild jungle man is with his condition, I get out of the line of fire—because you're all full of shit."

"There are important people working for the NAACP who would use every ounce of their influence to take your head for making that statement."

Tobey winked. "I'm not sure they wouldn't be successful, old man. They, and all the rest of the black man's messiahs, have been belly-aching for years that the Knee-grow's potential has never been successfully channeled because of the white man's oppression. The brains of these organizations never stop to realize that the cushy life they enjoy depends on the con*tinued* oppression of the black quarter—and then, again, maybe they *do:* that would explain their contentment with the wealth of small victories they trot out on exhibition from time to time."

"You'll have to admit, though, that they're *victories*."

"And great examples of the white man's psychological advantage—his way of dulling the viciousness of the big, dumb dog: a bone, with scarcely a bit of tasty flesh hanging on. Where he bumbled was in letting the savior organizations get out of hand. These served to make a facsimile of the black man—monsters like the *Weekly Messenger*.

Lee nodded. "For the first time you've said something I agree with. Papers like the *Messenger* have made the Negro obscene."

"The Negro has always been obscene in America," Tobey said, "simply because of what he was—and the Great White Father made him even more detestable by his proclivity for the dusky belle; he's made a crazy quilt of us."

"For this reason," he continued, "the Negro in the United States is only an amalgamated social fop, a cheating, conniving, back-stabbing little bastard who, because of his myriad heritage, is undeserving of any racial distinction whatsoever. He is allied to no one, not even himself. Because he is a bastard, his knife is perpetually sharp in anticipation of the throats of his other bastard brothers. I'm sure you can remember seeing exactly what I'm speaking of many times in the past. *This* is what the black man has accepted in the place of the mud hut, the headhunters and the tsetse flies, and I honestly believe it's a hell of an improvement."

"You're talking like Phil Meyer!"

Tobey looked at him. "I don't like to hear myself mentioned in the same breath with that man, and you know it, Lee. Are the facts so terrible? Why don't we have the necessary leadership? This is not the first time a race has been raped. There's not one clue to the thing that makes us tick. We are and we aren't, simultaneously. It seems as though somebody's paying us off to keep away from each other, spiritually. What do we do? What do we contribute? We're a race of *consumers*—we don't produce anything. What do we offer for consumption? You certainly can't eat a world's heavyweight champion or Nat King Cole. If the white man decided to starve us to death today, he could, because we don't even feed ourselves." He sighed. "The only other thing the amalgam called the Negro can boast of business-wise is insurance associations and funeral homes—and is that any goddamn accomplishment after almost four hundred years? And, really, it's an insult! The only thing we can offer ourselves is a nickel-and-dime insurance policy and a hole in some all-Negro cemetery on the edge of town."

Lee took off his shoes and wiggled his toes in the wet socks.

The Scotch was beginning to warm him, and he was stirred vehemently by Tobey's words.

"Consider the conditions we had to work under," he said. "The Negro *has* made progress in the United States; you're over-generalizing the great strides."

"Perhaps you'd like to cite the *Weekly Messenger* as one example of the progress we've made?"

"We can't summarily dismiss the good the Negro newspapers have done simply because of a few bad apples like the *Messenger*," Lee pointed out. "Look at the *Pittsburgh Courier*, the *Amsterdam News*—they're great examples of what the press *should* be."

"You picked out two of the best," Tobey concurred. "But the whiningly recurrent theme of these papers is 'acceptance,' that the white man *must* accept us, and 'equality.' This last point I go along with. Yet, no matter how slick and expert their presentation, they still play host to the curse. Using an effete sophistication, murder and mayhem is the focal point in their news stories."

"That's the second time I've heard that today," Lee said softly.

"The damnation of bloody news," Tobey said grimly. "The *Courier* does a reasonably fine job because it's not confined in its news interest—as in the case of the *Messenger*—having a string of similar mastheads in various cities. It can avoid the blood and guts theme with relative impunity because of its perennially 'clean' approach to Negro news. But the *Courier* and *Amsterdam News* are just two oases in the black desert, and, psychologically, they're two left shoes. Instead of Americanizing the Negro and showing him how to compete as an 'equal,' they try to *Negro-ize* him. This is like trying to put salt on the tail of a blackbird."

"But what else can the Negro papers do but appeal to the black man, try to elevate the *colored* role in America?"

"Don't miss my point, Othello. The black press is right in appealing to the colored people, but it is wrong in trying to instill, at this late date, a pride in something irretrievably lost: the Negro race, as such. It does not reconcile itself to the fact—purposely, I think— because to do so would be to entirely eliminate the *basis* of Negro press. It clings to the premise of *Negro* because to recognize it for what it actually is—an obsolete definition—would be to lose identity with it. There is no Negro race, Lee—not in the United States, at any rate."

"There is no Negro race," Lee echoed.

"Exactly," Tobey said. "I don't believe that there are really fourteen million of Negroes in America. With the exception of the black Puerto Ricans who've migrated to this country, I think it would be difficult to find even a million *true* Negro types. Look at my hand," he said, holding it out. "Could an anthropologist look at my texture and say without reservation that I *am* a Negro? Oh sure, I may have a few Negro-like characteristics, but I am essentially a member of no race, and this is the case with the majority of so-called Negroes in the United States today. The Negro press is aware of this, so it plays on the insecurity of the no-race peoples, trying to make them believe they belong to the same black rivers that gave birth to Hannibal, or the Moors who conquered Europe in the eighth century and left behind for the white man a powerful culture of art, medicine and other astounding concepts of civilization." He laughed. "The only thing we've got in common with those North Africans is the fact that we have no racial cohesion—and that's the reason *they* were eventually kicked off the continent."

Lee stared into his drink. He saw the tall youth get up and go over to his hiding place, then shut off the hi-fi, almost ruefully. "Have you heard the rumor that Beethoven was really a mulatto?" he smiled at Lee. "The rumor is belied in his music: his soul was intrinsically the chaotic restlessness of the Caucasian."

"It could have been acquired."

114

"Racial consciousness is indivisible, even through intermixture of the individual."

"Now you're contradicting yourself," Lee said, catching a point with relish. "You said the Negro in America is a no-race, a nothing. If what you just said is true, then he does have a heritage."

"A heritage, yes," Tobey said. "A heritage of slavery—a slavery inflicted by the white man and then by the Negro himself. But it's my contention that he has no racial consciousness, having been mongrelized time and time again. There is a great deal more difference between true black and true white intermixing than there is between two Half-Niggers. Don't try to get me off the track, Othello. Boo keeps me stable."

"Boo is a crutch for you," Lee snorted.

"Why, of course it is! But haven't we all inherited a club foot of some sort? Don't we all seek an artificial aid to our movement? Even you, Lee, the Puritan, have an undying affinity for Scotch." He came back over to sit once again on the couch.

Lee twirled an empty glass in his hands, confused now, not by the things Tobey said but by the tone of evasiveness in his voice.

"You said the Negro papers are always harping about acceptance and equality, Tobey, but aren't these the things they *should* bitch about? The things that should be the rights of all the people?"

"Of course," he agreed. "And I'm sorry I didn't explain myself. If the Negro paper is going to represent the so-called Negro people, why can't it give us good publicity? Naturally we *want* acceptance and anonymity within the white race, but how are we ever going to achieve them if we constantly point up the bad things about our race with picture stories of death, murder and crime? Is that good public relations? It's even morally deflating to the Negro himself." He paused for a moment. "Put yourself in the position of a gentile who is honestly trying to be objective about the race question. He picks up a Negro paper—say the *Messenger*. The lead story is about a murder. At least eight of the other twelve stories on the front page concern themselves with crime. How long is that gentile going to remain sympathetic to the demands of the black race after reading that sort of stuff? Consequently, when the Negro demands equality in housing, in education, in working conditions, he is rebuffed by that same gentile—and both of them are the victims of poor newspaper reporting. It's not because these papers don't have better things to say about the black people than murder and destruction, but because they are profitably laboring under the conception that the people who read the stuff *want* to read nothing else."

"You may be right about that," Lee confessed. "I've often heard Meyer talk about certain colored people who won't read the *Messenger* because of that."

Tobey smiled thoughtfully. "I recall reading in one of the columns in the *Messenger* where the writer pointed out that the white dailies also play up crime and murder at every opportunity. But is this to be used as a legitimate excuse for the black papers? The dailies are *dailies,* which give them the right to exploit those type stories. Not only that, they cater to all the people, making no particular racial distinction—although I have seen their news slanted to put the Negro in bad light. And conversely I have seen it slanted to put him in a good one. This is a poor analogy on the part of the columnist, since the Negro paper is only a weekly and intends to serve one special minority group. There is no justification for their methods, Othello, and they know goddamn well there isn't. That's why the columnist pointed his finger at the Great White Father in vindication."

"Well, I'm through with it!" Lee said suddenly. "I've worried and tried to figure the damn thing all I'm going to!"

"How's that, Othello?"

"I'm through with the *Messenger.* I knocked Ken Bussey down a little while ago. I don't know, maybe I killed him."

Tobey looked at him with surprise. "Then the wet shoes, no coat—don't tell me you're on the lam?"

"No, it's not that," Lee said, feeling his words ineffectual. "I just busted Ken Bussey in the mouth, so I don't have a job anymore."

He tried to explain about the Hardwicks family, the shock and death, the callousness of Scotty and Phil Meyer, the things he said to Meyer, the hypocrisy of Boss Hooker, of all of them.

And, reluctantly, he tried to explain the strange, mirage-like visions he had been experiencing all that day, the crazy words and explosions within, the complex fade-out of his mind, the terror, when he struck Ken Bussey.

"Does Diana know?" Tobey asked.

Lee shook his head. "I think I heard her holler at me in the hallway. I think it was her. Tobey," he said worriedly. "Tobey, do you think they'll get the cops after me?"

"Probably, Lee." His brow creased in concentration. "But from what you told me, it's no wonder you didn't do something before Bussey tipped you, something really serious."

"I wanted to *kill* Meyer, I told you. I really wanted to kill him! And I would have if—" He didn't go on.

"If what, Lee?"

"I don't know what, Tobey! I've never felt like I've been feeling today. What—what is it?"

"It's many things . . ."

"But *what*? How come, Tobey? I've never had these things happen to me before. Why today, of all days?"

"There's a campaign on to discredit Freud," Tobey said dryly. "But Jung remains in high esteem. I much more prefer the former, however, with due respect to the latter. *Cui bono?* These things you speak of are far beyond my discernment. Lee," he said, "Lee, come over and sit down."

Halting indecisively, Lee came back to the couch.

"I want you to listen to me carefully," Tobey said gently. "It's something I've been thinking about for a long time—that is, I've suspected it for a long time. Ever since we got together at State two years ago."

Lee was instantly alert at the grave tone of his voice. "What is it? Have I got halitosis or something?"

"Nothing as simple as that," Tobey laughed. "But I'm reminded of your background, being an orphan and all . . ."

Lee turned away from him. "I'm reminded of it too."

"Don't get puffy, Othello. It's the crux of what I'm about to say to you."

"Come on, don't build me up! Get on with it."

"All right, Lee," he said flatly. "I think you're an African—a pure-blooded African."

Lee didn't reply for a long time, staring at him incredulously. "You're crazy!" he burst out finally. "That Boo has blasted your brains!"

"And what's so horrible about being an African? Is it any more of a stigma than being an average, everyday Nigger?"

"It's impossible! I was born and raised in America! You're losing your goddamn mind! Just because I said those things I felt? Just because those things—*bothered* me? Just because I lost myself for a little while, I'm a goddamn black African, is that it? You go to *hell,* Tobey!"

"I'm in my twenty-sixth year of the journey, Othello. Hell is a long way off, you know, and you've got to walk all the way!"

"An African!" Lee spat, feeling the revulsion in his throat, knowing that what Tobey said was true, realizing that it was that elusive thing he had wanted to be brought face to face with all along. "A goddamn black African! How did I get to be an African, High Yeller, or can't you tell me that? How is it I'm an African and don't know it?"

"For one thing, you're an orphan . . ."

"That doesn't prove anything!"

"No, but *you* do. You've got the classic Negro features: the woolly hair, deep pigment, thick lips, a broad nose and prognathism. Maybe you don't know it, but a legitimate Negro doesn't ever shave, because he doesn't *have* to—and you've never shaved in your life. You're a perfect example of what is accepted by anthropologists as the 'true' Negro type, usually found along the southern shore of West Africa."

Lee lost his temper. "If you're trying to insult me, you're off to a damn good start! *Prove* to me how I'm an African!"

"I was thinking about those visions you told me about," Tobey said. "Do you remember me speaking of racial consciousness? I think you've experienced some of it."

"I've never been to Africa in my life!"

"But of course, Lee! That's the substantiation of racial consciousness. You've never been to Africa, but you *remember* it."

"It's crazy!" Lee said, turning his face away. "I won't believe it!"

"No, you won't believe it, because you've been taught in this society that it's most desirable to be a white man."

"I don't want to *be* anything. I just want to be myself and left alone."

"You'll never be yourself in peace. Today, something happened to you, Othello. You'll never be able to go back to where you were."

Lee glared at him. "I guess you know it all! Just go on—go on and tell me how I'm an African and don't know it!"

"I'll tell you," Tobey said calmly. "Even if you attack me because of the hypersensitive state you're in now."

Lee was chastened by the unsubtle hint. "Go ahead, Tobey. I'm sorry."

Tobey gave him an encouraging smile. "From what you told me, Lee, you were raised by a couple of middle-aged people on the Lower East Side . . ."

"I was one of nine other state wards," he recalled bitterly. "The only reason the Hollands kept us was because of the handout they got from the state. I hated that place. Old man Holland, a big fat bastard, used to come around like clockwork on Saturday nights and beat our asses—for nothing! I think he enjoyed it."

"That's the first time you've ever described that to me—those conditions."

Lee looked up. "It's the first time I remember it, I guess. I wanted to forget everything. Do you know, that's the first time I could remember those peoples' names?"

"What about the other children?"

He shook his head. "I can't remember them at all. The faces are blurry in my head. I know there was one little kid who died. He got real sick . . . Benny!" he said, his face lighting up. "Benny, that was his name! Me and him used to play mumbly-peg, but Mr. Holland took the knife from us one day. Isn't it funny how I remember it! Right after he took the knife, Benny got sick and died. That's when I ran away the first time. I thought Mr. Holland had killed him because of the knife and was going to kill me too. But they caught me and brought me back."

"What about before then, Lee? Before the Hollands?"

He shook his head. "I can't remember."

"Where did you get your name?"

"I don't know. I always had it, but I never had a birth certificate. Nobody ever told me who my mother and father were."

"Isn't Merriweather an uncommon name? Didn't you say something about a boat? A Merry Weather boat? Could be the S.S. Merry Weather."

Lee shook his head violently. "That was just something in my mind! Something crazy!"

"I'm reminded of a Negro," Tobey said. "An African pygmy type, by the name of Pork Chop Brown. This guy had a quirk of intestinal proficiency. Something in his metabolism enabled him to eat a pig at one sitting, and I understand the University of Michigan legally *owns* his body in the event of death, for research."

"Well, what has that got to do with me?"

"I was just thinking. Brown came to America on a tramp steamer, and was christened Brown, after the captain himself, who got a kick out of just watching the guy eat." He regarded Lee carefully. "Do you think something like that might have happened with your parents? I mean—they might have migrated from Africa years ago. Let's say they didn't have Christian names. Wouldn't it be one form of sentimental logic to name themselves after the boat on which they came to America?"

It was still too early for Lee to fully admit that he might actually be of African descent. "You figure it out."

"I will, if I can get any help from you."

"All right!" Lee said with agitated shortness, getting up to stalk around the room again. "If I came from Africa, how come I don't have it in my record somewhere? My parents had to apply for American citizenship, for me as well as themselves."

Tobey watched him with tender amusement. "Evidently you were born in America."

Lee came over to him with a hard grin of triumph. "Blooee! That blows your theory to hell! If I was born in America, how the devil could I know anything about Africa?"

"It's so complicated, Othello. I don't expect you to understand that it might have happened—that it *might* have been possible for your mother and father to have died or been killed shortly after they arrived here. If such was the case, it's no wonder that you don't have any records, since they were unfamiliar with the customs of this country."

"Don't insult me," Lee said. "I can understand anything reasonable."

"Okay. Try this on for size: *You* don't remember Africa—your *father* remembered it—or perhaps your grandfather."

Lee rolled his eyes with exaggerated sarcasm, but it didn't come off so well. "Boy, you're way out in the left side of the universe!"

"The right side is so crowded nowadays."

"You're asking me to believe something impossible!"

"I'm asking you to believe nothing. I'm only suggesting a probability."

"Let's start all over again. I'm an African and I'm seeing the things that my African father or grandfather might have once witnessed many years ago, right?"

"Precisely."

"*How* do I see these things? *Why* do I see them?"

"Racial consciousness vaguely explains the how. As to the why, I'd say that you were stirred mentally by the things that happened to you today—the death of those people, that rundown street, probably reminiscent of the street you lived on with the Hollands, which could understandably cause unpleasant memories—and the upheaval of your values, set off by Phil Meyer."

"Neat!" Lee said, turning away.

"*Copia verborum*," Tobey sighed.

"How true!" Lee said, whirling to face him. "I remember enough Latin to know that's all you've done so far—confuse the issue with a cloud of words."

"And what is the issue, Othello?"

"The issue . . . the issue is everything," Lee said uncertainly. "Right now, the biggest issue is the job I don't have anymore."

"But I thought you were glad to be rid of the *Messenger* and all it stands for," Tobey said mockingly.

"I *am* glad."

"Then why are you so desolate? Today is a good example of what the *Messenger* would have done to you if you had remained with it. It's given you cause for painful thinking, and one must always avoid that catastrophe, oughtn't one?"

"Do you think you're being funny?"

"Not in the least. Please believe me when I say that. What happened to you today can't be dismissed with some stock explanation. All along, I've been trying to tell you what the *Messenger* and the others like it were, how infinitely destructive they were to everything and everyone they touched. Unfortunately, the *Messenger* provided you the only means by which you could express yourself. I wish you had remained at college," he finished helplessly.

Lee went back over to the liquor cabinet and poured himself a fresh drink.

"You're going to get drunk, Othello."

"I already am." He tilted the glass and swallowed the mixture in one gulp, then looked at Tobey. "So where do I go from here? What do I do now?"

"You could go back to State," Tobey suggested. "I've got enough room here for you to shack up a while, and I could loan you the rest of this year's tuition."

"I couldn't do that—"

"Don't be a fool. Where do you get that ridiculous pride! You could pay me back when you got on your feet."

"You don't understand, Tobey. I've got a little money put away. But I had problems at State; I just couldn't get my work synchronized. I finished my last semester with a B-minus average . . ."

"I'm two years ahead. I could give you a hand with the bigger problems."

"That's not it altogether. There's Diana, for one thing—"

"What's the matter, Othello? Is Desdemona in a family way?"

"I'm not joking, Tobey."

Tobey shook his head understandingly. "You want to marry her, right?"

"As soon as possible."

"Then what's the problem?"

"If I went back to college, Diana'd have to keep on working."

"Doesn't she want to?"

"Oh, sure, she insists on it. But *not* at the *Messenger*," he added strongly. "I wouldn't let her stay on there."

"Then what's the objection?"

"Well—" he said hesitantly. "I wouldn't feel right, Diana working and supporting us, and me leveling off with a B-minus average. It wouldn't be fair to her."

"Marriage'll take care of that." Tobey decreed knowingly. "It'll give you the self-confidence you've been lacking."

"I'm not so sure . . ."

"If you're not sure about that, then you'd be a dog to get that nice girl into something you couldn't get her out of."

"You're right," Lee grudgingly admitted.

Tobey got up and went over to where he stood.

"Othello," he said gently. "You really love this girl, don't you?"

Lee looked up at him. "More than anything, you know that."

"And she loves you. It's just bursting out of her every time she looks at you. I've noticed it when you bring her here. I want to be sure you know your motives, Lee."

"What are you talking about?"

"I want you to *really* love this girl. You're the younger brother I never had, and I sincerely want to see you step firmly."

"You're not making yourself clear."

"I don't want to see you marry her because you think marriage to her is going to make you any lighter than you are," Tobey said. "Do you understand me, Lee? You're black. You'll always be black. To a girl like Diana, that doesn't make any difference. I don't want to see your ego capitalize on her love."

"It won't!" Lee snapped.

"My, you're full of sore spots today," Tobey smiled. "But you just heed me, brother. If you screw up that girl's life, I'm going to disown you. I'd never let you darken my liquor cabinet again."

Lee had to turn away from his vivid eyes. "I'd cut off my head before I'd do that, and you know it."

"Well, now, what about the *Messenger?*"

"I've quit, I told you."

"It's usually customary to inform your employer of your dissatisfaction and intent to terminate employment."

"I don't see the sense in it, but I could call Boss Hooker—"

"That wouldn't do at all."

Lee looked at him incredulously. "You don't mean I should go *back* to the *Messenger* and tell him?"

"That's just what I mean," Tobey stipulated. "You might as well face up to the music now as later. Go on back to the *Messenger* and take whatever's coming to you. Maybe you can talk Bussey out of prosecuting."

"I couldn't go back there!"

Tobey turned away from him. "That's up to you."

"But—but what could I say?" Lee said, following after him. "How could I explain myself?"

"I don't see how you could be forced to. Diana's the only one you owe an explanation."

"I just couldn't!" Lee pleaded.

"You're not afraid, are you?"

"Of course not."

"Then what are you bitching about? At the worst, the most you'd probably get is thirty days, for assault." He seated himself in the contour chair once more. "Go on back, Lee. Clear the thing up and start over clean, you and Diana."

"But it's almost six now. The office is closed."

"I guess you could do it just as well Monday, couldn't you?"

Lee paced the floor nervously again. "Mr. Sandersford, the publisher, is due at the office at ten tonight. I guess I could go around then—"

Tobey perked up in his seat. "You don't mean the big boy himself? Douglas Sandersford?"

"That's right. We were alerted today. He's coming in for his yearly check, and we're all supposed to be around to greet him. Why?"

Tobey chewed at his lips with a mysterious smile. "Ten, did you say?"

"That's what Meyer said."

"That's perfect!" Tobey said, getting up from his seat with unusual vigor.

Lee watched him suspiciously. "What have you got on your mind?"

"Huhm? Oh, nothing, Othello, not a thing! Did you say you were going?"

"No, I *didn't* say it. But I guess I will. I have to go over to the boys' club and let Ray Irving know there won't be any more articles. I think I owe those kids that much. Then I'll go home and get ready."

Tobey went over to the closet and came back with a blue, lightweight cashmere overcoat. "Here, you can give this back later. Where's your car?"

"I left it at the *Messenger,* in the parking lot."

"Then you can have my galoshes."

"No, that's okay. I'll catch a bus to the club."

"Okay, Lee, you go ahead. I'll see you a little later."

Lee caught the burr of urgency in his voice, the light of enthusiasm in his face.

"Tobey, you've got something up your sleeve. What is it?"

"Nothing, Othello! You're just imagining things. Now just go ahead and get at those things you've got to do."

"Tobey—"

"Lee, will you get the hell out of here? If you must know, there's a scrumptious piece of tail flying in from the campus. I just forgot I had an appointment to instruct her in the finer points of bedfellowism, that's all."

Lee watched him carefully. "You've never been this excited about a new piece."

"I've never met a piece like this before, Othello. She's something else again. Now, will you get out of here?"

Lee got into the coat and went over to the door reluctantly. "Tobey—"

"Now don't argue with me, Lee, just go on, will you?" He opened the door hurriedly and ushered Lee into the hallway.

"Tobey, don't you try any of your damn fool tricks!"

"Tricks? Tricks? I'm not up to any tricks, Othello."

"You sure as hell are," Lee said.

"Please," Tobey whispered hugely. "There're very nosy neighbors in this apartment building. They'll think I'm being evicted. Just go along, will you, old chap? Huh, Lee. Please? Don't exhibit the ass in your blood."

"You're the one," Lee said loudly. "Tobey, you're going to do something serious, and I know it."

"I always approach any situation involving a plump coed with some amount of gravity," he laughed. "Now get the hell out of here, Othello."

Still reluctant, Lee started down the hall. At the landing he turned back and called to his friend gravely, "Don't do it, Tobey. Whatever it is, don't do it."

"How can you stop it once it's started?" Tobey retorted with a smile.

Lee didn't know.

CHAPTER TEN

THE CHRISTIAN BROTHERHOOD OF WAYWARD BOYS, the sign read.

The four-story façade was drab, though neat, and the building stood out from all others in the East Side area, for it evoked a sort of life, an exuberance, the silent things it promised youth.

As a boy, this club was the sort of thing Lee had always dreamed of: a place where he could play and shout and run until exhausted; a place where he could mingle, unworried, with boys his own age; a place where he belonged in the world, where he could forget the difference of himself.

Maybe that was why Ray Irving had only needed to ask him down to the place once. . . .

He went quickly into the brick bosom of the club. From the pit of the gym, where the cries and screams of happy boys blossomed forth, the wealth of life was evident. Lee could look down the long corridor and watch the vague, dancing images through the open gym doors. The walls on each side of the hallway boasted pictures of the basketball teams, the baseball teams, the golden glove champions, of years gone by. In one glass-enclosed, sanctimonious niche, the trophies of the club were proudly displayed: the softball championships of 1943 (that had been the one Irving played on, as pitcher), the hundred-yard dash, 1950, and the golden glove trophy, won by a kid named Perry Moore in 1954. Moore was now the keeper of the club, and he was the first person Lee encountered on entering the gym.

"Hi, Mr. Merriweather!" he smiled, big toothy, Bugs Bunny grin—the smooth, dark arms too long, the T-shirted chest too wide. "How ya gettin' along?"

"Fine, Perry," Lee returned. Wistfully, he looked about the big gym, where some youths were heatedly engaged in a basketball game at the far court, their sneakered feet slamming with pithy insistence against the hardwood floor, their grunts and exclamations sounding out with echoes in the spacelessness of the interior. In other areas, the smaller youngsters were playing games of volleyball, badminton, or a variation of the game of tag, using a basketball to make the point of "It." In the corner, under the mezzanine-type practice track, two teenagers in trunks, T-shirts and headgear, sparred seriously in the elevated ring.

"Is Mr. Irving around?" Lee asked Perry.

"Not yet, Mr. Merriweather." He looked at the moisturized face of his cheap wrist watch. "It's six-thirty, though. He should be around real soon."

Lee looked around the gym. "These kids are having a hell of a time."

Perry wrinkled his flat nose distastefully. "I'm lettin' 'em run wild for a few minutes. In a little while, we're really gonna get down to work."

"How's the track team?"

"Some of 'em are over there in the basketball game. Just look at 'em! When it comes time to run, they gonna all be tuckered. But they needn't think I'm gonna ease up. I'm gonna run they asses off!" he promised.

"You've been training them all winter," Lee said.' 'They'll be hard to beat in the spring."

Perry shook his head doubtfully. "I don't know. The YMCA's got a hell of a crew, and they train all winter too. We got our first time to outpoint 'em in a meet. I'm hopin' we can do it this year. What I'm countin' on is my boxin' team."

"You shouldn't have any trouble. Smalley brought in the honors in the welter and middle divisions last year. I think he can do it this year too."

Perry frowned at him. "Didn't Mr. Irving tell ya? Smalley's in jail."

"Jail?" Lee said, surprised.

"Unarmed robbery. Cops picked him up a week ago, an' it looks like they got 'im cold, him and two other boys."

"But that doesn't make sense," Lee said. "Smalley was making such good progress here! You were even talking of sending him into the Golden Gloves next year."

Perry took a deep, boxer's breath of resignation. "I guess we just haveta scratch Smalley, Mr. Merriweather. I think he gonna git a stretch. You know, this ain't the first time he been in trouble; he's got a record. Just too bad."

"Yeah," Lee said dimly. "He had such a hell of a future in boxing."

"Sure 'nough," Perry agreed. "I was gone go pro this season— Mr. Irving was gone finance me and all—and we was thinkin' of makin' it a two-stable, when Smalley turned eighteen. Anybody who got in the ring with Smalley in his weight was born dead. He was a natural pug, and he wudn't through growin'."

"Maybe if Mr. Irving went down and stood up for him, Perry—"

"Wouldn't do no good, Mr. Merriweather. Mr. Irving tried all his connections, but it's just too late to do anything. Anyways," he said confidentially, "you know how they look on Mr. Irving comin' down to court, him in the numbers and all. Judge say, 'Hell naw!' They'll probably send Smalley 'way till he twenty-one, then it be too late for him to get in the game—like it's almost too late for me."

"Too bad," Lee said, but too bad was not enough: too bad was only the beginning for Smalley, and he knew it. Uneducated, untutored, unversed in any legitimate phase of society save boxing— and having only a rudimentary education in that—he would probably spend the rest of his life behind bars.

"I got another boy I wantcha to look at," Perry said, pulling him eagerly toward the boxing ring. "He ain't as good as Smalley, but he somethin'. He gone be a comer, you watch and see."

The whip-whap of the boxer's gloves resounded, smartly as they came over to the ring; the resin cried under their dancing feet.

"That's him," Perry said. "The boy in the blue trunks. Lookit them shoulders, huh? He just sixteen too. Gone be a heavy 'fore he eighteen, sure as hell."

Lee vicariously enjoyed the action. The two boxers, in blue and red trunks respectively, were of reasonably equal size, but the boy in the blue trunks was built like a wrestler across the shoulders. As he punched, the muscles bounced and bulged under the sweat-stained T-shirt, the shoulders humped with mastodonic grace. He jabbed at the elusive face of his opponent. He stopped. The muscles bobbed. The heavy-gloved right fist came from nowhere. *Whap!* Away they moved, finding the ring ropes, the resin crying underfoot. The pungent smell of sweat emanated from their briskly young bodies.

They were beautiful together, their bodies moving in unison, but they were much like a man and woman making love, the man knowing his power and strength, the determination of his loins, against the firm but submissive tenuousness of the woman. The blue boxer leveled a hard tattoo mercilessly against the belly of the red boxer; his big shoulders subdued the red boxer; his feet danced in accord with his relentlessly flailing arms. He stepped away suddenly, released a shotgun blast of left jabs, went from kidney to head with two blows that looked like one, crossed with the devastating right, left hook, a smashing right to the unprotected jaw, a dazzling left uppercut. The red trunks staggered and buckled, then caved, the long arms grabbing instinctively for support. The youth went to one knee on the canvas.

"Goddamn you, Cecil!" Perry yelled at the boy in the blue trunks. "You think you in the goddamn Garden? You think you kill somebody for nothin'? You get over there and pick him up!"

Sheepishly, the blue-trunked boxer went over to help his opponent up.

"Ain't that somethin'?" Perry said, unsuccessfully hiding his admiration. "You ever see a comer like that, Mr. Merriweather?"

Lee nodded in amazement. "He's the fastest thing I've seen in the amateurs, and he punches! How old did you say he was?"

"Just sixteen," Perry grinned.

"What's his weight?"

"Oh, he hovers 'round one-sixty-seven, one-seventy-one or so."

"Doesn't he settle?"

"Oh, yeah. He strips down to one-sixty-five, but he lose power. He be better 'round one-seventy-five."

"That's a difficult weight," Lee commented doubtfully.

"Yeah, that's the trouble," Perry said worried. "But he growin'. I think I'll try to fatten him up a little—maybe one-eighty—but I'm scared he'll lose his speed."

"He punches hard enough for the light-heavies. I think he punches hard enough for the heavies."

"Yeah, only thing is, I don't know if he'll come with two-hundred pounders. He never been tested. I'm sorta stringin' him along till I'm sure. A lot of two hundred pounders can make a boy lose faith in himself, make him scary. And that's the thing a man got to have most of in this world—faith."

For some reason, Lee had to look closely at Perry's dark, serious face.

"All right," he called to the boxers. "Cecil, you just go 'head and shadowbox for a while. I'll let you know when to quit. Davey, you took a hard knockin'. You go on back to the dressin' room and shower up. I'll be back in a little while to rub ya."

Lee watched the boxer Cecil dance around the empty ring agilely, snorting disastrously with the blows he rained upon his invisible opponent.

"He really somethin'," Perry said proudly. "I just hope to God he don't go wrong like Smalley. All those boys," he said, waving his arm to encompass the gym. "All these boys is poor, Mr. Merriweather. They git with gangs, they git with hipsters—they think they can make it 'fore they should. They lookin' for the easy way, but any fool knows there ain't no such thing. Take Mr. Irving," he pointed out. "Maybe he ain't altogether legitimate, but he worked hard to git what he got. He come up the same way a lot of these kids did, but he didn't go wrong, 'cause if heda went wrong, they wouldn't be no Brotherhood. He's a good man."

"You think a lot of him, don't you?"

Perry shrugged. "Sure. Maybe I don't care for what he's doin', but he's the top in my book. He gimme a chance I mighta never had otherwise. He's got faith in me, Mr. Merriweather, just like I got faith in that boy Cecil. I'm twenty-four now, real old to be turnin' pro, but I won't discourage Mr. Irving. Maybe I won't be no champ, but I won't be no bum. The most important thing is what it'll do for these boys here, the encouragement it'll give 'em."

"I understand," Lee said.

Perry nodded toward the ring. "That boy, he needs a lot of help, Mr. Merriweather. Maybe you could give 'im a little publicity, like you done for a lot of the kids here? Give 'im his first clippin', know what I mean?"

"Perry," Lee said haltingly. "That's what I came down here about . . . I—"

The other man felt Lee's reserve. "Ain't nothin' wrong, is it, Mr. Merriweather?"

"Well—I'd like to talk to Mr. Irving," Lee said guiltily. "It's something that happened at the *Messenger*."

"I hope it ain't nothin' serious," Perry said with concern. "I can't say I like the *Messenger,* for a paper. Matter of fact, all I read is the sports page and your articles about the club. But I hope it ain't nothin' serious for you, Mr. Merriweather."

"Thank you, Perry. Maybe it isn't."

Perry looked away across the ring, idly investigating the motions of his fighter. "I hate to knock the *Messenger,* Mr. Merriweather, but I just can't see the sense in it. Every other week or so, they got a contest on for the best churchlady or the best preacher in the city. How do they find out these people is the best, when the best is always kind of hid out in people's hearts?"

"You've got the wrong idea, Perry. Those are 'popularity' contests, that's all."

"But that's what I said," Perry went on. "Popularity means the best, don't it? If a preacher or churchlady is the best, they don't need to have no contest tellin' 'em that. Everybody knows it. I don't see no sense in it. Why don't they have a contest 'bout the best civic development 'mongst the colored folks, or somethin' like that, insteada what beautician burns the best head of hair?"

Lee couldn't answer the simple questions.

"Now, like I say, I'm not tryin' to knock the *Messenger,*" Perry continued. "But I think they could do more good tellin' 'bout the folks what's tryin' to live like *people* insteada a buncha jackleg preachers with long Cadillacs. And it seems like every 'churchlady' I ever knew who was real active in church affairs, was tryin' to sleep with the reverend, or *was* sleepin' with 'im." He shook his head. "I don't know nothin' 'bout newspapers and such, Mr. Merriweather, but colored folks does a lot more than deal in dope, cut each other up and knock each other in the head, don't they? Why, last week, I read in one of the white dailies 'bout a colored fella who designed a new type boat, and it was a real good story too. Then I looked in the *Messenger* and found the story 'bout him on page three. On the front page was a dope story. Why didn't they put that dope story on page three and the story 'bout the boat fella on page one?"

Lee couldn't reply. His vision was blurred by the quick one-twos, the skip-tap, grunt!, of the boxer.

Perry casually ground his big white teeth together, taking those deep breaths as he watched the fighter. "He good, ain't he?" he asked Lee.

"Yes."

"Yeah, he really good!" Perry said. "Now *that's* news to me. He kinda people the *Messenger* should praise, youngsters tryin' to go somewhere, fellas inventin' new boats and such. People like Mr. Irving, who's givin' up time and money tryin' to make somethin' out of our young people—them's the things the people need to know about." He turned to Lee suddenly with a fresh thought. "Now that's another thing that bothers me. I've seen our rich colored folks go to hundred-dollar dinners for the NAACP and stuff like that, but I got the first time to see 'em go to a hundred-dollar dinner what's gonna help our kids or our poor folks, or maybe build a project for the people in the slums—or any kind of program we can *see*. They's quick to give to any kind of benefit that'll help build another hoot-an'-holler church, or maybe some Egyptians five thousand miles away, but they won't help they own people." He shook his head woefully. "I just don't see the sense in it."

Lee turned away. "Maybe I better come back a little later, Perry."

"Oh, you ain't leavin', are you, Mr. Merriweather? Mr. Irving ought to be here before long."

Lee was obsessed by a heavy sense of guilt. In a way, he still felt himself a minion of the *Messenger,* and he hated himself for any past or present association with it.

"I'll be back in a little while," he said. "I just remembered something I have to take care of."

Perry pointed toward the gym doors. "You won't have to come back, Mr. Merriweather."

Lee saw Ray Irving, accompanied by a tall, willowy, high-toned woman in a mink stole, come into the gym. Irving carried a heavy gray vicuna over his arm, and the collar of his shirt under the expensive blue worsted was meticulously white against his dark throat. There was a gangsterish look about his ferret-like face that was contradicted in the softness of his eyes as he looked about the gym.

"Hi, Ray!" the boys called to him, pausing in their play.

"How ya doin', Ray!"

"Hey, there's Ray!"

Irving gave a victory salute to them, hands clenched above his neatly felted head. "Keep at it, guys!" he yelled, then caught sight of Lee and Perry and walked over briskly, the woman trailing obediently behind him.

He held out his hand to Lee, an exaggerated formality he always indulged in when they met. "How ya doin', man?" he asked, his small eyes flashing over Lee circumspectly, as if seeking to discover some wound or injury the world had done him since they last met. "I hear you had some trouble today."

Lee was genuinely surprised. "How did you know?"

Irving waved a small manicured hand, where a diamond flashed on the little finger. "Ah, I got ways! I know what they're doin' to ya!" He looked around at the woman, who was almost six inches taller than him, with a tinge of yellow in the blossom of hair over her forehead. "Hey, don't you know Maida Housely? Maida, Lee Merriweather. Her old man's the aide to the councilman. Ain't that right, baby?"

Lee was impressed with how this woman, evidently from a good family, was subdued by the coarse dynamics of the little man. Her eyes flared uninhibitedly as she looked down on him.

"I'm glad to know you, Mr. Merriweather," she said in a soft, perfect voice, obviously at her ease in the smell, the action, the movement of the gym.

"Lee works for that sonofabitchin' *Messenger*," Irving told her crudely. He grabbed Lee's arm with strong fingers. "C'mon, let's go back to the office. Perry, take care of everything, will ya?"

"Right, Mr. Irving."

"Hey, you kids!" Irving yelled at the basketball players. "Bounce dat ball! BOUNCE DAT BALL!" Then to his companions, sotto voce, "C'mon, let's move it up. I got things to do."

They went out in the hallway and down to a door at the far end, where Irving gained entrance with one of the many keys on his ring.

The office was small, with barely enough room for the cluttered desk and leatherette couch. The walls were plastered with pictures of well known Negro athletes, boxers, football players, basketball notables. All of them were personally autographed to Ray Irving.

Irving went over to seat himself behind the desk, motioning for Lee and Maida Housely to sit down on the couch. He did not take off his hat, and lighted the first of what Lee knew to be an incessant chain of cigarettes.

"Now, what's the trouble, Lee?" he said in a fatherly manner. "I wanna hear your story, huh? Yeah! I *know* what those guys can do to ya. When you know a bastard, you know him, right?"

"Well," Lee said, "for one thing, I punched Ken Bussey."

Irving laughed uproariously. "That guy's had it comin' for a long time! They were still tryin' to wake 'im up when I talked to Morrell and Hooker. You really musta nubbed him, man!"

"You talked to Morrell?"

Irving waved his finger about the room with erratic anger. "That punk has the nerve to call up and threaten me—*me!* He called Louie Viconetti first, but Louie wouldn't even listen to him. And here's me, up to my elbows in yesterday's hits, and that punk calls me

135

up. You know what I told 'im? I told him the spooks'd get him if he didn't stay out of my hair, and he knows how the spooks can carry a guy off to nowhere. Then he started tellin' me how Hooker was dissatisfied with the arrangement you and I had down here about those articles. Well, hah, hah, HAR! I says. You ain't gonna bleed me! I tells him. And you better leave my man Lee alone, I says."

"But why should they call you at all?"

"We got a working arrangement with the *Messenger*," Irving enlightened him. "Anytime one of the houses has to take a fall, the *Messenger* plays it down. We pay 'em good money to do that. Hooker and Morrell. So Hooker is pissed because he thinks I'm tryin' to beat 'im out of somethin' with your articles. I got so mad, I called him right up after Morrell slobbered over me. LOOK! I says. YOU GOT GOOD SENSE? YOU GET OFF MY BACK! I tells him. AND LEAVE MERRIWEATHER ALONE! That's when he tells me you punched out Ken Bussey, for nothing. Then he tells me you ain't got no more job. Look! I says, real low so he gets the message. You don't do nothin' to my man, ya understand? He-is-a-good-kid! Now you get off his back, I says. As long as I'm livin' in this city, he could punch *you* in the mouth and he'd still have a job!"

"But, Ray—"

"Listen, man," Irving cut him off, "you ain't got nothin' to worry about. Hooker was convinced. As a matter of fact, you go back to work with a ten-dollar increase in wages." He grinned whitely, apparently satisfied with himself. "Now ain't that bells? Huh? Yeah! Now you go right ahead with those articles whenever you feel like it, and don't worry about those rubbydubs at the *Messenger*."

Irving's verbal speed was dazzling, as usual, and Lee had difficulty getting his thoughts in sequence.

"Ray, you don't understand," he said. "I don't think I *want* to go back to the *Messenger*."

Irving blew out a wild puff of cigarette smoke and stared at him. "But you gotta go back, man! I fixed it! Whatta 'bout the articles?"

"There can't be any more articles if I'm not with the *Messenger,* can there?"

"Well, whatta you gonna do?" Irving roared. "Go to the *Eagle* or *Tribune?* You got too much talent for those guys, even a bonehead like me knows that much."

Lee was mentally unsettled by the change of events. "I just wouldn't feel—well, feel *right,* going back."

"Feel?" Irving said. "Feel? What's this gotta do with feelin'? Hey, look, kid, why don't you just back for a while? Huh? Just a little while. We'll think of somethin', Lee. I *like* you, man. I'll figure out somethin'. You just can't go to nothin'. You're not the kind of guy to go to nothin'—you got too much to lose." He leaned across the desk suddenly. "Hey, how's this? How about me settin' you up in business?"

"Business?"

"Yeah, yeah! The newspaper business."

"The newspaper business?" Lee said incredulously. "Ray, are you serious? Do you know what kind of business that is? You just don't *think* about a newspaper and then decide you're going to have one. Anyway, there're already three Negro papers in the city."

"Ain't this kid beautiful?" he grinned at Maida. "He even *talks* beautiful. Lee baby, I'm serious. What's it gonna cost, huh? Thirty grand? Fifty? Say seventy-five grand. Couldn't you get somethin' started with that kind of money? Not a shoppin' news, man, I mean a real newspaper."

"Well, I guess you could, but—"

"Then that settles it," Irving said, leaning back in his chair with his hands behind his head. "What this city needs is a good Negro newspaper, I've been thinkin' about it for a long time. A *real* competitor for the *Messenger,* somethin' that'll run it right off the stands. We want somethin' sweet and swift—somethin' any family would be glad to take into their home. Yeah, that's it—we want a clean, family-type Negro newspaper. Okay, Lee, you're the editor. I'll go down and talk to my lawyer Monday mornin'; you can go with me. Now all we need is a name. Can you think of somethin' good—somethin' real impressive, that's what we need! How about the *Avenger*? But that's kinda corny, ain't it, Maida baby? I tell you what, Lee—*The Monitor—The People's Monitor*. Sound, huh? And it's gettin' the people involved in it."

"Ray," Lee said, "are you sure you know what you're doing?"

Irving bounced forward in the chair, small eyes flashing. "Listen, Lee, I been in the rackets twenty years. I was pickin' up when I was fourteen. I got two Cadillacs now and a home what cost forty grand. Do you think I got all that by bein' *un*sure? All I ain't got is a wife and babies, but I think me and Maida's gonna take steps to correct that little point. Right, baby?"

Lee saw a flush come over the lovely woman's face.

"But why this?" Lee said cautiously. "Why the sudden interest in a newspaper?"

Irving gave his lips a forlorn twist. "I'm gettin' stale in this work, Lee. I need a change—a legit change. I think it's time I started goin' straight. I been doing a lot of thinkin' about it. But I want a business that's different and prominent in the community, somethin' to make those jokers at Congressional Baptist sit up and take notice. Huh? Yeah! Like a newspaper."

"But the expense," Lee pointed out. "Where would we get the reporters? We'd have to apply for the news services. What about the advertising personnel? We couldn't operate without them. Jobbing the paper would cost anywhere from five to ten thousand a week."

"We don't job *The Monitor!*" Irving said, turning thumbs down toward the desk. "We operate our own press."

"But that costs thousands, Ray! One linotype machine, second-hand, costs anywhere from two to four thousand a piece. We'd need at least four or five—and the union operators would cost almost five dollars an hour. And what about the press itself, which is fantastic? Not to speak of the typesetters, the trucks and truck drivers—"

"So *what?*" Irving grinned. "I got the bread, man! And if I get tired of spendin' it, my credit is good."

"But there're countless other things," Lee said helplessly. "What about them?"

Irving shrugged. "That's your problem—you're the editor. Reporters? Hijack 'em. Offer 'em better wages. There's that Marc Crawford, who works for Johnson Publications. I like him. Why not take a run over to Chicago and talk with 'im? What about A. S. 'Doc' Young for the sports page? Maybe he's about ready to blow *Jet*."

Lee shook his head weakly. "Ray, you're being—spectacular! We don't have the slightest chance of getting those people. They wouldn't even consider a virgin venture like *The Monitor*."

Irving winked at him. "You'd be surprised with how loud money can talk, man. Think it over. Chew up a couple of ideas, then spit 'em out. We'll make *The Monitor* the biggest Negro newspaper this or any other city has seen! And who knows—maybe after a while it'll be a daily!"

Lee started to protest again, but what good would it have done? Irving was speaking of an enterprise that could run way into six figures, and he was speaking of it with authority. Lee could scarcely doubt that he had the money at his disposal with which to make the wild dream come true, and he was infected with the forceful energy of the man.

Was it possible? Already he was considering *The Monitor*, the things it could do. Thinking of Tobey, he wondered if he might be able to rescue the cause of Negro newspapers with this bold new approach. Wouldn't he, as editor, be free to insinuate his own thinking?

What about a paper which would appeal to *all* the people, not merely the Negro? A paper which actually *looked* like a newspaper—an interracial paper—with first-rate printing and expert proofreading, a paper which escaped from the sloppy craftsmanship of the *Messenger* and the others like it.

Then he thought, a little viciously, Wouldn't Phil Meyer and Boss Hooker be surprised with *The Monitor*? And *him* as editor?

"You said I still had my job at the *Messenger*, Ray?"

Irving nodded. "Yeah, sure, I told ya. But what about *The Monitor?* You goin' back to the *Messenger?*"

"Please, just let me have some time to think about it. Let me have till Monday, Ray."

Irving lit a new cigarette. "Okay, we'll let it ride till Monday; we'll go see my lawyer together."

Lee got up. "I'm glad I stopped by. Perry let me take a look at the new fighter, Cecil."

"Yeah, he's a great little kid. He tell you about Smalley?"

"Yes. It's a shame."

"I'm tryin' all my angles, but it looks like the kid is goin' up to the joint."

Lee turned to Maida Housely. "I'm very glad I met you," he said, extending his hand.

"And I you," she replied, clasping it with an unashamed firmness.

Irving got up to come over and slap him on the shoulders. "You think about this, man. This is the chance of a lifetime."

"I will, Ray, honestly."

"See you a little later."

"All right," Lee said.

Irving let him out in the hall. "See you later, man!"

Going down the long hall, Lee wondered, Am I dreaming today? Is it all real?

Deep in his belly he felt a spark of happiness.

But there was also a spark of fear.

CHAPTER ELEVEN

HIS LODGING WAS A THIRD-FLOOR WALKUP in the drab little apartment building. The place might have looked as though it were centuries old, but it was neat and comfortable and, thank God, heated by gas.

As he went up the dimly lighted staircase to his apartment, Lee suddenly remembered that this was the day on which he was to pay his rent for the month, sixty dollars. He barely had forty dollars left from his pay, he realized with a shock, and he knew the caretaker would be up before long to see if there was a light under his door and to inquire in his croaky voice if Mr. Merriweather "felt like takin' care 'o business?"

Well, he could take care of it Monday. He'd go right over to the bank and draw out some of his savings.

Right now, he was too excited to think of such a trifling thing as rent. All the way home he had been thinking about *The People's Monitor,* and in his mind was reaping a crop of fertile ideas. Ray Irving had offered him the moon on a platter of gold. His imagined success of the proposed paper began to overshadow any hint of failure they might encounter.

Why have advertising at all? By distributing a paper which was unbeholden to the whims of its professional customers, *The Monitor* would be the first entirely honest paper of any race. No compromise—eliminate the advertisers and concentrate on news. Four hundred thousand Negroes in the city, Meyer had said. If they could build up the weekly circulation of *The Monitor* to around three hundred thousand, at twenty cents an issue, the overhead would take care of itself. And—if Irving was really serious about making it a daily—fifty thousand copies a day would make it a breadwinner. But he stopped here. In order to compete with the well-stanchioned dailies, the price of each *Monitor* would have to be comparable to theirs. Could they sustain such a loss for, say, three—maybe six months? Maybe longer.

What they needed was a strong, unique advertising campaign in behalf of *The Monitor,* prior to its first issue. This evidently would have to be handled by a competent agency. What would it cost in round figures? And would it be effective? Of course, with their own press, a good part of the battle was won. They could offer their services as jobbers and make up any deficit the paper might incur.

He was now unaware of the significance the proposition engendered: The moral value of *The Monitor,* the only real reason for its premature birth, was the lost in the wealth of potential financial tribulations.

He took out his key and unlocked the door to his apartment, failing to notice that a light shone underneath. Sitting on one of the sectional sofas of his modestly furnished living room, Diana waited with a worried look on her face.

She got up and came over to him wordlessly, the relief she felt better unsaid in the way her body melted into him, the way her lips roved over his face fitfully.

"I didn't know what to think!" she whispered. "After I saw you in the hall—after you ran—Lee, I told Boss Hooker I was taking the rest of the day off. I didn't care whether *he* cared or not!"

"Did the caretaker let you in?" he said against her hair, his mouth hungry against her skin against her full lips, his fingers digging into her body as though he might lose her at any second.

She freed her mouth reluctantly and looked up at him, her big eyes misty. "He didn't want to at first. He hinted around about your rent. After I paid him, he let me come on up. I've been here since about four-thirty."

"*You* paid my rent?" he said. "But that took everything you had, didn't it?"

"Baby," she grinned. "It's all right. It was worth it just to have you here now."

"But he could have waited until I got in," Lee said testily. "It's not as though I was behind in my rent."

"He probably just wants to keep his books balanced."

"The bastard," he said, pulling away from her and coming out of Tobey's coat.

"Lee," she said quietly behind him. "It's strange to hear you talk like that."

"I'm sorry . . ."

He went over to the hall closet and hung the coat up carefully. He came out with a grin that didn't set well on his mouth—a doubtful grin—a contortion of the flesh he could feel was unconvinced of itself.

"Are you hungry?" she said from across the room, a solicitous pall on her face. "I went out and bought some of those hot sausages you like so well. They should be ready by now—I'm roasting them." She started back to the kitchen.

"Diana, wait a minute."

He went over and kissed her on the mouth quickly. "I've got the story of the year. Maybe it won't win a Pulitizer Prize, but who needs a Pulitizer?"

He felt her body tense. "Have you been back to the *Messenger?*"

"No, of course not. But I'm going—tonight."

Fear danced over her soft features. "Lee, I'm afraid for you. You couldn't possibly go back there! They might have called the police."

"Don't worry—it's all forgotten. I've still got a job at the *Messenger.*"

"I don't understand . . ."

"My fairy godfather," he explained blandly. "Ray Irving. Hooker and Morrell have been receiving payoffs from the numbers syndicate. They called Irving up to complain about me writing stories about his boys' club—they thought I was getting something they weren't. Irving told them off very effectively; so effectively, in fact, that I'm supposed to go back to work with a ten-dollar increase in wages. They're forgetting that I even struck Bussey."

"Why *did* you strike Bussey?" she said, her eyes searching him closely.

"That doesn't matter," he grinned offhandedly.

143

"Oh, but it *does* matter!" she said. "You just don't go around striking people when you feel the urge—nobody does that! And it's something I'd never expect *you* to do."

"Diana, it's hard to explain," he said lamely. "I don't know why I did it. I went over to Tobey's and he cooked up some crazy idea about me being an African or something, but it's all wild and it doesn't explain anything, as far as I'm concerned."

"Then despite everything you're going back to the *Messenger?*"

"But that's the story I've got to tell you," he said animatedly. "Irving's willing to set up a new Negro newspaper in this city, and he wants me to be the editor. Maybe I *will* go back to the *Messenger* until we gets things straightened out, but—"

"He wants *you* to be the editor?" Her face turned a bit pale. "But, Lee, you don't know anything about newspaper publishing!"

"I've been around the *Messenger* long enough to know how *not* to run a paper," he said.

"But there're so many technical aspects that you can't even begin to imagine. Where are you going to get the personnel? There's the bookkeeping, for one thing—"

"You can take care of that."

"But I don't know *how*," she protested. "Certainly, I could probably keep the main desk business in line, but the problem of numbers is a tedious matter, something to be handled by an accountant."

"All that'll be taken care of," he said. "Irving's got the money to take care of everything. All I've got to do is concentrate on making the paper draw down an honest living. Diana, we need a good paper in this city—the colored people need it. More than anything else, I've seen that today. The people don't have any trust in the *Messenger* or any of the others."

"But don't you see, Lee? That distrust is going to be your biggest problem. It's something that's been growing for years. The people will be instantly prejudiced against another Negro newspaper."

"You're wrong," he said obstinately. "The people *want* a good paper. If you could have heard them talking about the *Messenger* the way I've heard them talking today, you'd know that! And

Tobey's right. Everything he ever said about the Negro newspaper is right. Do you think I should pass up this opportunity to prove that it can be different? Would you rather that I go back to the *Messenger* and suffocate in that filth?"

"I don't want you to go back to the *Messenger*," she said, looking away from him.

"Well, then, what *do* you want me to do?"

"I want you to be satisfied," she said. "I want you to *know* where you're going. I don't want you to bite into something too hard to chew."

"So this is too big a bite, huh?" he said sardonically. "This is too much for me? I'm not big enough to make a success of it! Or maybe I'm not white enough, is that it?" He instantly regretted his words.

"Maybe you're not mature enough," she said sharply.

"I'm sorry . . ."

"Don't be," she said, turning to go into the small kitchen.

He followed after her. "Diana, I didn't say I would take the job. Irving offered me the position, and I thought it would be a good idea. You've got to admit it's a sound idea . . ."

"That's just it," she said, looking into the oven of the apartment-sized gas stove, "it's *not* a sound idea."

He threw up his hands with helpless exasperation. "All right, it's not a sound idea! Just why isn't it sound? *The Monitor* would be a paper that couldn't be dictated to, couldn't be corrupted. We wouldn't even have advertising—just earn our keep on fat press runs."

"*The Monitor?*"

"That's the name of it. Irving suggested it. *The People's Monitor.*"

"Irving is one of the things I mean by instability," she said, taking a pan of steaming, red-jacketed sausages from the oven.

"Now what's wrong with Irving? He's putting up the money, isn't he?"

"For one thing, he's in the numbers. I wouldn't want you to be so closely connected with an underworld character. How could you even consider honesty when the backbone of the paper is a man like that?"

"He wouldn't be in the numbers anymore when we got *The Monitor* started," he told her with affected righteousness. "The man wants to live honestly, get out of the rackets. Anyway, he wouldn't have anything to say about how I ran the paper."

She came away from the kitchen table where she was laying out the plates and eating utensils and delivered a gentle but firm clout to his flat nose. "There's the hole in the wall, you big chump! Anytime somebody subsidizes something, they *do* have a say in it. They can run it any way they see fit. What have you to contribute but one hundred per cent editorship, which doesn't amount to a hill of beans in comparison with Irving's one hundred per cent capital? Lee, I know the *Messenger* is wrong, I've known it for a long time. But what would be the good in running from one *Messenger* right into the arms of another?"

"It wouldn't be the same thing. With *The Monitor,* I could print the news the way it *should* be printed. It wouldn't be anything like the *Messenger.*"

"Morally, it would be the same thing," she said. "Why? Just why does Irving want a paper at all?"

"He just wants it! Does there have to be any reason?"

"But of course there does, and you know it! Maybe the *Messenger* is nothing but a trashcan now, but when Mr. Sandersford first started it he had a strong spiritual goal. Nothing, whether it's good or bad, gets to become powerful unless there's a sincere motivating force. Any man who sits down and suddenly *thinks* he wants something as important as a newspaper is neither sincere with himself *or* you."

Lee had no reply for her, for Irving had approached the idea of a newspaper whimsically. Why? In dollars and cents, it was not a thing anybody, no matter how solvent, could afford to be whimsical about.

"C'mon," she said. "I've got some yams and sweet corn to go along with the sausages. You must be starved."

146

He sat down and ate silently, ravenously, more with a hunger of the brain than belly.

"Coffee?" she said, as he finished.

"Uh huh. Go real good."

"Go on in the living room and sit down. I'll put a pot on. Oh yes, you'll find some Scotch on the shelf of the closet."

"You think of everything," he said, bending over to kiss her. "Keep this up, and I might marry you."

"If I ever get you drunk enough," she laughed, "maybe you will."

He went out and took down the bottle of Martin's from the closet. He poured himself a small drink, downed it quickly, and started to have another. He decided against it. He needed to have his mind clear, to think.

He went over to sit in his favorite chair, a copy of Tobey's futuristic rump nest, and was reminded of the things Tobey had said that afternoon.

If he could only make Diana understand.

But then he knew to convince Diana of the importance of Irving's project would not be to convince himself. What was that Perry had said about faith . . . ?

The phone, which sat atop a middle-aged TV set that hadn't worked in months, began to ring insistently.

He hurried over and picked up the receiver. "Hello?"

"Hello, Lee?"

"Yes. Who's this?"

"Ray Irving."

"Oh—yes, Ray."

"Listen, man, I was thinkin' about that idea. Me and Maida talked it over, you know what I mean? We think it's great! I got so excited, I called my lawyer, and *he* says it's great—but he'd say anything was great, since he gets paid for everything he tells me."

"Listen, Ray, I've been thinking about it, too—"

"Now here's my idea, Lee. See, I know a lotta big names, guys in business and all—I even got an in with a county official. We get all this advertisn', huh? Yeah! We even hit the city up for its per annum reports to the taxpayers and all that other jive. See how fat the kitty gets with a little squeezin'? Now the editorial titty is solely your milkbag, man. Course, we go easy on the numbers boys—"

"I thought you were pulling out?"

"Well, I am, I am! But I wanna make sure this thing is gonna pay off, huh? Yeah! Now—you need a society editor? I got the solidest: Maida. She's in society and all, knows all the people. We'll make the *Messenger*'s society page look like the comic strips. Now I'm linin' up a couple boys for the distribution angle. They can talk straight business with the retailer, so you don't have to worry about that."

"Ray—"

"All you have to do is get your reporters lined up. Get professionals. Go as high as two-fifty a week if they're good. Expense is no importay, huh? Yeah! Now get at it, man. I'll talk withcha sometime tomorrow."

"Listen, Ray, I haven't decided about this thing yet . . ."

"Whatsamatter, huh? Whatsit, money? You need a little bread? Tell ya what—I'll start you in at three bills a week, how's that? You need a hundred or so now, you can get it. I *like* you, Lee. You-are-a-good-kid."

"It isn't the money, Ray—"

"Well, what is it? I can't waste my time while you ass around, kid? You know? Huh? This is my baby, you know; if I can't get you to put the diapers on, I don't think it'll be hard to get somebody who's willin' . . ."

Lee tensed. "No, I don't guess you would have any trouble."

"It's just a matter of good business, Kid. The idea's too good to blow, and I like to think of myself rollin' that kind of power around in my hands. Huh? Yeah!"

"Wait a minute, Ray," Lee said slowly. "Let me get this straight. Just what do you hope to accomplish with this paper?"

"We already *talked* about it—we're gonna rake off a little of the *Messenger*'s gravy—maybe all of it. Where's the end? In my business, I'd have a ready-made public mouthpiece."

"*Your* business? But I thought you said you were quitting?"

"Gradually, man, *grad*ually . . . A newspaper worth its weight in salt could shake a lot of hands in this town, make a lot of important friends."

"Then Diana *was* right," Lee said aloud.

"What?"

"Ray," he said suddenly, "I've been thinking—maybe you'd *better* get another boy to wetnurse your baby. I just remembered a previous engagement."

"Hey, look—"

"Thanks, Ray, for the offer—and thanks for giving me an eye-opening boot in the ass. I'll be seeing you around."

"Hey—do you know what you're throwin' away?"

Lee smiled to himself. "No . . . but I may be saving a few teeth."

He could hear Diana moving about in the kitchen as he hung up the phone and went over slowly to sit on the couch. Within himself he could feel a tiny fire burning angrily, but his heart was relieved. All the angers that had touched him this day could not compare with the fury he felt against himself when he realized what he had been prepared to do. Yes, Diana was right—but there was even more to the proposition than he had been prepared to accept consciously.

And now, consciously, he closed his eyes—but it seemed as though they were still wide apart, for they reviewed each event mathematically and candidly.

All day he had been running—and why? It was more than unknown fear that prompted him—it was apprehension of all which had, all the while, been too perfectly apparent. And, again, Tobey too understood.

It was true: the visions, the strange statements that rang in his skull, his violent behavior, Tobey's conclusions—it all had a sound basis.

His eyes snapped open and he looked piercingly toward the ceiling. Truth. The knife, the enslavement of a tribe—the guilt! He had needed only to face up to what his mind had been telling him in order to know.

Yes.

The stigma of coward. A blotch that had been etched into the very seed of a parent, perhaps his father. A man who had stood idly by, watching the death of his clan—a man who had run from the responsibility of his heritage. A man as treacherous as the betrayer by virtue of his knowledge . . .

Lee halted his thoughts; the thunder of them was too much all at once. Tomorrow, the next day—it would all come clearer. But today—today fate had *meant* that he should glimpse the key. The knife of truth.

Ray Irving had been the first step in a fight for redemption he had inherited. But so much remained, so much . . .

Diana came out of the kitchen with two cups of coffee. "Hey, how come the big smile?"

He almost jarred the liquid as he clasped her. "It's not a private joke, baby, but I'd like to tell you all about it later on."

She shook her head. "It's probably something ridiculous."

"It is," he said, kissing her. "My teeth . . ."

CHAPTER TWELVE

*A*LL EVENING SHE'D BEEN COOL. He couldn't help but notice her reserve, but he couldn't figure out the reason why. Wasn't it enough that he'd had to put up with Lee Merriweather and Boss Hooker today?

Stealthily, he followed her into the bedroom, aroused by the sight of her slim hips under the smart new suit, the provocative sway of her shoulders. Top-heavy, but nice.

"New suit?" he said, sitting down on the double bed to watch her undress.

"Any objections, Phil?" she asked sharply.

"None at all, Alene. Don't you think I have a right to ask?"

"It's your money, dear. You may ask whatever you like of its use."

"Listen, don't treat me like a public dole. I make damn good money, and you're free to spend it any way you want."

"Thanks for being so magnanimous."

He squinted at her. "Say, what's got into you?"

She turned to face him, unbuttoning the lacy green blouse, showing a bit of black brassiere and white flesh underneath. Damn, but she's beautiful! he thought.

"It'd be better if you asked what's got out of me," she said coolly.

She stood before him now, mocking him with the splendor of her semi-nakedness. Her breasts were high and large, and he knew they didn't need the assistance of the flimsy cloth which bound them. Her ribs were sculptured, sloping into the sensual curve of her belly, where over the top of her black lace panties the wrinkle marks of a past pregnancy showed livid on the soft white flesh. The big trunks of her long legs graced the pastel shade stockings, and the garter belt around her waist reminded him of the score or more French whores he had bought during the Second World War. The difference was that they had not worn panties, and he felt himself swell with the recollection.

Above all this erotic magnificence, Alene smiled down, a half sneer on her lovely wide mouth, at his breath coming quickly. "Do you like what you see?" she said.

She was a bitch, he thought. She knew what she was doing to him.

"Take off your panties," he directed with a short, involuntary gasp.

She began to do as he asked.

"No," he said, "leave your stockings on—the garter belt too."

She followed his instructions casually, making him wait.

"Where's Tommy?" he said cautiously, beginning to get out of his things.

"He went to a photographer's party being held for the Socialettes. Why?" she smirked. "Were you afraid he'd see something he shouldn't?"

He went over to the bedroom door and closed it, bolted it. "Hurry up, won't you?"

"I like your furtive manner when you get het up," she smiled. "You make it seem so dangerous—so illegal."

He went over to where she stood and pulled her to him. In her bare feet she was an inch or so over him, and he had to pull her head down in order to kiss her mouth. She submitted without returning the kiss.

"What's the matter with you?" he asked with annoyance.

"I hate spitty kisses, don't you?"

"You never hated them before."

"You get tired of *anything,* after a while—even money."

"What's got you in this goddamn crazy mood?" he said. "You're making everything awkward."

"That's the last thing I want to do, dear," she said tiredly. "It would wound me grievously to make things awkward for you."

An abrupt anger made him seize her roughly around the buttocks and lift her into the air. He took her unceremoniously over to the double bed and dumped her there.

She began to laugh uncontrollably. "You Tarzan, me Jane!" she giggled. "Oh, Phil, look at yourself!" She pointed to the wide mirror of the dresser behind him, where their actions were reflected. "If you could get rid of that paunch, maybe I could feel my role a good deal better!"

"Are—are you trying to embarrass me?" he said with sputtered indignation.

"Is that possible—*Doll?*"

He fell on her in a savage vengeance, entering her softness with a mad stroke.

"Easy," she said under him. "I'm not a professional, you know."

His fingers dug into her breasts.

"I wish I had a cigarette," her voice continued casually. "Isn't that what the girls do when you're hard at it, Phil?"

It was all over in a few minutes, and he rolled off her heavily, feeling dirty, humiliated and unrelieved, despite the wild flood which had just emerged from him.

"Feel better?" she said, getting up on one elbow to look at his flatulent face, that mocking smile still on her lips.

"Should I?" he said.

She shrugged. "I hope you do, dear. That's the last time you'll ever do that to me."

She got up and went into the bathroom that adjoined the bedroom. In a little while, he could hear the shower going. He dragged himself up from the bed, feeling weak, and followed her in.

"What the hell are you talking about, Alene?" he yelled through the shower curtain.

"What's that, dear?" And he could imagine her with the clean, hot spray of water on her mouth bubbling her words.

"You know goddamn well what I'm talking about!" he said.

"Why don't you wait until I come out, Phil? I'll only be a moment."

He went over to the washbasin and began to clean up. Then he went out in the bedroom again and selected a suit from the closet. He searched futilely for one of his new button-collar, executive-type shirts.

He heard the shower stop, and he called, "Alene, where are those new shirts I picked up last week?"

"What's that, dear?"

"My shirts! My shirts! The ones I bought over at the Gaymount's haberdashery. Where are they?"

"They're in your suitcase, Phil."

He looked toward the bathroom door, dumfounded. "In my *suitcase?* Just what the hell are they doing in my suitcase?"

"I put them there. You'll find your suitcases in the closet."

He went quickly over to the closet and saw that his leatherette set of three had been pulled down from their usual spot at the top and placed on the floor. He grabbed the largest of the three and found that it was packed. Experimentally, he nudged each of the other two. Packed.

He strode angrily across the room and opened the drawers of

his personal service. Empty. All his clothes, except for a lone suit of underwear, had been taken out.

Alene came out of the bathroom, gleaming freshly. He could see that she had on clean, sheer lingerie under a transparent silk gown.

"Aren't you dressed yet?" she said. "We mustn't be late for Mr. Sandersford, you know."

He came over to her, his thin lips pulled back over his teeth. "What are my suitcases doing packed? Are you out of your mind? I'm not going anywhere!"

She looked at him innocently. "Oh, but you *are,* Phil. Didn't I tell you? You're taking a long, long trip—away from me."

"Goddamn it, Alene, what are you talking about?"

She smiled at him, almost piteously. "It's simple, dear. You're getting out, and you're *not* coming back."

"Well, I'll be just a sonofabitch if I do!" he yelled. "Have you gone crazy? You've been talking and acting like it all evening!"

"For the first time since I've been married to you, Phil Meyer, I *am* sane," she hurled back, going over to her dressing table and seating herself. "For the past fifteen and more years I've been *un*sane. I've had a child for you, tolerated your silly inferiority complex and watched you carry on with any number of dirty women. Oh, how *un*sane I've been!"

The naked image of him swelled behind her in the mirror of the dressing table. "*My* inferiority complex! Mine? It was *you* who always felt inferior. *You* were the wallflower when I met you at NYU. What do you mean, *my* inferiority complex?

"Oh, sure," she said, beginning to apply makeup, dabbing at her cheeks angrily. "Poor girl from a poor family. I realize now that the only reason you married me was because I helped make you feel just a little bit bigger. And I was the absolute sucker, wasn't I? I *loved* you!"

"I guess I didn't love you?" he shouted. "I guess I didn't try to do every damn thing in my power to give you and Tommy the best things in life!"

"Only because that went along with giving *yourself* the best

154

things. Only because we allowed you another expression by being able to make showpieces of us."

"Listen, I've had showpieces all my life! I even had 'em in the Army, four years before I ever knew you existed. I've never known what it meant to be a really *poor* Nigger!" He went over to the service indignantly and began to get into the suit of underwear. "Is that why you're shot up? Because you think I'm making a showpiece out of you? You must be going into the menopause!"

"What a quaint observation," she said. "But when a woman gets to be thirty-five years old, she hasn't got much time left, you'll have to admit. And I'm not going to waste it with you, Phil—I'm going to have something out of life, for once."

"*Have* something out of life?" he said incredulously. "You think this twenty-thousand-dollar home is nothing? You think that two thousand a year for Tommy's private school is nothing? You maybe think that silly new suit you got today is nothing? Most women would cut out a maidenhead to be in your shoes!"

"Perhaps you think I can claim the distinction of *having* one!"

"By the way you acted just a little while ago, I'd be inclined to say you didn't," he replied brutally.

"Being an expert on such matters, I suppose you should know."

"Say, what is all this?" he said, coming over behind her again. "Is there another man? Is that it?"

"Yes," she said simply, looking his mirror image boldly in the eyes.

His mouth dropped open. It was the last thing he had expected her to say, and now he didn't know what to do after she had said it.

She resumed the application of makeup with a serious deftness. "As a matter of fact, there has been for over a year."

His voice sounded squeaky. "You're kidding!"

Her face was at last made lovely. She turned around on her seat to the gray pallor of his face. "I'm not kidding, Phil. I've been having an affair with another man for some time now."

"Then that's the reason!" he shrieked. "That's why you've been such a bag in bed!"

She shook her head. "That's not the reason. I'll confess that I have been to bed with him, but I've regretted every moment of it—until today."

"Who is it?" he yelled. "Who is this fine bastard of yours!"

"That's something I'm not going to tell you," she said calmly.

"You'd tell me if I busted your face!"

"I still wouldn't tell you, Phil. And why would you bust my face? Is it because you're stronger? Isn't it a shame I couldn't bust *your* face when I found out about your infidelities?"

He was practically speechless. "You're a dirty whore, do you know that? You're nothing but a tramp!"

"Since you evidently prefer tramps to your wife, I regard that as a compliment."

"I—I want a divorce!" he bellowed.

"So do I, Phil."

His face grew red. He turned away from her and hurriedly went over to the bed, where he'd laid out his suit. He yanked his legs into the trousers, then went over to the closet and pulled his suitcases out like a madman, throwing them on the bed.

He turned and shook a pious finger at her placid face. "You're going to regret this! I'm gonnna make you suffer!"

"I doubt if you can make me suffer any more than you already have."

His face flared like that of a petulant schoolboy's. "I was gonna save this news for later, but I'll tell you now: I was appointed to the mayor's commission on community relations today."

"Congratulations."

"Oh, you don't understand what you're missing out on, do you? Well, you can have that sonofabitch, whoever he is! You'll wish you had me back, one of these days!"

She got up and went over to her wall closet, where she took out a blue, dove-tailed dinner dress. "I don't think I will, Phil."

He came close to her, almost threateningly. "You understand what you're saying, don't you? This is the end, Alene! It's all over!"

"It has been for a long time."

"What do you think you're gaining?" he yelled.

"My freedom, for one thing." Her gaze was resolute. "Phil, I'll tell you exactly why I told you these things."

"I wish to hell you would!"

"I had a visit from Cathy Jones this afternoon . . ."

His face suddenly paled.

"Do you have any idea why she came over?"

He looked away guiltily, but his voice was still vehement. "Of course not. Why should I?"

"She told me about your affair, Phil."

He whirled on her. "What affair?"

"Your love affair, of course. And she brought along adequate proof. You've really made her hate you—or maybe—love you too much."

"Now, listen, you're not going to believe anything that *sick* woman told you, are you? She's emotionally unstable!"

"After what she went through with you, it's no wonder."

"The woman was infatuated. I had nothing to do with her—and even if I did, you've got no grounds to put up a bitch. You haven't been sitting on your hands!"

"No," she confessed. "But neither have I been having children by my lover."

"Now if she told you that, she's lying!" he declared. "All right, so I did lay her a few times, but she didn't get pregnant by me! It wasn't *my* baby!"

"Then why did you pay to have it destroyed?"

"I didn't pay a dime!"

"But she told me, Phil—"

"She's lying through her whorish teeth!"

"She showed me the check, Phil—a photostat of the check you signed."

He was instantly afraid. "What check? How did she get it?"

"I don't know, but she has it."

He grabbed her by the arms frantically. "What did she do with it? Did you get it from her?"

"No."

"Why didn't you take it! She could ruin me with that!"

"I think that's exactly what she plans to do."

"Alene," he said desperately, "we've got to get that check! Think what'll happen if she—"

"*You've* got to get it, Phil." She turned away from him and began to dress. "I don't care about it. I'm no longer involved with you."

"Look," he said, coming around in front of her, trying to make her eyes see the fear in his own. "If you don't care about me, care about Tommy! Think of what this could do to him!"

She glared at him. "Must you jump for the last straw so quickly? Tommy is a brat, and you know it. The scandal will give him a special distinction among the other snots he associates with. Don't start bleating about him."

"I'm trying to be reasonable about this!"

"You're only trying to save your skin!"

"Alene!" he said, grasping her tightly to his chest, beginning to feel the tears of desperation in his eyes. "You've *got* to help me! Haven't I tried to do everything I could for you? Look what I've done! Look at the power I've made of the *Messenger,* just for you! Look what I've done to it!"

"I'm well aware of what you've done to it," she said unfeelingly. "I've watched the *Messenger* for years, ever since we came from New York together. The *Messenger* was clean then, but over the years you've both become dirty. I don't have to see you to know you; all I have to do is read a bit of the dirt in the *Messenger* and I've got a perfect picture."

"Alene—"

"The *Messenger* is like dope; it's habit-forming. But it takes its addicts down much farther than narcotics ever could. Cy Venson is a good example: living like you, thinking like you and hiding behind what you represent, he's not even a man. Oh yes, I knew about Barbara, and he did too. Maybe we were both cowards . . ."

He crumpled against her. "Help me, Alene! I'll do anything! I'll even forget about that Nigger of yours!"

"I can't help you . . ."

"Just tell me what you want me to do!" he whined. "Just tell me what you want me to be from now on! I'll do whatever you say!"

She pulled away from him with revulsion. "I never thought you would act like this."

"My life is at stake!" he cried. "Everything I've built—everything I've done—all because of a little tramp!"

"Even life at the *Messenger* has its occupational hazards," she sighed.

He went over and sat on the bed with his head between his hands. The room became filled with his huge, breathtaking sobs.

She finished dressing and came over to where he sat. "You'd better get your clothes on. It's nine-forty. Mr. Sandersford should be there by now."

"I'm not going," he blubbered.

She crossed to the bureau and took out a pair of long white gloves. "If you don't, you're finished for sure at the *Messenger*. Perhaps, if you talk nicely enough to Cathy, she'll surrender the photostat. You were able to talk her into surrendering an article infinitely more valuable, from my point of view."

He looked up hopefully. "Maybe I could . . ."

"You're terribly persuasive, Phil."

"If I could get to her before she got to Sandersford—"

"She told me that you'd promised to marry her. Why not offer her that tidbit? I'd be willing to lend a verifying hand, for old time's sake."

"Sure, I could *tell* her that," he said hesitantly.

"In her state, you'd probably have to put it in writing." She sighed again. "But that wouldn't be so bad, would it? In sacrificing me, you'd be getting two things in return—the check and Cathy."

"But, Alene—"

"You really have no choice, Phil," she said firmly. "Zarathustra would have to speak before I'd change my mind about the divorce. I think Cathy would be very attractive as the new Mrs. Phillip Meyer. Moreover, *she* loves you."

He got up and began to dress himself hurriedly. In less than five minutes he was completely attired.

"Well, I'm ready," he said. "What about Tommy?"

"We can pick him up later," she advised, surveying him from head to foot. "You look very nice tonight, Mr. Meyer."

"C'mon, let's get the hell out of here," he said.

"Get a smile on your face, then. This is the last appearance we're ever going to make together, and I'd like for it to be an impressive one."

He opened the door and went out ahead of her.

A tear glanced her cheek as her eyes followed after him.

CHAPTER THIRTEEN

*T*HEY CAME FROM THE FAR END of Farrell Street, walking slowly through the deep snow. The night was dark but clear, and a light wind, undecided whether to become violent or vanish altogether blew succinctly at their backs.

There was a brutal, unpolished hue about Lee's black face, blacker still in the night, and the pressure of her arm in his seemed to hold him back. They knew that in a moment they would reach the *Messenger*. Their heartbeats rose expectantly with each step.

Finally the building hulked, half-lighted, on their left, and they paused.

"We're here," she said. "Are you sure you want to go in?"

"Yes," he said.

Her eyes tried to make out his face in the darkness. "Darling, we can forget about this. We can stop right here and turn around and go back."

He shook his head. "I can't turn around now. Would you want me to?"

"No," she said with a heavy voice.

They walked onward, then the crooked steps of the *Messenger* building came parallel with their feet, fifteen paces away.

"Oh, Lee, look! Isn't that Tobey?"

His head came up sharply. On the front porch of the building a young man stood with a placard affixed to a long strip of wood. The thing was carried casually on his shoulder like a rifle, and in letters of phosphorescent paint, the message cried:

INJUSTICE, MR. DOUGLAS SANDERSFORD
INJUSTICE IS THE WEEKLY *MESSENGER*
JOURNALISTIC INJUSTICE TO THE BLACK
PEOPLE OF THIS CITY, MORAL INJUSTICE
TO THE MAN WHO GAVE IT BIRTH

Lee broke away from her and ran to the steps.

"Damn you, Tobey!" he burst out. "I knew you were planning something like this!"

Tobey's face grinned down on him benignly. "How do you like it, Othello? I almost didn't get it finished after you left."

"You come down from there!" Lee shouted.

Tobey's deep voice rippled out in laughter. "Are *you* trying to order me away, too? Boss Hooker already tried it, without much success. I think he's in there now calling the cops."

"Tobey Balin," Diana said, coming up, "just what do you think you're doing?"

He bowed exaggeratedly. "Good evening, Desdemona. Thou bringest sunshine into the fool's heart at this dreary time. Mayest I dance thee a jig of appreciation?"

"Tobey, do you want to get in trouble?" she said worriedly.

"Ah, trouble," he sighed. "Thy sting is ever present."

Lee went up the steps to face him. "Tobey, stop acting like a fool and get the hell away from here before the cops come!"

And now Tobey was serious. "I can't, Othello. If I did, I'd be a fugitive from what I believe to be truth. I came here to picket the *Messenger,* and that's exactly what I'm going to do."

"But what if they arrest you?"

"The right to picket is an inalienable American privilege. If the *Messenger* can see to it that I *can't* enjoy that privilege, then whatever respect I've held for the Constitution up till now will be null and void. I'm not going anywhere."

"Tobey—"

"Now don't you two try to talk me out of it," he said. "Why don't you go in and join the other folks? There's Hooker and a fat guy, and I think I recognized that little worm you told me about—Cy Venson? We're all anxiously awaiting the arrival of Mr. Douglas Sandersford."

"Goddamn you, Tobey!" Lee shouted at him.

"Thanks for your blessings," he grinned. "Now onward, Christian Soldiers. I'll be here when you come out, I promise."

Diana took Lee's arm. "Let's go, darling. There's no sense trying to talk to him."

Tobey bowed before her again. "Desdemona, thy keen perception doth startle me!"

As they went through the front hall, the lights flashed on through the lower level, and the clumsy sound of footsteps came from the staircase. A gnarled little man in a pair of coveralls came down finally with a broom and dustpan in his hands.

"Hi y'all?" he said, looking over at them.

"Fine," Lee said. "You're the janitor, aren't you?"

"Sho' am," the old man grinned. "Mr. Hooker called me up, told me to come on down and clean up. Said he pay me extra."

"Where's Mr. Hooker?"

"He upstairs, him and Mr. Morrell and Mr. Venson—they all in the conference room." He giggled in a cracked little voice. "Why they call that dinky place the 'conference room'? It ain't no bigger 'n the ladies' ramble house."

"Hasn't anyone else arrived?" Lee said. "It's after ten."

The old man giggled again. "Nobody but who I told ya. They's just been sittin' up there, not sayin' nothin' to each other. Justa sittin'." His eyes got wide. "Mr. Hooker called the polices 'bout that fella out front wit' the sign. Ye ever see sich thangs? Why a man wonna come 'round this time of night wit' a crazy sign like that? Don't even make no sense, what it says. Some folks is jest plain crazy."

"I can particularly vouch for *that* fellow!" Lee told him.

"Why, how do, Miss Hill?" the old man said. "Didn't rec'nize you 'hind that big man."

"How are you, Jasper?" she said.

He put a sorry hand to his spine. "Oh, my rheum's gettin' me down a little. Wouldn't be so bad iffen I didn't haveta bend over so much. Why, first thang I seen when I come in tonight, somebody done strewed paper all over the City Room floor—tore it up and strewed it all over. Put' near broke my back gettin' it up."

Lee remembered the story about the Hardwickses he had destroyed that afternoon, and he felt ashamed of himself as he watched the old man. The act now seemed so childishly malicious.

"Do you want to go right up?" he asked Diana.

"We might as well."

"Wonder what's holdin' them polices up," Jasper croaked as they started up. "Been a long time since Mr. Hooker called 'em. I betcha iffen ittus me and my old lady called up on me 'cuz I was a little tankered and blowin' off steam, they'da come around in five seconds. But here we's got a crazy man standin' right in front of the door, and they takes they time."

They went up the creaking staircase to the second floor. The first door on their right was the conference room, and Lee hesitated but a moment before he put his hand on the knob and pushed it wide.

Sitting at the head of a huge, clover-leaf dining-room table, Boss Hooker looked up hopefully. Then his eyes faded and began to simmer as he recognized Lee.

On his right and left respectively sat Earl Morrell and Cy Venson, who looked as though he had been drinking. Next to Hooker's big fist on the table were the yearly report folders and, Diana was surprised to note, the file which contained all the canceled checks of the newspaper.

The room was solemnly draped, as though a wake were about

163

to proceed, and about the table some fifteen chairs stood arm to arm

"Please come in and be seated," Boss Hooker said with stiff formality. "You may hang your things on the rack behind you."

They did as they were told and had seats facing Boss Hooker and the others.

Cy Venson waggled his head at them half drunkenly. "I bet you just met her outside, didn't you, buddy-boy?"

Lee ignored him.

"Merriweather," Boss Hooker said stolidly, "your conduct this afternoon was unforgivable. Do you have an explanation?"

"I have no explanation," Lee told him.

"You shoulda seen him earlier, Boss," Cy smirked. "He almost chewed *my* head off! He's dangerous, if you ask me."

"Nobody asked you," Earl Morrell drawled, looking as though he were about to burst from the armpits of his tight-fitting suit.

"I have taken the matter under serious consideration," Boss Hooker went on. "It took some doing to get Mr. Bussey to delay filing charges against you until I had a chance to confide in Mr. Meyer and the others with whom you worked."

"I haven't got a thing against him," Morrell offered with unnecessary benevolence, beginning to light a fat, black cigar. "Through all apparent intent and purposes, the boy's been doing a fine job."

"Except for the understandable prejudice of Mr. Bussey," Boss Hooker said, "that's the opinion of everyone here. I checked past issues of the *Messenger* and read some of your work with a highly objective eye. I find you a writer of exceptional merit, Merriweather, and it would be a loss, both to you and the *Messenger,* if we could no longer find room for you here because of a—a temperamental manifestation of character; a clash of personalities, as it were."

"There was no clash of personalities," Lee said quietly. "The association Mr. Bussey and I enjoyed together was purely superficial. Today was the first and only time he had anything to say to me."

Boss Hooker ignored the remark. "In a private tete-a-tete with Mr. Meyer, we both agreed as to your basic recommendations. You're a hard worker and an unusually capable employee. In reviewing the facts, we found that the *Messenger* might have been intolerably remiss in its appreciation of your worth, and struck on the possibility that perhaps your meager earnings might have been the sublimated cause of your violent exhibition."

"I've never expressed any dissatisfaction with my wages," Lee said, faintly amused. "Not now, or in the past."

Boss Hooker was piqued by his lack of cooperation. "Nevertheless, starting next week, your salary will include a token of editorial redemption. Does ten dollars more a week suit you?"

Cy Venson raised up in his chair. "Ten dollars more a week, for busting Bussey in the mouth? What's going on around here, Boss? I've been working here fifteen years and *I'm* only making eighty a week! He smacks Bussey in the mouth after working here only a year, and he's making eighty a week already!"

Boss Hooker's burning gaze silenced him. He smiled at Lee with forced affability. "I guess you're a bit surprised by our show of gratitude, Merriweather, but I can assure you it was inevitable. As I said before, your conduct *was* unforgivable. However, unless there is forgiveness and understanding from my position, no amount of penalties will be conducive to the confidence our employees *must* have in the *Weekly Messenger*."

"What about me?" Cy poked his reddening face at the big man. "What about the confidence *I'm* supposed to have in the *Weekly Messenger*? Or maybe I'm not an employee!"

Boss Hooker flattened his big hands and made them slam out in front of him on the table. "I anticipated this reaction from you, Cy, and let me tell you I don't have much sympathy for you. The only time you *don't* drink is on the press day, which is the only reason you have a job right now. When you have *earned* a raise in salary, you'll get it, and not before. If you don't like that proposition, you're free to do whatever you choose!"

"Suppose I quit?" Cy yelled, forgetting himself.

Boss Hooker leveled a fat finger at him. "One more word, and you're *fired*!"

Cy would not be silenced. "Go ahead, fire me! You think you can get somebody else to shovel the crap I've been shoveling for the past fifteen years? Go ahead and fire me, Boss, and you'll have to type up the *Messenger* next week on the office machines!"

"You're not indispensable, Venson!" Boss Hooker roared. "I'm prepared for anything you might do. In view of your unreliability, don't you think I could have foreseen this or any other crisis? I've got a man to take your place whenever I say so!"

Cy sat back in his seat heavily. His eyes glazed over as he watched Boss Hooker; his hands began to tremble in front of him. Now a lowly obsequiousness came over his mouth, and his voice whined like that of a whipped dog. "Boss, you know the *Messenger* is all I've got—it's all I know how to do!"

"Then you'd better act accordingly," Boss Hooker said mercilessly.

"Where would I go? What else could I do?"

"That's no concern of mine, Venson. You've remained here only as long as you have out of the goodness of my heart."

Defeat overcame Cy. He slumped forward on the table, his head down. "I'm sorry, Boss . . ."

Boss Hooker turned brightly to Lee, "Well, Merriweather, now that we've got an understanding—"

"I don't think we do, Mr. Hooker," Lee said, and he could feel Diana's fingers dig into his arm.

The big man squinted at him. "What's that, Merriweather?"

"I don't think we understand each other," Lee said clearly.

"I'm not altogether sure I *want* to come back to the *Messenger*."

"You're not serious—?"

"It's all arranged," Morrell said, rolling his cigar around between his teeth worriedly.

"I don't think it is," Lee told him, then to Boss Hooker: "Suppose—just suppose I wasn't satisfied with the ten dollar increase, sir?"

Boss Hooker stared as though he were trying to see through him. "I thought we had agreed on that."

"Maybe you and Mr. Morrell and Mr. Meyer did, sir, but I haven't said I was satisfied."

"He wants more money," Morrell stated quietly.

"How much more, Merriweather?" Boss Hooker said in a strict business voice.

"Would you give it to me?" Lee asked casually.

"I'm asking *how much*!"

Lee pursed his lips thoughtfully. "Suppose I said I wanted a thirty-dollar increase instead of the ten you offered me?"

"That's ridiculous!"

"George," Morrell said, reaching over to touch his sleeve. "Why don't you sleep on it? The boy's good, we know that, and when you come down to brass tacks a hundred a week is only a living wage these days."

Cy Venson grunted dissonantly from his slumped position at the table.

"Well, Merriweather," Boss Hooker said with strained pensiveness, "I'd have to take the matter under advisement; I'd have to talk with Mr. Meyer, and particularly with Mr. Sandersford, who sets the wage scale here."

Diana suddenly spoke up. "But that's not true, Mr. Hooker. You set the wage scale yourself."

The big man harrumped embarrassedly. "Nonetheless, it's a matter I'd have to think over, you understand. We'd have to create new duties for you concomitant with the increase in salary."

"But I think I'm doing a hundred dollars worth of work for you now," Lee said stubbornly. "I wouldn't be willing to take on new duties."

Morrell sat up straight in his chair and threw Lee a penetrating glance. "Just who the hell have you been talking to?"

"What do you mean?"

"Who put these ideas into your head? You know damn well what I'm talking about."

"I put them in my own head. You act as though I've got a little hole in my head people can come up to and slip in a note. And by the way, Mr. Hooker—am I to discontinue my articles on the boys' club?"

"What articles?" Boss Hooker said, suddenly void of recollection. "Did I say you should discontinue any articles? I must have been thinking of something else. You're to proceed with your work as usual."

"He *has* been talking with him," Morrell whispered fearfully in the big man's ear.

"Let's get this straight," Lee said, feeling himself master of the situation, "I'm to proceed as usual, with a thirty dollar increase in salary . . ."

"I told you I'd have to think that over," Boss Hooker said.

"But I can't wait, Mr. Hooker. I've got another offer. You've got to tell me now."

"Are you trying to pressure me, Merriweather?" he said, raising his voice to an even higher register.

"Why, of course not, Mr. Hooker. I've just got to know before I leave here."

"You could wait just as well until tomorrow—"

"But I *won't* wait until tomorrow," Lee said adamantly. "I'll know right now."

"He's purposely being obstinate," Morrell snorted.

"That's right," Lee said.

"Merriweather," Boss Hooker shouted, "you're trying to put me in an awkward position! And I won't let you, do you understand that?"

"Yes, sir."

The cracks were plainly evident in Boss Hooker's composure. "I couldn't possibly promise you a hundred a week right now. Perhaps at some later date—"

"Now," Lee said.

"You won't get it!"

"I'll get it or else," Lee said.

"He's threatening us!" Morrell said in a fluttery voice.

"I certainly am," Lee said.

"Let me call Irving," Morrell said, starting to get up.

"You'll tell me before you call Irving," Lee said quietly.

Morrell's face was flushed. "And how're you gonna stop me?"

Lee shrugged, a slight grin on his face. "I simply won't be here when you get back."

"Merriweather—" Boss Hooker started.

"Now," Lee repeated. "Right now."

"We won't pay it!" Boss Hooker said. "It's blackmail!"

Cy Venson looked around in consternation. "What the hell is going on here?"

"Would you want to lose thousands because of a trifling thirty dollars?" Lee said.

Morrell plopped down in his chair helpless. "He's right. Irving's crazy about him. He'd make Viconetti let everything go."

Boss Hooker let his hands fall on the table submissively. "All right, Merriweather. A hundred a week."

"Go ahead, Merriweather," Cy prompted with a revengeful laugh. "Get 'em to make it retroactive to the first day you came to work here!"

The door opened and the wizened little janitor looked in.

"Mr. Hooker," he said, "the polices is here. They's takin' that crazy man off . . ."

Lee was up before any of the rest of them. He bounded out in the hall and down the steps. As he burst outside on the front, he could hear the arguing voices of the policemen and Tobey. They had dragged him down to the squad car at the curb. The placard lay on the snow-covered front lawn.

"Hey!" he called at them.

The policemen paused as he came over.

"I've been trying to explain to these gentlemen my inalienable right to picket," Tobey said with a smile, anchored on either side by the big, pale-faced officer. "They evidently think the only real *right* one of the proletariat has is to go to jail."

"Did you call up about this character?" one of the cops asked Lee.

"No," Lee said, "but I know him. Let him go; he's not doing anything."

"He's on private property," the cop said. "We understand he's making a nuisance of himself."

"Who are you?" the other cop asked Lee.

"Lee Merriweather. I work here."

"You say you know this guy?"

"Yes, he's Tobey Balin, a very good friend of mine. You've got to let him go; he's not hurting anything."

"Desist, Othello," Tobey said with theatrical gestures. "It is my destiny to be martyred in the name of justice."

"Tobey, stop it!"

"So you *wanna* go to jail, huh?" one of the cops said.

"If it will make Pharaoh let my people go," Tobey said, I'd gladly give up my head to the guillotine of political corruption."

"This guy's talkin' funny," the other cop said, staring hard at him. "Hey, are you on the needle?"

"We all have the needle of life rammed in our asses," Tobey informed him seriously.

Lee began to get frightened, for he knew now that Tobey was probably high from smoking marijuana. That would explain the crazy way he was talking, but not the preposterous way he was acting.

Boss Hooker and Earl Morrell tramped up heavily behind him.

"That's him, officer," Boss Hooker screeched. "That's the man. Watch him! I think he's psychotic!"

"Are you the Mr. Hooker who called us up?"

"That's right," he declared. "I'm the Editor-in-Chief of this newspaper. Your precinct chief and I are very good friends."

The first cop nudged his partner. "I think we better take this guy down."

A big black Cadillac came down the snow-covered street just then and drew up behind the police squad car. On its side was stenciled, *City Airport*.

"Oh, my goodness," Earl Morrell said. "Here comes Mr. Sandersford!"

Tobey was forgotten as Boss Hooker and Morrell went over quickly.

"Listen," Lee told the cops, "why don't you let him go? I'll be responsible for him, I promise."

The officers looked at each other doubtfully, then the first cop released Tobey's arm. "You look, fella, you just go over there and get that thing and get on away from here, okay?"

"Okay," Tobey said. "I'll go over there and get that thing."

"If we catch you parading around out here anymore tonight, we'll run you in," the cop added.

They let Tobey go and got in the squad car. They sat there watching for a moment, to see if he obeyed their orders. Lee followed his friend over to where the placard lay in the snow. He watched anxiously as Tobey picked it up and leaned it carelessly on his shoulder. The letters on the thing gleamed accusingly in the night.

"Hurry up, Tobey. Here comes Mr. Sandersford and the rest of them."

"Hurry up, I will," Tobey vowed. He went out to the sidewalk and began to march up and down resolutely.

"Officers!" Boss Hooker cried, espying Tobey again in full regalia.

"Tobey!" Lee yelled at him, running over to pull at his sleeve frantically. "You told the police you'd get the sign and get out of here!"

"Correction, Othello," Tobey boomed out. "I told them I'd get the sign—I didn't say I was leaving."

"Arrest that man!" Boss Hooker screamed.

The cops got out of the car and came over again.

"All right, let's go," the first cop told Tobey. "You ain't got no sense, fella. I think you're sick."

Both Tobey and the sign were swiftly ushered into the police car. The vehicle left the curb as quickly as possible in the deep snow, its siren careening through the night.

Lee felt a chill as he watched Boss Hooker, Earl Morrell and two other men whose faces he couldn't make out, come up the walk toward the building.

He clamped his mouth shut and started back in.

Upstairs, Diana waited anxiously. "What happened, Lee?"

He felt empty and useless. "The police took Tobey away. They gave him a chance, but he still went right on picketing."

"Oh, no!"

Still slumped at the table, Cy called down. "What is it you got on that bastard, Merriweather? You let me in on your secret, I'll let you in on mine."

"You'd better rise and shine," Lee warned him. "Mr. Sandersford has just arrived."

Cy's laugh sounded like a loud belch. "What a welcoming committee!"

The door burst open and Boss Hooker came pirouetting in, hands and eyes fluttering with a wild enthusiasm. Earl Morrell followed with stoic dignity. In their wake came a bright-faced, youngish man, who held onto the arm of a distinguished-looking man, whose skin texture was almost white. From all outward appearances he must have been at least sixty or seventy years old, but there was a proud carriage about his head and shoulders that suggested he was much younger.

"Quite a bit of excitement out there!" he said in a cracked but authoritative voice.

"Just take it easy, Mr. Sandersford," the younger man said. "I'll have your coat off in a minute."

The old man submitted meekly while his companion divested him of his heavy overcoat, and hat, and it was then that a profuse blossom of straight white hair was revealed, leaving no doubt as to his antiquity.

"Where is everybody!" the old man said. "Ain't many folks here, I can tell that!"

Boss Hooker danced about him nervously. "They'll all be here in a little while, Mr. Sandersford. I guess the weather held them up. Here, you just come right down here and sit down."

"Damn it, George, you don't have to be so almighty solicitous about me!" Mr. Sandersford said. "I ain't that old!" But he followed Boss Hooker's guiding hand to the seat at the head of the table. Once he had relaxed in the chair, Lee noticed that the old man stared straight ahead through misty gray eyes and did not turn his head from its set position.

"Where is everybody!" he said testily.

"They'll be right along, D.S.," Boss Hooker said, dragging Cy

Venson out of his seat and sitting down in it himself. Cy threw him a look of malice, but went to sit in one of the other chairs. Earl Morrell stood, like the young man who had escorted Mr. Sandersford in, behind the old man's chair.

The elderly gentleman's hand groped out and was quickly grasped by the young man.

"You don't know this boy here, do you, George?" he said.

"Why, no, Mr. Sandersford, I can't say as I do—"

The old man laughed squeakily. "Didn't think you would. Your mind's as short as the hair on a mule's rump! This is Clyde Joscelyn, the one I wrote you about a couple of months ago. Just got his B.A. from NYU. Gonna make a newspaperman out of this boy, just like I did with Phil."

Clyde Joscelyn smiled down on the old man fondly.

Mr. Sandersford's tone was serious suddenly. "Clyde, what was it you told me that sign said?"

The young man bit his lip. "It was nothing, Mr. Sandersford. Just some eccentric, I imagine."

"No, damn it, boy, you tell me just like you told me before!"

Boss Hooker moved about in his seat uneasily.

Clyde Joscelyn told him what the sign Tobey had been carrying said.

"Ah!" said the old man, when he finished, and that was all.

The door opened again, and the Jones sisters came in.

"Well, well," Teresa said, "if it isn't the old man!"

Mr. Sandersford's head snapped up. "Is that Terry?"

"Sure, it's Terry," Teresa laughed, coming over to him. "What's the matter with you? Blind?"

"That's it exactly," Mr. Sandersford laughed, but they could see he wasn't joking. "Blind as a bat. Happened about eight months ago. All of a sudden, bam! Couldn't see anymore."

Boss Hooker was shocked. "But, D.S., I didn't know—"

"Of course you didn't know," the old man said peevishly. "How could you know if I didn't tell you?"

"You could have written me, sir—"

"And what's the good in writing? There wasn't a damn thing

you could have done about it, if the best specialist in New York City couldn't."

"Well, you can't have everything," Teresa laughed. Her voice was light but her face was grim.

"That's the kind of talk I need to hear!" Mr. Sandersford croaked. "I knew you wouldn't let me down, Terry! Where's that snippy little sister of yours?"

"Right here, Mr. Sandersford," Cathy said, coming over to take his hand.

"I'll *bet* you are!" the old man said broadly. "Sit down, sit down, everybody! Where is Phil? Is Phil here?"

"Not yet, sir," Boss Hooker said.

"Well," the old man sighed, "I guess it's kinda hard for him to walk fast in those tight britches. I've got a couple of things to tell you folks—not pretty things—but you won't have to be worried about me taking up too much of your time. I never liked to take up too much of peoples' time because I never liked them to take up too much of my own. And I'm not a speechmaker." He stopped suddenly. "George who'm I missing?"

"Phil Meyer, Joe Richards—who said he had another engagement—and Ken Bussey, who's—indisposed," he finished, glaring at Lee.

"Is that Lee boy here?" the old man said. "That Lee whatsisname?"

"Merriweather," Lee called from his end of the table.

"Is that you, Merriweather?"

"Yes, sir, it is."

"Congratulations, boy! You've put a lotta life in this old rag. Clyde's read me everything you ever wrote, almost. I'm proud of you."

"Thank you, sir."

"Now!" Mr. Sandersford said. "Is everybody sitting?"

"Yes, sir," Boss Hooker said.

"I sure hate to go on without Phil," the old man said, casting his sightless eyes about the room. "But—well, it won't make much difference."

The door opened again, and Phil Meyer, with his well-dressed wife Alene, came into the room. His eyes were wide and fearful.

"Who's that?" the old man demanded.

"It's me, sir," Meyer said meekly, glancing over apprehensively at the expressionless face of Cathy Jones. "Phil Meyer."

"Come over here and shake my hand, boy!" Mr. Sandersford said. "First thing George tells me is that you've been elected to some sort of commission or something."

"Appointed," Meyer corrected.

"Where's Alene?"

"Right here, Mr. Sandersford," she said, coming over behind Meyer.

"Well, sit down, sit down! Now is *everybody* here?"

"Everybody but some of the advertising agents," Boss Hooker said, "and the bookkeepers, but they all said they wouldn't be able to make it."

"I sure hate that," the old man lamented. "What I've got to say affects everybody who works for the *Messenger*. I—"

The door popped open and the janitor peeked in timidly. "Mr. Hooker," he said, "that crazy man with the sign is back."

"What!"

"Yes, sir. He's right out front, walkin' up and down."

"Wait a minute," Lee said, getting up. "I'll go talk with him. I know him."

"*You* know him?" Boss Hooker thundered. "I should have known this was your idea!"

"You go bring that fella up here, Merriweather," Mr. Sandersford said. "Tell him I wanta have a few words with him."

"Sir?"

"What's the matter?" the old man snapped. "You hard of hearing?"

Lee left the room quickly.

Cathy Jones got up from her seat and went over to where the great man sat. "Mr. Sandersford, I've got something I want to show you . . ."

Meyer jumped up from his seat next to Alene. "Cathy—"

She turned toward him.

"Show me?" Mr. Sandersford said. "*Show* me? Didn't you just hear me say I was stone blind, sister?"

Cy Venson leaned across the table with marked indulgence. "Give it to me, Cathy, I'll *read* it to him."

"Mr. Sandersford—!" Meyer started desperately.

"It's a check," Cathy went on, ignoring them. "A *Messenger* check."

"A *Messenger* check!" Boss Hooker said. He leaned over protectively to the file of checks on the table. "What are you doing with a *Messenger* check?"

"Listen to me," the old man commanded. "I don't care what it is you've got to show me. I don't think there's anything you folks can tell me that's as important as what I got to tell *you*. I can tell from the way your voices sound that a squabble is about to come up, and please believe me when I say I ain't interested. Now sit down and stay that way until I've had my say."

They all returned to their chairs.

Meyer went over to whisper something in Cathy's ear, but she acted as though she hadn't heard, and her face took on a harder, more determined look.

Lee came back in with Tobey Balin, who looked none the worse for wear for his chilly durance vile in front of the building.

"I thought the police arrested you!" Boss Hooker cried.

Tobey grinned. "They did, but it turned out the desk sergeant knew the full meaning and significance of the United States citizen's right to picket—after I explained it to him. He even ordered the stepchildren of justice to bring me back to where they picked me up. He was a very understanding fellow."

"What's your name, boy?" Mr. Sandersford called out to him.

"Tobey, Douglas," he answered smartly, as if entitled to call the Great Him by his first name.

"You're kind of cheeky, ain't you, Tobey?"

"No more than necessary, sir."

"Come around here," the old man said, crooking an aged finger at the young man's voice.

Tobey came to stand by his chair.

"You a professional man?" Mr. Sandersford inquired.

"No, I'm not."

"Ever been in the newspaper business before?"

"Well," Tobey said thoughtfully, "I was vaguely connected with a similar business: my father was an undertaker."

The old man burst out in a creaky laughter. "Undertaker, huh? What was his name?"

"Mark Balin."

"Not old Put-'um-In-Dig-'um-Up Balin?"

"The same," Tobey smiled.

The old man laughed again. "I knew your daddy, boy! Knew your mother too. I always did wonder—who was it buried your daddy?"

"He did. He gave himself the thousand dollar send-off. You would have liked it."

Mr. Sandersford continued laughing, his sightless eyes dancing jubilantly in his hoary head. "Your old man was the stingiest human being I ever knew! I always said, if he buried himself, he'd, have the gravediggers come around after everybody'd gone home and substitute the regular wooden box for the one he'd been buried in!"

Tobey couldn't help smiling. "Dad went to rest in a stone coffin. I think he acquired an aversion for gravediggers *and* worms toward the end."

"He musta made himself a pretty penny before he kicked off," Mr. Sandersford observed genially.

"Oh, he did."

"Well, well, well," Mr. Sandersford said reminiscently. "Well, boy, I wish I could see you, but God thought I'd seen too much in this lifetime, so he put the lights out on me. What I want to ask you about is that sign."

"It's a very pretty sign," Tobey said. "If I'd known you were blind, I probably wouldn't have made it. I'm glad I did, because you saw it anyway."

"This boy here beside me tells me that the things that sign says are *not* so pretty."

"Well, I'd say that depended on how you look at it."

"Depends on how *I* look at it, huh?" Mr. Sandersford said. "Boy, you got quite a tongue in your head. Get a seat—get a seat and bring it over here next to me."

Tobey found a chair and did as he was told.

"Now," the old man said. "You just go ahead and explain that sign. If I get the complete picture in my mind, then maybe I *will* see it."

"It means just what it says," Tobey began. "Injustice. The *Messenger* is an injustice to this city, to you and to everyone who comes in contact with it. Meeting you now—seeing you here—I know the *Messenger* is not the thing you intended it to be."

"You're not going to listen to this—this maniac, are you, sir?" Boss Hooker said.

"George," the old man said with quiet patience. "You just keep still. If what this boy says hurts, it's only because it's true."

Tobey looked around the room at all their faces, and Lee felt his heart soar when the probing gaze reached him. Diana tightened her grip on his arm.

For a moment, shame touched Tobey's face as he said, "I came here tonight, with that sign, thinking I was going to ridicule you in full view of your creation, the *Messenger*. But I realize now I came here, not actually to indict you or this paper, but to try and cleanse myself of a little of the guilt I felt—a guilt in helping to promote the *Messenger* and everything it stood for."

"Guilt?" the old man said musingly. "How could you be guilty, boy?"

"I'm guilty, just like thousands of other people in this city are guilty, of remaining silent, by wordlessly consenting to the deplorable exhibitions of this paper." He lowered his head. "Today, I tried to tell my friend, Lee Merriweather, of the futility of Negro newspaper publishing. In telling him, I discovered *why* it was futile. I discovered I had known the reasons all along—perhaps like everyone else knows them—but that I didn't really *care*. In painting that sign, I neglected to include that an injustice has been done the *Messenger,* by the people, the intelligent people, who read it and don't *care* about it." He looked up. "Mr. Sandersford, I want you to accept my most humble apology. Now if you'll excuse me—"

"Just a minute there, boy. Sit down." The old man turned his face in the vicinity of Tobey's voice. "Just let me do a little saying before you pull out of here." He waited a few moments before he continued.

"I know that what you say is true, and *I* feel one hell of a need to apologize, but I don't know who to do it to. Yes, you're right—the *Messenger* is an injustice. And I can't blame anybody but myself. I can't blame George, or Phil, or any of the rest of you. The responsibility of the *Weekly Messenger's* moral integrity was solely in my hands. I neglected it—I criminally neglected it. Maybe that was why God put the lights out on me: so I could fully *see* my neglect." He reached upward, tentatively, and Clyde Joscelyn took his wrinkled hand. "For the past several months, Clyde's been reading me the *Messenger*—every word of it. I was able in this way to finally get a good look at the dirt and cheapness that I'd let get out of hand—almost three decades of it. And it made *me* feel really dirty and cheap. I was always pretty proud of the fact that I was a rich man, with several newspapers in my hip pocket, but I wasn't too proud after what I listened to in the *Messenger* and the rest of them. You said on that sign that the *Messenger* was a moral injustice to me, boy. Well, you're wrong—I was a moral injustice to the *Messenger,* and six other newspapers." He stopped again, and when he went on, his voice was full of strength. "Now, after I say this, I want it to be ended. I don't want everybody hollering and shouting for Gabriel to come. I made up my mind and nothing's going to change it: I'm disbanding the *Messenger;* I'm disbanding the chain."

The room was stunned.

The old man bobbed his head at the faces he couldn't see.

"Now, I've done a lot of thinking about this," he said. "It's not off the cuff. I'm going to give you all an adequate severance pay—one year's salary. And I've already picked out new positions for you with business friends in this city who can pay you just as well—and in most cases better—than the *Messenger* ever could. You'll all have the best references."

Still no one spoke.

"I want it clearly understood that there'll no longer be a *Messenger*," the old man continued. "I'm selling everything, font by font, and I'm going to let Clyde start up a new paper in Texas, or maybe in my hometown of New Orleans, which could do with a respectable medium for Negroes. And I'm not worried about this paper degenerating into another *Messenger,* because my lawyer's drawn up a contract to see that it doesn't. Maybe you'll wonder why I don't start some of you people on this thing, but if you'll look closely you'll see why I don't: You'd only be carriers of the *Messenger* germ. Now, George," he said finally, "if you'll lay out the checkbook for me and guide my hand to the line, we'll take the first steps in obliterating the name of the *Weekly Messenger.*"

Boss Hooker got up as though in a trance. He went out of the room and came back presently with a large, ledger-sized book of checks. In gold letters on the front of the green cover were the words, *Weekly Messenger.*

The room had been adequately decorated. It was now a room of death. As each check was signed and delivered, a portion of the *Weekly Messenger* crumbled.

Teresa Jones was crying.

"Terry!" the old man called. "I'm gonna miss you!"

"I'm gonna miss you, you old slave driver!" she said, bending to kiss his forehead.

"And, Cathy," he called. "Do you think this check will tide you girls over until you find something else?"

She looked at the check incredulously. "But this—"

"You don't think I'm going to leave without giving you folks a bonus, do you?" the old man said indignantly. "Oh yes, you had something you wanted to tell me, didn't you?"

She smiled down on him, and Teresa was surprised to see tears come to her sister's eyes. "I didn't have anything to tell you, Mr. Sandersford. Not a thing."

The checks were signed, another and another. Boss Hooker, who could not speak now. Earl Morrell, chewing dazedly at the cigar holder with its dead cigar. Cy Venson, a harsh, too-sober look on his gaunt face. Phil Meyer. Diana. All the other names on the *Messenger* rolls, each and everyone contributed to the dying.

"And finally, Merriweather," the old man said. "Since he's the youngest in seniority."

Lee stood by his chair.

The old man handed him the check.

"This is too much," Lee said.

"Don't argue with me. You take that. You do something good with it. Mold that talent of yours, build it. You should be in school."

"Well, I was going to State, sir . . ."

"Then go back to State. Learn all you can. If you have time, come over to New York in a few years and see me. If I haven't kicked the bucket by then, maybe we'll be able to get together on something."

"Yes, sir."

"Good luck, Merriweather," the old man said. He struggled to his feet, aided by Clyde Joscelyn. "Well, everyone, goodbye. As I said, I'm not a good speechmaker, and I hate to be maudlin about these things. I'll just say goodbye . . . and I love you all very much."

He was helped on with his coat. In a few moments, his white head disappeared through the door.

There was an unbroken silence in the room. Presently they all began to file out: Boss Hooker, Earl Morrell, Phil and Alene Meyer, Cy Venson, the Jones sisters, Diana, Lee, and Tobey.

And soon they were standing in the snow, and the *Messenger* building was empty except for the janitor who remained behind to give it a last clean-up.

There was no longer a *Weekly Messenger*. The sleeping city did not see.

There were many things that died which were not men.

CHAPTER FOURTEEN

TOBEY MONOPOLIZED LEE'S CONTOUR CHAIR no sooner than they came into the apartment. Diana stretched out on the couch, and Lee went over to the closet to find the Scotch. He went into the kitchen and was back in a minute with three glasses.

"Drink, anyone?"

Tobey slouched tiredly in the chair. "Even I'll have one tonight, Othello."

Diana looked up at him. "You may pour me one, Baby. A big one."

They sipped their drinks silently.

"Well," Tobey said, "to quote a famous poet, a Nigger is a Nigger is a—"

"Human being," Lee Merriweather said.

They sat sipping their drinks in cadence to the passing night.

Yet Princes Follow

The ordinance of god,
How inscrutable it is
And goes on for ever.

He makes no show of moral worth,
Yet princes follow in his steps.

From the *Book of Songs*

CHAPTER ONE

ROBERT JOE TEESE was the biggest, blackest, ugliest man anybody ever saw. Even after you looked at him a hundred times, you still thought that he was. He was the kind of man people disliked instantly, on first contact, at first sight—that is until they got to know him.

Teese had a saving quality that offset that first sensation of revulsion: he'd open his big, thick lips, he'd show those pearly teeth, he'd growl out that deep rumble of sugar-and-honey-smacked laugh—and whoever witnessed this phenomenon immediately belonged to him.

Teese was the miracle of Lomax Street, the big, black sugar-baby of all who knew him. The grinning football of his hat-tipped head daily greeted every rat-infested hovel, every barber and beauty salon, every whorehouse, bar, grocery and sweetshop; he met every pimp, every dancing-hipped pimp's lady, every sweat-worm of the thunder mill called a steel plant, that sat on the hill of the city.

Teese, the numbers man, was known and loved by all. And life might have gone on too, too sweetly for him.

Except the damn fool had to fall in love.

Now hear me, brothers,
for I speak. I am the voice
within and without; I am the Knower
of all things knowable, the Seer
of all things unseeable,
the Taster of sweet delights,
the definitive of man
and man's blood and flesh.

CHAPTER TWO

"**Y**EAH," SAID TEESE, grinning broadly to his first stop of the day—the Rt. Reverend Thaddeus A. Jones—"Yeah, Rev," Teese said happily, "I do think I'm gonna have to set a date with ya."

An early riser to the morning, Rev. Jones blinked sleep from his eyes and made sure the door to the bedroom dividing himself and Teese from the main floor of the church was closed. He said, "Ahem," as he did so, acute discretion written on his slim, neat brown face.

But Teese wasn't fooled. Several mornings he had arrived here late for his pickup and seen Sister Rosy Dawn sneaking out by the back way, stepping on tiptoes, her skirt up high around her fat yellow thighs, as though she were walking through the rose bushes her husband grew in his little shop on Lomax, avoiding the thorns.

"What did you say, Brother Teese?" Rev. Jones asked in that funny way of his, reminding Teese of a hound he used to own in Arkansas as a boy, an animal cursed with the task of fleas as Job with boils. "I didn't rightly hear you."

"I was talkin about my marriage," Teese said.

Rev. Jones gave an incredulous grin, his eyes opened fully now. "Well, don't tell me, Brother Teese!"

Teese beamed. "It's sure enough."

"Well, I say," Rev. Jones said, clapping his hands smartly, an exciting gesture when he did it in the pulpit, but somehow a little sarcastic and mocking now. "Don't tell me it's the truth, Brother Teese! Happy matrimony! And is the young lady a member of Christ's Redemption?"

Teese nodded his huge, happy head. "Yes, sir, I think she is. She's Miz Grace Anderson."

"Grace Anderson! Not Brother Pete Anderson's little daughter— God rest him—of the Anderson Moving Co. Andersons?"

"That's her, all right."

Rev. Jones recollected, licking his lips. "That *is* a peach of a girl, Brother Teese! The prettiest thing on Lomax Street—and that hair—!" But he was digressing in his constant appreciation of woman-flesh, and the hard, inquiring look from Teese served to pull him up short. "Well, I say! And when, may I ask, is this happy, happy event going to take place?"

"Well, we ain't decided yet," Teese said. "But I got her word, and her brother's word—Ely Anderson—and I'm waitin for my lucky number to start things rollin."

Rev. Jones was suddenly solemn advisor. "Marriage is a serious thing, Brother Teese, as I don't guess I have to tell you."

"I'm forty-one years old," Teese said, not complaining. "I've seen more marriages than minnows—never takin part in any of 'em, though—but I've had my sweet and sour."

"Then you know the taste," Rev. Jones said, rising to a sermon. "The only thing that can stand between a happy union is a cruel heart, Brother Teese, remember that. You must have *love*."

With a grain of salt, Teese consumed, and nodded. "Yes, sir. Love is what I got plenty of for Miz Grace."

"And faith," Rev. Jones added. "And fidelity."

"Yes, sir, Rev."

"And love of Jesus Christ!" Rev. Jones went on, clapping his hands sharply. "And happy honesty!"

Teese said, "Can I have your numbers, Rev? I'm kinda in a hurry—"

His voice brought a furtive, Earthbound look to Rev. Jones's dark face. He went to the back door, opened it and looked out. The slowly rising, hot August sun stared back at him over the sagging little morning city of Lomax Street.

He closed the door and came back to Teese. "You don't think nobody saw you, huh?"

"You always ask me that, Rev. You know I wouldn't let nobody see me come in here. Course, I can't see why it matters so much, since everybody on Lomax Street plays the numbers."

"It just wouldn't be fitting," Rev. Jones said, without further explanation. Quickly he went into his bedroom and returned with the small pad and carbon strips, on which he tallied and directed the play of his numbers and money.

"I haven't wrote 'em up, Brother Teese, but if you'll wait a minute—"

"Go ahead," Teese said, only too glad to wait, since Rev. Jones usually played from ten to fifteen dollars daily. Teese worked on ten percent commission, and it followed that the more was played the more he made.

Rev. Jones went back into the room for his dream book, and Teese had time to fall into a dream with Grace again—only one of the millions he had had about her since she had said she would last Saturday night.

Man O man! Gee, jump! jump! He was the luckiest big bastard who ever stood over a rod and balls!

He never stopped to wonder why Grace Anderson, the prettiest, the ripest, the hippiest young hussy on Lomax Street had consented to henceforth share her daily bread and nightly bed with the homeliest man in the city, if not the United States of America and Canada —and big, happy, smiling, flat-footed (from cotton-picking in Arkansas), forty-one-year-old R. J. Teese did not give one holy damn.

Let them laugh, let them haw-haw behind his back. No one would ever know how lucky he was. Not even he could fully grasp the power of his good fortune.

It only demonstrated what Teese had always told his lynch-complaining, trampled-poor-Negro friends: America were opportunity, boy, yes, yes, rhythm, jump, jump, with a Rev-happy beat— opportunity and love for a big black man lost in the dark.

Teese was ecstatic this morning.

"Snake," Rev. Jones mumbled over his dream book, while sitting at his makeshift kitchen table, a humble affair that served adequately for his hurried meals.

"Shake," Teese said, caught up in the cadence of his love.

"No, snake, Brother. Like that tempter, that defiler, in the Holy Garden. That's what I dreamed. Plays for 5-2-6."

"Never could figure out why," Teese said, "God let that rattler in, in the first place."

"Didn't *let* him," Rev. Jones objected. "*Put* him. And I don't think they had rattlers in those days."

"Couldn't nothin be that vicious but a rattler," Teese opined, "the way he led that poor little Eve on."

"Temptation!" Rev. Jones said, snaring a key word. "What does that play for?" He looked it up between the green covers of his dream book and wrote the numbers on his slip.

"Yes, temptation, Brother, the beguiler. And iniquity. Ah, yes. And vanity! That's what destroys marriages, Brother, those are the havoc-wreakers. 5-2-6 and 6-2-9," he said over his numbers. "The devil's mobsters!"

"Them sounds like pretty good figures," Teese said, recording the numbers for his own use, since he knew Rev. Jones hit the numbers correctly at least once out of every ten tries, and it was about time for him to hit again.

"Is that all you're playin, Rev?"

Rev. Jones regarded the figures he had written on his slip for a long time, then he tore the slip from the book and handed it to Teese, who gave a little start when he saw how much money the Reverend was playing.

"You playin twenty dollars on 526 in the first race?" He whistled through puckered lips. "You sure must have a lot of faith in it—and in 629, too!"

"Faith!" Rev. Jones said, capturing the word. "Yes, *I* have faith—in Jesus Christ. I'm playing 629 in the box, Brother," he said, returning to the subject of numbers.

Teese figured quickly in his mind. "You playin 629 for five dollars in the box—that number can come six ways, so that's thirty dollars played. Thirty cents off each dollar means you owe me twenty-one dollars. On 526 for twenty dollars, that's fourteen dollars to go. Altogether you owe me thirty-five dollars."

Rev. Jones gave him the money, and Teese put it away with the numbers slip in one of the secret pockets of his suitcoat.

Silently, he was figuring out his commission on this play, which

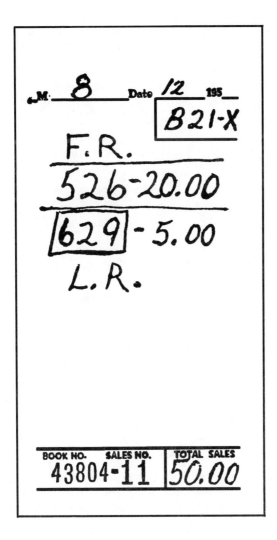

normally took only a second for his practiced sense of mathematics; but it took him a little longer now because he was debating the choice of a smart red dress Grace had told him about downtown or a down payment on a wedding ring. He honestly couldn't make up his mind.

"I certainly hope, Brother Teese," Rev. Jones was saying, "that you will render me the privilege of presiding at your matrimonial fete." He smiled at his choice of words, and—just a little—at his image of how ridiculous Teese would look beside the ravishing Grace Anderson—*if* such a trick did come off.

"Oh, yeah," Teese said. "You know I wouldn't have nobody else but you, Rev, to latch us up."

"Seeing as how you're an *honorary* member of Christ's Redemption," Rev. Jones said, a bit accusingly, "I knew you'd say that."

Teese fidgeted a little under the righteous stare. "Honorary? Well, Rev, you know I'm a regular member. I just been takin, what you might call, a holiday."

"The *devil* doesn't take a holiday," Rev. Jones said darkly.

"Yeah—well," Teese said, giving that big, white, people-melting grin, which was wasted on Rev. Jones. "Well . . . I guess I'll be gettin on, Rev. You know how it is; money callin me."

"I surely do," Rev. Jones said, escorting him to the door. "And I want you to be real careful."

"Huh?" Teese said, and saw that Rev. Jones was smiling a little.

"With all my money, Brother!" he told Teese with a laugh. "Satan's dues to the Lord. The way I see it, if Satan's going to run that numbers racket in the face of the Lord, we might as well make him pay for it!"

"Yeah," Teese grinned, thinking Rev. Jones's excuse for playing the numbers just as weak now as it had been three years before, when he'd pulled Teese surreptitiously into his empty church and announced he'd like to play a few figures in the Lord's behalf.

At the moment, however, Teese didn't care about man, babe or bull, as long as he could saunter carefree along his route with rapturous dreams of Grace.

Rev. Jones watched his errant parishioner cloud-walking away, and gave an amused shake of his head.

Grace Anderson. Ummm-ummph!

Little secret kept quiet, was that Rev. Jones had been working toward that plump goal for some time now. Still, Brother Teese wouldn't complicate things any.

Anyway, hadn't Grace been fritting around with that half-pimp, Roy Beavers, of the boarding-house Beaverses?

Happy knowledge!

He went back into the bedroom, where Rosy Dawn was just wiggling into her corset. Upon finishing, she came right over and planted a big, wet, smacking kiss on his musing lips.

"Jesus saves," she grinned.

"Hallelujah," he chuckled, making his hands do body-rising things below her back.

"Who was that?" she said, smelling thick of last night's love and fresh morning lipstick on her yellow, fat face.

"Teese, the pickup man. Do you know, Teese told me he's gonna marry Grace Anderson!"

"What?"

"It's the truth," he said. And I think Brother Teese wouldn't tell a lie about something like that."

Rosy Dawn shook her head, grinning. "I can't believe it! That Teese is the *ugliest* man in the world—even uglier than my old man Sam, bless his soul."

"And that's saying something," Rev. Jones agreed. "But I still can't figure out how Brother Teese did it; it's God's own mystery. He hasn't got any money to speak of, and he's living in that rat-trap of a hotel old man Favors owns."

Rosy pursed her wide, red sex-mouth with secret knowledge. "Teese useta fool around with Bea Green, you know."

"You mean old Horrible Hannah?" the man of God yuk-yukked.

"That's who I mean! They say the Lord don't love ugly, but I swear He gave a many black soul a pat on the head."

"Well, I say!" Rev. Jones said, enlightened. "Bea Green!"

"She came into the shop to buy some goin-away flowers for her de-parted aunt, and, child, did we get to talkin about one thing and the other—and men. She got to goin on Teese, and the way she carried on you woulda thought he was Harry Belafonte or Sidney Potti-eh, the things she said that man could do!"

"Good, huh?"

"Pure sin!" Rosy Dawn declared. "Which is why a young filly

like Grace Anderson could do a flip or two—if she kept her eyes closed."

"I can't decide to believe in that girl," Rev. Jones said thoughtfully. "She isn't any more than twenty-one—"

"Twenty-five," Rosy Dawn told him, with a suspicious eye.

"And she lives in fast company. You know that Beavers boy's daddy was full of life until one of his women cooled him off with four or five airholes about fifteen years back."

"He sure was," Rosy Dawn said, recalling the juicy stories she had heard about Roy Beavers's dashing dad—and she also had good reason to know that the father was a small hunter compared to the son.

"Yes, sir, it provokes a lot of thinking," Rev. Jones said.

"Well, you think," Rosy said, giving him a last kiss and getting herself together. "My old man's gonna be raisin hell 'cause I had to stay all night again with Cousin Lena, poor sick soul."

Rev. Jones watched her briskly wiggling buttocks as she went hurriedly about the room, rather pleased at what he had accomplished with her last night, those soaring peaks of glory!

Happy memory!

At forty-five, he was still devilishly formidable in bed, though that might have been stretching the description just a bit; and it was really one of his lesser talents.

Thaddeus A. Jones, PPS, M.T., S.S.B.—all roughly translated to mean a self-made man—was a gifted individual, and he was only waking up to the fact. For more years than he liked to remember, he had been unaware of his singular, hypnotic rhetoric and—most special of all—his premonitory blessing: a thing which an article in a magazine and a professor of City College confirmed as ESP.

Only casually did the members of his church remark now that Rev. Jones hadn't given out a good number in three years, and little did they realize that three years had been sufficient time for the Rt. Reverend Jones to prove a newly conceived "system"—or a type of freedom of dream association he had borrowed from the works of the late Dr. Freud on one invaluable trip to the public library.

In three years, Rev. Jones had put four thousand dollars into the numbers, and had been rewarded five times over. Of course, this had been at the sake of the church treasury, which he controlled, and which was now depleted with the last thirty-five dollars handed over to R. J. Teese, the pickup man.

Many times Rev. Jones asked himself where had the money gone—all of it—but that was really a silly question.

There was the Cadillac limousine out in the church garage, a trip to New York with one luscious Sister two months ago, about a dozen silk suits in the wardrobe—and don't forget the Beefeater, Old Taylor and Grand MacNish, with which he liked to toast his various fleshy conquests. And, oh yes, the county racetrack.

More than thirty thousand dollars—and the interdenominational head of the ministry was coming today, Monday, to check his church and records.

Unhappy realization!

Still, Rev. Jones wasn't too worried. He had faith—yes, *it.*

He knew his power and the power of God Almighty. Last night the snake had come to show him the way, and he had felt that dream pull as he'd never felt one pull before—not even some of his more successful ones.

That's why he'd played so heavily, hanging himself for the pig rather than the piglet.

Rev. Jones felt so sure of at least one of the numbers that he had played, he would have staked his career on it—as he surely was.

If 629 came, he would be able to replace the couple thousand missing from the treasury and still live a little. And if 526 came— happy blessing!—it would be the concrete foundation of a thing that had only been a dream, the beginning of a reputation unheard of since Jesus Christ! With ten thousand dollars he could really build the church he needed, really herald himself as the religious scion of the city.

False gods . . .

The words from the Bible worried him, but he made a fair attempt at shutting them from his mind. Instead, he justified his every action—even his embezzlement of church funds—with the words, *God's image*. He, in God's image, was no less than a god. He could do no less than a god would do.

Materialistic Christianity, oh happy!

The real devil was the one of denial, he thought—and there had never been a more religious man than himself. So religious, he loved every quiver of Rosy Dawn's heavy behind, every peach-blush of her springy young breasts—and he was not niggardly in his heavenly love, mark that: he loved all women and the essence of good living with celestial passion.

Yes, the women—truth: that's where the money had gone, and it was where a great deal more would go if he ever got his hands on it.

Women like Grace Anderson.

And here he paused, thinking un-reverendly thoughts about Grace Anderson.

"Well, I'm on my way," Rosy Dawn said, woman-warm and cherry-pink next to him. "My sweet preacher's thinkin about that young chicken, I can tell," she chided with mild rebuke.

"I shall not be moved," he said.

"Yeah," she said, putting a hand to him. "But I got to go, so I can't prove you *can*."

He patted her fondly and took her to the back door, where he looked out first to see if the coast was clear.

"All right," he whispered.

"I'll come tonight, if I can," she said as she went past him.

"Not tonight," he called after her. "I'm going to be busy. I'll let you know."

He watched her vanish into the heat of the young day, then he went back to his room to dress in one of the silk suits, singing to himself:

> I shall not,
> I shall not be moved,
> Just like a tree that's
> Standing by the water . . .

The cities of the Earth are the bowels of the universe; within them-selves they take the meat of man's spirit and consume it with the acids of Life; they creak and grind their mortared muscles against the frame and substance of consciousness, and when they are done a laughable fac-simile of what was is all that is left.

CHAPTER THREE

R. J. TEESE WHISTLED, and oh how he could whistle today! Languidly strolling down the hot bricks of Lomax Street, each familiar sight was a new thing seen with new, glorious eyes. Joe Caldwell's Harlem Market was a windowed green-grocer's oasis; Bessie's Bower of Beauty held a harem of early-morning, frizzled-wigged damsels, all glowing and smiling on him lovably; brown-stoned, patriarch faces of elder dwellings stood far-reaching castles before his dazzled gaze; and the street—*the* Lomax Street—was the golden road that led to the holy city of Jerusalem.

Never had Teese felt such poetry in his soul; not even that wondrous day of escape from Arkansas twenty-five years ago had made him feel this way.

Though he was well over two hundred pounds, Teese felt as light as a feather; he felt as though he were capable of rendering a creditable soft-shoe in the style of the inimitable Bojangles Robinson, right here on the hot, blistering pavement of Lomax Street, and was tempted for a moment to do just that.

Instead, he sang, without any personal derogation:

> Just because my hair is curly;
> Just because my teeth are pearly;
> Just because I always wear a smile—

"Shine!" yelled a voice from the Three Aces Poolroom.

"Man, dig Teese!" cried another.

Three brown-faced youngsters—all not yet twenty—whom Teese knew, lounged importantly at the glazed-glass front of the billiard hall, hair slicked and twirled in the fashionable konk—six-dollar jobs—while their baggy hustler's trousers silently, sadly, spoke of better days seen long ago.

Instantly Teese was on his guard, for the young "ragheads," as he called them by dint of their habits of tying kerchiefs about their marcels to keep down sweat and protect the sheens, were items of youth he felt were fast going to hell with their reefer-smoking and wine-drinking and gang fights—or to the penitentiary.

"Man O man!" grinned one baby-faced youth. "Like, daddy, that is one happy-O Teese-man!"

"What's happenin, Teese baby?" inquired a pimply-faced, fuzzy-chinned tyro, who was illogically mis-nicknamed Papa John, acknowledged leader of the dashing trio.

"Numbers," Teese replied, with some hesitation. "What you-all think is good today?"

"Man," giggled the third boy, "like, I mean, my man, numbers is way out, like the Atlas, happy-O, like I mean, single-action is it."

Teese was able to comprehend the last part of this. "Well, I don't take care of the single-action, boys—Lulu Haynes handles that; you can see her. How about you, Papa John? You usually got a nickel or dime on 707."

"Man," Papa John began a lament, "you cats been changin the figure too much on the lay-away side. I mean, dig: I had seven-O straight for a quarter last M-day, and it came that way at a five and a three-O after the buzz-boy faded. I liked to flipped! That hundred and a quarter was in my fist almost, and I went blood-houndin after you. Then a cat tells me at six-three-O, like, 'Man, they changed it—the joy gem's 701.' I blasted then, really blew my wig!"

In this way, Teese was apprised that Papa John had played 707 last Monday for twenty-five cents, and was elated by the news at five-thirty in the evening that 707 *was* the number. Knowing the House paid off at five dollars for every penny played, Papa John could practically feel the hundred and twenty-five dollars in his hand. Suddenly, and joyfully, a member of the nouveau riche, Papa John set out to pick up Teese's spoor and collect the windfall. Then, an hour later, almost in sight of his goal, a friend told him the number had been changed to 701. This news, of course, had a negative and very violent effect on the youth, though changes of heavily played numbers were not at all uncommon.

"Well, it weren't my fault," Teese said, excusing himself. "All I do is pick 'em up and lay 'em down."

"Yeah, baby," the boys said sarcastically together, like a Greek chorus.

"That's God's truth," Teese told them, though he didn't know why he felt it necessary to convince them. "Sometimes folks want a number to come so bad, they put out the wrong figure themself. The House, as far as I know, don't put out one figure, then change it like that."

"Yeah, baby," the boys sang.

"Well, I can't argue wit'cha all day. See Lulu if you want to play some single-action." He started down Lomax.

"Hey, Teese-man," Papa John called. "Don't be runnin off that way."

"Boy, I got to move," Teese said. "Money callin, money cryin to be played—numbers money."

"Yeah, man-baby, I know all that; like it's what you gotta do to cop the three-square, kee—"

"—rect?" crowed his two accomplices.

Teese had to give that big, pretty grin, that honey-rumbling laugh. "You boys is crazy!"

"They talk about *beat*," said one of the boys. "We're *re*-beat!"

"We got a peaceful co-existence," Papa John declared. "We got like moral re-armament—re-beat, happy-O? Kee—"

"—rect!" chimed the others.

Papa John closed his eyes and smiled beatifically. The others followed suit, and all began to sway sensuously before Teese's astonished stare.

"Man, get together," Papa John said. "Dig each other—white folks, black folks, yella folks, pink folks—they got to dig, spy! Get mellow, like: re-beat!"

"Crazy!" said his friends.

"Like *feel* it!" Papa John bellowed, looking ridiculous.

"Crazy!" said the others.

200

"Like put out feelers to Teese-baby and get inside him!"

They stretched out their arms to Teese, who was watching them now through half-lidded eyes.

"Feel him!" Papa John ordered. "Like, that man is real happy—*feel* that happiness!"

"Crazy!"

"Dig that wild pattern," Papa John commanded.

"Crazy!"

"That man is *happy!*"

"Crazy!"

"He is co-existing in peaceful bliss!"

"Crazy!"

Papa John opened his eyes and squinted at Teese. "That man is in love: look at him!"

The others swayed without speaking this time.

"My sweet baby, moral re-armament," Papa John said. "I can look right through him!"

"Spy!" demanded the swaying two.

"I see a broad who is a devil—man!—like she's the mellowest bulb-baby on Lomax East. But, men, I see evil!"

"Spy!"

"Now wait just a damn minute," Teese said, feeling for a moment as though the young Papa John actually were looking in on his thoughts. But the boy ignored him.

"Grace!" he said in triumph, and the others stopped their swaying and looked solemnly at Teese.

"You just keep your mouth shut about Grace," Teese said, surprised at his vehemence.

"Don't get excited, happy-O," Papa John said soothingly, in view of Teese's size. "I can't help it if we got rap-port, rap-rhythm, kee—"

"—rect?" said the two, who were now grinning.

Teese was speechless. Was it possible that Papa John and his fellows were in some wild, twisted way clairvoyant?

He was positive that Grace and her brother Ely hadn't told anyone about the coming marriage or that Teese had been courting Grace for the past few weeks. As a matter of fact, they had been hesitant when Teese insisted on telling only the Rev. Jones, who was particularly popular on Lomax Street because of the confidence he kept (and thus his own escapades were rewarded with secrecy).

Then how could Papa John know anything about Grace, unless he was indeed blessed with some power of foresight?

Teese felt a respect for the boy—half tinged with fear—that he had never felt before, and, for one wild moment, was seriously considering applying for membership in the youthful clan.

Still, the big man wasn't a complete fool. As careful as he had been in visiting Grace in the rooms she and her brother shared over their moving establishment, he might not, in his anxious love, have been careful enough. Silent feet drew silent ears, and eyes, you know, which he himself had proved in the case of the Rev. Jones and Mrs. Rosy Dawn.

This explanation calmed Teese's suspicions to some degree, but he wasn't at all sure. He started to go a bit farther, but Papa John's grinning young face said he wasn't answering any questions.

With a shrug, Teese grinned back at the strange trio, honey-laughing.

"You boys is crazy as hell!" he said, and started off about his business.

"Fare thee well, happy-O!" Papa John called out behind him, but Teese didn't answer.

"Poor chump," one of the boys said, looking after the big man. "I kinda go for that happy mark, like."

"Me too," Papa John admitted sadly. "That happy-O is one righteous people—square and a good daddy."

"He's so ugly like, he's beautiful," the other boy put in.

"But, men, I don't think we got through to the cat," Papa John said. "He's so square, he *can't* dig. He won't dig—until that hot bitch takes him."

"Mannnn, that's gonna be one sorry cat."

"Yeah, it's like death."

202

"People like him is rare," Papa John said philosophically. "He's like Parker was to Gillespie."

"Look," one of his companions said, pointing. "Here comes Roy-man Beavers."

Down the twisting street, rapidly filling with day people, their eyes found Roy Beavers as he passed Teese.

"Look at the way he's lookin at happy-O," Papa John said. "Sorrow, men, *sorrow!* And the happy-O not knowin he's bein fronted off."

They watched Roy Beavers approaching, sharp and neat in a white summer washable straw stingy-brim with red band around the crown. His light brown face bore the most surprisingly thick, heavy black mustache, hiding the broad upper lip and accenting the straight-lined weakness of the lower. His eyes were small and keen-staring brown, like those of a store dummy, and they seemed to make his head top-heavy with light on his small frame. Just broaching thirty, Roy Beavers was as handsome as he was indolent.

And he was also a man of mink-like violence, as he demonstrated with his first action on reaching the boys.

He collared Papa John and gave him a vicious shake. "I saw you talkin to that fool," he said. "What did you tell him?"

The other boys moved up to Papa John's aid, but he waved them back.

"I didn't tell him nothin," he said. "What could I tell him?"

Roy Beavers half relaxed his hold and squinted at the boy. "You coulda told him about what I said Saturday night, while I was shootin pool."

"You said it, I didn't, baby-O. I can't help it if you get juiced up and shoot your mouth off." He snatched out of Roy's relaxed grip. "And from now on, keep your hands off me, baby-O," he warned, putting an emphatic hand into one of his pants pockets. "Like, I never liked you no way, big man, *or* your style. And I didn't like the way you was braggin about what you and your hot doll was gonna do to Teese-man. I don't know how you're gonna pull your hype on happy-O, clean daddy, but everything about you stinks! I hate you like Hitler, man, but I wouldn't snitch out on ya;

203

I gotta rule against that. But the next time you collar me, bad man, I'm gonna have a whole hand for a souvenir!"

Roy straightened his lapels calmly and tried to grin disarmingly into the grim young faces.

"You misunderstand me, kid," he said. "You know how an operation is—you know what the game is. I just have to be real careful."

"Yeah, baby!" they all said together, but this time it wasn't in fun.

Roy took a neat, hesitant step, looking at them a bit worriedly and cursing his indiscretion of Saturday night.

"You boys just go along with me, there's somethin in it for ya," he promised.

They merely watched him.

Roy turned quickly on his heel and continued down the street, in the direction of Grace Anderson's boudoir.

"That is one evil man," Papa John said, looking after Roy, and the others agreed.

"But I got my pledge," he said, looking again in the direction Teese had disappeared. "I say us, me and myself, we don't meddle, kee—?"

"—rect!" his minions finished.

Papa John slapped his thigh disgustedly, and a cloud of dust filtered from the worn gabardine.

"Who's with me?" he said. "I got three dollars that's tellin me to go over and see Carl-O, the reefer man, and get about a half dozen joints."

"I got the wine money," one of his companions pledged.

"Then let's go," young Papa John said. "I *gotta* get happy after all this sadness."

My eyes are the eyes of all men:
They see the treasure, the hope
and hopelessness, the optimism
and pessimism of countless legions:
They delve the I and the It, and
they conclude the sum total of
all in confusion.

CHAPTER FOUR

OH, DAMMIT, TEESE THOUGHT, coming out of old Clyde Matthews's shack by the railroad tracks with Clyde's favorites, triple 3's and 023, in hand for a nickel in both races—*here comes Bea Green!*

Bea Green's eyesight was as sharp as his own, and she homed directly across the track, like a hound on the scent—an action which lent believability to her sad, hound-dog's face. A flicker of immediate pleasure came over the whole, disconcerting countenance as she closed on Teese, and he moaned to himself as he saw the little dog's legs bear down relentlessly on the graveled terrain.

If Teese was the ugliest man in the United States of America and Canada, Bea Green was surely his female counterpart.

Her marital status might have belied this fact, however, since she had been twice married and twice widowed before reaching her thirty-fifth year—yet her unhandsomeness could have very well been the cause of her widowhood. Teese, for example, could not imagine awakening from a deep, untroubled sleep, morning after morning, to face the troubles Nature had placed on the neck of Bea's crudely assembled body.

In fact, as she tromped deathlessly toward him, he was amazed that he had been so bold as to enter, and make use of, Bea's ancient but springily cooperative bed for even *one* night.

In the light of day, and an involuntary comparison to the young, soft, gorgeous Grace Anderson, Bea's long, flat nose, big red mouth, short kinky hair, ski-ramped forehead and more than dark complexion—adding to this a pitiable gaze of myopic distraction—were an unconquerable deterrent to any man's lust, not to mention R. J. Teese's.

True, in the dark of her room and bounce of her bed, Teese had been expertly and pleasurably recompensated for his bravado with a long-drawn, sensation-tickling, satisfying excursion to the nether regions of love-making.

Indeed he had to admit Bea stood head and shoulders above any women in this respect—though, of course, he hadn't yet tasted the sweet cherry juices of Grace Anderson; had been afraid, in fact, to even dare the thought in her presence. He fully expected the young girl, on their marriage, to provide him with the beauty of Venus and the hot, leg-twining torrents of a Bea Green.

—Which made the space closing between them now even shorter.

Kneading his mind with a mental fist, Teese tried to squeeze out some of his formerly fond regard for the woman; but it was dull and clouded by thoughts of Grace, and he could no longer remember the goodness of Bea, the sense-cooling balm of her soft, incongruous voice, the burning, needing life her fingers gave out when a man thought he'd die if he did it once more, then found to his unsated, masculine surprise that he'd die if he didn't.

Yes, such is the callous forgetfulness of a man in love, and Teese was not unlike other men.

"How do, Bea?" he said as brightly as he could, tipping his hat.

"Well, I declare!" Bea twinkled in her soft voice. "Is that Robert Joe? Well, bless me! Where *have* you been keepin yourself, Mr. Teese?"

"Oh, I been around," Teese said guiltily. "Been meanin to stop over to your place . . ."

"Well, you know I'd be glad to have you, Mr. Teese," she said, leaning hard on formality. "All alone in that great big old house at the end of Lomax, where nary a soul cares to even look, I sure could use a little company now and then."

"Yeah, I know that's true," Teese said.

"Why, I were just thinkin about you, Mr. Teese," she went on, as though the meeting was an especial occurrance. "Yes, I were thinkin that I ain't seen you in over three weeks, and what a stroke if I could run into you today."

Teese was wary. "Truth is, Miz Bea, I been intendin to come around for your numbers, but—"

"Hush!" she ordered gently. "It weren't the numbers so much—why, I don't even play numbers no more, Mr. Teese, not since you became such a stranger." She gave a reproving giggle. "No, Lord—I know how you dote on black-eyed peas and hamhocks, Mr. Teese, and I were just on my way to the Harlem Market."

Teese saw the trap. "It were nice of you to think of me, but—"

"And I were sayin to myself," she went on over him, " 'Mr. Teese would bust his gut on this meal I'm about to fix, and it's a shame I'll have to throw most of it away.' "

"Yeah, I know that's the truth, Miz Bea, but—"

" 'Now if I run into Mr. Teese pickin up his numbers,' " she cut him off, " 'I'll straight-away invite him over for supper this evenin.' "

"You're sure the nicest woman in the world, Miz Bea, but—"

"Gonna have that sweet cornbread you like, too," Bea tempted in desperation. "And tomatoes, and a side dish of collards and bacon left over from yesterday, along with cucumbers, and a great big pitcher of lemonade. Now don't that sound nice, Mr. Teese?"

"It sure do, Miz Bea," Teese said, unable to keep from licking his chops, "but—"

"You just say the word, Mr. Teese," she interrupted hurriedly. "I got my husband's—one of 'em's—Army check this mornin, bright and early, and I'm sure enough ought to be able to stand the expense. If you want, I can get a dozen or so ears of fresh corn and fry that up goozle-drippin in butter, and if you don't want lemonade I can get a six-pack of beer for you, since you know I'm an abstainin woman. Still, I sure do like to see a man enjoy hisself."

Bea Green was not without artifice. She knew the inroads to a man's heart by way of his stomach. Yet she could not reckon with Teese's plans—or his appointment with Grace Anderson that afternoon—for the evening, or how much it meant to him.

He blurted out a half-honeyed, apologetic laugh. "Miz Bea, you sure tempt a man crazy—"

She smiled expectantly.

"—but I just can't make it."

"Oh," she said, and the droop of her homely head drove a stake through Teese's heart.

And not being a cruel man, he lied, "But if you'll put all that together for one day next week, if it won't be a bother, I'll sure try to make it."

This helped some. "That's right nice of you, Mr. Teese. How's Monday-week?"

"That's fine," Teese said. "A week from today. You see, Miz Bea, you know how this numbers business is—money callin, money wantin to be played."

"Oh, you know I understand, Mr. Teese," she said with that reproving giggle.

"Well," he said, with one last polite tip of his hat. "I got to be gettin on. See you next Monday, Miz Bea."

She gripped both hands over her heart, and she couldn't help calling as he started away, plaintively, half frantically, "Teese!"

He pulled up his frame's momentum and turned to her sad, doggish face. "Yeah, Miz Bea?"

"I just—" she said, choking on the words. "I just wanted to send you off with caution."

His laugh bubbled out in reassurance. "I ain't worried about the cops in this part of town—they belong to my bossman."

"Good-bye, then, Mr. Teese."

"Good-bye, Miz Bea."

She watched him leaving her.

She did not raise her thin legs to resume her course until he had vanished around the path through the high weed clumps that led from the tracks back to Lomax.

And, O Lord! she was hurting! Hurting for Robert Joe and herself.

She started toward the high end of Lomax Street, toward the Harlem Market, thinking she would die if only it would help to keep Robert Joe from harm.

Bea Green was as sensitive as she was ugly, and she knew the sure signs in the shift of a man's affection—she knew man's unsubtle methods of severance from those things he did not care to have any longer—and it was because of her deep love and knowledge of Robert Joe Teese that she feared the outcome of his obsession.

Fortunately—or unfortunately for Teese—Bea had met that wench Rosy Dawn trucking home with her pants cooled from some all night lay-to with some man (didn't her husband Sam have no sense a-tall?), probably that Roy Beavers she was so hot for. Through this chance meeting Bea had become the third party that morning to find out about Teese's forthcoming marriage to Grace Anderson.

Was Teese as big a fool as Sam Dawn? Bea wondered woefully. Couldn't he see that young switch-tail didn't mean him any good? That she was just leading him on in some fateful plan, not unlike many she had perpetrated against gullible, and now tight-lipped, elder gentlemen of Lomax Street's fading generation?

Lord in Heaven, what was the matter with men nowadays!

Was love a board you had to slap them in the face with? Couldn't that Teese *see* that Bea had practically laid her heart and every penny of her resources at his big flat feet just for the privilege of loving him?

For two years, almost, she had led him—or he she—to the summit of connubial bliss, and it was impossible to think, even considering her ugliness, that theirs couldn't have been an idyllic union. She and Teese, to use the well-worn cliché, were *made* for each other, and it didn't seem fair that Grace Anderson should bare her claws on the innocence of him when Bea knew there were at least ten other men on Lomax Street who could have given her more. And were much more available; some of them were even good-looking.

Bea trudged along sorrowfully, knowing Teese would not come next Monday, or any other Monday, as long as the enchantress Grace Anderson held him under her spell.

Bea stamped her feet down hard, and turned her ankle in the anger that swept over her, but she didn't feel it at the time.

Grace Anderson—as it was everybody's knowledge except R. J. Teese's—would never stop carrying on with that woman-hopper,

Roy Beavers, Bea knew that for a fact. How Rosy Dawn could keep right on running after him, when it was plain he didn't give a whit about her, Bea didn't know!

She sighed. She would put her trust in the Lord, and her love for the fool that was Robert J. Teese.

Notwithstanding, her meal tonight would be a lonely one.

The senses of man are tinkle-bells,
alternately steering him from smooth
courses to rough, with warning knells;
and the man who asks for whom the
bell tolls indeed asks a valid ques-
tion: For how can the races of man
know it tolls for all humanity?
The bells they hear are many, and
each important.

CHAPTER FIVE

*T*EESE REACHED the halfway mark on his route, and it found him with a hundred and thirty-seven dollars, and as many numbers slips.

It was turning out to be a fine day, and he would be able to meet Grace with confidence later on.

For a man in love, the world always takes on newer and brighter dimensions. At each stop he made Teese exuded a conviviality over and above his normal capacity; his grin was electrifying.

And don't think his patrons had no clue to his happiness, for Rosy Dawn had been busy since dawn spreading the unbelievable news to countless unbelieving ears.

To disseminate motives in broad black and white, Rosy Dawn had an interest in—and hope for—the consummation of the marriage that would shock many people. With her rival Grace out of the way, Rosy knew who Roy would turn to—yes, she knew!

She had only taken up with the Rev. Jones out of spite (although he was kinda nice, and wasn't tight on the moolah), when Roy-boy started paying so much attention to Grace.

Now she was on the way to recapturing her throne, and she was going to make sure that the world knew what she knew, and in that way plunge Grace completely out of the running, at the same time indirectly binding her tighter to her pre-marital obligations.

A few citizens of keen perception, and a high regard for Teese, spotted the real reason for her ready information, and when the big man came around to pick up their numbers they played a little more than they usually did out of friendship—or sympathy—for him. They also had the good sense to keep their mouths shut about what they knew.

Teese, of course, had no way of knowing of the growing undercurrent of developments, although he was being carried unwittingly along by it. Therefore, he attributed his heavy play as the first sign of a propitious day.

When he entered Mohammed's Temple No. 6, on the corner of Lomax and Central, to pick up the plays of the handyman, Lucas West, it followed that unhappiness and foreboding were the farthest things from his mind.

Waiting to meet him, however, in the dark recesses of the reconverted bank building, was not little Lucas but Mohammed's number-one chieftain, Badr al-Din Kahzib, better known as Michael X.

"S'lum aliekum," the tall, turbaned, black, fiery-eyed, goateed man intoned at him ominously. "There is no god but *the* God, and Mohammed is his prophet!"

Teese couldn't help flinching at the thunderous voice—he had always thought Michael X and his followers a little crazy. What's more, Lucas had warned him to always be careful about coming into the Temple and never to let Michael X catch him there.

"He says numbers is the devil's invention," he recalled the little man-of-all-work telling him. "He'd go crazy if he ever found out you was comin around here to pick up my figures."

Equipped with this unsavory remembrance, Teese had a vivid instant of uneasiness, and prepared himself for the bodily assault he felt certain was forthcoming. Many times he had noted Michael X on the street as being a beautifully muscled, amazingly lithe young man, and he wasn't at all sure that his own soft pot-belly, nurtured by butter beans and salt pork from the boarding fare of old man Favors's cookstove, or his pugnacious chin, with the wobbly lower bridge, could withstand sustained punishment.

He felt himself tremble with apprehension, but he managed to say, "Ah—"

"Silence!" roared Michael X, his eyes gleaming. "Apostle of evil and minion of Ummi-Amir, the hyena, you will not be permitted to speak in the haven of righteousness!"

"But I—"

"Silence, I say!" Michael X lowered arms from his chest that looked to Teese like the arms of an ape. His eyes flashed under the pyramid of his turban. "You will follow me."

Then he turned his back and started slowly down the outside aisle. Teese was tempted to turn and bolt through the front door, but he was almost convinced Michael X was capable of springing over the twenty or more feet that separated them like some man-eating tiger and murder him with madman relish.

He followed after the man, strictly against his better judgment, but he felt he was doomed anyway.

The bank building had been reconverted with some thought, and Teese was not so unnerved by Michael X as not to wonder about the impregnable and puzzling mazes leading through many locked doors—all of which Michael X seemed to *command* to open with careless gestures of his hand—into the inner sanctum of Mohammed's Temple No. 6. And, with the pang of the condemned, he knew he had come too far—so far that he could not return without Michael X's aid or consent.

The click of each door closing on Teese's increasing fear seemed the final curtain to his short happy life on Lomax Street and the near-grasped love-dove that was Grace Anderson.

Yet Robert J. Teese was a bearer of a stout, if erratic, heart, and he silently vowed a fight to the death with the imposing black keeper of Allah's Lomax Street estate.

They reached the final door, and, with an elaborate Ali Baba's flourish, Michael X beguiled the heavy black door to open without visible means.

"Enter," he told Teese, and the big man stepped with unheavy feet through the portals of what he imagined might well be hell.

Hell was tolerably civilized, with a neat desk and chairs in one corner, and Lucas West, the handyman, busily applying himself with mop and bucket near the back window. His nubby, roach-like face fell almost audibly when he looked up and saw Teese.

"Peace," Michael X purred to the room at large, raising a wide orange palm and looking directly at its backside.

"Peace," croaked Lucas, looking as though he were trying—and somewhat successfully—to hide in his worn, overlarge overalls.

"Praise be to Allah," Michael X invoked.

"The Beneficent King," Lucas returned.

"Creator of the universe," prompted Michael X.

"Lord of the three worlds," said Lucas, brandishing the mop in what Teese thought was a strange way.

"Blessing be upon our Lord Mohammed!" thrilled Michael X.

"May his wrath fall on the heads of all devils!" Lucas said, with some violence.

In a lower voice, the master of Mohammed's Temple No. 6 said, "Prayer and blessings enduring on Him and grace which unto the day of doom shall remain, amen."

Teese stood mystified and a bit leery of it all. Only last Saturday Lucas had been telling him he was thinking of leaving his wife Emma (and would if he hit his number, 711) because he seemed unable to satisfy her in any way, form or fashion. Now he bellowed along with Michael X like an enraged lion unleashed.

The transformation defied all description, and in his plodding—but not so slow—way, Teese knew Michael X had brought him here expressly to view the weird metamorphosis.

Except for the part where Michael X had something to say about Grace, whom Teese was sure he knew nothing about, Lomax Street's numerical nursemaid was baffled by what he had just witnessed between the two men.

"Be seated," Michael X told him, and gestured to a chair. Reluctantly, Teese sat, and Michael X went to sit majestically behind his desk.

Long fingers tip to tip, he made his eyes burn over the space separating himself and the pickup man.

"You are wondering why you are here," he said.

Teese nodded without answering, intimidated now because Lucas was looking at him with the same accusing stare that sprang from the master's eyes.

"It is Allah's will that you are here," Michael X said matter-of-factly. "Inshallah, it is the wish of the Glorious that you be brought forth from your ignorance and the snares of the devil."

"I ain't snared by no devil," Teese objected. "Maybe you got me mixed up with somebody else."

"Lo, it is written in the holiest of holy books, the Holy Ku'ran," said Michael X, " 'Know ye not your sins in truth, for the devil's diverse guises cloud thy eyes as the sea spray.' In Allah there is liberation, the Wonderful, the All-knowing." He half turned to the little man behind his chair. "Speak, Lucas X."

"Allah is re-demption," Lucas said, speaking as though he'd memorized the lines. "I have been con-verted to the True Faith, the *only* Faith—Allah is right, everything else is wrong!"

Teese looked at him wryly. "I guess you said all that to say you ain't gonna play no numbers today. I don't have to be run down by no beer truck to see the light, Lucas West—I can take a hint!" He started to get up.

"Wait!" Michael X ordered. "So bedazzled are you by the false gems of the devil, you disbelieve *truth*. Hold your peace, son of Ummi-Amir."

Teese sat, but he was becoming a little indignant. "My daddy's name was Napoleon Amsterdam Teese, and I'd be beholdin if you'd remember that fact," he said with anger of pride. "So you can keep your mummy-mammies to yourself!"

For a brief instant Michael X showed a wide row of gleaming, even teeth, like a dog getting set to snap.

"You are the bile of your brothers," he sneered. "You are the lowest dung of the dungheap, and your stink is poisonous! Will you not listen to truth? Will you ever be yoked, the slavering slave, in everlasting bondage to the blue-eyed devil? Yaku, save us!" he thundered. "Strike down this gibbering slave!"

And with this he flung out a long stiff arm with pointing finger, as though to impale Teese.

On finding he was still unstruck, the big man said with encouraged defiance, "I ain't no slave. I live in a free country, and as long as white folks leaves me in peace I got no quarrel."

"In the name of Allah, the Compassionating, the Compassionate," Michael X shouted, "awake! Awake as Lucas X has awakened, as all the Lucas X's in this devil's land have awakened, and fall to Allah before you burn along with your pink gods!"

"Ain't got no pink gods," Teese said stubbornly. "My mother taught me to believe in Jesus Christ and the Good Book—though

I don't follow after them like I should—and that were the only things I cared to believe in."

Michael X laughed in loud disparagment. "The garbled mind-shackle of the rogue King James, and the foolish carpenter. Allah destroy them! Open your eyes, you tail of the back-biter Ummi-Amir, open your eyes and see his hate, his derision of you! He takes your women and makes colored clowns of their sons! He teaches you hate of one another and foreigners, but *love* of him! He uses your labor and toil to dig his bloodied loot, and yet will not let you live in the same neighborhood with him! He thinks of you as filth and causes you to live in it, while making sure the Jewish leeches sap out your soul with rotten meats and products, house you in overpriced dwellings which rightfully belong to the rats who inhabit them! Prostitutes he makes of your daughters, drug addicts of your sons—criminals! And you *love* him!" A thin white froth had risen to the corners of Michael X's mouth, and despite himself Teese couldn't help but be frightened at the wild sight.

"Turn to Allah, fool!" The master rose, pounding his desktop with the power of his next word: "Hate! Hate! *Hate!* Hate the devil as he hates you! Turn from him to Allah's protective wing! Give not your dollars to enrich the whorehouses that sell his cancers! By the beard of Yaku, who, in his kindness, lifted down the white monkey from his treetop home one million years ago and gave him Europe—*hate* the enemy of the Sovereign of the three worlds!"

"Hate!" Lucas cried, his usually mild face now distorted with emotion. He raised the mop handle over his head. "Hate 'im! Hate 'im! He's the cause of it all! Raped my grandmammy, my great-grandmammy! *Got* to hate 'im!"

Michael X trembled, a thin stream of saliva coursing to his neat, pointed goatee. With an effort, he pulled himself together, eyes flashing irrationally in his dark face.

"Infidel!" he threw at Teese, but it was controlled. "Turn from the ways of evil and take unto your soul the Almighty Allah. Forsake your numbers-carrying and tip-sheet-touting, throw down your dream books. Free yourself from the white devil before it is too late, before Allah breathes down His fire of vengeance on him and consumes all who share his bed. Turn, turn, Inshallah! Come unto the sons of Yaku, join the great black wave that will one day soon sweep over the earth, obliterating the unholy one. Yea! all remnants of him! Turn to Allah before you too are sucked up in the mouth of destruction. Allah is right, *you* are wrong!"

It would be an understatement to say Teese was merely moved; Michael X's ear-shattering rhetoric had him tingling with a strange sense of power.

Not even at revival meetings—and he had been to many of them in his day—had he been so moved; and everybody knew how easy it was to get upset in the jangle of tambourines and the ecstatic cries of the plump, bouncing sisters: if a man didn't feel God then, he came mighty *close* to touching Him.

Michael X could not be compared with anything like that, however. Where Teese had felt exhausted at the end of a rivival meeting, he now felt weirdly exhilarated; where evangelical zeal had prompted him to act in the spiritual cause of God, he was now prompted to act in the materialistic name of man.

Understandably ignorant of the origin of Michael X's expert and exhaustively directed plea, Teese did not know that the master was playing on a general racial predicament that appealed to most black brothers, that however much the harangue seemed personally fitted to Robert J. Teese it was in fact the collective first act of all the growing black men in America, on which the curtain had not yet fallen and a better scene was still promised.

Being a race man, and a staunch believer in the Brother's cause, Teese adhered—against his will—to the magnetism of Michael X. But only briefly.

Little did the master, now waiting stone-faced for some reply from Teese, realize that he *almost* had a convert. If he had gone on, if he had detailed the crimes of lynching and police brutality in the big cities, he would have gained a loyal and invaluable subject.

But he gave Teese time to think, and when the big man was set on such a track he was as indomitable as the Maniac. He reasoned that Michael X was right, and that his words were true, as far as he could see—but he saw no immediate solution, and knew the master had none.

Teese's incredulity stemmed from a lack of faith in his own God on the subject of race: for didn't they say God was a righteous God, that He would one day right the white man's wrongs to his black brethren? Yet here they were, three hundred years later, and while they had a Ralph Bunche and Thurgood Marshall, *they* might as well never have existed as far as Lomax Street was concerned.

No, Teese couldn't buy it. If his God saw fit to take His time—and He was known to be a slow but *sure* worker—then he was pretty positive some fella with three worlds to take care of didn't have time for the poor Negro.

Nope, R. J. Teese had to get on with his numbers pickup, and earn his keep. That was all he knew how to do, and he had been doing it now for a good many years. If he gave it up, where would he be? Could he go to Allah for three squares a day?

He shook his head silently. God hadn't sent down any manna from heaven for several thousand years, and if Allah could do any better than that He'd woke up quite a while back to the fact He was making a soft touch of Himself.

"Well," he said, rising, and throwing a glance of wonder at the changed, aggressive countenance of Lucas X. "I guess I'll be gettin along, Mr. X," he told Michael. "I sure do appreciate you talkin to me this way."

At these words, Michael X was done with Teese. It was just impossible, he thought, to change many of the devil's slaves over to the slavery of the growing, pulsing movement that would one day soon take the United States by the throat—the whole world!

He had kept his eye on Teese, picked out his ugly face in one or two of the crowds, and, from hiding, watched him sneak into the Temple to pick up Lucas X's numbers—and had thought him perfectly fitted, after conversion, to the corps of the Temple bodyguards. Allah knew, they would one day have to make use of them.

Evidently he had misjudged the man, and he even went so far as to put his innate perception up to intense scrutiny. Teese bore a quality of independence that was quite unusual for a man of his sort. He was beyond doubt economically pressed, as were most so-called Negroes, and his lack of response to Michael X's verbal purge made the master feel unworthy in the eyes of Allah.

Perhaps it was for the better, he reflected. Teese would probably balk, as had so many others, at the idea of giving up the identifying mark of slavedom, the surname, in lieu of the anonymous X.

Why it meant so much to them, Michael X would never know. But it was not his place to know: such obstinacy was assuredly the will and wisdom of Allah, separating the wheat from the chaff.

"You may go," he told Teese, reseating himself with finality and going into a deep meditation.

Teese was led to the door by Lucas X, who seemed in a trance.

"Infidel," Michael X called out of his meditation. "You may return here as you please; perhaps you will find truth, if Allah so permits."

"Thanks," Teese said, able to perform that easy grin once more, now that he was leaving.

Lucas X raised a hand, and it was at his slow, groping movement that Teese saw the little lights in the door jamb, just like they had in the doorway of the Harlem Market for folks who had their arms loaded with groceries and couldn't open the door themselves. On discovering the electronic eyes, he felt even better.

He gave Lucas a poke in the ribs as they went down the hallway. "Boy, you sure got a good thing, Luke! If you act at home the way you did in there you'll scare the *hell* out of Emma."

"Allah is the only God," Lucas said. "Allah is right, all else is wrong."

"Aw, c'mon, Luke," Teese said. "You don't have to put on with me. You just converted to that Allah-ism so you could play your numbers in peace and bulldoze Emma."

"Allah is God," Lucas said.

When Teese saw the blank look in his friend's eyes, he knew it was no use—Lucas was lost.

It only convinced him more that Allah and Michael X were not for him.

And it were a damn shame about Lucas, he thought. Never done nothin or bothered nobody—and havin to get Allah-ed up this way.

Ah, well, Teese had his Grace—despite what Michael X had said about her—and that was religion enough for him, though he still couldn't beat down that sorry feeling he had for Lucas.

Then, thinking of Grace, he remembered their appointment, and knew he'd have to hurry if he wanted to be on time.

At the entrance, Lucas admitted the noon sunlight to the many-chaired hall and Teese stepped out with a sigh of relief.

Before he had gone ten feet he heard a sharp whisper, and turned to hear Lucas X-nee-West hissing at him:

"Put me a nickel on 711 in both races! I'll pay up when I come around to the poolroom tonight!"

Teese thought, with a smile, that the only thing man could successfully convert was a furnace. And even some of them were hard-headed.

*Woman is subtle, mystic proto-
plasm, through which a man might
place a hand and draw forth smoke;
inherent guile and self-preserving
fantasy compose the whole, and when
a man feels the innocence in a comely
face, mark down the proof of his basic
ignorance: for there is where the
evil surely lies.*

CHAPTER SIX

*N*ow GRACE ANDERSON, at twenty-five, can be described with only one word: delicious. At least, that's what most men would say of her, because of that mouth-drooling sensation they got when gazing on her young, man-motherly breasts and those aggravated feminine accessories.

Her sisters, world-renowned for their wretched appreciation of other women's attributes, referred to Grace's qualities in more precise, if not flattering, terms.

Yet they had to admit that what Grace had could not be duplicated, just as there is only one Mona Lisa in the world, one *Rites of Spring*. There is a chance Eve might have been Grace's original blueprint, and if she was it's no wonder Adam defied God for her.

Grace was a conglomerate that was both interesting and startling to see. Somewhere down the Anderson family line, perhaps during the Indian wars, some cautious and softfooted Blackfoot buck had come and gone unseen to the pallet of a trembling Anderson mammy and left his mark nearly a century and a quarter later in the long, black, straight hair of great-granddaughter Grace. Evidently the great-grandmother had contributed both white and black blood to the strain, for Grace had hazel eyes set over high cheekbones and curving, fat, blood-cherry cupid's bow lips.

Her coloring also gave proof that whites, blacks, Indians and Mexicans came closer together in the days of yore than our history books would have us believe. In moments of stress—or denouncement—Grace could chameleonize alternately from shades of spring peach, to summer MacIntosh, and complete the cycle with autumn cling and fall Jonathans.

And as to her body, some said she could have been sired by a bull, though Pete Anderson, before he died, was more likened to an exhausted burro, what with the tribulations he had in raising two motherless, hell-raising youngsters, and trying to operate a thriving moving business to boot.

Folks said poor Pete would turn over in his grave if he could see how his efforts had gone to pot.

Son Ely's mismanagement of the business verged on the criminal, what with his extravagant nocturnal sorties against every bar in town, accompanied by a couple of free-loading cronies and four or five willing females. Notable also were his invariably losing forays at the notorious Roundhouse gambling den on Lomax.

And Grace—little Grace whom he had counseled like a mother, which indeed Pete was at the time—had turned into just the swivel-hipped, conniving Jezebel he had prayed God she wouldn't.

Grace, however, was victim of her own beauty. Ever since she could remember—even as an overly developed pre-teenage girl—men had paid her unusual attention. Before she realized she could take advantage of all the fun she was having with them, she had run, and defeated, the gauntlet of some fifteen or so irrevocably and eternally smitten swains.

Immediately she revamped her tactics and began to play the game for what it was worth. But Grace was a demanding consort, and it wasn't long before her disgruntled Lomax Street beaus had passed the word around that her kind of love was most expensive and never lasting.

Enter here handsome Roy-boy Beavers, bearing in his classy skull Grace's first defeat. Call it love, call it madness; whatever it was Grace was lost in the frigid, unscrupulous, mercenary vise of the aspiring young pimp.

"Baby," he confided to her at the peak of their lovemaking one night, "you got to take care of me to keep me."

"Oh, yes, Roy!" she had cried, and from that night on she had been inescapably bound to her promise.

Now that the shoe was on the other foot, Grace was aware of its pinch. Roy created new, and deadly, vistas for her talents, and whatever reluctance she felt was quickly extinguished by his current threat:

"There's plenty women would do for me, baby. Now you take

that Rosy Dawn—she loves my B.V.D.'s. I snap my fingers, and she'd lick my shoes."

Therefore, Grace *had* to apply herself, didn't she?

Vigorously she captured every well-to-do stranger who unsuspectingly stumbled into her various Lomax Street traps, and led him to the Beavers's boarding house, where Roy awaited. His end consisted of waiting till the last possible moment, then rushing into the transient room the couple had engaged, the indignant, knife-wielding husband.

It had all worked fine, and very profitably—but Roy had been a trifle late on several occasions.

The idea never crossed Grace's mind that Roy would one day fail to appear at all and that she would be painlessly initiated to the famous club, in which he had already reserved for her a first-class membership.

No, all Grace knew at the moment was that she and Roy had sheared the wrong lamb too close, and needed money to leave town right away, before the lamb carried out his threats to go to the police.

What to do?

Roy's aunt, who owned the boarding house, certainly was too wise to put any funds at Roy's disposal, even with the happy knowledge (to use a phrase of the Rt. Reverend Jones) he would leave town with it: she trusted Roy about as far as she could take him on her sixty-year-old shoulders and carry him out of town herself.

No, Roy had said, she was out for certain. And he hadn't been paying enough attention to Rosy Dawn lately to put the bite on her, although he told Grace he'd probably call her up, just to make sure, sometime today.

The moving business? Ely didn't earn enough money to keep gas in the truck tanks. Furthermore, the trucks no longer belonged to the Andersons but to the Second National Bank.

They were in a funk until Grace thought about the pickup man, Teese, the only individual on Lomax who hadn't directly or indirectly been touched by a Roy-Grace scheme. What's more, Grace recalled that awed, lightning-struck look Teese gave her every time he came up to get brother Ely's good-money-after-bad list of numbers.

They began working on Teese three weeks ago, in cooperation with the spineless, money-hungry Ely, who was currently in rather dark esteem as far as the proprietors of the Roundhouse, who held his IOU's, were concerned.

Roy had been able to put off the lamb till tonight, with the information that Teese had popped the fatal question Saturday night.

"It's perfect," Roy had gloated. "There's always a heavy play on Monday, and he'll have just what we need to leave town with. Boy, I can just see that lamb's face when he finds out we're gone tonight!"

But Grace wasn't at all sure she was as good an actress as she needed to be in order to get Teese to release his plays to her.

Switching her hippy way down Lomax now in that black, buttock-gripping silk dress she used in her business ventures, she couldn't help slowing her pace as she neared the point of rendezvouz, Bill's Bar.

She felt kind of sorry for R. J. Teese, though this feeling lasted for only a moment.

She had to remember the lines Roy had coached her in so carefully, or they would both be sorrier than moose-faced Teese could ever be.

Pumping up her convictions with false justification, Grace entered Bill's air-conditioned, velvet-plush hideaway, ignoring the leers and silent astonishment of the Monday-noon bar patrons. Her eyes searched the back booths, near the empty bandstand

Yes, there he was, exactly where she'd told him to be eyes lighted up on her like hundred-watt bulbs.

She went over and slid into his booth, facing him on the other side of the table between.

"How do, Miz Grace," Teese said, fairly electrocuted by her presence, not quite able to believe she was sitting here with him.

"Hello, Bobbie-Joe," she said, and made her voice sound distracted.

Teese's wide grin faded. "Why, is anything wrong? You look kinda under the weather."

"Oh," Grace said, with that same, faraway voice, eyes lowered. "Oh, no, Bobbie-Joe. I guess I'm all right."

Though not convinced, Teese grinned once more. "Well, maybe a drink would pep you up. It's so hot today . . ."

"I think I'll have a Bud, Bobbie-Joe."

He called the bartender over and gave him the order, making sure he ordered Coke for himself (didn't want Grace to think he was a lush, though she was free to drink what she wanted).

After the drinks came, Grace merely twirled her fingers about the bottle, adding to Teese's concern.

"Oh, Bobbie-Joe!" she said suddenly, lifting those big—now sad—hazel eyes to him.

"Yeah, Miz Grace?" he said, startled by her voice and ready to leap over the table to her aid.

"Bobbie-Joe—" Her voice trembled. "I don't know how to tell you this . . ."

"Tell me what, Miz Grace?" he said, fearing the worst.

She forced her words out, studied pain in her big eyes. "About *us*, Bobbie-Joe."

Teese, staring at her apprehensively, could not urge her on. He felt his heart choke up his throat, and a drink of Coke only served to make him sputter and strangle.

"Oh, Bobbie-Joe," Grace wailed, sotto-voce. "You know I love you, don't you?"

"Yes, Miz Grace," Teese said, eagerly shaking his head like a mechanical man at this tremendous revelation.

"You *know* I wouldn't do anything to hurt you," she said, looking at him with filmed eyes.

"Yes, Miz Grace!"

"I think you're the nicest, finest man in the world, Bobbie-Joe."

"Thank you, Miz Grace—"

"And I think I could make you a good wife."

"So do I, Miz Grace!"

"But I couldn't—" And here she paused for emphasis, shielding her eyes with heavy lashes. "—let you become the husband of a woman about to go to jail!"

Teese's mouth fell, and the wobbly lower bridge almost dropped out on the table.

"*What* did you say, Miz Grace?"

With exceptional bravery and dignity, Grace continued, "Today I will go to jail unless I can raise five thousand dollars."

Teese closed his mouth with an effort. "Five thousand—" *Click*, his mouth shut, teeth nipping tongue.

Grace tossed her long black hair with doomed finality. "That's why I cannot ask you to be my husband."

"But, Miz Grace—"

"Oh, Bobbie-Joe, I don't know *how* it happened! All I know is I signed some papers for a delivery or something—furniture—while Ely was away, and it all disappeared. I *know* I shouldn't have done it, but—I'm willing to pay for my mistake."

"Ain't there no way—?" Teese started.

"None. We didn't have any insurance. The way it looks, I was in on it some way." She hung her head. "Now I'm going to jail!"

"Oh, no, you ain't," Teese said protectively. "Not if I can help it, you ain't!"

Grace gave him a dry, beaten smile. "Bobbie-Joe, I know you'd like to help, but I know too you can't raise five thousand dollars."

"Well, naw, maybe I can't, but—"

"I'll just have to *pay* for the crime. Prison is the only thing left for me."

"Now, wait a minute," Teese said. "Maybe I can raise a little money."

Her eyes brightened. "You can? Oh, Bobbie-Joe, how much? How much have you got right now?"

"Well . . . about a hundred and seventy, but—"

"That's just right!" Grace told him happily.

"But I thought you said five thousand," Teese said. "And, anyway, this is my pickup money."

"No, Bobbie-Joe, what I meant is, it's just enough for us to leave town together—go someplace where we can get a good, fresh start together."

"Now, wait a minute," Teese said, shaking his head. "You just can't run away, Miz Grace—"

"Wouldn't you want to come? Don't you love me?"

"Well, sure I do, but—"

"Or would you rather have me stay and go to jail for something I didn't do, for ninety-nine years, then come out an ex-convict and an old bag?"

Perish the thought from Teese's mind. "I know you know better than that, Miz Grace, but—"

"Just think, Bobbie-Joe," she implored him. "Tomorrow we'd be married; about this time tomorrow we'd just be waking up in our bridal suite, loving each other . . ."

Teese's eyes faded with the delectable dream, but reality would not be so easily backhanded. "Still—"

Grace burst into tears, the final stratagem against his stubbornness. "You don't love me!"

"But I *do*, Miz Grace, I love you more than anything!"

"Then prove it," she demanded. "Give me the money so I can go right down to the train station and get the tickets."

Teese writhed in the trap. "Miz Grace, you know I can't do that—"

"I *told* you you didn't love me!" she sobbed.

"Oh, Miz Grace," he said with pain. "If you knew how much I loved you, you wouldn't say nothin like that. But I just can't up and run off with other folks' money."

She fixed him with a wet, accusing stare. "You could if you loved me enough. But that's all right, Mr. Teese, I'll always remember you were a good friend, while I'm serving time in prison."

The "Mr. Teese" did it. He reached a huge, comforting hand across the table to cover the lily of her palm.

"Don't you worry," he said. "I promise I'll have some money together. I'll see my bossman, Mr. Canelli."

"What time?" she said, interested again. "*Those people* might come to get me any time."

230

"Just as soon as I turn in at the House," he told her. "I been workin for my bossman a long time; he's got confidence in me. He knows I'll pay him back."

"But how can you pay him back if you go away with me?"

"Go away?" he said in surprise. "Can't I just get a couple hundred for you to hold 'em off till my number comes through? I ain't hit in about two months, Miz Grace, and I don't think it'll be long before I do."

"Well, I guess so," she said. "But you'd better hurry it up if you don't want to see me go to jail."

"Oh, I *will,* Miz Grace," he promised. "I'll have the money for sure."

"Well, you just better be sure you do," she warned. "Or maybe there won't be any marriage at all."

The thought made Teese shudder. "Don't you worry, Miz Grace."

She rose. "I guess I'll be going, Bobbie-Joe."

"But you ain't drinked your Bud, Miz Grace, and I thought we were gonna talk some more—sorta plan things."

She smiled down her pretended anguish. "You understand, don't you, Bobbie-Joe? I'd better be there . . . in case they come for me."

"Don't you worry," Teese said. "I'll take care of everything."

"I know you will, Bobbie-Joe."

With one last, weak smile, she turned and started out.

Rigid, Teese watched—as did everyone else in the place—Grace wiggle to the exit. His breath came hard as his eyes followed the molded, senuous backside, and it was all he could do to keep from dashing after the flashing high heels.

He drank his Coke in a daze.

Of the incongruities of Grace's story, he did not think—nor would he permit himself to see them.

The only thing that was important to him was that Grace needed money—and he was going to get it for her, some way—any way.

Idly he touched the secret pocket wherein reposed the hundred and seventy dollars, thinking that it would indeed be paradise to be lying with Grace tomorrow in the bridal suit of some sumptuous hotel.

That would really be something!

He drained the last drops from the bottle and got up to leave, as sure of getting some money from his bossman, Boots Canelli, as Moses was of leading his people across the Red Sea on dry land.

He had to: Grace had said she loved him, and that was the first time anyone so wonderful as her had told him a thing like that.

It is recorded that Xenophtex,
a heathen god, went to prove his
greatness in moving a huge and
very ugly mountain on the landscape
below his heaven. When
all had failed, the sweating Xenophtex
asked impatiently of the
uncooperative, age-old spire:
"Why do you balk?" And replied
the mountain calmly: "You give
me cause."

CHAPTER SEVEN

THEY SAY A GOOD MAN is hard to find nowadays, but a man who can hold his temper and pride in the face of gross insult and perfidy is just as rare.

Such was the fiber of Samuel Dawn, an individual who was not the fool Bea Green and Rosy Dawn thought him to be.

For eight years—the tenure of his marriage to Rosy, whom he had courted in the Land of Cotton—Sam had taken especial pains to give people the impression that he was oblivious of his wife's extra-marital activities, and her army of admirers.

It wasn't that Sam didn't *care*—in fact, he loved Rosy better than the prize dahlia he had been grooming for the annual florists' show in Phoenix—he was just a man who loved peace and content-ment, Rosy's as well as his own. As long as nothing interfered with the operation of Dawn's Floral Shoppe, or Rosy's casual but warm affection toward him, Sam, who had on several occasions attended one of Father Devine's churches in Chicago and heard the fat God on Earth give an inspiring delivery, was at peace with the world (Peace! it's wonderful!).

But when he was not at peace, which meant his pocketbook was involved, that was another thing.

Rosy had just received a phone call from that fella Roy Beavers, the conversation of which Sam had overheard on the extension phone (secretly installed) under the tulip bed in the hothouse.

All right, he said to himself, that call was all right and good enough.

He knew about Roy Beavers, about the Rev. Jones, too. Sam allowed that he wasn't a good-looking man at all, what with the livid razor scars that crisscrossed his black face, the winner's pot in a crooked backwoods poker game twenty years ago—in which he was the innocent, if somewhat misunderstood, bystander.

That was all right with Sam—Roy Beavers and the Rev. Jones, that is. Lord knew, Rosy was a good-looking yellow woman, and, just like a flower, she could wilt quite easily if she didn't get the right working around the roots.

But, now, Sam's hard-earned money—that was another thing! He didn't mind Rosy having a good time—could not find the power in himself to deny her a good time—but his money—!

At first he had cursed himself for a snoopy-nosed old man when he had the phone installed in the hothouse. Rosy had been getting more than the usual calls lately on the phone at the front of the shop, and he couldn't help getting a little jittery about them.

So he had put the phone in while she was away on one of her jaunts with "Cousin Lena," not to snoop, mind you—just to *listen* a bit. He knew she never came to the hothouse except to call him out, so he wasn't too worried about being discovered.

He had felt guilty about it at first, but be-damned if he wasn't glad now!

Softly, he put the phone back on the hook and wiped warm, moist soil from his fingers.

Of all the things he thought Rosy capable of doing, he didn't think she'd almost beg to give *his* money to another man! A woman like her, fine-looking as she was, could name *her* price, if it came to that.

Sam got up from his knees, shaking his head sadly.

Two hundred dollars!

He picked up his potting trowel and drove it into the tulip bed thoughtfully. Jesus knew he'd done everything he could for that woman, except give her what she needed to stay home nights—and his work with the flowers took most of that out of him during the day.

Two hundred dollars!

He began to burn with the thought. He could just see her tonight, the money clutched tightly in her fist, skulking off to the rear of the Anderson Moving Co. *His* money for some other man!

But, then, hadn't it always been some other man before him? *Remember,* Sam prompted himself, *remember Alabama? Remember how you'd been courtin her for nigh on five years, then she went out with that high-steppin Tarlow Hightower and got knocked up? And who married her before the little boy were born dead? It sure weren't Tarlow Hightower!*

But Sam Dawn's tolerance bordered on the saintly, and he really couldn't blame Rosy for that. She was twenty-two at the time, and he forty-four. During the first couple of years, she had tried—she had really, honestly tried.

He blamed himself mostly: because there hadn't been another baby, because he just couldn't seem to fall into the married scheme of things and earn them a Southern living.

She had been patient, and in the first years after their sojourn to the North she had helped direct and add prosperity to his consuming love of flowers.

"Still, that don't excuse it!" Sam found himself saying aloud, digging the trowel in the bed violently and unearthing a few bulbs.

All that didn't excuse this new thing! She didn't have any right to take his hard-earned money and give it to some tramp who didn't give a damn about nobody but himself!

The flowers tried to talk Sam out of his anger, but this time it didn't do any good. It wasn't just some little case where he could come in and talk over his troubles with them, smell their fragrance of reply, their wise, human-knowing answers.

No, this time, for the first time in years, Sam had been stepped on where it hurt, and he wasn't going to just lay and take it!

He saw Rosy come out of the front building and glide voluptuously across the short space of yard to the hothouse.

He turned his face away and made himself think peace. Time enough later, he thought. Later.

She rapped on the window, and he threw down the trowel and took off his earth-stained apron.

Outside, he could feel her happiness. Her face was beaming, and her fine lips had the healthy glow of fresh roses.

"Teese is here," she said. "You gonna play?"

"I guess so," he said.

"Wait'll I tell you," she said with a giggle. "Teese is gonna *marry* Grace Anderson!"

"Do tell?" Sam said. "And who told you about it?"

She hesitated but an instant before telling the lie. "Cousin Lena just called; she told me. She said the Rev. Jones passed on the news when he stopped this mornin to find out how she's gettin along."

"Do tell?" Sam said, going into the shop. He wondered how *big* a fool Rosy thought he was. Only yesterday he had met her Cousin Lena on Lomax, near the sanctified church she attended, where he was delivering flowers for a funeral. She had been as hale and hearty as a racehorse, with that same turntable bird jabber—and she'd mentioned that she hadn't seen Rosy in over a month.

Teese did indeed look like a man struck dumb, Sam noticed when he entered: dreamily Teese was staring at the window display and a wedding corsage.

"Hello, there, Mr. Teese," Sam said.

"Oh—how do, Mr. Dawn?" the big man said, turning. "What you figure for the first race today?"

Rosy had come in behind Sam.

"Adultery," he said in a bland voice. "Dreamed it last night."

He could almost feel Rosy stiffen.

"That plays for 319 and 932," Teese informed him.

"Yeah, I know," Sam said. "I looked it up in the dream book." He rung the cash register and took out his numbers slips, written earlier, and money from under the change drawer. "Here y'are, Mr. Teese. And it sure is about time you started bringin insteada *gettin,* all the time."

"Ain't that the truth?" Teese laughed in that honeyed rumble. He took the slips, investigating them idly, and put them away with the money. "Sure wish I could hit my number—I'm gonna need it."

"Yeah," Sam said. "I heard you're plannin to hitch up with that Anderson girl. I hope you know where to bring your flower business."

A brief look at Rosy told Teese that the news was now well

along; no doubt she had heard him tell the Rev. Jones that morning, or the Reverend had told her.

"I sure do," he assured Sam. "If we're gonna live together in this old world, we might as well scratch each other's backs."

"That's a good thought, Mr. Teese."

"Well, I got to be gettin, Mr. Dawn—gettin late. If your number comes you can count on me bein around this evenin."

"I'll sure count on it," Sam said.

There was a wild, unreasonable warning for Teese on his lips, but Sam let him walk out, puzzled by the feeling.

He wasn't one for gossip, but you couldn't help hearing some of the things customers brought into your shop about people like Grace Anderson and Roy Beavers. It didn't matter that ninety-nine percent of the tales were pure fabrication—it was the one percent that counted.

He retraced his thoughts to the name Roy Beavers. Hadn't Grace Anderson been going with him? Someone had mentioned it to him—probably Rosy, in one of her spurned, malicious moods.

Grace Anderson, Roy Beavers, Rosy and Teese—and *his* two hundred dollars, sucked away by that smooth voice—could they all be hooked in together some way?

Sam hovered over the open cash drawer, torn by the inner ambivalences of anger and fear—fear for the homely, innocuous, gregarious Teese.

"Ain't that somethin?" Rosy giggled behind him. "Teese marryin Grace Anderson!"

Sam shut the drawer a little too hard and went over to stare out the window after Teese.

"It's almost unbelievable!" Rosy said, unable to hide her rapture.

Sam began to arrange some of his floral displays, thinking, trying to put it all together.

Behind him, Rosy shuffled restlessly. He heard the snap of the delivery clipboard on the counter.

"You got a bouquet for Shriner's Hall at 2:30," she reminded him.

"Yeah," he said vaguely. "I'll take care of that."

"Then Rev. Henderson's church, a funeral."

"Uh-huh."

"And what about Mrs. Calloway's daughter's weddin?"

"Yeah," Sam said.

"Are you listenin to me, Samuel Dawn?" she said snappily.

"I sure am," he told her without turning.

"Then you better see to these appointments."

"They'll take good care of theyselfs," Sam said. "Don't you worry about 'em."

"Wel, if *I* don't, you, sure as Martin Luther King's a black man, won't! Quit fussin with them flowers and get to it, now."

He stopped and came around the counter to get his coat.

She looked at him closely as he put it on. "You feelin all right?"

"Just a headache," he said thoughtfully.

"Why don't you stop in the house and get an aspirin before you leave?"

"That's what I were thinkin on doin." He started out by the side door that led to the living quarters of the shop.

"Oh, Sam," she called.

He turned.

The happy glow of her skin made it look as though it were on fire. "Cousin Lena said when she called she were still feelin poorly. She wants me to come over to sit with her a spell this evenin."

"That's okay with me," he said.

"Just thought I'd tell ya, in case the shop's locked up if you're late."

"I'll be back before you go."

Without another word he went directly into the house to their neat bedroom.

It had really been only a thought, but her last words had convinced him.

It were always my thinkin, he reflected, *that if trouble were to come at all, it might as well be big trouble as small.*

There were some things a man just could not stand, even if he had to sacrifice the peace and security of his position and home. This was one of them.

With the one-tracked thoroughness of a non-violent man forced to action, Sam searched his and Rosy's room for the thing that would equalize and avenge his circumstance.

In a dusty shoebox, in the far reaches of the closet, he found it.

The Owlhead .32 glistened in all its deadly, hammerless beauty under his hesitant fingertips.

Now that he had found it, he put it back and straightened every article he'd disturbed.

It had been a long time since he had even thought about the pistol, but he hadn't forgotten how to use it.

When he came home later, he would tend and grease its parts as carefully and as lovingly as though it were his prize dahlia.

*In the high grass a snake may
lurk, coiled, grinning, fangs
bared in waiting.
It is only a fool who would leave
the certaintly of his world to ac-
cost the serpent in the tall, green,
well-known shelter of his own.*

CHAPTER EIGHT

CALL ROY BARTHOLOMEW BEAVERS what you will, he never represented himself—unless it suited his immediate plans—as anything other than he was: a hustler.

While still a boy, Roy was as certain of his calling as most men of their sex. And he hadn't been without encouragement: the escapades of his flashy father, Jim Beavers, were still talked about up and down Lomax. It was these which were said to have driven his wife Sadie to an early grave.

Despite the admonitions of his old maid sister, Chloe Beavers, Jim did not counsel the boy to a straight and narrow path. Roy could remember going many times with his father to the Lomax Inn, a now-defunct establishment, and watching him whip several hefty females for their "laziness" and failure to "come through" for him. The boy never ceased to be impressed by his father's power, the almost life-and-death omniscience he held over the women who worked for him.

But Jim's iron hand and Don Juan characteristics inevitably led to his downfall. Roy could recall vividly the night on which he'd heard the *pop-pop* of Katie Thurmond's .25 in his father's room of the boarding house, the screams of Aunt Chloe and Katie herself, the blood that had splattered the wall over the bed when one of the two slugs that entered his head struck Jim point-blank above the left eye.

It was a nightmare Roy had sometimes; every bit of it came back to him—but with a difference: *he* was both Roy and Jim, and he felt in that last moment of dying the terror, the fear and the soul-wracking *need* to live on.

Sometimes he would awake with whomever shared his bed at the moment, sweating and trembling, thanking his twisted idea of God that it hadn't been real.

Perhaps it was this adhesion, this death-wish, that gave him his fear and loathing of all firearms; his skin crawled on seeing them, as one's skin might crawl on seeing a snake or some other slimy reptile.

Thirty in five months, Roy, when he was a bit younger, had been drafted as a matter of course during a blunder of national importance, and had been shipped overseas, where his commanding officers found his fear of combat and all methods and machines antecedent of combat was exceeded only by his native talent for goldbricking.

Therefore, it wasn't long before he was brought to home port with his undesirable papers in his hand, and was able to return to a career that had been nipped in the bud by military service.

This did not mean that Roy had an aversion to all forms of combatant skirmishes, however; he was, as a matter of fact, quite effectively vicious against love-struck women, small boys and sexagenarian aunts.

In actuality, shucked of his hard-talking, threatening well-dressed facade, he was the plain, everyday coward with whom one comes in contact during the course of an afternoon.

You couldn't have told this to Grace Anderson, though, or Rosy Dawn or Aunt Chloe, who had been verbally stormed into silence when she objected against the badger game Roy and Grace were operating in the boarding house. Though she was cowed, she was equally tight-fisted, and Roy met an unbreachable wall when he attacked her financial defenses.

He was confident, however, that she would die soon and leave him everything—though what he couldn't know was that Aunt Chloe had willed everything to the National Negro College Fund, in the hope it would help a Roy Beavers who had stumbled that far, and so mend his ways with her milk of human kindness. She had long since given up any hope for her nephew's moral rehabilitation.

Of course Roy did not know this, and he felt pretty certain in his knowledge that he could travel the ends of the Earth and still come back to claim his rightful inheritance, since he was the last of the Beavers line.

And to the ends of the Earth he might well have to go, if his current scheme didn't come to its projected head.

Sitting now with bug-eyed, slick-haired, tallow-skinned Ely— the antithesis of sister Grace—a tall glass of Scotch and creme de cacao mixed in his expertly manicured paw, Roy felt pretty certain, after his talk with Rosy Dawn, that things would work out.

"That gal's gonna take care of everything," he grinned from his prone position on the couch, at the doubtful, pacing Ely. "With what baby Grace brings home from the fool, we'll all be sittin pretty!"

Ely rubbed his hands together nervously, and buzzed out in his high, dissipated voice, "Man, I sure hope so! Them Roundhouse boys ain't gonna like it if I don't come up with their money tonight."

"I told you me and Grace'd take care of you before we left. Don't worry," Roy said calmly.

"I can't help worryin!" Ely said. "Them Roundhouse boys mess a man up if he welches."

"Then you should play poker with gentlemen," Roy said gen-teelly. "Leastways, you ain't got the brains to gamble with them Roundhouse sharpies, Ely, you know that."

"I just thought I could win—thought I could get some of these haints off my back."

"You put 'em there," Roy said with contempt. "Don't blame nobody but yourself."

"There you go," Ely accused, "talkin just like Grace! When a man gets to be twenty-six years old, he don't need nobody to chastise 'im!"

Roy laughed and sipped at his drink. "He *do* if he act like he's six years old."

Ely twisted his hands impatiently. "You and Grace just won't understand! This bad luck's decided to hang onto me, and there ain't nothing I can do to shake it off."

"Ssssht!" Roy said in disgust, raising up to a sitting position on the couch. "You been crying about bad luck since the day I saw you! Don't you know you got to *think,* man? Ain't you got no idea of what the game is?"

244

Ely took two mad steps toward him, bug-eyes bugged incredibly. "Yeah, I know what the game is! I know what kinda game you're gonna play on Grace. I know all this business with Teese is just the start of somethin she'll never be able to get out of."

His blind insight struck its target.

"Just take it easy," Roy placated. "I ain't got nothin but good thoughts for your little sister. I plan to make her the belle of New York—this little jerkwater town cramps her style."

It was certainly necessary to ease Ely's worry at this point, Roy reasoned. An hysterical outburst like this in front of Grace could do a lot in the way of blowing his meal ticket right out the window. She still needed a lot of tutoring before she was ripe.

"Sit down, boy," he soothed. "Rest your nerves. Grace'll be back with that heavy green in a few minutes, and you'll be too excited to do what you got to do with it."

"Yeah," Ely said, seating himself in a chair that seemed to bounce gently with his inner turmoil. "If I could drop fifty bucks on those boys, maybe they'd let me slide for a while."

Roy got up and found the White Horse on the dining-room table and made Ely a drink.

"Take this," he said, coming back. "Get right with the world, man. Thank the Lord for a sucker!"

They toasted that, and a thin smile began to spread across Ely's pallid face.

"I just hope—" he started.

"Don't worry," Roy said, going back to the couch.

"But what about that Teese?" Ely said, discovering a new dilemma. "Suppose he comes up here after he finds out you and Grace are gone? Suppose he gives me some trouble? You know he asked me if it was okay for him and Grace to get married. Maybe he'll blame me, and I'm too small for that big man to get mad at."

"Didn't I tell you not to worry?" Roy said irritably. "I got a little plan all set up that'll take care of Mr. Teese, the pickup man. He'll be too busy to worry about you."

Ely wasn't convinced. "Maybe I better get outta town too."

"Are you a complete damn fool?" Roy snapped at him. "You

got the business to take care of, and if *it's* no good you still got the building; your old man was smart enough to pay it off."

"It's mortgaged too," Ely revealed glumly.

"Well, I'll be damned!"

"So I ain't got no reason to stay on," he said hurriedly.

Roy got up. "Well, you sure as hell ain't goin with us! I'll have enough trouble lookin out for Grace, less more you."

Ely silently agreed, although he couldn't help thinking he was being made the scapegoat in some way.

Roy strode around the room with the satisfied knowledge that all his plans would soon be consummated. The two hundred dollars from Rosy Dawn would cover expenses till he had lined Grace up for the right action, and what she got from Teese would more than cover their train fare.

It was a pity that they couldn't set Teese up for more—indeed, Roy had envisioned a long-range con of the pickup man, under more suitable circumstances—but perhaps Grace would surprise him.

And surprise him she did when the door opened and she came tentatively into the room, her eyes burning with failure and begging forgiveness of him.

"You didn't get it!" he barked.

"Roy, honey—"

"Shut up! You let that stupe crawl out! I got a good mind to clear out right now and leave your silly butt!"

Grace tried to touch him, but he shoved her away.

"Please, Roy," she begged, "let me tell you what happened."

"Did you get the money?" he shouted.

"No, but—"

"Then you can't tell me nothin! If you don't want me to shove a fist in your big, dumb mouth, keep it closed!" He fumed about the room.

Ely sat ineffectually by, gripped in horror by thoughts of what the Roundhouse boys would do to him. Grimly, he was trying to decide between hanging and a dose from the can of Drano Grace kept in the kitchen.

"You're the stupidest woman I ever met!" Roy trumpeted wildly at Grace. "Didn't I tell you what to do? Didn't I tell you how to rub that sucker up? Ain't you got even an ounce of brains? I shoulda stuck with Rosy Dawn, that's what I shoulda did! At least *she* can scrape up some money for her man, when he needs it!"

This charge caused Grace to bow her head briefly, since she was not allowed to speak in her own defense. Silently she waited while Roy ran through his colorful and humiliating list of adjectives, heaping them all generously on her, and only after he'd finished and yelled at her, "Right, stupid?" did she speak.

"Teese is going to get the money for me right now," she said. "He wouldn't touch that numbers money for me or nobody. He says he's gonna borrow some from his bossman."

Rage faded from Roy's face. "He did, huh?"

"He promised me. As soon as he gets it he'll bring it right up here to me."

"Well," Roy said in a different voice, and she drew to the tone of it.

"Roy, honey, you knew I'd do all I could," she said in small rebuke, eyes fired with love.

"Yeah, yeah," he said impatiently. "You did okay. He said for sure, huh?"

"He promised. Teese'll come with the money, you can count on it."

"Well," he said again, going to get himself another drink. "I guess we can relax, huh?"

"I told you, honey—"

"Yeah, yeah," he said, annoyed at her cloying devotion. Much as he had cultivated the seed grown into affectionate slavery, he was revolted by it at times. "When did he say he'd be by?"

"I don't know, but I told him to hurry it up."

"Yeah. Did he say how much?"

She nodded. "He said a couple hundred, more than he had on him when I saw him."

Roy chewed at his lip thoughtfully. "That kinda messes things up, that borrowin. I had somethin else planned for Teese; I want him completely out of the way. If I ever come back to this thick town, I don't wanna be runnin into him."

"But do we have to, Roy?" she said. "Couldn't we just leave it like this, without hurting him more?"

He squinted at her. "What's the matter? You gettin soft for that fathead?"

"No, but—"

"Then shut up and let me do the figurin." He went over to the window and stood there silently for a long while. Then Grace saw his slim body stiffen as he gazed out.

"Hey," he said. "Here comes Teese now. He must be on his way up here!"

"It's too early," she said, looking at her watch. "He doesn't turn in for another hour."

"Then he must be comin up to get Ely's plays." He whirled, his handsome face bright with inspiration. "Ely . . . *Ely!*"

Ely jerked from his trance as though he had been mortally wounded. "*What?*"

Roy pulled him up roughly. "C'mon in the kitchen with me. Hurry it up!"

Ely stumbled wildly into the dining room, half expecting the arrival of the Roundhouse boys.

"Now listen," Roy told Grace in a strict whisper. "This is what I want you to do: when Teese comes up, fall all over him, go crazy. Tell him them people've already been by and they won't take nothin but *all* the money."

"But, Roy, Teese can't—"

"Shut up!" he hissed. "I know what I'm doin! Tell Teese you're sure as hell goin to jail if you can't raise the money by this evenin. I know he can't get nothin *like* five thousand, but he may be payin off some hits this evenin—and if you play it right we'll have more than a couple lousy hundred, and I'll be able to take care of him the way I figured."

"But how *can* I, Roy?"

His eyes bore a sneer as they traced her round, plump young body. "With what you got, do I have to tell you *how?* All I got to say is you'd *better!* Go the limit if you have to—you've done it before."

He left her standing there just as Teese's knock sounded on the door.

In the kitchen he pushed aside the blubbering, petrified Ely and leaned an ear against the door.

"How do again, Miz Grace?" Teese's deep, slurring voice came. "Just stopped by to pick up your brother's numbers on my way to the House . . . Why, what's the matter, Miz Grace?"

"Oh, Bobbie-Joe!" her voice sobbed.

"Has them folks been by, Miz Grace? Is that it?"

"Oh, help me, Bobbie-Joe! I'd do anything if you'd just help me!"

Roy's thin smile allowed Grace was learning fast. He had, at last, twirled the right combination.

"*Anything,* Bobbie-Joe!"

"Miz Grace, you know I'll do everything I can—"

"I couldn't stand it! I'd die in prison! They say they'd give me twenty years if I don't raise the money by this evening!"

A shocked silence from Teese.

"*Help* me, Bobbie-Joe!" Her voice sounded muffled, as though she were crying into his coat.

"Miz Grace, I do love you awful, you know I do, but—Miz Grace, where you goin? Miss Grace—"

Roy could hear Grace's bedroom door slam, followed by a long silence. The hall door clicked, and he knew Teese's hand was on the knob.

Then a long, drawn-out, deathly, chilling scream tore from Grace's room. Teese's flat feet slapped back into the interior like blasts from a shotgun, propelling his big body toward what he knew to be certain suicide.

Grace's door snapped open and slammed shut behind him.

It did not come open again for a long, long time.

Pushing the numbed Ely to a chair, Roy lit a cigarette and waited, smiling to himself.

Though there be ninety and nine demons, and ninety and nine saints, and though they be engaged in battle against each other that rumbles and shakes and tears the universe, even they take respite in combat to look down on insignificant man, rolling and spitting harmlessly against himself in the dust.

CHAPTER NINE

*A*s bossman Boots Canelli's industry neared the close of a brisk and reasonably profitable workday, he sighed in relief and lit one of the eight-inch cigars forbidden him by his physician.

All through the entire fourth floor of the Traverse Street office building, employees sighed along with their employer and recharged themselves toward the five o'clock hour. Today at least, they collectively thanked God, bossman Boots had not exploded and spewed out his madman spleen on their innocent heads.

All forty-seven members of the Three-Star Enterprises, a doubtful but perennial business that concealed its actions behind barred front door, rear and emergency exit, heralded the end of their first workday of the week with loud, enthusiastic resonance.

As the field men—a motley corps, but all stamped with the zest and diffidence that mark salesmen the world over—began to make their entrances, bringing with them the countless order blanks of their trade, the faces of the girls who ran the adding machines brightened; the cashiers' fingertips snipped and clinked like lightning in counting; the man who operated the short-wave radio tuned to Santa Anita turned up the volume so no one could mistake the running of the last race.

Onto this strange playing field of commerce, bossman Boots Canelli strode with the mien of a college coach who had just led his team to the Rose Bowl of financial prosperity.

The combined clicks of the adding machines added up to thunder in his triumphant ears, and—

"Rounding the far turn now—"

—it was Boots Canelli who knew the inner thrust of victory.

Of course it hadn't always been like that for Luigi "Boots" Canelli, and perhaps that's why defeat rankled so sharply in him today. Anyone who is poor, who had lost the marrow of living because he was poor—anyone who has starved and felt his belly shrink—on reaching the top and winning through a persevering if not well-educated mind, cannot stand ever to lose again.

The thrill of this knowledge, the sound of his conquest, flowed with drunkening effect through Boots Canelli's mind, as much a part of him as the sweet, soothing cigar clasped lovingly in the half-sneer of his thin lips.

No longer was he the dirty-faced, apple-snitching kid of the 1900's, no longer did he carry bricks or lay them alongside his father, smelling the onion and pepper of the sandwich consumed at noon—or turning to look up into the wine-flushed, discouraged features of a man enslaved by the job.

No longer sweat, and three dollars a day, and people cursing the "dumb dagos" who had come with their cheap labor to wrest the jobs from those who merited them by virtue of their native American citizenship.

No, hell no—not that again!

Now Boots, through affiliations with the Old Country Mafia, which had transplanted so effectively to the New World, had a ticker tape, "just like them Wall Street bums."

He had a Cadillac for himself, a Chrysler for Maria and a Thunderbird for the collegiate scampers of young Paul.

He lived in a forty thousand-dollar home, and he realized a net profit of twenty thousand dollars a week from Enterprises. After handouts and greasing of the right politicians and cops, he was left with seven or eight thousand clear.

Boots had everything he'd ever dreamed he would, even an undreamed-of duodenal ulcer that did much to restrain his love of good food and fine wines.

And there was the rub: the only thing he didn't have was freedom from worry.

This properous son of poor immigrants found his temperament ill-suited to his present occupation.

Sure, he could retire—he had laid by enough money to satisfy his own needs and the Department of Internal Revenue, when they came calling—but "looka alla the money some other mug'd be gettin!" by *his* fleshy and spiritual sacrifices.

Unh-unh. Boots was a good Christian and a devout Catholic, but he was also a patriotic American and avid Capitalist, believing with the credibility of a hungry man made rich that nothing should stand in the way of the system—not even a duodenal ulcer.

Boots was sixty-six years old, though he confessed to fifty-nine and looked seventy-five. In his doughy little hands and half-bald white head, he held the numbers bank of the east side of the city.

He was known for his scalding, screaming tirades when his bank was hit heavily of a week, and, at one time during the thirties, as the vengeance of the Lord on un-bona fide elements of competition.

Though this violent past was behind him, the pickup men who worked for him walked a straight-arrow line of honesty and integrity, for it was general information that the thing which pleased Boots least was a double-cross.

Under these auspicious conditions the bank ran oil-smooth and trouble-free. Boots was not a tightwad despite his fondness for Sam's silver, and it was on days like today, when he was pleased with himself, that the runners and others of the organization made their bites—and were promptly, but unforgettably, rewarded. Boots was an ambulating computer of "who owes-sa me what." Indeed, his nickname stemmed from the fact that, as a younger and much huskier man, he had forcibly extracted debts from fellow workers contracted through his "loan shops" on construction jobs with the convincing aid of the large and heavy seaman's boots he affected.

But, again, these things were behind *Mr.* Canelli, and his confident and familiar air with bookkeepers and mathematicians alike bespoke this fact.

"How-sa it look?" he asked one of them, a bright little shy genius who had been only recently hired.

The young man snapped to attention under his green plastic visor. "Pretty good, Mr. Canelli." He tapped a sheaf of papers on his desk with the butt of his pencil. "We've got a 5 and 2 leading in the first, and my computations indicate another 2, led by a 6 or 7, in the last race. The returns from field men allow for light play on 6-2, and very little in other areas, almost negligible. I'd say—" and here he consulted his slide rule "—that we'd have three to six hits, with a run-down total of seven hundred fifty-five dollars."

Boots chewed at his cigar with satisfaction. "Only a buck anna fifty-one cents play, huh? That ainna bad. Thatsa good." He clapped the young man on the shoulder. "Thatsa real good, kid!"

He went on, thinking he wasn't a slouch with numbers himself—but these college kids!—they could tell you where the hair was short, huh?

He went over to the cage of the head cashier, a drab, prim, middle-aged little woman who wore spectacles.

"How-sa my gal Alice?" Boots inquired in a booming voice, and the woman was startled from her counting. She knew the boss's fits of rage and elation, and hers was to commit herself with only a brief, distant smile.

"I'm fine today, thank you, Mr. Canelli," she replied.

He peered in her bulging cash drawer hungrily. "How-sa it look?"

"Fairly well, Mr. Canelli. This is one of our better days."

Boots put his hands behind him and pouted the cigar at her pugnaciously. "Whaddayou mean, 'fairly well'? Talka to me in dollar signs."

Having worked for—and tolerated—Mr. Canelli more than ten years, Alice did not lose her composure under his threatening stare. "You know better than that, Mr. Canelli. I can't you give an official figure until the last field man is in—and we're due several yet."

"Field men, schmeel men," Boots snorted. "C'mona, Alice, justa gimme a *leetle* hint."

"I don't believe in counting chickens, Mr. Canelli," she said, returning to her counting of money, "as I've told you for more years than I like to think about."

"I'ma not countin the goddamn chickens," Boots said, losing some of his good humor, since Alice was one of the few—and invaluable—employes he could not intimidate. "Justa give me an estimate, that-sa all I'ma askin!"

She sighed, stopped counting, and turned a patient, bespectacled gaze on him.

"All right," she said, taking up her ledger. "This is it, and don't blame me if it's off a hundred or so on the final tally." Her eyes traced the entries, then she turned to her adding machine and, with slow, methodical fingers, punched out the result.

She tore off the slip, read it and handed it to Boots.

"There you are," she said. "Seven thousand eight hundred thirty dollars and sixty cents—and the single-action plays have only begun to come in."

"Single action, single smaction!" Boots grinned. "This isa good, huh? This ainna bad? *Mama mia,* if I could only have a thirty-day week like-a this, huh?"

He shoved the information in his pocket and continued his tour happily.

Adding machines and typewriters clacked and rumbled over the wide, busy room; the chik-chik-chik-chik of the teletype and ticker tape sent out their valuable news in staccato voices; "*And in the stretch . . .*"

Boots listened to the music of it all like a man demented in the chaos of sound, a particularly pleased potentate of the penny-and-nickel monarchy called the numbers game.

In this daily game of speculation, which was surer than General Motors of paying a dividend—and as likely of hitting the ground floor as Northern Natacha Plutonium Mines of Upper Siberia, Limited (U.S.-owned)—Boots knew his five dollars-for-a-penny-played corporation was the closest thing to war any man could approach in peacetime.

And it was his side that invariably won against the hungry, disorganized mobs storming his financial fortress.

But when he lost—sometimes he *did* lose—intimates marveled that a man could be so wrought by a defeat among countless victories, or—considering the violence of his distress—that he should even think of taking up arms the next day to drive the enemy from the captured hill.

It is necessary, to understand Boots Canelli, that one looks at him through the microscope of military metaphors. On the account of one who has fought endless and innumerable battles, all in the name of Luigi "Boots" Canelli, there is no other way.

Boots was indeed a flamboyant personality as he entered his office late Monday afternoon, and, because of this, he lit another cigar and got himself a good stiff drink of equally forbidden rye from the bottle in the bottom drawer of his desk.

A man who had no appreciation of good furniture, he leaned back in his chair and planted one heel atop the other on his desk.

Seven thousand dollars now (he looked at his Omega) meant ten thousand by five o'clock. And, if the college calculus genius was correct, the House should clear better than three-fourths of that, not counting the sure money of single-action numbers. Single-action was a smiple form of playing the numbers, in which a bettor laid his money against picking one, or all three, of the main numbers correctly.

A guy put a quarter on a 2, which may have been leading after the House turns were practically all in. If he hit his 2, he got $1.50. If he didn't, he had two more chances, or five, if you counted the last race.

Because the odds were reduced, single-action didn't pay off too heavily. A dollar hit, for instance, would bring the lucky player only six or seven dollars.

This was the House's make-up money, and it never went under a thousand a day.

But this was an exceptional day for Boots, and despite his first objection to the syndicate that single-action would entail too much extra bookkeeping, when the idea was introduced not too many years ago, he was now glad to have the money along for the ride.

He knew what his evident happiness would bring, and he didn't have long to wait.

George Nichols, the little gray-faced man who scored the big board at the rear with race results, came in fifteen minutes later, with chalk on his conservative vest and fingertips.

"Georgie!" Boots roared with a big grin. "The besta goddamn

man ina the joint, huh? He-sa maybe can tella me who won at Pimlico, huh?"

"It was Miles Ahead, Mr. Canelli," George said, smiling unsurely at Boots's good humor.

"Miles Ahead! Fine!" Boots swung his legs down with a yell. "That-sa my horse, boy! I got fifty smackers onna his nose!" His eyes turned lovingly to the ceiling. "Whatta lucky day, huh? Boy-O! Boy-O!" He clapped his hands hard on the desktop.

"Er, Mr. Canelli," George said, knowing that the iron had never been so hot. "Mr. Canelli, I wondered if—"

"Ah, what? Whatchusay, Georgie-boy? Speaka, man, get it offa you chest!"

"I wondered if I could get a raise, Mr. Canelli," George blurted.

"Raise, schmaze!" Boots beamed at the bearer of good news. "Sure, you can getta raise, boy! How much am I-a payin you?"

"Seventy-eight fifty, Mr. Canelli, and I've been here three years, and the wife's gonna have a new baby—"

"No kiddin? A new bambino, huh? Why didn't you-a say so, Georgie?"

"Well, I was, Mr. Canelli, but—"

"Shuttup," Boots said fondly. "Congratulations! Have a cigar!" He went over and shoved one of the long projectiles between George's lips.

"A sweet-a little bambino, huh? Congratulations, Georgie! I'ma payin you seventy-eight fifty? From now-a on, you're makin eighty-five fifty, Georgie! You tella that prune-puss Alice whatta I say, huh?"

"Oh, *thank* you, Mr. Canelli, I don't know how—"

"Shuttup!" Boots growled, grinning. "It's-a justa baby present, huh?" He put a hand on George's shoulder and pushed the stunned man into the outer office.

Fricassee-fricassa! Boots sang to himself. What a good day this was turning out to be, with Miles Ahead the clincher to his premonition of luck!

He started over to his desk to call up and laugh in the face of Benny the bookmaker, but the door popped open with another visitor. It was the calculus student, with slide rule in hand and a rather puzzled look on his face.

"We just got the final figures in, Mr. Canelli," he said.

"Hah? Wella, what is it, kid?"

The young man flushed. "I was evidently off a bit in my peripheral calculations, but—"

"C'mona, c'mona, kid," Boots said impatiently. "What'd they pulla outa the fishbowl in New York?"

"526 and 629."

"Hah?" said Boots. "Wella, how does that look?"

"It doesn't look bad at all, Mr. Canelli. About like I told you it would be, though I haven't checked through all the plays yet—"

"Then whata you worryin about? Becausa you didn't hit it right ona the nose? Yi, yi! Relax-a, kid, you ainna no Einstein."

"I know, Mr. Canelli, but I was so *sure!*" He didn't tell Boots that his worry sprang from the fact that the peripheral numbers were those to be feared most, those 937,331 to 1 shots; he knew also that Boots wouldn't understand if he tried to explain the flexible law of probability that operated in higher mathematics.

Both the first and last—especially the last—races had defied his thoroughly rechecked calculations, and he was almost sure that outside, on that big wide table that held the day's numbers receipts, which were all being checked now by the screeners, there was a bit of paper, or several, that held the fatal numbers.

The question was for how much? And, given time, the postgraduate student earning his tuition through City College here in the carnival of a numbers house could probably have figured that out.

Only no one was giving out extra time—particularly Boots Canelli—and he couldn't very well ask for any under the circumstances.

"Rest yourself!" Boots advised him heartily. "Ainna you said the hit was small? Ainna you told *me* there ainna nothin to worry about?"

"But, Mr. Canelli—"

"Rest yourself!" Boots ordered. "Here, hava cigar!"

258

"Thanks, Mr. Canelli, but I don't smoke—"

"Then give to you Papa, kid. Relax-a, huh?"

"If you say so, Mr. Canelli . . ."

"Fine! Now get outside and give 'um a hand with thema slips, huh?"

He shoved the youngster outside and slammed the door behind him.

"Aie, aie!" he lamented. "Can't they-a see for theyself? This isa *my* day!"

He went back to his desk and had just seated himself when a knock sounded on the door.

"C'mona in!" he shouted.

R. J. Teese, hat in hand and wide white grin on big black face, sauntered into the office, fortified by news from the grapevine that Boots was in an exceptional mood today.

"Looka my big man!" Boots shouted affectionately. "My bee-u-tee-ful pick 'em up-a and lay 'em down Teese!"

"How do, Mr. Canelli?" Teese smiled.

"Sitta down, sitta down!" Boots said, putting out the old stub of cigar and lighting a new one, as Teese sat facing his desk. "How-sa it look, Teese?"

"Oh, fine, fine Mr. Canelli! Oh, there ain't no trouble at all, I'd like to tell you."

"Then that-sa good," Boots said, in stern approval of the gods who controlled such things. "We can't aska for nothin better when there ainna no trouble, right?"

"That's right, Mr. Canelli."

"Then whatta you do in here?"

Teese jumped at the sound of his voice, but when he looked he saw that Boots was grinning.

"Oh," he said, following through with a laugh. "I'd like to ask a favor of you, Mr. Canelli."

"Yeah?"

"Yes, sir."

"Okay, aska."

"Well, Mr. Canelli," Teese began carefully, "I'd like to know if I could borrow five hundred dollars from you."

He saw that Boots's face hadn't changed, and hurried on, thinking the man had been shocked into silence by the request. "The truth is, Mr. Canelli, I'm plannin to get married, and, you see, this girl is kinda up tight against it, and I wondered . . ."

"You wondered what?" Boots said.

"Well . . . I wondered if you could let me have the money," he said in doubtful summation.

Boots leaned back in his chair and looked at Teese for a long time, puffing at his cigar slowly. "How long-a you been workin witha me, Teese?"

"Over twenty years, Mr. Canelli."

"Anda, me and and you, we treat each other right-a, huh?"

"Yes, sir, as far as I can figure, all the way down the line. I were without no work, fresh outta the South, when you took me on. Nobody else would."

"Yah," Boots said, remembering those days. "So you knowa how I work, huh?"

"Oh, yes, sir, Mr. Canelli!"

"You knowa I like to geta my money back? People who-a worka for me, I don't charge no commission, no interest—but I lika to getta my money back."

"Mr. Canelli, I promise I'll give back every cryin quarter. I ain't never borrowed nothin from you before, but I promise to pay back just like anybody else."

"Okay," Boots said, grinning suddenly. "I trusta you, Teese. If it's-a anybody I trusta more here, it's-a you."

"Mr. Canelli, thank you—" he started.

"Shuttup," Boots said, with a wave of his hand. "Wait justa minute and we'll go outa to see thata stove-faced Alice. Leta me make a call first."

Glowing in his benevolence, Boots picked up his phone and dialed Benny the bookmaker.

"Hallo!" he said when he got his connection. "Benny?"

"Yeah, who's this? Boots?"

"Who'd you thinka it was, you-a poor sap!"

"Whaddayou talkin about, Boots mio?"

"Miles Ahead, you-a poor sap! He's a payin me $12.50 for every two bucks! I tella you my long shot come in one day! Send one of-a the boys over witha my three hundred bucks."

"What the hell's wrong with you, Boots? Don't you get the pickup from Pimlico over there?"

"Sure-a! That-sa why I'ma tellin you to senda me three hundred by fast mail, kiddo!"

"Don't tell me you don't watch yer own board, Bootsy-boy! It was a photo finish, with Miles Ahead and the favorite Summer Paradise neck and neck. Summer Paradise nudged M.A. by a nose."

"*What?*"

"That's it, Boots my boy."

"That-sa the goddamndest thing I ever hear!"

Benny laughed hilariously. "Write your congressman, my friend—I'm three thousand miles from the scene of the crime. Oh, yeah—thanks for the fifty. See ya tomorrow."

The phone clicked in Boots's ear.

Perched in anxiousness by the bones of his butt on the edge of the chair, Teese could see the explosion coming.

The eruption was volcanic in intensity. "Goddamn-a, the sonofabitchin crooks-a! The dirty, a-lousy, sneakin bums! Aie! the stinkin bastards!"

Teese waited patiently, but Boots had just begun to fight.

"Jesu, Guiseppe é Mari! That-a goddamn-a ashes-ass nag! That-a putrid glue mill! That-a bastard of a friggin jockey! Aie, aie, aie!" Boots tore at his hair and got up to storm the room, while Teese sat helplessly by.

The door popped open and the young mathematician came back in. His face was a study in terror, and the green visor was awry on his skull.

"Mr. Canelli—"

"Whata the goddamn hell do you want!" Boots cried, throwing his arms up wildly.

The youth seemed to shrink visibly with his words. "Mr. Canelli, we've got seven hits on 526 and 629."

"Seven hits! Seven-a lousy hits!" Boots said, beginning to feel a trifle better. "Isa that alla you got to tella me, huh? *Huh?*" His eyes closed into angry slits. "Maybe you-a gotta somethin else to tella me, huh? Jesu! I can see it ina you stupid face! *How-a much?*"

The youth swallowed, licked his lips, felt it almost impossible to find his voice.

"C'mona, c'mona, *give!*"

"The-the first six hits aren't so bad, Mr. Canelli—just seven hundred eighty-five dollars."

"The firsta six hits! the firsta six hits! What about the last-a one?"

"It . . ." The young man hesitated.

"Talka you mouth, man, before I choke-a you eyeballs outa you head!"

"It—it hit for—" And here he gaped like a fish drowning in air. "For twelve thousand five hundred dollars. One ticket."

If Boots had been able to disintegrate in small, pinhead bits, he would have surely done so. But, being merely human, he could only stew in the bilious inferno of his own blood.

Students of medicine would have found him an interesting, if not frightening, specimen. Boot's hair actually rose in a white cloud above his slowly reddening skull, and seemed to shimmer like the fur of an angry cat. For a second his eyes turned their pupils to the rear of his head and exposed only the blood-lined whites.

Gripped by a strange, wracking palsy, Boots wiggled and shook like an A and T freight trying to cross a western desert in the face of a sixty-mile-per-hour headwind.

All life was suddenly extinguished from his face, as it immediately turned black as Teese's, then on to a pinkish orange and jaundiced yellow.

The cigar he had just lit, an unsuspecting victim in the phenomenon that was just occurring, was snipped off neat as a Tootsie Roll section between his clattering false teeth.

Teese, who was no stranger to these amazing fits, waited calmly for it to end, but the young college student, never before subjected to such transformations except in the fictional premises of movies entertaining lycanthropy, fled in mortal fear of his life before the monster, and was not ever to be seen again by any of his co-workers.

When he had at last found his voice again, Boots wailed like a wounded bull elephant, *"Twelve-a thousand five hundred! Twelve-a thousand five hundred!"*

The day, which had promised to close so beautifully, was annihilated.

Like an escaped lunatic, he dashed to the door, left open in the horrific wake of his former employee, and bawled, "Manny! Alice! Come-a in here!"

The room at large was stricken with deadly silence as the voice of the master seemed to shatter the four walls, and there was no movement save for the frantic, scurrying forms of those whose names had issued from the human loudspeaker.

Manny, the table maestro, in suspenders, rolled-sleeved white shirt and burnished Old Crow nose, crept into the office like a whipped dog under the stalwart, unfearing form of Alice.

"Now look, Boss," he said. "I didn't have anything to do with it! All I know is the slip's layin there on the table. I give it to Alice, and she passed it along to the boy genius. That's all I know!"

"Shuttup!" Boots shrieked. "Whata I wanna know isa what squash-head took a fifty-dollar play on one-a slip! What-a squash-head! Tella me! Tella me, before I spit up great-a green snakes what'll chew you both alive!"

"Here," Alice said, handing him the slip. "The pickup man's code is right on it."

With firey eyes Boots read the cipher. "21-X! Who the hell is 21-X?"

Teese looked up in surprise. "Well, beggin your pardon, Mr. Canelli, but *I'm* 21-X."

Boots's eyes widened like saucers. "You donna *mean* it! You-a mean *you*, Teese, you-a do this to me? Jesu! Guiseppe!"

"But, Mr. Canelli," Teese protested, "you know I took fifty

dollars worth on a ticket before—even a hundred, one time. I didn't think—"

"You-a didn't think! You-a didn't think!" Boots screamed. "You-a damned right, you-a didn't think! You-a helpa my House get hit for-a twelve-a thousand five hundred bucks, and *you-a didn't think!*"

"Mr. Canelli—Boss—"

"Shuttup! Alice, you-a give this tomato-head that twelve-a and a half grand, for the payoff—and he-sa *fined* the fifty-buck play!"

Alice was shocked. "*Fined?* But, Mr. Canelli, you've never done that before. It wasn't Teese's fault that he got that hit."

"WILLA YOU DO WHATA I TELLA YOU, HANH? NOW GETTA OUT!"

Teese rose in confusion. "But, Mr. Canelli, about that there loan you were gone give me—"

Boots began to go through an uncontrollable fit of shaking. His teeth clicked like drumsticks on a drum pad. His feet trembled and danced together as though he were a missile held firm in the last stages of countdown.

Teese shook his head sadly and left the office with Alice and Manny.

Just as the door closed there was a horrendous crash in the office, followed by lesser violent destructive noises.

Alice patted Teese on the shoulder consolingly. "Don't you worry, Teese. It wasn't your fault. He'll see that soon."

"Thank you, Miz Alice," he said, but right then he was thinking that Boots Canelli was the least of his worries.

Listen to the sound Life makes:
listen to the bubbling roar, the
lilting, eternal scream; listen
to the muted passage of Death:
your ears are the ears of all hu-
manity, and can hear even that,
that part of life . . .
Listen, and with your eyes see,
the pleasing, unpleasing, dream
of sleeping God.

CHAPTER TEN

THE ELECTRONIC SPEED of the numbers grapevine would dazzle the inexperienced eye, and it is futher amazing that the information is transmitted largely by mouth.

Granted, the House dispatcher does phone the evening's results to key pickup men, and the machine of communication is thereby set in motion.

But from that point on, the use of telephonic means is practically forgotten in the frenetic translation of what those six sexless personalities mean to the hopes and despairs of the teeming city.

Grumbling inwardly that his route has managed to hit for one hundred and fifty dollars, putting a large dent in his commission, one petulant pickup man by the name of Granger stops off at Leeman's Barber Shop to relay the news to the heavy-playing proprietor.

"It's 5-2-6 in the first, and 6-2-9 in the last," he yells to the sparse Monday crowd, and eyes look up from *Ebony* and *Tan* and *Jet,* filled with a variety of emotions.

"Goddamn," somebody says, in a curse on someone, or something, they know not what.

Leeman's "Sonofabitch!" is a trifle more vindictive, however, and the gentleman whose nose is unfortuitously in the path of a soapy razor at the moment finds that the headrest of a barber chair could, in some instances, be easily indicted as an accessory to manslaughter.

"That goddamn snake again!" Leeman says. "It already come 562 two weeks ago!" As emphasis to this claim, he waves the razor wickedly, to the distress of his patron.

Leeman is a man who fared well from the numbers in earlier

years, being able to acquire a two-family flat and his present business establishment, to the eternal chagrin of Boots Canelli.

But Leeman's luck had changed some time ago, and he is presently considering experimenting with the saw advocated by a good many Negroes, "A change in bed is a change in good stead." He has a suspicion, however, that such an idea is nigh on impossible for him, in the light of his second, and most tryingly ironclad, marriage to a Seventh-Day Adventist widow of a Seventh-Day Adventist minister. As this restricts his activities on Saturday, which is his only reasonably free night of high adventure, Leeman is uncontentedly resigned in the knowledge that his bad luck will persist for quite a while to come.

"526," he spits disconsolately at Granger's exiting back. "The Lord don't love nothin but a white man, I can tell you!" And returns, to the relief of his lathered patron, to the labors of his trade.

But though he dispatches forthwith the Magic Six from his mind, one of his patrons rises with the recollection of the slip he'd wrote out on his job in the steel mill that morning.

Didn't he play 562 for thirty-five cents? He is *sure* he had.

Quickly he follows Granger out on the hot, evening-simmering Lomax.

"Hey, man," he says, catching up. "Didn't you say 562 and 629?"

"Didn't say 5-6-2," Granger says uncooperatively, with a scowl. "Said 5-2-6 and 6-2-9."

Turning on badgered heel, he leaves the man to ponder his mistake.

Just passing, a piqued passerby catches a bit of the repartee and slows his pace before the wondering one.

"Did he say 526 and 629, just now?" he inquires.

"That's it," the other replies with a sigh and nod of regret. "I sure did think I had it, too. Shoulda boxed that number, and I'd be a hundred and seventy-five dollars richer this evenin! Ain't that somethin?"

The stranger nods his sympathy and leaves directly to carry the news to Bill behind the bar of Bill's Bar.

"You just can't win," says red-faced Bill, glad that he hasn't played today, for he surely would have missed by miles. "Ain't no need of a man thinkin he can beat the numbers—it can't be done!"

In a little while, the man leaves the establishment, but not before he has informed ten individuals, most of whom have left before him, carrying the germ.

One of these is a slick little whore by the name of Josephine, who shares quarters with a half-dozen scarlet sisters in the "rest home" run by old lady Maxwell at the juncture of Lomax and Division.

Out to give Lomax an early and expectant reconnoiter, Josephine is brought up short by the news. She is pretty positive she played 629 for a nickel with Teese the pickup man that morning, and it is one of those about-time blessings she won't have to split with her dapper man of the hour, pimp Johnny.

Or so she tells herself. She knows she is powerless against that sweet-meat young'un, that Hershey Bar Daddy, that gold-throated peacock that passes for a man, and however adamant her resistance at the moment, he needs only to flick one brown, half-carated finger at her when he comes around for his dues later in the evening, and she will willingly heap all on him.

With this unenthusiastic knowledge tucked comfortably forgotten on one shelf of her one-tracked mind, Josephine twitters like a school girl as she swishes toward home in sweeping tides of eau de Man-Catcher, realizing happily that this is her first hit in two months.

It naturally never crosses her mind that she has had to play fifty to get twenty-five, or how hard that fifty had been to acquire in the competitive unrest of Mme. Maxwell's Rest Home (for the Aged & Invalid).

Like most numbers players who give their all for the remunerative fluff of a hit, Josephine feels a power likened to that famous damsel who ruled over Napoleon.

Quickly, ignoring the inquiries of fellow inmates as to "how the streets look?" this evening, Josephine rushes upstairs to her little room under the east eaves of the big house and empties the contents of her top dresser drawer on the bed.

Her write-up book, worn and well-used, is the first thing she spies among the sundry articles. And inside, on today's page, she finds confirmation.

The thing Josephine experiences is the joy felt by a novice who drives the king of a master chessplayer to the wall and accomplishes checkmate.

It is more solace than a sense of conquest, a satisfying thrill that even she can cause a crack in the mammoth dike of some numbers baron. It is this feeling now suffusing Josephine that sweeps through all holders of a successful hit this evening: all the little people who are not otherwise allowed to pit their strength, or luck, against a thing bigger than all of them combined.

With her flush of success, Josephine epitomizes them all. She has gambled and won; tomorrow she will gamble and lose, but that doesn't make any difference.

It is this sense of being garnered by the several anonymities like Josephine that makes numbers a billion-dollar business.

Is is they who encourage the faceless mob to, day after day, pour their luckless pennies in the bottomless, futile abyss of impoverished hope.

Without these erratic, once-in-a-while hitters, the numbers racket would lose its best and most effective propaganda, and would soon expire.

But, in her joy, Josephine gainsays that she is about to let anything of the sort happen.

In mad happiness, she runs downstairs and collars her dearest whore friend, Big Ethel, who is engaged, as always, in a raid of the well-stocked and obliging community refrigerator.

"Honey!" Josephine cries. "I hit it! I hit it!"

"Humh?" Ethel says through a fat face, a bit of yesterday's chicken in her mouth. "Hit what, baby?"

"The *number,* damn fool! I told you this mornin 629 was comin!"

"Was *that* it?" Big Ethel says.

"526 and 629," Josephine says breathlessly.

"Well, I'll be damn," is the big woman's only comment. Money does not easily excite her, as she has seen more than her share. Anyway, all it can buy, as far as she is concerned, is a roof over her head and a modicum of food, to which she now holds access in plenty.

As she returns to her eating, it is with no slight or dig at Josephine's happiness. It is just that numbers are one of the things Big Ethel never had a need for—like men.

Turning in disgust, Josephine rushes to every other level of the house, exacting praise and jealous disparagement respectively from the lodgers.

"629! Honey, tomorrow I'm gonna play your book with ya!"

"Twenty-five bucks! Is that all? Your sweet-man'll blow that in ten minutes with one of his women!"

But Josephine is not discouraged. In fact, she returns buoyed to her room.

In her mind she has already spent the money she has coming, and two-fifths of it has gone back into the numbers.

Josephine is not alone in her happiness. All along Lomax Street, as though sprayed on the facade with some massive water pistol, several drops of elated personalities drip effusively through their well-known haunts.

Joe Hibbs, the shoeshine man, has hit for ten dollars, and his black rag smackity-smacks over a customer's shoes with a bright, thundering eloquence.

Sally Caldwell, the beautician, joins the chain of communication in the bower of Bessie's Bower of Beauty, with the joyous cry to a customer, "962 in the box! Lord, this is my lucky day! *Fifty dollars*—just wait till I tell my old man!"

And the customer rejoins with a laugh, "Keep your mouth shut, girl! Money is somethin you should *never* tell a man about!"

All along the street the numbers drawn from the New York fishbowl are met with scowls, injured howls, grave disappointment tempered by an almost-hit, deflation, extreme joy, silent and audible thanks to God, and various other forms of psychological inebriation.

Finley Thompson, a pickler operator in the steel plant on the hill, has hit for one hundred dollars by correctly picking 526 in the first race. His immediate reaction is to set up the bar in Bill's beam at the congratulatory you're-an-all-right-guy pats on his liquor-slumped back, and, without one thought to the five needing children and work-worn, tousled-haired wife awaiting him at home, blandly proceeds to give back to the wind the windfall just handed over to him grudgingly by the pickup man Granger.

But, in another niche on Lomax, a place where two half-naked children and one diphtheria-struck infant lie sleeping fitfully in a single bed, a deserted mother cries brokenly into her hands as R. J. Teese, a tense, gentle smile on his big mouth, slowly makes her fingers wrap around two fifty-dollar bills, the reward of twenty cents she had stolen that morning from the mouths of her babes, praying that God would make a way for them all by nightfall.

And she cries, knowing now that He had planned to, all along.

Crying along with her, but in other sections of town, are a man whose mentally retarded daughter can be boarded a little longer in the fine atmosphere of the state home, because of his luck; a woman who now has the money to bury her uninsured three-year-old son, struck down by a car last Saturday; the unemployed, injured workman, who can now obliterate and reinstate with confidence the large bill run up at the Harlem Market in the behalf of his wife and eight children.

In these people, the numbers racket finds a sort of redemption, no matter how few they are. The gain realized by numbers' unscrupulous chairmen loses some of its taint when held in the light of mass hopeless, when redeemed in the glow of individual attainment.

One wonders if it is not a good thing, when he looks on the small, meaning-full gifts the numbers give back to the scores of deserving have-nots from time to time . . .

Accompanied by the Rev. Howard T. Perriwinkle, one of the ruling chairmen of the interdenominational conclave (native of Valdosta, Ga.), the Rev. Jones was driving his Caddie slowly down Lomax when a hailing voice from the street pricked up his ears.

The message wasn't directed at him, but he was very much interested in what the voice said, and the numbers it hawked.

It was some time before his heart stopped pounding in his ears and allowed him to hear the gray-haired, dignified little man sitting next to him say for the second time, "Nice town you have here, Reverend."

"Oh!" said the Rev. Jones. "Oh, a joyous town, Reverend!"

"But such a neighborhood—" the Rev. Perriwinkle began distastefully, as they passed the poolroom, where Papa John and his fellows leaned like three wooden Indians.

"A wonderful neighborhood!" Rev. Jones chimed happily. "A God-struck neighborhood, Reverend!"

"Yes, of course," the reverend investigator said. "There is a lot of work to be done here, however. You've chosen a formidable proving ground for God's word, Reverend."

"A happy proving ground, Reverend—a happy proving ground!"

Oh, happy snake—*happy* temptation!

Hadn't he felt it? Hadn't he felt that dream pull and tug from him the happy knowledge?

Up till now he had almost resigned himself to his fate. Though he knew he could probably stall Rev. Perriwinkle for several hours, he realized that would be the limit and the man would insist on the "tour" that would inevitably lead to Rev. Jones' ouster from the conclave.

He had been considering running the Caddie—which was paid for—over to Arthur's Auto-Home, but even then the red tape involved would not give him access to any cash until the next day, and the Rev. Perriwinkle would have surely found the shortage by then.

Anyway, he'd best hold onto the car, in case he had to make an abrupt departure.

But—happy ESP!—now such a move was unthinkably unnecessary.

The Rev. Jones settled back under his driving with a liniment-like glow stealing over his entire body.

Yes, sir—with the Lord, and faith—a man who was washed in the blood of the lamb could venture past the black shadows of the unknown unafraid—he could plumb the happy depths of the universe.

With an elated burst that surprised him—and the Rev. Perriwinkle, who looked on quizzically—Rev. Jones began to sing a spiritual in a rumbling, effervescent bass,

> Amazing grace, how sweet
> It sounds! that saves a
> Wretch like me;
> I once was lost, but now
> I'm found—was blind,
> But now I see!

An Honest man is
Ofttimes led
From paths of Right
To paths of pain;
Forsooth, 'thout love
And honour
Might he never find
His way again

CHAPTER ELEVEN

WHAT TO DO? This was the biggest question R. J. Teese had ever faced in his entire forty-one years. Rarely had he been torn this way, between love and integrity; never had he been forced to such a precipice.

Having tasted the pleasures of Grace Anderson's body that afternoon, he was irretrievably lost in a maelstrom of passion.

The universal victim of love's fatal sting, Teese was a man on the verge of insanity. Now Grace Anderson meant more to him than he'd ever imagined, as the consummation of their planned marriage slipped further and further from the bounds of reality.

What could he tell her?

What could he do?

Suddenly the timid personality of R. J. Teese reversed itself under the extreme external pressures, and he found burning in him a deep resentment for Boots Canelli. Of all the things Teese held most sacred, a promise claimed first position.

Didn't the bossman have any respect at all for a promise—what it meant to the promised? Couldn't he realize that he held Teese's heart—his very life—in the delightful confines of "I will"?

It wasn't fair, and, ratonalizing automatically, Teese still could not find the means to excuse Signor Canelli.

He was a man on the edge of a waterhole, finding it a mirage; he was a winded gnu, fleeing toward the woods and sheltering twilight from the lion, and finding himself awaited by the lion's mate; he was the throbbing, Sunday-morning headache from Saturday night, in the skull of a man who awakens to find himself without aspirin.

How to describe these things Teese felt with any word less than "anguish"?

How to tell the pathos of a man who had asked for the world and had been refused the comfort of even a tiny swamp?

As he trudged down Monday-darkening Lomax toward his last payoff stop, with twelve thousand five hundred of the Canelli House's begrudging dollars in his pocket, Teese was in a profound, funk-filled quandary.

He knew his mission, but he hesitated over it with common bewilderment.

Tomorrow morning we could be waking up . . . loving each other . . .

The soft moss words fuzzied his mind, causing him to waver a bit drunkenly as he walked.

. . . Loving each other . . .

Oh, how he could visualize it! Grace, his very legal, God-given own! Again he smelled the musky scent of her smooth, golden skin, felt the tiny touch of her tiny fingers tangled in the crazy wire brush of his chest hair, that soft, crushing kiss of her bowl-of-cherries mouth on his own!

Teese trembled. Unbidden, his fingers touched the thick packet of maybes sucked into the House, the tens, twenties and many ones of today and forever.

Walking, pace ever slowing, he wondered what the Rev. Jones would do with all this money. Women? Drinking? Another Cadillac?—all that was as nothing compared to the glory of Grace.

With twelve thousand dollars (and he was surprised that he'd permitted himself the thought) he and Grace could storm the ramparts of happiness with every confidence of victory.

But he trembled again with the illusion. How could that be? Unless he—took the money?

No! he thought. *Maybe I were many things, but I were never a thief!*

Not to be outdone, his less scrupulous alter-ego argued that bossman Boots Canelli had done him wrong—hadn't he? Hadn't he been just an everyday Indian-giver, a thing Teese had thought he could never be?

Had Teese *ever* asked him for anything before? No!

Didn't Teese have one of the biggest pickups in the House, and had never been hit too heavily before? Yes!

No, there weren't no cry when Teese picked up fifty- and hundred-dollar plays, and the plays lost, but when he picked up one—his *first* big hit—Mr. Canelli blamed *him* for it, as though he'd arranged the hit in some way.

Yes, sir, it would serve him right if Teese packed up, him and Grace, and took off for Brazil, Spain, or some such place! With over twelve thousand dollars—

He had an ague with the audacity of the spontaneous plan.

Could he? Would he be able to? Wouldn't he lose everything if he didn't?

Standing there, trembling like a dunked dog in the middle of dark-now Lomax, Teese sweated with more than the heat. He knew he didn't possess the fortitude or lack of conscience to carry off such an operation. Also, there had been talk of what bossman Canelli had done to runners who tried to slip off with a heavy roll—and the talk hadn't been pretty.

But Grace . . .

There sat his resolve.

He began walking quickly toward the abode of the Anderson Moving Co. Andersons.

He would see Grace, and then he would know.

Sam Dawn slipped five lead-nosed projectiles into the chamber of the Owlhead and snapped it shut. The harsh metallic click did something to him, and he shifted a bit where he sat on the bed.

Well, Lord, there didn't seem to be any other way. Talk? Talk to Rosy?

No, that time was past. Maybe if he'd done his talking a long time ago—been *able* to talk, explain the eccentricities of his love toward her—this wouldn't be happening.

In his peaceful mind, Sam was beginning to see he was as much to blame as anyone—even Roy Beavers. Yes, he had denied, he figured, his rightful love to Rosy. That's why the giving of his money to another man—her purchase of that man—meant little or nothing to her if she got the love she needed in return.

Still, this was not Rosy's, or Roy's, complete absolution—this mistake Sam had made toward his wife.

He stood up from the bed, his face burning, shoving the little pistol under the belt of his trousers. He put his suitcoat on to conceal the small bulge, and started out to the front of the shop.

If a man made a mistake, he thought indomitably, he had to clear it up some way—even if it cost him everything.

Rosy was just packaging a bouquet when he came out.

"Oh, Sam," she said, looking up. "The Masonic lodge on Eighth Street just called up, and they want this took over right away."

"Okay," he said, taking the box out of her hands.

"Now, you gonna be all right?" she said, pulling her light summer dress—a new one, he saw—down a little lower over her luscious figure, making it neat about her hips. "I'm on my way over to Cousin Lena's."

"I'll be all right," he said. "Don't worry about me."

"Now you be sure to lock up tight," she reminded him, going to the door.

"Don't you worry about me," he said again, a little sharply.

The door opened before her hand reached the knob and a flushed-face Rev. Jones came in.

"Well, Reverend!" Rosy twittered delightedly.

"How're you people this evening?" he said with a hurried tip of his hat.

Sam nodded unsmilingly.

"I just wanted to inquire," Rev. Jones went on, "if you folks happened to see Mr. Teese this evening?" Then, remembering Teese's occupation and Sam's ignorance of his numbers-playing, he added a proprietary lie, "I've been considering Mr. Teese for the board of deacons, and I'd like him to meet Rev. Perriwinkle, who just—"

"No, we ain't seen Teese," Sam said, not believing any of the story and thinking it only a convenience by which the good Rev. could set up an assignation with Rosy. This surmise gave him a sudden impulse to whip out the Owlhead and find out whether God was in a mood to retain His philandering salesman.

But he quieted himself; Rev. Jones wasn't the one he wanted.

"Much as we'd *like* to see Teese, Rev. Jones," Rosy said grinningly, "he ain't showed up here this evenin."

The Rev. impatiently tipped his hat. "Well, I'll be on my way. Sorry to bother you folks. If you see Mr. Teese, you tell him I want to see him right away."

"Sure will," Sam said dryly.

Sensing the Reverend's anxiousness, and good fortune, Rosy followed close behind him. "I'm on my way to see my Cousin Lena, Rev. Jones. If you're goin my way—"

He looked at her distractedly. "Yes—well, I'm in quite a hurry, if you don't mind, Mrs. Dawn . . ." He hurried out of the shop ahead of her, jumped into the Caddie parked at the curb, and roared off, almost airborne.

Rosy stared after the flashing tail-lights. "Well . . . I guess I'll be gettin on, Sam. You be sure to lock up tight."

"Don't worry," Sam said, watching her exiting back with hard eyes. "I'll take care of everything."

He stood for a long time behind the counter after she had gone, reviewing their past life together, the strength of his resolutions.

Two hundred dollars in her purse . . .

He locked up the shop carefully, arranging the floral displays with care.

With a deep sigh and uncomforting pat of the pistol under his belt, he ambled back to the hothouse to say goodnight to his friends.

He knew it was the last goodnight he would ever give them.

Was that Teese?

Bea Green whirled as the big figure pushed unheedingly past her on the street.

Why, it sure was! Now where was he hurrying off to that away?

Drawn, she turned to stare after him perplexedly, her errand after a bottle of Sloan's Liniment for the ankle she had twisted earlier in the day forgotten.

Without a reason, her small, ill-constructed body was clutched with a fear for Teese as she saw in which direction his feet led him.

That Grace Anderson!

An unproud hussy, Bea turned her steps after the big man. Should she call to him? What could she tell him? Was there any way to explain this queer feeling—and her love—to him?

Lord, if a man didn't surprise a woman in turning out to be twice the fool she figured him to be! The more she thought about Teese's supposed-to-be-about-to-happen marriage to Grace Anderson, the stronger were her convictions that there was an oil slick on the water.

Like a fledgling detective, Bea gauged her short steps in an effort to shadow Teese inconspicuously. But she knew there was no need to be overly cautious: that man's eyes were stuffed with the lies of an evil woman; he couldn't see anything or anybody but Grace Anderson.

A thin, humped guardian angel, she trailed behind him, a prayer on her lips that life would not treat him unjustly, and a vow to herself she would see him through and stand beside him—to the end.

Papa John and his entourage of two, all high on cheap wine and a few quick whiffs of the last bit of marijuana they'd purchased that morning, eyed Teese's and Bea Green's vanishing figures on the street with keen introspection.

"Man," said Papa John, from his usual spot of honor in front of the poolroom, "that is the kinda *woo*man I'd like in my corner."

"Yeah," said the two appreciatively.

"Ugly but righteous," Papa John commented. "The perfect broad for Teese-man. Men, I don't dig why he *don't* dig."

"Evil," said a companion.

"Grace," said the other.

"Man," said Papa John, with a shake of his head. "I feel real bad and sorry-O for that unhappy cat."

"Yeah, man," said the two, in sorrow.

Papa John nodded sadly to the night. "What I tell us, me and myself—man, that bears lookin into right now."

The two looked at him expectantly, but Papa John didn't go on.

In silence they watched the night advancing.

The sound of running feet and exhausted breath assaulted their ears, and they turned to see the Rev. Jones come up to them frantically, the driver's door of the Caddie gaping open at the curb.

"Evening, boys," he said quickly. "Can you tell me if you happened to see Mr. Robert J. Teese pass this way?"

The boys looked at each other.

Then Papa John said, with some show of hostility, "Why, man?"

"I just *have* to find him," Rev. Jones implored. "It's a matter of life or death!"

They looked at each other again. Then they turned and merely stared at the Rev. Jones as though he had disappeared.

After an exasperating silence, the minister turned and jumped back in the car. The tires squealed as he pulled off in the opposite direction Teese had taken.

"Wasn't that that holy daddy?" Papa John said. "The one with the church?"

"That was him," one of the boys confirmed.

Papa John looked after long-gone Teese. "Men, somethin stinks, kee—"

"—rect!" chorused the two.

Papa John pushed himself away from his perch and took a walking stance in the direction Teese and Bea had gone.

"Let's stroll," he ordered.

They started purposefully down the street.

Over at the Anderson Moving Co. Roy Beavers looked at his watch with angry perturbation. Grace and brother Ely sat motionless, watching him apprehensively, like blank-faced China dolls.

"Goddamn it!" Roy growled. He turned on Grace. "You said that dumb bastard'd be here before now!"

"Roy," she pleaded. "It's not *so* late. Teese'll be here."

Anger unslaked, he pounced on the cowering Ely. "If you don't stop lookin so goddamn silly, I'll kill you before those Roundhouse boys do! Get downstairs and watch out for that lamb. If he comes around, tell him me and Grace ain't in."

"But, Roy," Ely protested, "what if the Roundhouse boys—"

"I don't give a damn about the Roundhouse boys! Just do what I tell you before I break your stupid neck!"

Numbly, Ely got up and left.

Grace came over to him, tried to soothe, him with the rounded comfort of her body. "Roy, honey—"

"Just leave me alone!" he barked at her. "All you broads is the same—*all* of you! That sonofabitchin Rosy Dawn—"

The door came open and Ely dashed in. "Teese is comin upstairs!"

"God bless a monkey!" Roy said thankfully. "C'mon, Ely, in the kitchen. And you remember what I told you, Grace!"

No sooner than the kitchen door closed on them, a knock sounded on the other. Grace was there at the second rap.

Grace, though she tried to deny it to herself, had found things quite pleasant in Teese's arms that afternoon—that brave moment of truth—and under different circumstances—without a Roy Beavers . . .

She was surprised to find Teese no longer ugly and repulsive to her. The broad, bright grin, the electrifying goodness and innocence of him, oddly inflated her sense of guilt. In him she saw—too late now—that thing Pete Anderson had drilled so unsuccessfully into her head many years ago: plain, unpolluted honesty. And it was a thing that surpassed her motives—even Roy—and made her feel quite filthy.

"How do, Miz Grace," he said respectfully, and a little self-consciously now.

Beating down a sudden urge to tell him to go away, she let him come in.

"Oh, Bobbie-Joe!" she said on cue, but this time the tears were real, something she could not help.

She had no idea what this did to Teese. He gathered her into him, his big voice purring over her. "Don't you worry, Miz Grace. I got the money . . ."

She looked up. "You've got it? But—Teese—"

He tried to smile, but it was not one of his characteristically warm ones.

"I got some money, Miz Grace," he said. "A whole lot of money. But—"

He mistook the look in her eyes, and took the packet of bills from his pocket and pressed it into her reluctant hand.

"Now, Miz Grace," he said slowly, "you take this. I want you to hold this while I—Well, I still gotta make up my mind, and the only way I can is to see you and that money together."

He stood back, as though to truly see her for the first time, and said with the same, hesitant smile,

"I can't hardly explain it the way I want to, Miz Grace, but I wanna tell you how I feel. You see, if we takes that money, we won't be able to pay them folks you owe—and that'd be just another debt we'd owe together. Because I *got* to pay this back, don't you see that? I just can't steal, no matter how much I love ya. I'd never be no more good until I give back what I took." He shook his big head in confusion. "We'd have to run, and that don't seem rightly the thing we should do. I don't know, Miz Grace, I just can't explain it the way I should. I wanna go away with you more than anything in the world—still, I wants to be an honest man more than anything. It don't seem like the two go together, and I know they should." Torn and severed in countless pieces by the problem, he groped to the end of his speech.

"I believe you know how much I love you, Miz Grace. I'm gonna leave it up to you—what *you* wants to do," he said.

This innocuous sentence tore through Grace's hard exterior.

"You damn fool!" she cried, and rushed from him into the kitchen. "Here!" she hissed at Roy. "Take it! It's dirty; I don't want any of it!"

Roy's fingers dug into her arm. "Goddamn you, get back out

there! If you don't do what I said, I'll kill you! Keep him out there until I make this phone call!"

He pushed her through the door at Teese's stricken cry, "Miz Grace!"

He listened to make sure Grace followed his orders, then he opened the packet, whistled softly at the contents, and went over to the wall phone.

Ready at any signal to dash down the backstairs, Ely heard him dial a number and speak in a rapid monotone.

"Mr. Boots Canelli?" Roy said. "I know somethin you might like to know . . ."

In the other room, Grace was crying unconsolably on Teese's breast.

Sam Dawn saw Rosy disappear into the alleyway behind the moving company.

Unaware that he was being observed by Bea Green, who had taken up a post across the street, he unbuttoned his coat and followed his wife.

Rosy paused and waited for a good while at the bottom of the stairs that led up to the second floor of the Anderson flat.

Concealing himself in the shadows, Sam finally saw a flurry at the top of the stairs. Rosy tensed. A body hurtled downward, almost falling down the stairwell, but Sam saw, to his surprise, that it was Ely Anderson, who seemed to be in a mad hurry.

Behind him came his sister, who was evidently being forced by Roy Beavers.

Sam extracted the pistol and began walking slowly toward them.

The next few moments were blurred in his mind. Afterwards he recalled his intense feeling of hate when he saw his wife break toward Roy, the rising cry of her voice as she shoved something to him and tried to hang onto him at the same time.

Then the *crack!* Was that the pistol? No—it was Rosy's maddened palm against Grace Anderson's cheek.

Then Rosy was on the ground, pushed by Roy, and Sam's arm had raised the deadly piece to position and lined up on the shocked, terrorized features of the handsome man who had just caught sight of him.

Not knowing Roy's rabid fear of firearms, Sam was naturally startled when the young man bounced high as a fear-struck gazelle, turning, in mid-air, against all the laws of gravitation, and propelled himself in life-saving flight, emitting wild little *eeks* of horror.

Perhaps that was what caused his finger to tighten involuntarily on the trigger and send the slug that was intended for Roy's high, smooth forehead into his smartly tailored rump.

This, of course, he could not know, since Roy was encouraged to supersonic speeds by the hot fire in his butt, and the trail of garbage cans he left littered in the insane swath he cut through the alley aided in convincing Sam that he was bearer of a mortal wound.

In his wake followed Grace, crying after her injured lover, and Rosy, wondering if her lungs would last the long sprint to Cousin Lena's house.

Prostrate with fear, Ely found unexpected haven in the shelter of two tall, odoriferous receptacles.

During the scuffle, Sam had noticed Roy drop a packet, and he bent quickly to retrieve it. The two hundred dollars, he thought.

It felt rather large and bulky, but he paid it no attention as he started out of the alley, thinking it was probably mostly ones. It would help him to get started somewhere else, until he got a job and worked enough to start another floral business: the only true purity he could ever look forward to.

He had already taken what money they had in the shop, but he was sure Rosy would make out, since he was leaving her the shop and car.

The only regret Sam had as he came unknowingly out on Lomax, was that he'd had to kill Roy Beavers.

Sadly, he pointed his scar face in the direction of the train station.

Upstairs, still waiting on Grace to return from her errand to the kitchen, Teese had an uneasy period.

Convinced now that he would not be able to take any part of money that was not his, he was sure Grace would see it his way; that she would consent to stay, with him beside her, and face the music of the criminal courts.

He was pretty certain, now that he thought about it, that they would go easy on her.

He twisted a bit on the couch.

What was that *pop?*

It sounded from the alley, and he rose.

Grace?

"Miz Grace?" he called, but there was no answer. "Miz Grace?"

The money! She still had it, didn't she?

Hesitantly he went back to the kitchen and pushed open the door. "Miz Grace . . . ?"

Then he saw the back door gaping open.

Oh, Lord! Had Miz Grace took the money and run, scared to death of what might happen to her? Oh, *Lord!*

He dashed heavily over and saw nothing in the darkness of the alley below.

On frantic feet, Teese hurried down. "Miz Grace!" he cried. "Please, Miz Grace, you gotta come back!"

Nothing. Only a sound from two garbage cans under the steps, which he figured for rats.

He ran down to the Lomax end of the alley, hoping he would catch her before it was too late.

"Howdy, Teese," somebody said, and as he turned expectantly, a fist crashed into his mouth, jarring him to the shoulders.

In shocked wonder, Teese felt the wobbly bridge loosen altogether and pop out into the alley, like the mouthpiece of a stunned fighter caught flush with a good right hand. He tasted blood on his palate.

Dumfounded, before he could focus on his attacker, the fist slammed into his mouth again.

Teese fell to his knees, stars dancing in his vision.

"Boots sent us over," the "howdy" voice said. "Boots said you crossed him, Teese . . ."

He felt himself dragged farther into the alley, then a pair of sharp-toed shoes dug into his ribs simultaneously.

"You fellas are hurtin me," Teese said dumbly through the pain. "I didn't do no-nothin . . ."

Somebody dragged him up. A fist buried itself in his stomach, and, suddenly without wind, he felt consciousness sliding away from him.

"You're real lucky, Teese," the voice laughed. "Boots thinks you're an all right guy—he don't want you completely rubbed out. Ain't that nice?"

"Didn't do wrong," Teese gasped. "Didn't . . . steal . . . Just loved—"

He felt now that the fists were covered with leather gloves. They tore the skin about his eyes and mouth.

He collapsed, pleading without words that he hadn't done what Boots Canelli had thought—that he *couldn't* when brought face to face with himself, steal—not even for Grace.

Then, as suddenly as the attack had begun, it ceased. He heard a garbled cry, and the wild scream, "I been cut!"

Feet danced about him, and he could tell men were struggling. On the outer fringes of reality, he heard running footsteps. Hands were lifting his big body gently.

"Easy, Teese baby. Everything's gonna be all right—it's gonna be just crazy."

Papa John!

Teese tried to open his swelling eyes.

"Oh, my Teese!" Bea Green's voice cried. "They hurt my Teese!"

He was standing now, leaning against her tiny, rock-hard strength.

"My house," Bea told the boys. "He'll be all right at my house. Please help me—"

"Don't worry, Bea baby," Papa John said in a soft voice. "We're gonna look out for Teese-man."

Dimly, Teese was aware of the importance of this. For one painful moment, he was rather glad of the beating he had received.

Oh, God!—these people around him, helping him, loving him—didn't it *mean* something?

Slowly, down the hot, gawking, night-time Lomax, they carried him tenderly.

A Cadillac intercepted them a few moments later, roaring up to the curb, and the Rev. Jones jumped out.

"Teese!" he said. "Thank God! I been looking all over for you! My money—" Then he stopped, sobered, seeing Teese's battered face. "My money?" he said, with fast-fading enthusiasm.

Teese could hardly face him. "Rev, I—"

"He got robbed," Papa John said, with an inward perception born of the streets. "We just pulled two guys off him."

In the words, Teese could tell that Papa John—that all of them—had known all along what he'd been too blind to see.

"I'm sorry, Rev," was all he could say as they continued with him down the street.

After they had vanished, the Rev. Jones stood for a long time with his mouth open.

Not so much was it shock as complete realization. Thunderstruck, he knew this was the way everything was *supposed* to happen today.

Knowledge, not so happy, filtered through to him. His career, of course, was over; though he might be able to replace what needed to be replaced. Tomorrow. Too late, tomorrow.

Yet the hit he felt now was much greater than the one he had accomplished in numbers—in the *losing* of the great sum he had won from numbers.

What were those words he had sung so jubilantly just a little while ago?

> Amazing grace . . .
> I once was lost, but now
> I'm found—was blind,
> but now I see!

For the first time in his life, he truly understood those ways in which the Lord was said to work.

And he thanked heaven that he had not seen the truth too late.

With a bowed, and sincerely humbled head, he went over to replace himself under the wheel of the waiting Cadillac.

Not We Many

There is a place at Heaven's
Gate for those who wait;
For waiting is the waiter's
Faith—
That Heaven's there for just
A few such waiting souls—
And not we many . . .

CHAPTER ONE

I TOLD THE CAPTAIN OF THE FRUIT, Brother Harvey, that I just didn't give a damn. Those were my words, and I could hear the gasps from the ordered black lines of my brother Muslims.

Brother Harvey had been quizzing me on my listlessness, my uncertainty of direction, not only in the ranks of fleshed blue suits and sun-red ties and forefront eyes, but in quite evident inner-mind.

It was youth, and impatience, he said, and lack of faith in our Leader's way, and inbred Devil's ignorance, he added; those were my ailments.

And that's when I said I didn't give a damn.

And that's not all I said.

I said, You're lambs, too, just like that dead nigger in the street who *hasn't* heard the message of the Prophet and prefers the white man's boot, and loves his pork chops—but that's not all I said:

"If I'm to die or live for Islam, then let it be *now*. Not waiting for some goddamn eastern cloud to show up on the horizon. If Armageddon's to come, then let *us* bring it to pass—here, now!"

Then I shouted, in a way that made his shocked black face wince, raising my fist as though it held a slashing sword of vengeance,

"*Allahu Akbar!* In the name of God!"

I was immediately expelled for ninety days and denied all contact with the Temple.

CHAPTER TWO

THERE WAS RAIN ON THE ROOF, and I was poor. Plus my mother was sick; and the white man at the grocery store on 80th wouldn't increase my salary.

Man, I loathed this shitness of living!

I loathed Brother Harvey, Brother Minister, who called all shots in the Temple's policy subject to He Most Knowing, and I hated Craig, my friend from boyhood, who'd introduced me to Islam months before and was more shocked than anyone else at my obscene explosiveness—who could not, damn him, understand my pain and need, and demand, for expression of the gall that boiled, seeking access from my throat.

I even hated my dying mother, who'd brought me into this hell, who now whiningly sought surcease and vindication through her dying.

"David . . . ?"

It was her; and the plaintiveness of her voice—the not-understanding faint timbre of it—made me feel ashamed of the things I'd been thinking.

I listened to it, sitting by the window in my small room, watching the haze of evening blackened with rain and cloak-like above the crap-pile crowns of the dirty city five stories below our tenement tower—and felt a kind of inside gnawing, kneading, mouth.

"David . . . son?"

I couldn't understand what was happening to me. At twenty-five, I didn't feel *too young*, too withheld from a *knowing* of myself and what I wanted:

That was just the trouble—I wanted more than merely the vision of early-autumn gold and silver intermixed in the rain and dust-lifted, mote-laden halo of my city's filthy crests—I wanted the gold and silver alone, without the dirt of people's making and pain.

And more—much more than I could know at that moment—I wanted peace, and an awareness of something other than hate, something that would spring with sweet freshness to my morning's tongue—something I couldn't understand just then.

Slowly, I rose and went into the apartment's remaining room, my mother's, the dining, living and everything-else place, made secondary by her presence.

"Yeah, Ma?" I said, standing over her.

"It's you I want, David," she said slowly.

"I ain't got time for talkin, Ma."

"Don't put me back, David—I'm your mother . . ."

"I know who you are . . ."

"Then sit," she commanded.

And I sat.

"We have things to talk about, my son," she said in a voice stronger than I had heard in many years.

I waited, trying to close my heart.

"We're not close, David—we haven't been close since your father died ten years ago."

"I don't remember him."

"Yes . . . I know."

I had not seen her face, and now when I looked purposely I found it in shadow.

"Want me to turn on a light?" I asked.

"No, please . . . there's another sort of light we need, you and I."

And now I waited again, anticipating in wonder, yet knowing all the while what was about to come, dreading the words I'd never heard spoken.

I'd lied deliberately about my father—I remembered him only too well—his strength, the fount from which I'd drawn my height, the clear bright goodness that was invulnerable to everything but the tuberculosis bacilli.

But now I waited, lying. To her, to myself, to my inner yearning yet unknown.

"David, I know your feeling . . ."

"Do you?"

"Please, let me finish."

"Go on."

"It's because . . ." She paused and shifted a little on the bed so that her face revealed itself in the listless light, starkly. "It's because having a white mother is not an easy thing—"

"I gotta go, Ma." I stood up, watching the pain erode slowly over the sharp angles, the soft breast-bows, of her features. "I'll be late for work."

"David—"

"I only gotta work a few hours—"

"Please . . ."

But I cruelly ignored the word, snatching up my jacket from the couch, where I'd thrown it angrily arriving home from the Fruit meeting.

"David," she said softly, that second before I could fully close the door behind me, ". . . your father and I loved each other."

And I had to hurry, before the flood burst entirely and I rushed back to her arms and comfort . . .

Like the night my father died.

CHAPTER THREE

HERE'S MY WORLD—Niggerville—my sore, my shame, since the first time I realized it as a thing of fact and not some Cracker's cartoon strip:

Greasy Bones 'N' Cracklin's, the Shine epicure's constancy of eternally chopping jaws; the lighted neoned otherworlds, where whiskey-whining woes found expression in B.B.'s blues and *Blinky's* hues of black and low-trash white; those slinking Johns, consorting with sly-eyed, fearful laughs, futilely measuring their acceptance here, dickering with some black Horror's whore for that slice of ecstasy that was not life unto themselves, *was* oblivion to the whore and what she represented to her environment—like screwing death, I thought disgustedly.

My world, man:

Yes, dopeys and drugmen and dapper mocking Dans—the fuzz and pussy and pussy-collared: the *Jesus, please* exhorters on cornerfronts, in candy stores converted; the hurried, harried, hungry, for whom despair and life composed a litany—a dirge—preceding, yes, overlasting, their damned-faced passing.

Mine.

And me. I'm them.

So see as I have seen, have been, am now, will remain:

When I walk streets I see with different nigger's eyes . . . The pool-packed, pulsing poolroom is no longer fraternity house, where clicking balls in undulating unbroken colored continuity caused by reefer's exciting illusion, and inconstancy, is now a mortuary replete with stupidly staring, insipid-eyed corpses—with nowhere else to be but here and being dead this way.

Lazarus, the Prophet called us.

Hi, Laz, old buddy, I say to myself in passing—all you Lazs in *Abraham's Pool Emporium* . . .

His bosom.

Niggerville, Hooverhill, Stupidstill.

That was it—*still*, rather than anything else, forever, like allways, always this way, unchanging, without the usual boredom of such things, *like* things (though not another world is *like* this one of mine), undifferently different, daily.

I walked and felt the cooling night-time stink against my cheeks and saw myself reflected sadly in the garish glass facades. There was no other world in which I could escape my fate, no ash or sackcloth to redeem my father's guilt, his father's past, that pasttime savage's acquiescence to slavery's sloppy mouth, her whorish kiss . . .

Seventy-fourth Street.

Oh, my people's city within the black bloated white whale's belly! Unmasticated, swallowed whole in dirty, acid bilish unfelt torment—

I see here an Avenue of lavish lights, of luscious, lazy abstraction—of irresponsible life—and I goddamn its refusal of me, of my question, of my quest for identification—

"Because you could *tell* me," I say, in a way that makes a passing man turn as though he really could.

—and denying me, in its complacent comfort, that pit-small piece of peace which is my heritage's right.

I despise and loathe you, each and every nigger, now, before, to come, who make me prisoner and shameful recipient of a deeper unrealized repulsion.

Only your deaths—and mine—would make me accept the way things are!

CHAPTER FOUR

"Listen, Dave, would you tell me straight? It's just a thing that crossed my mind, and you and me are pretty tight around the store—just a question to prove my point 'bout progress, and brotherhood and such."

I looked deep in Arnie's light blue eyes and saw the lecher gleam. Another question about sex—and me.

"You ever had a white woman, Dave?"

It was the same, the question that was not asked by them for knowing's sake—more for self-substantiation. It was one that always rankled me, nothing like the "how big's yours?" or "can ya really strike bottom with a colored girl?" kind: this query demanded self-incrimination, and it left no fifth-amendment exit.

I looked at him, his face, the palishness that was a glow to *know*. His covering skin was the same as my mother's, but the differences here was a distention of abstraction that dissolved into complete racelessness. I mean . . .

I felt the burn of it—I *hated* him. And her, too, my Ma. But still, they didn't seem to be the same, her and Arnie: she, in her hiding, bed-ridden twilight of prolonged dying, and he—he the cousin of my boss, my co-mate superior in the supermarket's well-stocked stockroom of floresced people-needs.

He—this—here—was what I seemed to *know* in her, but couldn't ever see in fact. It was frustrating, and I was helpless. Futility,

That drove my fingers into hard-rock black fists.

That made me rise—actually *rise*—as though to sunder Murder's virgin cherry.

"You know what I mean, Dave? Huh?"

Again I looked at him, examining his flushed, pink throat: his talk of women's asses, tits, pussy, hungry, consuming mouths—had drawn hot blood to his reddish skull, and caused a shiny wetness at the corners of his mouth.

I raised a carton to chest level and placed it on another just the same.

"No," I said, avoiding him, unsure of myself as I'd never been before.

"What?"

"You heard me."

He wiped the moisture and stockroom dustiness on his apron front, and sat on two ass-high cartons of Campbell's soup.

"Aw, Dave, come off it . . . I know you City College boys—"

"I only went for a couple semesters . . ."

"But that's enough! You musta met *some* hot young blonde—they've got a reputation over there."

"They didn't earn it because of me—I went to CC to get an education—" I was angry now, and I turned on a pivot that warmed my calves and thighs, clear to my chest and pounding heart,

"—not a piece of tail that all it knows how to *be* is tail—that means no more to me than *your* ass!"

"Now listen . . ." he said, rising.

"No, *you* listen—" And I saw him back away a little, shocked by the thing in my eyes.

"My religion tells me you're scum," I said in a low, steady, unmistakable voice.

"What are you talkin about, Dave?"

"That you're filthy. From your sex habits and psychosis to your useless effort to return head-first to the womb through some brother-faggot's rump—"

"Hey—" he said in an almost scream, as though I'd struck him.

"*Now!*" I said, impressed with our aloneness, the inspiration of death in my hands. "It's gotta come now—not when Fard decides it's ready—*our* time is ready!" My head was buzzing with a surging new strength.

"What's the *matter* with you, Dave?" Arnie said, aghast. He moved behind the boxes, trembling in a manner that gave the gutty stone at the pit of me an urgent implosion.

We both knew it, what was about to come, in a way that was more than fear, or orgasm—or death: even more than the thing itself. I found myself crouched, somehow overly huge and anticipatory, like a jungle animal that had surprised its natural prey breaking thirst, and now there was no shelter or escape for it, as though there had *never* been, as though God had never meant there to be a haven from its natural death.

"Dave," Arnie whimpered, "for chrissakes, pull yourself together!"

As I had sensed natural death, so now did I sense an innate, almost historic, fear. A congenital thing, just as Brother Harvey and the Leader had apprised us of in the teachings. Before me was the face of a *criminal*—a murderer and rapist—who had been caught in the act, and now dreaded the final, absolute, consequences of his acts . . . Revelation's Beast of the Bottomless Pit who would cry to Heaven on the day of exposure, seeking mercy where there is none—the serpent of the original garden: Baal, Satan.

The Devil.

"Dave," he said, trembling uncontrollably, "the way you're lookin . . . you're *scarin* me! Dave, I never did *nothin* to you—why do you wanna do this?"

Involuntarily, my mind and body were released from the strange—yes, *selfish*—tension, and it was as if my eyes had been opened after a week's slumber. And what I saw, through the dying storm of my lust, was not a devil at all, but merely a prefab human— certainly a prototype of the Master of the World—a cardboard Tarzan whose hard-ons came vicariously . . . who, for some indefinable reason not completely explained to my satisfaction in the teachings, bore an insuperable weight of guilt, of envy, of masochistic love-hate, in the person of a contradictory personage—the black man.

Why I stopped to grapple with, to rationalize, my *hatred* (but was it *mine?* I wondered; wasn't it shared by others?) I didn't know.

My anger was unceasing—indeed, it had increased, soared, in an illimitable abundance, not upward but Heavenward, eastward, toward Mecca, receiver of my five-times-a-day genuflections—and the God of another age whose evil black mind had predestined my torment presently with His creation—*glad* creation—of a plague-race, and the current-day Allah, W. D. Fard Muhammad, whose patience in the divine city was my pain.

And I cursed aloud, and the quivering, pre-ordained Adam before me quivered anew, mewlingly, so sickeningly humbled by his own unknown fear that I felt like retching.

I turned away in guilty disgust.

This was not the kind of thing that I, if God's seed I was, could make war on.

Yakub, the God of Genesis, had been successful in his command, "*Come, let us make Man in our own image . . .*"

For an *image* was all he succeeded in creating.

CHAPTER FIVE

THE BOSS REGARDED ME as though I was mad—and I guess I was, maniacally—when I told him to shove his job, and collected the pay I had coming. I didn't see his face—it had idiotically grown too pale to realize, diaphanous—nor hear his words of not-understanding: nor even, really, feel myself as a person—more as a dissociated entity that was *eyes*, watching *me* go through a series of motions at the checkout counter, glaring low-browed in a way to cause the watcher to feel that *me* was staring inwardly at some inward horror, or had, finally, terrifyingly, come aware of a rot that had existed there unnoticed all along, too long, and that putrescence was steadily, intransigentl*y*, occupying the *all* of *me*.

I watched *me* come slowly out of the market, shoving the few bills to the coarse pocket bottom, separating the few coins from the crinkling mass so that they came between the first joint of each finger, tediously.

He glanced over the long, black, brighted, night-time street pointlessly, for he knew now there was nowhere to go from here. Above, the sky had grown black as his thalamic pit; the wings of his heart fluttered accusingly. Yes—and *his* soul was tightening about his entire being like a garrote.

His eyes, darting ahead of his brain, recognized the next, people-cluttered, block as the one nestling the Muslim restaurant, Shabazz, and he knew many Brothers would be there now, indulging a good-night's repast. The urge to enter was almost overpowering, as he passed, but he knew their voices would lower if he did, their eyes would not see him, their minds would deny his outcast abstraction.

Inside (his heart sped with longing as he came staring by) were the brightly-lit, sterile cleanliness of Brotherhood, and Brothers' close-cropped heads, neatly nodding to sup, the smell of onion-sopped beef expertly cooked by Sister Dahlil, Brother Harvey's fat, jolly ebony-skinned wife, which brought saliva bitter and yearning to his tongue—and he quickened the passage of his feet a bit in going by the luscious place of belonging.

Behind him, he heard footsteps discreetly chasing his, and turned to see Brother Forest, tall as a Watusi, and his sister, Famat, who was but an inch or two shorter, led in a mild, soldierly trot by Brother Carl.

"Brother David . . ." he called.

But he already waited, weirdly empty, as they came abreast.

"As salaam aliekum," Brother Carl said, and so did the others.

"Wa 'liekum salaam," he answered.

Brother Carl was somehow abashed, rather ashamed, it seemed; and the others—their eyes watched him with expectancy—and for the first time he knew Famat's intense white smile, the way it was embossed by large, generous lips; the way her nose flared, like a doe that has been frightened suddenly—the way that her smooth skin was, now, not black and monotonous as he believed all black skins to be, but lustrous, myriadly brilliant and kaleidoscopic with the variance of night-lights, and abruptly it was one of the most beautifully pigmented tissues he'd ever seen.

"We saw you pass by Shabazz, Brother," his friend told him, now so different from the embarrassed, facially reticent young man he'd spoken with after the Fruit meeting, earlier.

"You shouldn't have left your meals," he told Carl quietly, supernaturally aware of himself *above* himself, hovering, it seemed, like some message of black importance.

Concerned. Yes, their faces watching him, the looks in their eyes, were concerned.

"Is anything wrong? Brothers? Sister?"

Famat tensed visibly at his reference, and boldly set precedence by answering before any of the males, invoking quick, obvious displeasure from her brother.

"Brother David . . . we wondered—at least, we . . . *I* . . . heard about what happened tonight. I'm sorry."

"Of course we are," Brother Forest said, putting emphasis on "we."

"We weren't eating," Brother Carl told him. "We were just talking when you came by. Brother Forest intends to record a little of the Teachings . . ."

"We wondered if you would like to come by," Brother Forest said politely. "We don't feel, because of your suspension, you should be denied Allah's most abundant food—we don't feel any black brother should be ostracized, in this respect."

"That's kind of you," he told them.

Famat's face brightened. "Then you *will* come along?"

"I'm sorry . . ."

"Please, David," Carl said kindly. "It'll take your mind off things."

"My mind isn't troubled, Brother, thank you."

He saw Carl's face flush, an accent of lemon on thin, sensitive, Asiatic features, and felt ashamed of the pain he'd caused his only friend.

Now his eyes shifted to Famat once more, and there was something about the way she watched him, not that prim generality of surveillance used by the modest Pearls of Islam, but a frank, open gaze, white and clear, which accentuated her full, unpainted character of face; and the trunk of her, he saw self-consciously, with a tiny tickle of physicality, was full to bursting with youth under the plain dress emulated by all Sisters of the Pearl: breasts high, full and proper over the wide, receptive pelvis, carried on thick thighs and slim smooth legs he had come to recognize as those belonging to the pedigree of black female blood—the mark of an honored tribe.

And he wondered what had kept his eyes from seeing her before. In this peculiar, pleasing, way.

"I was on my way home," he began, watching the way her lids raised at the sound of his voice.

"Oh, please, Brother David—Allah would be pleased if you came along," she said.

From above, from a plane, an aerie perspective, that seemed to sway his heart irrepressibly in a way he'd never felt before, he saw, and felt, his mouth form the words.

"If . . . I won't bother anyone," he agreed.

"You won't," Famat said, showing a wide, comforting smile.

They struck a pace, and Carl fell in beside him.

"I stopped by your place not long ago," he said quietly. "Your mother told me you'd gone to the market."

"I quit tonight." But he offered no further explanation, and Carl did not press. He turned to Brother Forest and Famat, who followed behind, and directed their attention to an eastern star.

"Mine," he announced, like a song. "Brother Dawud cast my horoscope, and that's my direction, he said. The star of faith."

Brother Forest nodded with dark inscrutability. "You have as much of that as anyone I know, Brother Carl."

"Thank you, Brother."

They walked in silence up to 112th Street, then over a block past the teeming nightshade tenements, where black men and women and running, playing, children lived in unlikely prosperous vivacity, enthusiastic, perhaps for tomorrow, perhaps the next day, in love with life's living and each personal moment, contained in the fallacy of God's benevolence, in a kind of drug-like deprivation that induced a false, comforting elation in an immediacy that was really death. And more.

Was really the World in miniature, was frightening, truly, if one stopped to look at it. And he *had*—suddenly had.

Carl noticed the slight change in step. "I'm glad we saw you tonight, Brother . . . I didn't have a chance to speak with you as fully—after the Fruit gathering—as I would have liked . . ."

"Yes. I'm sorry now. What I said," he told Carl in a funny, different voice he'd never heard his mouth make before.

"No, Bro—David." He watched Carl's profile and, when he could see them, the small, radiant eyes, that seemed to emanate a feeling of sincerity, of brotherly dedication to the cult of—brother-hood.

And he smiled with the thought, not with discovery but with a heavy weight of judgment. For he had known all along that there was something each man endeavored to achieve—something, he didn't know what, that even *he* desired over and above the very fact of life.

In simply knowing this, he knew what it was Carl wanted—and he despised Carl for it. But if Carl wanted it . . .

Didn't Brother Harvey? Brother Forest and all the other Brothers?

Even the Leader himself?

Were it not for his detachment, he could have answered the most important questions. But it didn't seem to mean so much now, not now that he was aware of Carl, and his hunger, and the hunger about them as they walked, and the black above, with Carl's star dimly insinuated, and his own heart thumping wildly as he made himself aware of Famat's full, blossomed presence behind and how much he would like to touch her flowered skin, to know its warmth with his own.

Perhaps . . .

"This is my place, Brothers," Forest said, pointing to a stoop just ahead, where several black people sat drinking beer, two women and a man who was cursing one of the women unangrily but steadily and did not pause as they came up and entered.

"Sometimes the dead Brother is disgusting," Brother Forest commented in the dark, unlit gloominess of the hallway.

Like his own apartment building, Brother Forest's was a musical of despair; the stairway looped rather than ascended to the third floor, around hedges of battered-faced doors and limp iron railings, where the darkness grew more penetrable as they went higher, shafted by beams of the night-sky's varied illumination from the dull skylight above the fifth floor.

"The darkest part of the temple," Brother Forest noted grimly, referring to a Masonic ritual.

At one of the rear doors on the third floor, he stopped and inserted a key. The room was neat and plumpily furnished. In one corner was a television set, with a black plaster bust of a long-dead Egyptian queen atop. On one wall was an almost full-sized eastern tapestry of a desert scene—two camel drovers trading with what appeared to be a rich merchant, whose eyes on their wares were greedy and lascivious rather than brotherly—very beautifully and expertly done.

All the couches were purposely fat, cushioned in the opulent eastern harem fashion, and he felt misplaced, the softness sucking at his rump as he sat, and much out of place.

A tall, dark-skinned, smiling woman came through the kitchen doorway, bowing slightly. "As salaam aliekum."

"Wa 'liekum salaam," they replied.

"I heard you come in," she said in a gently deep voice. "I have some coffee ready."

"That's fine, Mother," Famat said. "I'll help you with it."

They both bowed almost imperceptibly in united grace as they left for the kitchen.

"Your sister is a fine-looking woman, Brother Forest," he heard himself say involuntarily. "And your mother is quite handsome."

He noticed vaguely Carl's glance in his direction, that seemed to make his skin prickle, and he turned his eyes toward the door the women had entered. Over the archway was the blood-red Muslim flag, the sun, the crescent of the moon, the tranquility of the stars. Freedom, Justice and Equality.

Brother Forest went into an adjoining room and returned with a portable tape recorder and a sheaf of papers in a manila folder.

"I'll have to review a bit, Brother Carl; Brother Dawud and I did quite a lot of recording earlier today." He set it down next to an overlarge easy chair, unlatched the top, and plugged the cord into one of the wall outlets.

"Here's the coffee," Famat said, entering again with a tray. "I hope you like it black—there's no cream."

He watched her as she smiled at him, handing over a cup and saucer tentatively. "Brother David . . . ?"

"Thank you," he said, and watched the salience of her long dark legs as she took a seat facing him. And he could not take his eyes from her face, knowing all the while she was aware of his attention.

"There it is," Brother Forest said, with a final tape adjustment.

He consulted the typewritten pages in the folder. "Where shall we begin, Brother Carl? Brother David?"

"Well," said Carl, "the European evolutionary stage—the Devil's development there. I don't think we've done it yet." He sipped hugely of his coffee.

Brother Forest objected with an upraised finger and polite smile. "I have the tapes by Brother Charles X, which were done last fall."

"They're kind of shabby now, Brother," Famat addressed her blood. "Why don't we begin with The Creation? We're all familiar with it, and maybe you Brothers can contribute taped portions without the benefit of the Leader's notes."

Whenever she spoke, he noticed, a certain quiet prevailed afterward, accentuating the tone, the resonance, of her rather deep voice, giving the words an impact of forwardness and presumption he was sure she did not intend to convey.

"Why not let Brother David begin?" she added, and it might as well have been the sharp explosion of a pistol.

Carl looked at him quickly. "Yes, David, why don't you start it off for me?"

And he felt himself saying, against his will, "I don't know how it'll turn out . . . but I wouldn't mind trying."

Brother Forest stood up from his seat. "Sit here, Brother. I'll adjust the machine as you speak."

He saw himself rise, take the place, take the microphone along with Brother Forest's brotherly smile, and, with one last glance at the calm-faced Famat, and a signal from Brother Forest, he was surprised to hear himself begin:

"As salaam aliekum. By the benevolence of Allah, the One God, the following is an interpretation of The Creation, as revealed to our Leader by Allah the All Merciful, in the voice of Brother David X, devotee of Muhammad's Temple of Islam, eastern district."

Brother Forest snapped the off-button. "Now, Brother David, that was a fine introduction. Take your time; there's thirty minutes of tape."

He cleared his throat, not nervous as he'd expected himself to be, and, peculiarly, not even aware what his first words would be. He took a deep drink of the bitter Arabic coffee.

They waited expectantly. Brother Forest started the machine again.

"About eight thousand years ago, in the Holy City of Mecca," he began, "there occurred the birth of a man, whose name, Allah tells us, was Yakub—the God of his time. Yakub's birth had been foretold through the prophets in the twenty-two-million-year-old dynasty of the black man.

"Now. When Yakub was born it was, therefore, no secret. The people, as well as the Sidi and the twenty-four prophets, knew of his coming and what his coming would mean to the world and countless generations to follow.

"Yakub, in fact, told his uncle, at the age of eight, that he would create a race more powerful than any the world of Godmen had yet seen . . . and his statement was not taken lightly. For even his destiny had been foretold also—even so the evil it would bring . . ."

His voice now took a branch of discourse they were not familiar with, indelibly stamped in the twisting spool, and he felt the strange warmth in the eyes as they watched him.

"However, no action was taken to prevent the coming of this scourge, predicted to last six thousand years, neither by previous Gods, who could have easily misdirected the genetic stream, or the God of Yakub's day, who could have blunted the seed, telepathically, in his mother's womb . . ."

Unconsciously, he stopped. The statement was unpremeditated but far from subtle. It was a rebuke, a criticism, plain and simple, an irritating granule of thought that had grated his whole conscience since the day he'd embraced Islam, the unasked *why*, that could not, as Brother Minister and Brother Harvey claimed, be "explained mathematically, as could all things in Islam," for no mathematical solution seemed sufficient enough an *excuse*, a *vindication*, of the Godheads who were supposedly aware of the havoc this new devil race would disseminate on ensuing generations.

No.

Mathematically, he was forced to see, it was imperfect—and ridiculous to consider it any other way.

Six thousand years of hell as balanced against *what?* Tomorrow, which was an abstract one could not compute along with yesterday's facts and today's reality—was, therefore, the imponderable fraction, the key denominator in a final solution?

No, he told himself impassively.

No.

"Go on, Brother," Brother Forest said softly, watching him. They all watched him, like stuffed drovers anticipating a wealth's barter he could not yet fully honor.

Brother Forest waited with finger on key, having deigned the full, raging, thunderous catharsis of enlightening silence they'd just heard.

He raised the microphone close to his lips again, and licked them.

Click.

"Yakub came to be," he heard himself say, "the first God of evil, Baal, the first black Devil ever to exist in Heaven-Mecca. He was a genius of dissension, sedition, subterfuge, coming at a time when a certain portion of the world's population was socially satisfied while a smaller percentage was not. It was to these malcontents he appealed when arranging his master-plan. They followed him unquestioningly into the whirlpools of political unrest he fomented, never doubting his assertion of their own *special* divinity under his leadership, and even, when Yakub was no longer tolerable to those of ruling authority, followed him into exile—a small island off the coast of North Africa.

"As a result of Yakub's concentrated attacks and other ingenious methods contrived to create turmoil, the civilization of the Original God suffered schisms of belief; new faiths arose; Godman isolated himself in groups on other portions of the globe and went into wild tangents of religiosity . . . the clashes were enough to draw attention away from the insidious God Yakub and the Frankensteinian scheme he set toward consummation.

"Yakub—or, as the Bible calls him: Luther, the Archangel—

you see, was followed by fifty-nine thousand nine hundred ninety-nine believers, whom he was to employ in this Gargantuan plan. And it took four hundred and sixty-odd years."

Brother Forest snapped the recorder off. "Brother David, I think you ought to say a word or two about the pre-Yakub world."

"It's pertinent," Carl agreed. "Anyone hearing this for the first time, David—say, one of the dead Brothers—couldn't help being a little confused."

Famat smiled at him. "You're doing beautifully, Brother David." *Click.*

"A footnote should be added here," his voice rang solidly inside his head. "Before the coming of Yakub, for thousands—yes, for millions of years—Original man had existed upon the Earth in complete sensual serenity. He was the *mind* of the universe, the God of Perfection, capable of self-reproduction, the like of which is observed today in certain amoebic life forms; it was much later, after realization of his intellectual supremacy, that he decided to form the female entity separate of himself. No one knows, save Allah in His greatness, how Original man evolved. But no one doubts the facts of his unique dominion for countless centuries. From the life force of his mere being he had caused the existence of the Earth, moon, and surrounding planets through a calculated explosion of our nova. Even the crinkly hair of certain black people is directly attributed to one of these Original men—a casual whim of his.

"This was a period of total oneness, a time in which man communicated with his brother through the medium of telepathy; when he traveled by the light-like instantaneousness of teleportation; when one thought, one discovery, was simultaneously flashed to the corporate mind.

"One may ask why man didn't continue this indescribably perfect state—and that one has every right to have his question answered."

But here Brother Forest stopped the machine and looked at him a long time before speaking. "I don't think we should stray too far off the point, Brother David."

"I don't intend to."

Brother Forest nodded in a way that did not necessarily indicate concession. "Let us continue, then."

He licked his lips and felt his voice lower to a throbbing, strengthful octave of emotion.

"It was because," he went on, "that Original man was *not* as perfect as he led himself to believe . . ."

Click.

Brother Forest now stood from his kneeling position by the machine. There was almost a vibratory emanation of quiet confusion in his rigid stance, unwavering eyes and dark-set black face. "I think we'd better erase that part, Brother David."

"Wait," he heard Famat's soft voice say. "I don't think Brother David completed his thought."

"What he's saying is not doctrine," her brother said, with what was now an unmistakable chill in his voice. He looked to Carl for— not *support*—confirmation.

And Carl said, not looking at his friend.

"Yes, sir. We're listening to personal interpretation."

"But I thought that's what we agreed on from the beginning," she protested, "a rendition of *personal* perspectives." She shifted her bulk, the fineness of her living electric beauty, to him where he sat waiting with the microphone. "How else are we expected to gain the *essence* of the Leader's truth other than by interpretive individuality? No one truth is the same in the eyes of all the people, Brother, because each man's conception is colored by his *own values* and experiences. But this doesn't change the truth from being *truth*—nothing, no one, could do that. No matter how you dress it, no matter how many lying drugs are injected to make it stand at a false attention—not even artificially changing its sex or origin."

She paused now, and seemed about to go on for a moment. Then she smiled at him under the glowering cascade of her brother's distemper.

"Please go on, Brother David," she said softly.

He cleared his throat, not feeling nervous at all—actually anxious to go on, embraced by the necessity of expression and the pulse of a foreign passion.

After a brief hesitation, Brother Forest stooped to start the machine again.

"Somewhere, during his various metamorphic stages, Original man lost his originality," he said unflinchingly. "After countless years of duplication of his perfection and him*self,* the first God became more *man* than God, for through his own formulation, his basic cognizance of the unavoidability of—the primary prerequisite of all creation—the cycle of three hundred and sixty degrees, man-God *inversed* himself, taking on more manlike atributes at the sake of aggravating the God-core—originality—thereby fusing the flesh and that which was omnipotent into an unholy alliance. In other words, there were too many Gods for God's own good—too many omnipresent pretenders for the throne of omniscience.

"Mathematically, then, there was little these unfused God-intellects could do, in the eons falling on the coming of Yakub, to keep from degenerating into mere men.

"And so concerned they were with the inward contemplation of the wonders in the evolution of their slowly vanishing Godseeds, the growing inaction of the God*seat*—the brain—that there was damned little they cared to do about it."

"That's about all," Brother Forest said harshly, cutting off the machine with a loud snapping noise that rang around the void of All-things and yanked the past, the present, into the *here* . . . and *me* into *myself.*

"But I'm not finished," I said, looking at him in his eyes until our four eyes were glued, and I could feel the fear as he hovered menacingly above me, from both of us.

"You are as far as I'm concerned," he said rather loudly.

"Brother—" Famat started. "Forest . . . Brother David is our guest—we *won't* show him any discourtesy."

"It's Brother David who's shown the discourtesy," he said lividly. "He's shown it to the Holy Koran, our Honorable Leader and Allah Himself in that order—any one of which is excuse enough to take his blaspheming head!"

"Forest!" Famat said.

Carl stood to go over to him. "Brother . . . peace, Brother, *please.* It's only that Brother David's interpretation of known truth isn't as exact as it *could* be—he needs further study . . ."

"He needs total expulsion from the Temple," Brother Forest said venomously, and I knew he hated me—but the hatred was because of another thing, because of his sister, whose plain prim dress I had raised over her hips as soon as I knew that the wrongness I was experiencing was the dress itself, the doctrine, the *peace be with you* in hell, as though there could *ever* be the sudden, good, human-again feeling. . . . Someone, some voice, some*thing,* was laughing at us, at all of us, at *me,* because of some vague, shadowy, goddamn lie we'd been conned to believe in.

I could see the sides of Brother Forest's cheeks bunching in sharp muscles, rocky, black huge mountain definitions, as he looked down on me. "This young man is dangerous to himself, to us, and to the cause of the lost-found black nation here in the hell of North America. I heard him earlier tonight, with his filthy devil's mouth, heaping abuse on Brother Harvey in the midst of a Fruit discussion, and if it hadn't been for you, Brother Carl, I'd never have allowed him in my home."

"Brother—" Carl started.

I now stood myself. "That's all right, Carl. Brother Forest, I want you to know something—"

"I don't want your apologies . . ."

"I wasn't about to give them."

"Then you can get out of here."

"Forest!" Famat said.

Her mother came through the kitchen door and stood watching us quietly.

"Now I've got something to say," Famat's voice rose surprisingly, and I could see now a glimmering coat of anger in her smooth features that somehow gave me a feeling of extreme excitement. "And I'm going to say it whether you like it or not. You Brothers all seem to feel that we Sisters have no right to think. Well that's wrong. That we have no voice—that we're merely receptacles for your holy seed and the teats for its nourishment. Well, you're wrong again!" she said feelingly. "We *do* think, and we *are* more than homemakers and brood cows—"

"Famat," Brother Forest said tensely. "I command you to shut your mouth."

"And I refuse to!" she said defiantly. "And from now on I'm going to refuse *all* commands I think are unjust. Don't you provoke me, Brother," she warned, "because I'll go further than Brother David and question the tenet called Freedom, Justice and Equality under Islam. I thank Allah for the capacity to make my own judgments and to *seek* my own answers." Her ire caused her to appear lost for words for a moment.

Then she glanced at me, a soft thing, feline and heartful. "If you're going to expel Brother David from the Fruit, then you'd better expel *me* from the Pearl."

"Famat!" her mother said, shocked.

"That's the way it must be," Famat went on strongly. "Because I have questions, too, and I'll never stop asking for the answers until I have them—to *my* satisfaction. Even though we were raised in Islam, Forest—please. Even though our father raised us in Islam, he never established—no, decreed—our positions as his children—"

"*I* am Allah's spear of judgment," her brother said proudly. "I offer my life to the war, and victory, of Armaggedon."

"Yes, you," Famat answered dimly. "You're a warrior of Allah—you know your place. But what about me? What about me. Mother?" she said, looking up. "Us? Why is it we've got to take the back seat? Is my only duty to Islam to teach day after endless day fourth-grade classes in the Temple classroom—when what I want to do is use my mind—contribute what I *know* is a good intellect—to a common cause, a common good? Is it only to birth strong black babies whose only purpose will be to give up their lives in some stinking war whose cause—whose background—whose beginning—is too profound for them to understand? So that all they've got to feed their warfire is a bunch of slogans and thrilling semantics? No! I refuse. Again I refuse! Because I don't know— and I've *got* to know before I follow *any* command. Allah says that

315

I am his separate self. That under the law I am equal, free and subject to every justice rendered my male counterpart. I choose, as Brother David apparently does, to *demand* confirmation of my heritage, and as long as I don't get it I'm going to question the dogma of men—because God, not man, is the only infallibility." She stared unafraidly at her brother. "I hereby assume my better judgment to be the final decider, and from it *only* will I follow orders—because, of all things I know to be God-given and *mine* only, this is most obvious."

Brother Forest, without a doubt, regarded me as sole cause of his sister's impassioned rebellion, and I began to hope fervently that I *was*.

The chill had increased in Brother Forest's eyes. "You've said quite enough, Famat. I'm sure you don't want Brother David's departure to become any more complicated."

I went to the door, nodded slightly, "As salaam aliekum," and left.

I noticed that no one, with the exception of Famat, wished me peace in going.

CHAPTER SIX

We wore silk robes and slippers of gold;
We were the finest people, I'm told;
Now we're the poorest of the poor . . .
Nobody wants us at his door.
    So, my friends, it is easy to tell
    White man's heaven is a black man's hell.

The loudspeaker outside a record shop on Eighth Avenue defiantly blared the deeply emotional voice and haunting melody. I paused for a moment and listened, moved against my will as the rhythmic strains flooded the lull of the late night-time, existed in sweet deprecation:

> With his white woman and firewater,
> Tricks and lies he stole America . . .
> The Original owner of this nation
> Is cooped up on a reservation.
> So, my friends, it is easy to tell
> White man's heaven is a black man's hell.

I walked slowly toward home, strangely calm and introspective in a way that seemed in accord with the night and all its things. As though, a moment before, I hadn't been locked in self-conflict, hadn't engaged and warred within myself to strict and gruesome culmination. *Had* been the victor.

Now the taste of it—this first victory, the only one I'd ever won—overcame me, and I tasted it hot and sweet-bitter, like the wonderful soothing taste of Famat's good black coffee.

I crossed over to the mall, where an empty bench faced the traffic, and sat down, feeling washed and free—possessed of an alien knowledge that had come under my control through a cultivation I had not been aware of.

I listened intently for a while to the message from the loudspeaker, listened to it trace a history of slavery in chilling, graphic detail right up to the present day, which saw the status of the slave unchanged—in fact, more deeply ingrained through a process of indocrination that deadened the collective senses and hardened the arteries of mass response.

I wondered at myself, compared my new audacity of self-awareness to that of a molecular chain, framed much like the scheme of stars overhead pointing the way to the arid answers of space.

I now had my path indicated, unspecified, but happy, and I

wondered about it all, intoxicated, like the first time I had tasted liquor hidden discreetly by my father from my mother's attention: frightened yet exhilarated, sickened yet cured, warmed and cooled simultaneously, both inside and out, in gut and epidermis.

Brother Forest had said I was dangerous. And he'd been right. I was. But more than anything else, the Nation included, to myself— to my sudden sanity. And the thought of this suddenly made me quite afraid. Suppose I should lose it?

I got up and strode slowly into the street and traffic, narrowly missed by roaring convertibles loaded with carousing, drunk-eyed teenagers, chased without pretense by grinning juggernaut trucks.

Slightly out of breath, I made the other side, standing now in front of the record shop, Muslim, I saw now, by the fact of the young black woman sitting behind the counter with her hair covered, in the traditional Pearl manner, with a colorful silk bandana.

> The greatest crime is his
> Who kills new dust of the womb,
> Sterile father of Death and the Tomb;
> The snake of the Garden and Tree,
>   Despiser of Man's trunk and Earth;
>   But in Love we find truth and rebirth.

The words were strange to me. I stopped and listened closely.

> We find ourselves a part of plots
> So desperately made,
> But love is not easily swayed;
> Our task is a one to be praised,
> Allah has directed our ways,
> To roads that the future has paved.
>   Come flee with me to new land,
>   Where evil disdains our way and kind.
> Someday, my darling, we will gift our
> Kinsmen with passion's harvest:

New men who'll rule the world and stars—
Our sons, the Children of the Outside.

Something about the song caused me to linger to its finale. Unlike "White Man's Heaven Is a Black Man's Hell," it spoke of love, and woman, and an end to all iniquity through adoration and physical delight.

"That's called 'Outsiders,'" someone behind me said, and I turned with a thrill of recognition to look in Famat's smiling eyes. "It's very beautiful, isn't it?"

"Yes," I said.

"The author is unknown."

"Perhaps he isn't."

She lowered her eyes, but not in a way that was shy—was, oddly, a gesture meant only for me. "Would you like me to tell you the story of 'Outsiders'?"

"I'd like that more than anything else."

"Let's walk," she said, taking my arm.

I hesitated. "My mother is alone. I should've *been* back to see about her. I was on my way home when I met you at Shabazz."

"I'll walk with you," she said.

"It's late. Too late for you to be out, Sister."

"I'm not afraid, David," she told me with a confident smile. "This neighborhood, these people, are mine; they know me. They wouldn't hurt me in any way."

I looked at the dress parade of slouching winos and whores as we passed, the peanut hawkers and profane children, the neat pimps in ambiguous Cadillacs, the other twisted sores of Harlem's blackened face, and said, "These people belong to someone else—not you, Famat. The Leader's right—they're zombies, the walking dead—slaves of the Devil."

"What did you mean?" she said suddenly.

"About what?"

"About the song—about its author possibly being known?"

"I'll have to wait, to hear the story you're going to tell me; I've heard them all and know their creators. There're just so many story roots, even in Islam."

"This isn't Islam, David . . ."

"Then what is it?"

She lowered her eyes again as I glanced in her direction. "It's a love tale. It's simply about two people."

I waited—because it wasn't embarrassment she felt, but a tenuity that abruptly trilled through us both.

In silence we walked, in silent agreement, in solitude of self, if that is expressionable; this was an outlying venue that did not at all portend an eventual disaster, but was much like a fairy forest full with need of *having*: the need to be *had* by another individual, that should be a coupling of two differences into one fact.

As we neared the place I lived in, I felt a new fear pull accusingly at my knowledge of the present.

"Carl has spoken of your mother," I heard her say dimly. "I hope my neglect in introducing you to my mother formally won't stop you from making me known to yours, as your friend."

"She might not be yours," I said frankly.

"Why shouldn't she be?"

"Why was the white man created?"

"That's such a difficult question, David. That's why we're here together, tonight. Maybe that was the reason—to bring us here together."

She turned her eyes as I met them.

"It's a question that Islam . . . attempts to answer," she went on softly. "But the explanation has always puzzled me and seemed— *sadistic*. I guess you've felt the same way."

"I've felt . . . confused," I confessed.

Now her eyes brightened, impish flashes, and I grew warm in their glow. "Have you ever felt—not quite right, David? I mean . . ."

"What *do* you mean?"

"Well, as though—" She struggled for the evasive words, clutched them resolutely. "As though you were where you belonged but didn't really belong there at all."

I smiled, "I've never known how to express the feeling—till now."

My street arrived, like a dirty laugh, a carousel of crude buildings, and denuded life sucking at long-emptied bowels of contrived surcrease advertised as *newly redeckorated* or *money, love, happiness peace Madam Nosall Basement front Lucky Spirits;* gallons of uncapped noisome garbage that belonged now—had belonged for more than three days—to the City of New York, and had multiplied, as though by some celestial command, until it reeked in worship, in a way that was sacrificial, the gush of its own fierce, filthy immortality.

"This is where I live," I said quietly—but no longer ashamed in the way I had been at one time—which had only been a few hours before.

I sat on the stoop, and she placed herself closely beside me, so that I could feel the heat of her and the unfamiliar thing it seemed to stir in the pit of my belly. "Now," I said. "Tell me about the Outsiders."

"Well," she said, in a voice I could imagine as one she used in her classroom with the Godseed of the Fruit and Pearl, "the Outsiders are two people aware of the Devil's evil and his attempt to annihilate them. But rather than fight him, they find it easier to escape his reservations and make the outer world their home: *We two, we few, we Nomads, must love desperately, use love's disguise,* they tell themselves."

"I noticed you sang that, and it was beautiful." I touched her long, relaxed fingers. "I feel there's another stanza following that. Please sing it."

After a moment's hesitation, she purred softly, "*Thus when our bodies meet in fusion comprising a total one-ship, we know our home: the heart of destiny—existing on the Outside . . .*"

And then, for a long time, when there was no sound in the street, or the world, we stared at each other.

Silently, I took her hand again and held it firmly in the mouth of my palm. "Sing, Famat, sing . . ."

And her cooing words enveloped me:

It's true, my darling, you're the finest
Treasure I've owned;
No precious stone breaches your tone:
Contrasting black skin, whitest soul.
My ending life isn't hard when
Love's the best place to go,
And I've been . . .
I've won, I've failed, but you know:
They don't get along, Man's laws and mine.
So when you pray for me, remember our
Good feasts and love mem'ries *as* me;
No man or God may touch what is to be:
 Our hearts are on the Outside.

Now the stars grouped in, and the night, and all things indeed became a solitude of our one existence.

"Do you understand?" she asked me.

"How can one understand something he's never known?"

"David . . . you didn't ask me why I followed you tonight. Why I've come this far."

It wasn't the question so much as the realization that I knew the answer, not even really that her speech was not a question at all—more like an accusation that drew me into a frightening, unplumbed vortex.

And I said, "I didn't intend to be the reason—"

"But you *are*, David, whether you want to be or not," she told me. "You can't—if you have the slightest belief in Islam—help believing in destiny, in fate, in predestination, David," she said firmly, and I could feel her breath warm and Famat-fragrant against my cheek. "We both felt it tonight. I could tell it, oh, so long ago, when I first saw your face and the pain on it, in the Temple—that first Sunday you came, do you remember? When you came to the rear after Brother Minister spoke, to accept your letter of entrance into the Temple: I was passing them out . . . Oh, David, I knew you then, and you *looked* at me, for such a time, for such a time that seemed so long a time . . . *And I was warmed through with you—*"

She stopped abruptly.

"Please . . ." I said.

"You probably think I'm mad . . ."

"But I *don't,* Famat."

"I don't know what's wrong with me," she said vaguely, turning her head away. "I'm just acting like a fool . . ."

"Listen, Famat, how can I tell you how *I* feel?" I said desperately. "Because what you say *is* true . . ." But now my words would not come, and I sat with her in silence, waiting for the flood of our emotions to pass. And they *would* not; they grew huger, monolithic, and sweet. Her hand was warm and moist in mine.

"David," she said at length, "do you think—do you think I've been shameless? I mean—I don't want you to *think* I'm not without shame, because I feel it about so *many* things—about the way my mind refutes so much of the Leader's testaments—which *must* be good, for Allah has seen fit to reveal them to us—that confuse me. In my prayers, I beg for forgiveness, but Allah doesn't see fit to give me comfort from this torment . . . David, my Brother," she said passionately, turning her face close to mine, "my *self—tell* me!"

"There *is* peace, Famat . . ."

"But where? Is it really on the outside? Are *we* the Outsiders?"

I felt a strange and sobering fear. "Why should we be? All we need to do is keep our mouths shut. Keep our minds shut, opening them only to what *should* be absorbed by them. Stop thinking." Then I suddenly saw the fateless futility of that fear. "Walk to the beat of that certain drummer, remain just one of a billion faceless faces. Stay harmless, and lambs—the way we were born to be!"

"Stop it!" she said harshly.

So I stopped, but merely stopping did not restore the ungentled plane of balance.

"How can—we—compromise, David?" she said finally.

"Ourselves?" I asked. "That wouldn't be the end."

"No, but it might make a beginning."

I smiled. And she smiled, too.

"It's the first time I've seen you look so beautiful," she said.

Now I blushed.

I stood. "Would you like to meet . . . my mother?"

"I couldn't think of anything I'd enjoy more," she said, rising in a single fluid motion.

But now I paused, anticipating, imagining her reaction to the place I called my home—the woman who was my mother.

Now, she did *not* know, and the magnetism I felt between us was not false, nor did it stem from some cataract of illusion; it was a bond, the caul, in fact, of a newborn entity that superceded our very existence, thrust from a womb of non-identification. But there *was* a spectre of identity between us, and I wondered at her response once she set eyes on it.

It was a very difficult moment for me. I was on the threshold of discovering Famat, as a woman who had come to represent something unutterably valuable among all the things I had, up to now, considered tinsel and gilt, the tender of desiccated demigods. Yes, and discovering *myself* as a man—not merely the inflation of the genitals: yet more, the inflation of the heart to painfully gigantic and pleasant proportions I'd never before experienced.

I was afraid of losing her, and yet, more afraid of losing myself.

"David . . . ?" I heard her voice probe at my indecision.

Without another word I took her hand and led her into the fetid building, she bringing along a warmth beside me that, curiously, was chilling to my flesh.

When we entered, I could see that my mother had found the strength to rise and turn on the lights. There was a residual scent of cooking, left-over spoils that mixed sourly with the ever-present smell of my mother's strange sickness.

Now she reposed in bed, limp and tiredly pale, eyes shining fitfully as we entered, and I felt the guilt of my neglect pounce unmercifully on my mental shoulders, heavily bending its back. I remembered belatedly that I had the unsavory task of telling her that I'd quit my job.

"David," I heard her say. "I was becoming worried . . ."

Behind me I felt Famat come to an abrupt halt, and I was almost frozen, as I said, without turning,

"Famat, this is my mother, Mrs. Kane."

"Oh, *hello*," Ma said, trying feebly to rise, to preen herself, to become other than the semi-invalid she was.

I felt Famat brush past me, and, strangely, watched her bend over the bed to take my mother's half-raised hand. And Famat was smiling down—*smiling*.

"Mrs. Kane," she said in that soft voice, "I'm very happy to meet you."

My mother's face seemed electrified with an unusual surge of new life. "*Famat*, did you say? Oh, you dear girl! David, get Famat a chair and put it here by the bed. Oh, you dear girl," she said in a totally happy way that was strange for my ears to hear. "Are you a friend of David's? But that's silly—of *course* you are! My dear, you don't know how happy I am that you came by. David doesn't bring many friends by. Carl, of course—but *you*: child, you're the first girl David's ever brought home to me!"

I went and found the chair. Then I made coffee while they talked of inconsequential things, women things, and I sat on the couch and watched them as Ma bubbled on and the night crept slyly to ravish morning, and the thing between them developed, until I hungrily realized they were two women I desired intensely and was not, because the laws of other men said I could not be, allowed to have, and I strained at the chains until I felt the snapping of a link, a vitally important one, that bound the biceps of my brain, till the free formation of my *own* new laws expanded their vast, clumsy arms to embrace the two differences of those living, human, souls to the point of oneness, and there was no longer distinction, nor distillation, nor detraction.

"Famat, I've kept you *so* long," Ma said at last. "Please go home, child, and rest. But promise me you'll come back."

"Any time you want," Famat smiled. "I'll stop later this evening, if you don't mind."

I saw Ma shoot me a hesitant glance. "I'd be very happy if you did, Famat . . . I don't get many visitors."

"Well, you've got a regular from now on, Mrs. Kane—before it's over, you'll have a stomach full of me."

My mother's smile was vivid and fond. "Have no fear about that. I've got a year of conversation for anyone who'll listen."

I couldn't help feeling relieved as I led Famat out and down the stairs.

Outside the day had come with an early ferocity that soundly slapped the cheeks of the dirty sidewalks.

We walked silently up to Eighth, where the motorized sweepers and street-washers had already begun their early-morning dirty work.

Finally, as we walked, and the marvel of the new day, with an ambivalently clean fresh smell of the city, surrounded us, I couldn't help saying what I knew Carl had thought all along but would not reveal to others because of our friendship:

"Now, it's plain what my sin is . . ."

Famat's face was surprisingly radiant as she looked at me. "There *is* no sin, David."

My laugh was dull and tarnished by what I considered an irreconcilable fact of origin. "Having just come from the den of the Devil, you can say that?"

I felt the pressure of her arm as it passed through mine.

"It is not the Devil within that matters, my David," she said softly, "but the one without."

CHAPTER SEVEN

TWO WEEKS LATER I had found my way. With Famat's help, studying with her in my room after she'd left the Temple in the evening, I came to grasp an ology that was an intermixture of Ax, orthodox Islam and theory.

Sometimes Famat would stare inexpressibly at me for long periods, which usually ended with, "You need so desperately to *believe*, David."

I took the Ax Muslim mathematical equations and reviewed them:

One:—The Beginning.

Two:—A nation: man and woman.

Three:—The light of the world: the sun, moon and stars.

Four:—The square by which all things are equal, i.e., $4 \times 9 = 36$, which points to 9 as the beginning of One.

Five:—The number of Allah, Who is just to the obedient.

Six:—The Dragon's number—the number of a man who was six hundred years in the making, has six thousand years to rule, at which time his cycle of life will be complete—and he will die forever from the face of the Earth.

Seven:—Is complete in itself, causing the first to come last and the last to come first.

Eight:—Yakub's number, signifying the maker and the made.

Nine:—Is exact and the beginning of One.

This was an advocated formula, panacea for all the black man's ills. But study as I might, I could not adjust its semantics to any practical use.

"It's not applicable," I told Famat, after a few interminable sessions.

"Maybe we're trying too hard, David."

"It's not that," I protested. "There *is* truth in its numerical sense, but there's fallacy in the semantic denominator. All right, let's look at One, the Beginning. I've searched the teachings, the Koran, the Bible, and they all only *allude* to it."

She nodded. "That makes it an unknown factor."

"And possibly the key," I agreed. "I'm sure death will reveal the answer, but death takes us right back to One and Nine. Two and Three are incontestable truths. Now, look what happens when we come to Four, the oddball, which subtly inveigles Nine into its scope of reasoning."

Famat concentrated, her brow creased beautifully. "This could be the root."

"But how?" I said, showing her my list of contentions. "Where was the Beginning, in One, Two or Four? Not only do these suggest origin, but so do Seven and Nine. Why?"

"Go on to Two," she smiled. "That's the one I like best—and I didn't make a pun on purpose."

"What can I say about Two that we don't already know?" I said softly.

I saw her begin a speech, but she paused and started again. "What do you think of Three?"

"The sun, moon and stars? The flag used by *all* Muslim followers the world over. But it's something to be considered of unusual importance. Whether it's of mythical or original significance will involve further study, Famat, and I'd like you to dig up all you can about the subject."

"Four?"

"Isn't *Two* just as practical? It's easier to arrive at 36 two times eighteen than 4 times nine. I wonder . . ."

"What about Five?"

"We've been taught to look on the One God as an entity rather than a divisible quantum—unless—and I say this hypothetically—Five represents the five senses possessed by man: the pillars of the

328

human temple. But we know that man may be in charge of *more* than five senses, so it's difficult to proceed on the God-man theory when we know Allah is the All-knowing, All-bountiful, All-giving. Let's go on."

"Six, the Dragon's number, the number of a man," she said.

"This is *knowledge,* Famat. I've seen provocative references in the Koran. And there's something to it; what, I don't know. A profounder intellect than mine'll have to point out the nuances and cement the seams of my logic."

"What about the Caucasian's proclivity for burying his dead six feet underground," she said, "his sailing measurement of sounding, using six fathoms of depth as the gradient?"

I agreed with a nod. "There're numerous others, the six-thousand-year reign, et cetera. There's no doubt his racial history is scanty, at best, past six thousand years. But there's also the fact that the black rulers of Egypt had Caucasian slaves in abundance, and this goes back more than eight thousand years. I can't find any mathematical consistency here—"

" 'Six hundred years to make, six thousand to rule . . . ' "

"Exactly. But I'm not so concerned about this fallacy as I am about the stress it puts on the imagination of the uninitiated. It's like giving a dog the bone first and the meat later."

"Seven," Famat went on with a relentless little pleasure. I shrugged, and then she said, sharply, "Eight."

"The year Eight Thousand, right?"

"I'm asking you, David. It's *you* who must answer these questions, so that I'll know, and be able," she said, looking away self-consciously, "to teach my children."

"We're told Eight Thousand was the year of Yakub's coming—"

"*More* than eight thousand years ago."

"Okay. We *know* this is the year Fifteen Thousand and Forty-five, which should have put the final creation of Yakub's mutant around the year Nine Thousand and a little more, since Yakub's *exact* birthday was Eight Thousand Four Hundred. This I'll accept at face value until investigation changes my mind."

"But you don't like it."

"I didn't say that. It's not a question of my liking or disliking this wealth of submitted evidence, but whether or not I *accept* into my personal values items which are, thus far, poorly substantiated."

She pouted at me. "What about Nine?"

"It's *unexact,* since its root is 3, not 2 or 4. *Unless*—" I became excited with the thought. "Unless One and Three are indicative to some chemical composite in relation to Five, Seven and Nine."

"I don't follow you, David . . ."

"Look, Famat, what makes *active* life? I mean, atomically?"

She studied for a moment. "Well, there's the proton, neutron and electron . . ."

"The sun—energy, alias proton," I said. "The moon—the feminine gender, the neuter, the receiver of life's seed; and the stars, that unknown binding quotient of all life, the thing that intersperses man's void and connects each living tissue. Famat—!"

"I understand, David," she said intensely. "Two, in conjunction with Five—no, with Three—that gives us *Five*— man and woman, the nation: *Allah.*"

"Seven," I rushed on, unable to contain myself, "gives us— procreation, male and female births out of the nation, making the first come last and the last come first!"

"And Nine—" She suddenly clasped me about the neck and rained sweet, new kisses on my glowing face.

"Oh, David," she said, as I took her in my arms. "We've discovered *God* . . ."

CHAPTER EIGHT

I GOT A JOB near the close of the summer which was sufficient to pay the rent and feed my mother and myself. It was a semi-white collar position as ledger-filer in a Negro insurance company, where I came into first-hand contact with the unscrupulous exploitation employed by one brother against another—and a huge black brother who was my superior, and who (it was my misfortune to reveal it unthinkingly one day) knew I followed the Muslim faith. His name was Charles Benson.

"Yall teach hate over there, doncha?" he asked me early one morning in the filing storeroom.

"What?"

"Yall Mooslums," he said impatiently. "Don't yall teach each other to hate the white man?"

"I don't know what you mean," I answered vaguely, going about my work, not wanting to get involved in an argument.

"Well?" said Charles Benson.

"Well what?"

His pancake face, black and pious, crinkled a little comically. "Well, *do* ya or *don*cha teach hate, you Mooslums?"

"No, we don't," I said, wondering at a way to tell him I no longer attended the Temple, by my *own* choice, now that my suspension period was up. "We teach merely that those things which go against our survival are the ones to be shunned—not hated."

"Like the white man?" Charles Benson said craftily, reminding me of Arnie, but in a more malicious, more insidious, way.

"If he threatens our survival, yes."

Charles Benson laughed and sat next to the filing cabinet where I worked. "Boy, you sure is dumb—all you niggers!"

"Okay," I said, promising myself not to get angry, "suppose you tell me why."

"Because," he said, stabbing a pink and black finger into his palm, "the white man give us everything we got, that's why. If it hadn't been for him, where'd we be today?"

"You tell me."

"In Africa, that's where!" he said violently. "Agitatin ain't gonna get you nothin, don't you know that? Look at it the way it is: see how far we've got since slavery days? The black man ain't never advanced so much, so far, at one time. And integration's on the way."

"And what does that mean?"

"It means freedom!" Charles Benson said indignantly.

"But don't you already *have* that?" I asked him in the strictest seriousness. "The Fourteenth Amendment guaranteed—"

"You *know* what I mean . . . freedom to eat in the same place the white man does, go to school where he goes, swim where he swims—not be discriminated against."

"But look—integration doesn't change your color: you're still *black*. How can anyone imagine that a law can, overnight, convert a man who wasn't a man yesterday into a man today?"

Charles Benson bristled. "Are you sayin I *ain't* a man?"

"No—but the white man *is*, by the very insinuation of his integrating laws." Now I warmed. "There may be some sad things said about Islam in the U.S., but the thing you can't deny is the fact that its followers stand on their own two feet and don't need a bunch of laughing-up-the-sleeve laws to tell 'em they're free and *equal*—not through white men's laws, but God's!"

Charles Benson laughed in a way that infuriated me momentarily. "I hear that talk all the time, up on 125th Street, but it ain't knockin down no walls the white man don't *want* down."

I was a little amazed. "In one breath you say the white is the black's last hope, and in the next you admit he is a supressor who allows racial walls to fall at *his* discretion."

"Well, it's *his* country, ain't it? You Mooslums talk about how *inferior* he is—but I want to thank ya, he *ain't* no punk. It took a *man* to raise this, the most powerful country in the world. How can the black man, with nuthin, stand up against the maker of the A-bomb and H-bomb?"

"Who said anything about standing up against him?" I said. "The black Muslims of America ask for *separation*."

Charles Benson shook his head mockingly. "And what's that gonna getcha?"

"*Freedom,*" I said harshly. "That thing which you seem to think integration will bring you."

"All right, suppose you do get separation like you want—two or three states just for the black man to live in: how ya gonna get along without the white man's goods, his machines, his factories, his food?"

"Well *make* them ourselves."

"Don't make me laugh!"—and he did so, derisively. "You'll never get a bunch of niggers to cooperate in somethin like that. I know from my own experience, from workin right here in *this* place." He squinted up at me.

"The way it is, with the nigger, he's used to followin the white man's orders, and he'll be lost without the bossman to tell 'im what to do."

I was about to speak, but saw he was going to continue.

"I don't care *what* you say, man, you or none of them people on 125th—a black nation here in America won't ever work."

"Why?" I said.

"Why? *Why?*" His eyes got big. "Because *the black man stopped bein a black man a long time ago—in this country.*"

Now I had to stop working—the little I was doing—and take a seat facing him. At the moment, he and I were the only ones in the filing room and the opening of the outer office door would signal a new entry with the hum and clatter of office machines.

"What do you mean?" I asked Charles Benson, carefully.

"Just what I said," he told me adamantly.

"No, explain yourself. You said this country's black man is no longer black. If I've got the right understanding, you mean he's become a *white* man."

"That's *just* what I mean! That's where you Mooslums goin wrong, can'tcha see? The nigger's been chuggin uphill for more'n a hundred years after equality through—through *association*. Hell," he said, stabbing his palm again, "look at magazines like *Ebony*, where they got niggers in ads doin the same things whites do in the identical ads in *Life*, or *Look*. This just goes to show ya . . ."

"What?" I insisted.

"That yall is *wrong*," he went on fervently. "You think after all this strugglin and strivin to be like the white man, you could get more'n a handful of people to throw 'way that hard work? Boy, shit!" he said disgustedly, "you'd better take another look at it for the way it *is*. Even your Mooslums, dedicated the way they say they is—give 'um one week away from the subways, hollerin Harlem and the easy-pay plans on 125th, and they'll be *scramblin* to get back."

"But, *why?*"

"Because they got a germ in 'um," he told me sagely. "You got it, I got it, everybody and everything with a drop of nigger blood in him's got it. It's a thing that won't allow no *separation, brotheration* or *concentration*. The same old self-sickness we fed on right out of our mothers' tits—and even before that, the bossman made sure we knew how to use this sick germ 'gainst ourselves, first and forever. And that's why I know not eatin pork, smokin cigarettes or prayin to Mecca ain't gonna make a damn bit of difference."

Now I shifted, and when I looked in Charles Benson's wide, stark white eyes, I knew he wasn't the fool I took him to be.

After a while, I asked the question he was waiting on.

His eyes twinkled. "Don't you know, boy? It's that thing you first denied knowin anything about: hate."

Famat met me after work and, as I anticipated, sensed the current of new thought running rampant in my mind.

"What is it, David?" she said, as we threaded our way through the evening crowd on 125th.

"Nothing serious. A man just gave me food for—seeing, I guess you'd say. . . ."

"Tell me about it."

I smiled. "I will, but not now, honey. We'll take a walk later, okay?"

She smiled and took my arm without another word.

When we arrived home, I was surprised to see my mother up and arranging a cold salad on three plates. "Hi, there," she said brightly. "I didn't expect you two so early."

"We took the tram," Famat said with a resonant but deep-soft laugh—and again I was surprised, for I never suspected their relationship would touch on secret-joke elements that concerned my mother's adolescence in England. As a child I had been fascinated by her endless tales of a strange, pale, proud, powerful people, and cities that were composed of heathers and moors and vales and sheep, and an unfeminine person called a Queen, who was loved by everyone she ruled and ruled by a church called England.

Too soon—and impatiently, after my father died—I'd come to look on her stories more as fairy-tales than fact. But now I couldn't help envying Famat, knowing she had entered a phase of my mother's life that I had spurned—and it was an emotion that quickly grew to an almost physical sensation of pain, as I watched them talk animatedly over the meal. And I could appreciate fully now the solitude and loneliness this white woman who was my mother must have suffered in the years following my father's death, how it had been intensified through the uncommicativeness of her *only* link with humanity—her son. . . .

Because she could never be accepted fully by the black brethren of her husband, and because she had shorn all ties to have him, she was never again acceptable to the peers of her natural origin!

Each minute, studied cruelty I had exercised against her came back to me vividly. I'd always felt like a freak—but not because my skin color or tone was different to show the oddity, which they were not—but primarily:

Primarily because she *was* my mother and white and you could look at me and not be able to tell a damn bit of difference. I tried once to explain this to Carl, but I'd never been able to make him see what I meant, he never failing to reply maddeningly: "One drop of God's blood makes you whole, Brother."

That wasn't it at all: I wasn't solely my father's child . . . I was my mother's, too, there was no getting away from it. But yet I *wasn't* at all, can I make myself understood? With my coloring belying my maternal heritage on one side, and certain Gaelic features casting aspersions on the identity of my sire, there was really *no racial classification reserved for me.*

Yet my environmental acclimation was Negroid, my thoughts, my motivation and militant impetus—even the basic mistrust of my mother.

It's hard to explain here . . . for it went—and goes—much farther than what I've put down here: to tell of the *black* feeling one black experiences at all times; the tenacity and choke of racial somnambulism because of that same innate blackness; the panorama viewed by *black* eyes, that may not consciously regard but cannot help psychosomatically registering, which shows plainly the *difference,* the injustice, the pain, physical and psychic, the lust writ on the faces and hands of the pale executioner, whether in the midst of a lynch mob or white citizens' public orgy, or firm stroke of a slum landlord as the tip of his pen nips the roof from the heads of a rent-delinquent family, that makes *being* black, a Negro, Nigra, Spade, nigger—any of a dozen colorful synonyms—nothing less than a crime.

Shit, I said to myself, watching Famat and Mrs. Kane carry on as though there were no such things as racial propriety or pride, I would rather be a tree or rock or a clear white drop of cloud moisture with a moment's life, than be an American so-called Negro, who can be compared to a pig who'd suddenly found himself within the Holy City of Mecca.

I ate silently, relishing the self-loathing Charles Benson had warned was inescapably incident to all like myself.

It was getting dark when Famat and I walked down to Riverside Drive, and the park. From the battlement hedging the green growth below—while around us young couples with new, stumbling, first-stepping children and aged Jewish haves, and ancient have-nots, hot-blooded, running, yelling children attacking flat-skulled water-fountains near the staircase to the lower level, swarmed interminably—we watched the shimmering Hudson in the dying blue-gold of the sun's depressed half-moon (cool orange now over Jersey and pleasant to look at directly), and saw the lights from the other side's city flicker on in fear of insurgent night.

She took my hand in hers, and I turned at the gesture to look levelly into her big, becalmed eyes, and see a moment's peace there.

"What are we going to do, David?" she said quietly.

"I don't know," I admitted.

"I . . . saw you, when we were eating. You were thinking so deeply."

I didn't answer.

"David," she said, and the tone, the tightening, of her voice made me turn to her. "There's something I've got to tell you . . ."

"Yes?" I said, noting that the tempo of my heart had accelerated.

"Forest . . . is going to—he and some others of the Fruit, including Carl—recommend that you be expelled permanently from the Temple."

"Oh . . ."

"Did you understand me, David?" she said anxiously.

"Yes . . ." Then I took her arm and guided her to the lower level, coming close, down the flagstone paths, to the guard-rail fronting the river and time-and-water-rotted wharves of another era. I found a bench and we sat in silence, watching, feeling, smelling, night approach.

"It doesn't matter, Famat," I said, after a long while. "I've come to realize that the real Temple is the soul—what you feel inside, the thing that overrides the laws and orders of other men." I shook my head. "They can't take anything away from me."

Strangely, as had more frequently been the case with us lately, I could feel she had more to say.

"What *is* it, Famat, please . . . ?"

When she turned to me, it all came in a rush. "Forest has been following me—I told him I've been coming over regularly and don't intend to stop, how much I love your mother—" She stopped, and when she did I took her in my arms and cast her body into the mold of myself, made her mouth mine, made it yield its passion's fruit, until mine was full of its sweetness and need.

And the coming night became a cloak to time our love, where we found it on the featherbed of grass and protecting overhang of rock formation God had made a million years before to serve this moment.

"You're mine, Famat," I said over her, at last, "my flesh, my woman. Any man who tries to take you from me will risk—and lose—his life."

CHAPTER NINE

T HE NEXT WEEK, early in the evening, I took a kitchen ladder— borrowed from a neighbor on my floor—and went down on 125th, right across from the Hotel Teresa.

It was Saturday and brisk along Seventh. Sidewalk hawkers, junkies with hot suits, trousers, dresses, winos and whores, had plunged into the evening's river, struggling, some successfully, against the tide.

I hadn't told Famat what I'd planned, and now, as I watched the steaming, surging, people-flood, I felt the first tinge of doubt.

Allah is with me, I told myself resolutely, and crossed to the vacant corner facing west and downtown and set up the ladder. I climbed to the wide flat top and looked about me. Two white-faced patrolmen on the east side of the street watched me disinterestedly; they were used to the racial harangues of nationalist and Ax Islamic speakers, and probably considered me no more dangerous than the rest.

"Watcha gonna do up there, man?"

I looked down and saw a crooked, bent little old black man staring up at me.

"You gettin ready to preach?" He carried a worn black shopping bag, the top of which exposed the limp fluffy heads of tired lettuce.

"No," I told him, smiling down, "I'm going to speak, if I can get anyone to listen."

The old man cackled a pleasant laugh. "Well, boy, you'll get plenty people to listen—all you gotta do is start talkin." He raised his toothless chin in a listening position.

I rubbed my sweating hands together and stretched my arms outward, Christlike. "Brothers . . . Sisters . . . give me your attention!"

"Yews got it," laughed the old man. "Start talkin, boy."

A few passersby had stopped—two teenage girls licking flavored ice chips in paper cones, a soldier in summer khakis and an old woman carrying a bag, who might have been the old man's wife, or twin sister.

"I want you to know," I began nervously, "that I come to you this evening on a mission of the gravest importance . . ."

"Mebbe, mebbe not," said the old man. "You let *us* 'cide how important it is."

"You bringin God's word?" the bag-carrying old woman inquired snappily. " 'Cause if you ain't, I kin get right on home to what *is* important."

I cleared my throat. "The word I bring *is* God's," I said strongly, "Whose real name is Allah . . ."

"I knew it," said the old woman, turning stoutly to walk away with her bag. "Any man callin God by two names *couldn't* know what he talkin 'bout!"

Her exodus caused a snicker to ripple through my slowly growing audience.

"Go wan, boy, I'm witcha," the old man laughed. "Some calls

339

a spade a tool, an others say it's a man, but that don't change neither one of 'em from bein what they *is*."

This statement encouraged me, and I looked out at the spray of new black faces with a growing confidence.

"Brothers and Sisters," I said, "it's only fair for me to tell you that I *am* of the faith called Islam." I saw the torso of the crowd begin to shift and sway. "Wait! I know what you've heard of the black Muslim movement, and I know what you've heard *from* it. But what I want to tell you about Islam is another thing—maybe it's crazy, maybe it's unreasonable—but it's mine: one man's belief in the reality of his own existence—and I want you to listen, if you will."

Somehow, through some affinity peculiar to crowds, they collectively assented to stay, and I was assailed by a new problem: what to say next.

"Well, go wan, boy," prompted my accomplice—or Nemesis— the old man. "Tell us whatcha been thinkin 'bout."

"I just want to dispel some common notions, first of all," I went on bravely, "that most people connect with Islam. It doesn't teach hate; it doesn't teach intolerance; it doesn't teach revolt. But it does teach love, acceptance and compatibility; cleanliness, both physical and mental, and union, through brotherly recognition."

"You talk good, boy," the old man said, "but the words is so big they bust a dumb man's brain. Just tell us in plain words whatchu learned from all this teachin."

I glanced sharply at the old man, for he had touched a chord that had been eluding me, a sensitive and slightly painful one—yet all the while I knew it was the very thing that had brought me here, as though before some *en-masse* receiver of my confessional.

For this was guilt, wasn't it? This need to reveal my aching total and sums of indigenous skepticism?

"Go wan, boy, time's a-gittin! We all be dead and gone 'fore you get through."

"Maybe he's got nothing to say at all," said a new but familiar voice, and I looked over the heads of the crowd to recognize the

340

expressionless face of Brother Forest. Carl, and another grim-faced Brother from the Temple, were flanking him.

The crowd was waiting. For a fiery instant Brother Forest and I threw our eyes together.

Then I began to speak.

"I came into Islam many months ago. I came because, like so many of you Brothers and Sisters here today, I needed belief to tide me over the swells of the white man's unfailing supression—or his constant attempts at supressing—my basic sense of individuality and the need to be free.

"Now, that may not say much, the way I've put it, and there may be a tighter way for me to make plain what I want to say . . ."

"What *do* you want to say?" Brother Forest's voice rose threateningly over my last words.

"That, when I say I wanted to be free," I went on strongly, "I didn't necessarily mean *physical* freedom. I've always been told that Lincoln *gave* me that—not God but Lincoln. What I want to make plain is, I knew I *was* in a special sort of slavery that required no shackles or chains, or any other physical restrainer—but detained its prisoners through subtler, more ingenious, methods. Methods that involved the book called the Bible—which invoked fear of The Great One and adherence to commands better suited to gods than men; indoctrination, utilizing this same book, which proposed that those without, those meek and poor, and *black,* should suffer the slings and arrows of outrageous hell without rancor or despair or hate, in anticipation of the Promised Land, where all the atrocities ever committed against them would be righted in the greatest war-crime trial ever held, and the enemies of man would burn in the everlasting hellfire of The Great One's judgment."

"Amen, boy, now you sayin the Word!"

"All right," I said, voice trembling a little. "So this was the way it had to be. The Book said so. And who was I to suggest that it wasn't quite justice enough, from *my* way of looking at it? . . . That's what I want you to remember—that this is just *my* way of looking at it . . . Or that there wouldn't be much of eternity left after this trial of trials, since *billions* of defendants, from time immemorial, had to stand before the bar of the Almighty. Or, for many of those defendants, their crimes were determined by the Almighty Himself in the eons before they were born. Or, in *my* opinion, it should be the Almighty *Himself* standing in the judgment of men, since He had started the whole unholy mess in the first place."

The crowd swayed again, a huge black serpent now, with angry growlings in the dark pit of its bowels.

"Let me remind you," I went on, "that these are *my* feelings— not anything that's taught in Islam. Not any belief held by any man I know . . . I am the only man I know who suggests God is a war criminal." I looked around me, not afraid—in fact, elated—but tentative. "May I go on?"

"Speak yer piece, brother," a woman's voice hollered up at me.

I tried to find Brother Forest's face in the black, rippling pond, and when I did it was indistinct, but it seemed to have grown in size and appeared now like a huge black balloon hovering masklike, the face of a witch-doctor, over the unpeaceful attention of my audience.

"So I came into Islam," I said.

"Why?" was Brother Forest's angry voice.

"To board the transport to a *new* outlook toward the Supreme," I shouted back. "One that exposed *my* roots as those among the countless which are inextricably linked to the One God, Allah. But—"

"*But* what?" cried Brother Forest.

"But I found *duplication* amid the truth!" I answered. "I found man had inserted his ego here in the same manner white man had inserted his in Christianity. I found Allah the same knowing criminal, the same omnipotent originator of this present Earthly hell, the same Promiser of Peace through Armageddon's final bloodshed— the same great Big Daddy overseeing each beginning and end with the relish of his divinity: but, unwittingly, He had given me the formula to the composite structure of *all* things.

"*And I saw Him.* No longer could He hide behind the sacred cloak of Godhood, because it had been rent by the lighting blast of His own indiscretion—I saw Him and knew Him, and *see Him now.*"

I pointed my finger at the black belly of the crowd. "Take your genitals in hand, you Great Deceiver, for they are the crown of Him Who was, Who is, Who *will* be—to the end of eternity!"

CHAPTER TEN

*T*HE MOON HAD COME DOWN. Thunder rolled across the muted sky. From the east, a chiding shatter of angry rain had risen to briefly drench me where I stood, the ladder folded and held under my arm.

I stood trembling from some inner violence.

Looking toward the chastening east, the sharp rain daggers, cold and accurate, stabbing my vision, I could see vaguely the blinking neons of theaters and bars and novelty chains, and people and dogs (one stopping to crap happily in a well-trained gutter manner) and slickered cops smoking on duty——and westward, the heavens were lit sickly by some upper ozone, twinkling in dying: and it haloed the skyscrapered trillion-bricked dwellings, like the wand of the Devil had passed over its brow, as it had touched the crown of Sodom.

And I stood trembling. The night grew blacker. My audience had left—Brother Forest and the others quickly, after I'd finished. And I had answered the questions of tired, wrinkled black women and men smelling of charm water and galloping death, assuring them I had no "church," and did not want their alms or blessings, or a good "figure," and had felt good when they thanked me for speaking, even though they didn't understand half of what I'd said.

I stood trembling in the rain, resigned in the cleansing eastern reprimand. I'd said too much to gain so little, for what I'd earned was baptismal and simply each man's right. I'd carried my public confirmation to dangerous lengths, and I began to sense the—to anticipate the—consequences of my actions. It wasn't myself I was worried about, but Famat . . .

I began to walk in the downpour. Famat would be coming by now. Surely she would. She *must*.

At 123rd Street, a little man, a midget, a black little gnome-faced creature, came up and plucked at my sleeve.

"As salaam aliekum, Brother," he greeted me in a crackly voice.

"Wa aliekum salaam," I replied.

He double-timed to keep up with my pace. "You Ammaddiayia Muslim, Brother?"

"No," I said, hurrying on.

"But you's a Muslim, right?"

"I follow certain tenets of the Muslim faith, Islam," I said.

"Well, I heard you talkin, that's all. See," he said in the sharp voice, snapping at my sleeve again, "I'm *bein* a Muslim myself."

The rain became stronger, and I ducked into an open doorway for shelter, the midget on my heels.

"Man, it's really rainin, ain't it?"

"It'll let up in a minute," I predicted.

"Now, listen," said the midget, "I heard you speakin, like I say, and I'm just learnin Islam. I want you to help me, Brother, 'cause I got a problem."

"Well, I'll help all I can, Brother," I said, looking down in his wide, almost cat-like eyes, full with something that bespoke shock —or pain. "What is it?"

"Jazak-Allah, Brother," he thanked me. "What I wanna know is this: In Islam, I is supreme with God 'cause I is black, like the Original man, havin seven layers of skin, seven-an-a-half ounces of brains, and comin into my own in the seventh-thousandth year. Is that right?"

"I have been taught that, Brother, yes."

"Jazak-Allah. Now, look here: if I is God, like you say, how is I gonna keep from over*lookin* myself on Judgement Day?"

When I looked down, he was looking up at me and bursting, a fat black toy panda, with his own hilarious, cackling laughter.

"David!"

It was Carl who grabbed my arm as I came around my corner. The rain obscured my mind's picture of him, and it was only the stark angry yellow skin that stood out ominously.

"I'm in a hurry, Brother Carl—"

"So am I, David. Listen to me—you're no longer my Brother! And Famat has been promised to me—leave her alone!"

"Let me go, Carl . . ."

"You've blasphemed, David! I should have known that Devil mother of yours—"

"If you don't release me, Carl," I said tightly, "I'll forget that peace *has* existed between us. I wouldn't want that to happen."

I felt his hand drop from my arm. "You'll pay for this treachery, David . . ." I saw his head turn toward the tenement I lived in, and I was suddenly overcome by an unknown menace.

I squinted through the rain at Carl, feeling my fists clench and bulge the muscles of my forearms. "What are you talking about?"

"Allah demands the heads of all Devils, therefore—"

I reached out blindly and before I realized it his face was level with mine and I could feel his breath of fear. "David . . . you're choking me!"

"Where is Brother Forest?" I almost screamed at him.

"I don't know!"

I squeezed until there was no resistance, and the flesh of his throat was escaping the prison of my maddened fingers.

"Wait," he gasped. "*Wait*, David!"

The vise of my fingers relaxed and I could hear the babbling of his terrified voice. The red-hot insanity found exit in the wild dash I made toward the apartment. Twice I stumbled over the garbage cans lining the walk, rising, filthy and reeking with the slush of discarded human waste, to plummet on, not daring to imagine the scene I might find in the apartment.

Almost out of breath, I stumbled up the staircase and onto the floor that was mine.

The door moved inward at a single twist of the knob, and I froze inwardly.

It was not caution that made me enter slowly—not even fear. It was more than that—not death, no, not the condemned finally meeting the instrument of his execution—not even that exquisite moment . . .

How can I explain the way my insides had *flown?* Had deserted me laughingly?

Death was here, surely,

I first saw—*first*—my mother. On the cot. Eyes closed. Mouth partly opened, pale, thin lips. Faded hair cascaded nobly about the sheet-whiteness of her face. Worry-wrinkles relaxed, muscles sagged. Like a ghost, even now, not tomorrow's but yesterday's remembered wraith.

Then in the shadows cast off the lamp's periphery, I saw Brother Forest, abnormally tall, cloaked, it seemed, like a master messenger of fate.

And I knew she was dead—perhaps not now, not yet, but dying, and dead, because of what he suggested, and was.

"Your mother was kind enough to permit me to enter," he said, at length.

"What have you done?" I said slowly.

"Nothing, *Brother* David," he said, advancing out of the shadows and into the light of the room. "I haven't touched her." He looked down at her, almost amusedly. "Of course, I *wouldn't,* you know. I stopped by simply to inquire after Famat—she seemed quite glad to meet Famat's brother. We had an interesting chat . . ."

"About what?" I said, feeling that thing rise within me that Charles Benson had spoken of.

He shrugged. "You. Famat. Your mother. Her background. Her *history*—her racial history—"

I took a step toward him.

"Peace, Brother," he said, smiling.

"Never again," I said.

"Be rational, Brother David. After all, she was highly enlightened—and excited—to find that you had studied the facts of her origin." He smiled again, and I felt a chill come over me, numbing my brain. "Such things as, well, finding out how Yakub arrived at his final creation through a series of birth elimination experiments from the guinea-pig following of 59,999. How he murdered each black baby, driving pins through their heads and lying to the mothers about the fates of the newborn, until his doctors delivered the first all-white children . . . Oh, she was very glad to find out your studies were so broad—"

He was suddenly sitting on the floor and my fist was aching, the fingers locked.

"David . . ." It was her voice, and I rushed over to the bed.

"Ma . . ."

She opened her eyes briefly, then she saw me, and I watched her mouth tremble into a frightened smile.

"Please don't hate me too much, my son," she said in a voice I could barely hear. "I just didn't know . . . I didn't know God made mistakes, too . . ."

"Ma . . ." I said. "*Mother!*"

When I looked around, when I raised my head from her breast, there was darkness in the lampglow, Forest was gone . . .

And she was dead.

I stood and looked at her, this wax-white, doll-like dead thing, eyes closed to the world—the womb of my coming. No more.

Lost. Strength in the loss that shored my ignorance and claim to manhood . . . child tears, like those of my first moment's birth, and a man's voice to sob them out.

I turned and left, closing the door of that other world.

I met Famat coming up the staircase. I did not have to tell her. I saw the shimmering loss in her eyes for a moment only, and then she said, "I have left my household and the people of my birth. I come to you with my arms open and the dowry of my heart. I come to weld my life with yours, my David. Forever."

I took her, and we went into the hell of the night, walking, and she once asked, not really caring, "Where?"

And I answered, with a dream of tomorrow and the knowledge of our good marriage in the eyes of Allah:
"The Outside . . ."

Black! brings together three short novels by Clarence Cooper, Jr., a rediscovered genius of African-American writing. "The Dark Messenger" is a short, sizzling novel in which a reporter for a black newspaper discovers that truth and justice are no match for the next handout from the corrupt powers that be. "Yet Princes Follow" and "Yet We Many" are both sardonic crime novellas set in the worlds of the numbers racket and Black Muslims, respectively. All of them demonstrate the hard-edged, ultra-hip style of realism that was Clarence Cooper's trademark.

Clarence Cooper, Jr.'s other novels include *The Scene* (1960), available from Norton, and *The Farm* (1968). He died in 1979 in New York City.

edited by Marc Gerald and Samuel Blumenfeld

W. W. Norton
New York • London
Cover design by Marc J. Cohen
Cover photograph courtesy of the
Pittsburgh Courier Photographic Archives

ISBN 0-393-31541-X

9 780393 315417

90000>

$12.00 U.S.A. $15.99 CAN.

Old School Book